THE HAWKSBRIDGE WORM

By Julian Smart

The Hawksbridge Angels
The Train To Hawksbridge
The Ramsburgh Variations
The Hawksbridge Worm
Emma Vernon's Northminster Ghost Stories (with Harriet Smart)

THE HAWKSBRIDGE WORM

A THOMAS RUFFORD MYSTERY: 4

by

Julian Smart

Published by Anthemion

First Edition

This is a work of fiction. Names, characters, places, brands, media, and incidents are either the product of the author's imagination or are used fictitiously. The author acknowledges the trademarked status and trademark owners of various products referenced in this work of fiction, which have been used without permission. The publication/use of these trademarks is not authorized, associated with, or sponsored by the trademark owners.

ISBN 978-1-907873-84-3

Made with Jutoh

PREFACE

In the autumn of 1849, no sooner had I emerged from the grip of one danger, than I was plunged headlong into another. I barely had time to get used to the happy state of matrimony when the sanctity of my home was compromised, and tragedy struck once more in Hawksbridge.

You may well imagine how small my appetite was for further investigative entanglements, given the preoccupations of a fresh marriage. Still, fate gave me no choice, and also burdened me with an odd riddle a century and a half in the making, courtesy of my friend Francesca Campbell and her new venture. A desperate cry from the past, and a hint of double murder, could hardly go unexamined.

I am not a person susceptible to the charms of fairy stories. But delving into these human calamities, I was forced to consider certain local myths that each had a disconcerting resonance with present events. As the filaments of science and industry increasingly reached into the lives of our citizens, perhaps it was no surprise that men and women sought the comforts of the old stories.

And yet these tales were not so much comforts as lures that beckoned me deeper into the gloomy realms of human depravity. It seemed to me that we awakened one myth's terrible protagonist, so that it manifested itself once more, stretched its claws across the town, and cast upon us the corrupting shade of its scaly hide.

Any solace I might have taken during these traumatic affairs was ruptured by further demons, born of my own past folly. Youth draws its exploits as if upon a slate, to be effaced on graduating to maturity; alas, how I know this to be false, and what misery bygone sins can bring!

You may judge for yourself who or what is most monstrous in this story. But as ever in my memoirs, the darkness of sorrow is mitigated by the far brighter light of human nobility. I therefore submit my fourth volume to your discerning gaze in the hope that it shall prove as illuminating as its predecessors. I am grateful that you have come with me this far.

— Thomas Rufford, August 1865

Thus unleashed to gorge with frenzy on love's feast,
Twisting in the glass I spied not man, but beast.

Allan Lawrence

PROLOGUE

The Grand Opening of
Tanner's Magnificent Wonderland
by His Worship the Mayor of Hawksbridge
will take place on September 8th, 1849 at
Ten O'Clock
A Unique Assortment of Amusements,
Gymnastic Activities,
and Educational Exhibits
Something for Everyone!
Row With your Friends on the Patent
Hawksbridge Giant Worm,
Ride the Merry-Go-Round,
Or Take a Gentle Trip on the Boating
Lake
Exotic Animals – the Remains of Ancient
Monsters –
And Many Other Attractions!
Tickets Tuppence at the Door
Refreshments will be Available

CHAPTER ONE

September 1st, 1849

"WHAT have you done now?" I said as Francesca guided the trap through the moss-covered stone piers that guarded Halfpenny House, and onto the road to Hawksbridge. "I know that look – you're up to some mischief!"

Francesca smiled enigmatically at me. "You'll find out soon enough. Not mischief, exactly – although I suppose it could turn around and bite me if I'm not careful. Oh, it's wonderful, Thomas! I can't wait for you to see it."

I felt mounting curiosity, but also trepidation, knowing as I did how easily Francesca fell into this or that enthusiasm, often with unfortunate – if not scandalous – consequences. But she was glowing with happiness, and since life was never dull around Mrs Francesca Campbell, I decided to let myself enjoy the mystery and anticipation of the moment.

"You haven't told me about your honeymoon," she said. "How was Florence?"

"A little hot and noisy, if truth be told," I said. "But beautiful, of course. Almost too beautiful."

"Oh?" she said. "How so?"

"So many exquisite frescoes and paintings and statues... it becomes exhausting. One can have too much of a good thing."

"Perhaps, with dishonourable exceptions," she said. "You being a passionate man, I dare say Phyllis will already be expecting."

"Really, Francesca!" I protested. "Must you be so direct? No, we're being careful. We're not ready for a family."

"Careful?" Francesca said. "Oh dear! How unromantic. You're both far too young to be careful. And how is that even possible for you?"

"The usual way. Self-control."

She looked at me with a combination of incredulity and pity. "Self-control? You? I don't think that's good for a young married man. Or indeed, for his wife. But I expect you know what you're doing. Still – I give you two months at most before your resolve crumbles, and nature takes its course."

I shrugged and said, "We shall see." In fact, I very much doubted I could even hold out for another week. On returning to our hotel in the languid heat of the afternoons, surrounded by the decaying romance of old Italy, and having gazed on innumerable walls and ceilings depicting half-naked, rosy-cheeked, voluptuous women, carnal discipline had been nearly impossible. But having achieved the long-yearned-for goal of capturing my beloved Phyllis, pacing the course of our union was surely a small price to pay.

We were silent for a few minutes, as the trap rumbled onwards between hedges that were starting to hint at the autumn with occasional dashes of yellow. I stole a glance at Francesca as she looked ahead, smiling and lost in secret thought, elegant fingers curled around the reins. Devoted as I was to my new wife, I had – especially in the Pitti Palace – frequently been reminded of Francesca by the masters of the Baroque and their fleshy, twisting, stretching, and delightfully naked subjects. It was obvious that such paintings had inspired the angels in the Town Hall, and Francesca's angel in particular.

We had reached Hawksbridge, and had now passed through to the southern side, an area with which I was not especially familiar. We were nearly into open country again when my guide stopped the trap outside a run-down inn covered in scaffolding. Detached from its bracket and leaning against a wall was the inn's faded sign bearing the name 'The

Veiled Sisters' and showing two ghostly, white figures.

I looked quizzically at Francesca, and she flung a hand in the direction of the inn. "Behold!" she said, and climbed down. "This is mine, would you believe?" She tied the reins to a post and said, "Come on! I'll show you around."

"You've bought an inn?" I said, following her. "Good Lord. Whatever are you going to do with it?"

"Do it up and open it, of course," she said. "I have some railway shares – part of my arrangement with the North British Railway – and the dividends have been... well, a little shocking. So I thought I'd have an adventure with them."

I stood and peered at what I could see of the building behind its corset of poles and planks. Although the external walls seemed mostly sound, the window frames were either in poor condition or entirely absent, and the roof looked as though it had been neglected for many decades. From within the building, I could hear hammering sounds, whistling and the odd curse. Francesca had evidently lost no time in making her mark on the inn.

"Two buildings for the price of one," I said, looking at the different styles in which the building had been constructed.

"Yes, the seventeenth century stone part is the original inn, and the larger brick part on the right is a later addition. Early eighteenth century, or perhaps late seventeenth. I know it's hard to tell in this state – but is she not simply gorgeous?" Francesca clasped her hands and smiled broadly at me.

"Well, yes," I said. "Very elegant. You're bound to restore it to perfection. I just can't imagine you as an innkeeper."

"Then you must try harder, Thomas. You know how fascinating I find people – and think how many amusing characters will pass through these doors!"

"I hope so," I said. "I truly do. But the railway... won't it affect business?"

There had been anxious talk in Hawksbridge's drinking establishments about the inevitable reduction in coach business once the North British line was established. It occurred to me that the previous owner of 'The Veiled Sisters' must have been relieved – indeed, pleasantly surprised – to sell up.

"The railway doesn't faze me. And I have some ideas about that. But let's not stand and jabber – I want you to see inside."

Francesca opened a sturdy oak door in the newer part, and I followed her into a foyer, and then a guest parlour with an austere but impressive stone fireplace. Everything else had been stripped out; plaster was falling off the walls, and some floorboards were missing.

"Rotten," Francesca said, pointing to the hole in the floor. "But John will soon have it looking as good as new."

"John?" I asked.

At that moment the whistling stopped, and a genial-looking but very dusty man in his mid-thirties stepped into the room. He smiled, wiped his hands down on his overall, and extended his hand.

"John Hutton. Very pleased to meet you, sir."

"Thomas Rufford," I said, shaking his hand and resisting the urge to wipe my hands on my own clothes.

"As you probably guessed," Francesca said, "John is my builder. He's doing a marvellous job, considering his client is fussy and always changing her mind."

"As is her right, ma'am. Happy to oblige." He gave a bow and a flourish of his hand, with a well-judged balance of exaggeration and respect. His soft accent owed a little to Northumberland, and a little to the Scottish Borders.

"I thought we could patch the gutters," he added, "but on closer inspection, I'm afraid they're all pretty much shot, ma'am. Best replaced, in my view. You don't want to risk it. But our smith will make a good set of new ones for not too much."

"Then please do replace them all," Francesca said,

unperturbed by the news. I imagined she had had far greater shocks with this project.

"Have you had any ideas about a new name yet, ma'am?" John said. "Just so we can get you a sign made. I can't say I ever cared for the old name." He shivered. "No wonder business weren't brisk, ma'am. 'The Veiled Sisters'! It's macabre."

"Was there a reason for it, do you know?" I asked.

"Oh aye," John said. "A reason, and a story that'll curdle your blood."

"Now, John," Francesca said, "I'm trying to persuade Mr Rufford of the wisdom of my purchase. If you tell him ghost stories, I may as well give up now."

"Very good, ma'am," he said. "I'll skite back to work. But let me know about the name."

He quickly disappeared, and Francesca raised her voice: "'The Angel Arms', John!"

John's head appeared around the door again and he grinned knowingly. "Of course, Mrs Campbell! 'The Angel Arms'. Of course. What else could it be?"

The inn's new owner made a shooing gesture; the builder once more vanished and the whistling started again, followed shortly by banging noises.

"How sweet," I said. "You seemed to have gained both an inn and a loyal puppy. I believe he'd do anything for you."

"Yes, what luck!" Francesca said. "We do seem to have hit it off rather. In a purely professional sense, obviously."

"Intriguing," I said.

"Not really," Francesca said, although I noticed she avoided my gaze. "Now, the kitchen!"

My tour continued, and the dirt and shabbiness seemed only to fuel Francesca's zeal. Hutton's men were busy ripping old plaster from walls and removing window frames. The proportions of the inn's rooms were good, which was fortunate as this quality – bar the fireplaces, the doors and the odd pair of shutters – represented practically all that remained of the original building. The previous owner had evidently lost all interest in his business and let it decay. But John Hutton had exuded such competence and confidence that I had no doubt that it would soon be as good as new. Perhaps better, as here was an opportunity to banish many of the inconveniences of the past. Francesca's staff and guests might enjoy modern plumbing and even a luxury of which Ramsburgh was not yet availed: gas lighting.

The original sixteenth century inn was now relegated to an annexe. I stopped in one of the back bedrooms and peered through a grimy, broken window pane. In the courtyard, I could see the stables, but set further back, there was another substantial building whose form and purpose I could not quite make out through the dirt.

"That's the best part!" said Francesca, pulling at my arm. "Come!"

~

I was standing in a chapel that had evidently been used as a store-room for some time. It was full of the debris of maybe a hundred years: tea chests, broken farm implements, chairs with no seats, old beds, pottery, and filth from the pigeons that now called it home, coming and going through several holes in the roof.

The victim of much neglect, it seemed a miracle that it had survived as long as it had. Perhaps it was under divine protection as it waited patiently to be restored to its original use. Although the chapel was modest in size, the number of faithful that could be accommodated was swollen by the wooden gallery that was wrapped around the interior. It, too, was filled with rubbish, and several pigeons were perched along the handrail, observing us suspiciously.

I returned my astonished gaze to Francesca, who was beaming as though I had been admiring the Sistine Chapel itself.

"Isn't it thrilling?" she said. "I can't believe this belongs to me. The potential!"

I scanned the building again, trying to see what she saw. Admittedly, it was a fine example of Puritan architecture, with beautiful rafters – in what state of decay, the Lord and Hutton only knew.

"You're not going to form a sect, are you?" I said. "The Francescans, perhaps? I'm sure you would have no trouble finding devotees. John Hutton would be the first member of your congregation, I think."

Francesca laughed. "Not you? I'm devastated."

I shook my head. "Alas, no. I have a wife I must worship."

"You mustn't put ideas into my head – but no, I have no plans for a sect. A theatre, of course, Thomas! Don't you think it would make an absolutely gorgeous little theatre?"

She went to stand in the centre of the chancel, and raised her arms dramatically. "We'll have a stage here. And a fancy proscenium arch above. We can charge more for the gallery. It's all so perfect!"

"We?" I said, alarmed.

"Oh, forgive me, Thomas! But I had this fantasy that you might help me with the theatre. You need to be diverted from the events of this year, and kept well out of trouble! And you can let Phyllis get on with her book."

She came up to me and took hold of my hands. "Oh, I know it's silly of me. But we could have so much fun. Might you consider it?"

I had to smile at her enthusiasm. "But I have no theatrical talents," I said. "What on earth could I do?"

"You wouldn't have to act, of course, unless you wanted

to. You can help me design the theatre furnishings, create a company, commission plays... and give me moral support when it becomes fraught! You're so good at that." She squeezed my hands. "Besides, you have already helped to start a successful business – Myrtle's! I need someone to advise me – and ground me a little."

The notion was not entirely without appeal. I had been worried that I would become frustrated with no more cases to occupy me, while Phyllis became absorbed in her writing. It was true that I needed something new to get my teeth into, and this was as good a distraction as any.

I looked around again. "You really think you can rescue the place?"

"Of course," Francesca said. "John says it can be done – it won't be cheap, but I don't care."

"And you think we can attract an audience?"

"I know we can!" said Francesca. "I have lots of ideas. Oh, you said 'we' – you're considering it! Thank you!" She embraced me, and then said, "Let's go back to Halfpenny House, and I can tell you everything."

~

"You're taking on a lot," I said, putting down my coffee cup. It was agreeable to be out of the dust and must of Francesca's eccentric new empire. From the comfortable vantage point of Francesca's drawing room, the scale of my friend's ambitions seemed daunting, even reckless. "An inn and a new theatre? Will it not wear you out?"

"I need it," Francesca said. "I get bored quickly. Besides, since both businesses are on the same site, I can look after both more easily. And I'll hire plenty of staff. I'll need a theatre director-cum-manager."

"And the railway?"

"The railway will bring us guests for the inn, and an audience for the theatre. Some will be customers for both. Hawksbridge is going to be a wonderful place for people to take their holidays: it has its natural beauty, its stories – not least due to your recent adventures – and the theatre will be another reason for people to come."

She frowned. "And we must counterbalance that dreadful vulgarity – Tanner's Wonderland." She spat out the name. "Ugh. I can barely bring myself to say it. It will be like a permanent fair, with its caged animals, penny shies and goodness knows what else. Mr Tanner plans to help himself to the wages of the railway navvies. How can we let Hawksbridge be notorious for that? We must offer something uplifting and edifying."

"True," I said, "though I have to confess that Tanner's venture does sound intriguing. I gather it's also a gymnasium –"

"Ah yes, just so he can claim the moral high ground, and get his licence!" Francesca said, buttering her toast. "But it will be little more than a collection of fairground entertainments. And the 'Hawksbridge Worm'! Who wants to sit in a giant machine with dozens of other people and row in circles? It's ridiculous!"

I nodded, trying to visualise this strange contraption. It sounded rather jolly. "Why 'worm', I wonder?" I mused.

"Surely you know the story of the Hawksbridge Worm?" said Francesca. "It's such a shame it'll now be associated with the awful Mr Tanner. Anyway, the Worm, or Basilisk, was supposedly a monster that menaced the town hundreds of years ago. It had to be propitiated with maidens, who were tied naked to a post at night – one a month. In the morning, they had vanished without a trace. All gloriously horrible."

"And was this thing vanquished?"

"Yes, by fairies!" she said. I sniggered, and she frowned

and said, "I see you're not in the mood for fairy tales, so I'll tell you the rest of the story another time, if you wish. But I assure you, you're out of step with the town – folk lore is becoming more popular. People see the monstrosities of industry, and yearn for the monsters of old. Who can blame them? And I would like to explore this in my theatre."

"I underestimated you, Francesca," I said. "I should have known better by now – you've obviously thought it all through. I believe you'll have a success on your hands."

"You mean, *we* shall have a success on our hands! Let's drink to it."

~

When I returned to Ramsburgh, I found Phyllis in the library surrounded by several piles of books. She was absorbed in a history of the Jacobite uprisings, and did not immediately stir when I entered the room. I sat down in an old wainscot chair and waited, reluctant to break into her thoughts.

After a moment she looked up, frowning. "Sorry, I just need to finish this chapter," she said. "There are some excellent things for my story."

A little disappointed, I withdrew to pour myself a glass of port. I wanted to tell her my news, but I was having to acclimatise myself to my wife's work habits and her frequent scholarly detachment. After all, I had promised her that our marriage would not be the death of Phyllis' literary alter ego, Iona Tavistock. It was not entirely what I had imagined a marriage would be, but I could at least look forward to her undivided attention in bed, a pleasant moment that finally arrived.

"A theatre?" she said as she snuffed out the candle. "Francesca is opening a theatre?"

I forgot my earlier annoyance and revelled in the pleasure of cradling my warm wife in the darkness. It now seemed extraordinary that for so much of my life, I had gone to bed alone, silent and often cold.

"Yes, in an old chapel, next to her inn."

"Her *what?*"

I explained as best I could Francesca's new domain and ambitions. "And she wanted to know if I could help her – organize a few things, and act as a sounding board. I've been wondering how I'm going to fill my days – the Pottery and the estate don't take up much time."

"I'm sure I could find something for you to do now, at least," Phyllis said, turning over and kissing me on the lips. Inflamed, I started to kiss her cheeks and neck before I realised I ought to finish the topic I had begun.

"Do you think I should do it?" I asked. "Help with the theatre, I mean?"

Phyllis considered, tracing my features with an elegant index finger. "It could be satisfying. You should. Besides, it will keep you..." She hesitated.

"Out of your way while you're working? That's what Francesca said."

"How acute she is! It's not that I want to banish you, of course, but if I feel you're stomping around the house searching for something to do, it will make it hard to concentrate. So yes, why not?"

"Thank you," I said, resuming my kisses. "You're very generous."

"I do believe I am," Phyllis replied softly, removing her night-dress and tossing it on the floor.

CHAPTER TWO

THE muse having descended overnight, Phyllis kissed me and left me in the dining room to my toast, coffee and thoughts of the night's pleasant exertions. I considered the injustice that Francesca had no bed-mate. It was a terrible waste. But what about John Hutton? Did I detect a spark between them, or was this simply my prurient imagination? Hutton's mischievous humour, his energy and his engaging smile must surely be a temptation, especially for such a romantic soul as Francesca, and she would be inclined to overlook or even enjoy the difference in social standing, for a while. Against my will, my brain conjured up an image of the two in a passionate clinch, and, disgusted with myself, I rose and gazed out of the window at the south lawn, recently dampened by a shower.

As I emptied my thoughts of forbidden visions, a carriage came into view. I was irritated by the intrusion, and tried to recall if Phyllis was expecting anyone. But as two figures dismounted and the carriage was dismissed, I realised with dismay that I recognised both of them: a pair who belonged not in my present life, but firmly in a past I had been thankful to outgrow. What the devil were they doing here now? Was this some ghastly, misconceived surprise that my wife had arranged?

Despite my sense of dread, I knew I had to act the genial host for what I trusted would be a short interlude. I did not like the fact that the carriage had been sent away as if in the expectation of a protracted stay. It was all thoroughly disagreeable, but hoping to get it over with quickly, I reached the hall just as Shipley was opening the door.

"Tom! How are you, my old friend? I assume you got my letter." The unwanted guest strode into the hall and my heart sank as he put down a large travelling case. With an apologetic expression, his companion put down her own, smaller case.

"Peter," I said with as much enthusiasm as I could muster. "What a pleasant surprise."

Age had already taken some of his hair, but an unkempt beard – showing signs of premature grey – attempted to distract from this fact. He was also thickening around the waist, and it all gave the impression of a much older man than he was. He was almost a caricature of the boy I once knew, and it was disconcerting.

"And Louise, how are you?" I continued. I shook their hands, noting Louise's obvious discomfort, and added, "I'm afraid I didn't get your letter, no."

"Oh, Lord," Peter said, handing his coat to a stony-faced Shipley. "How embarrassing. So you had no idea we were coming until just now?"

"None whatsoever," I said, forcing a smile. "But please come through to the dining room and have a drink and a bite to eat."

"Wonderful," he said. "We're both famished, truth to tell. Didn't really fancy the food at the inn last night." Louise stared at him, and I guessed that there was another reason for their lack of sustenance. She caught my eye, and we seemed to come to an understanding that her brother's statements were not to be taken at face value.

I smiled reassuringly at her. "Shipley, I believe bacon and eggs and coffee are called for. Will that be amenable? I'll just have some more toast."

"That would be most acceptable," Peter said. Louise nodded miserably and managed a faint smile.

Shipley left, and we took our places at the table. Almost immediately, Peter rose again to absorb the view from the window.

"Splendid lodgings you've acquired, Tom. You're a squire now! King of your own little castle. Who'd have thought little Tom would become the celebrated Thomas Rufford, fearless scourge of Northumberland's criminals?"

Coming from anyone else's lips, it might have been a compliment, but here there was more than a hint of insincerity. Louise did her best to cover her brother's tone.

"The Times had a piece about your ordeal," she said. "That dreadful woman! But perhaps I shouldn't..."

"It's all right," I said. "With luck, I'll never have to do the police's duty for them again. It's neither to my taste, nor theirs."

Peter turned sharply from the window. "Oh, come now, Tom. Such false modesty. Doesn't it make your heart pump faster when the Grim Reaper is breathing down your neck? Doesn't it give you a little thrill? I bet it does. And of course it doesn't harm your standing with the ladies. Am I wrong?"

Before taking his chair again, he gave me a slap on the back, and Louise winced.

"Peter," she said, "you really need to explain why we are here, and ask Thomas..." She trailed off, mortified.

"All in good time, Lou," Peter said, putting his elbows on the table and making a show of being at his ease. "Oh, very well. Would you mind awfully putting us up for a few days, old man? It would be a great kindness. We've had a spot of bother with our landlord. Couldn't reason with the stupid fellow at all. Inbred, I should say. And we needed a break from London anyway – Louise never shuts up about the noise and smell. And what better to combine a trip with seeing a good old friend from long ago? We can reminisce about our escapades."

Before I had time to reply, Phyllis appeared in the doorway. "Thomas is still getting himself into trouble," she said. "Good morning! Shipley tells me you are Peter and Louise McNulty. Thomas has mentioned you. You're most welcome."

I was proud of my wife's forbearance; she did not like her writing to be interrupted by surprises. I felt glad, too, that I had made a good marriage. It was the return of a competitive streak I had always felt with Peter, and which I now realised was an immutable feature of our relationship, such as it was.

"You are very kind, Mrs Rufford," Louise said, standing and bowing her head. "I'm so sorry that we did not signal our visit in advance. There was some confusion."

"Think nothing of it," Phyllis said. "I'm afraid I can't stay – I must finish a scene. But I look forward to getting to know both of you."

"A scene?" Louise asked when Phyllis had left and Mrs Felton had laid breakfast on the table. "Does Mrs Rufford paint?"

"My wife is a novelist," I said. "Yes, of course you may stay here. It will be a pleasure." According to the habit I had lately formed, and against my better judgement, I was beginning to see her current situation as a puzzle that I needed to solve.

Peter grunted and after chewing noisily for a moment said, "Novelist? Surprised you didn't make her put away her scribbling when you married. Seems quite distracted by it – would drive me mad. Nothing published, I take it?"

I made an effort to control my annoyance. Peter had never been a sensitive youth, but in adulthood he had evidently become insufferable.

"Some," I said. "Nothing you would be interested in, I expect. She writes as 'Iona Tavistock'."

Louise put down her cutlery and her eyes widened. "No! You're teasing us, surely? As in 'The Author of Kingshorne Priory'?"

I nodded, and a blush coloured her pallid complexion.

"Peter," she said earnestly, "did you know this? We have disturbed a great writer! We have barged into the home of the wonderful Iona... It's too..." She was unable to finish her sentence as she forced back tears of humiliation.

Peter looked at his sister with contempt and said, "I need a drink. You don't happen to have any whisky, Tom? I'm parched."

I nodded at Shipley, who had just come in, and with the trace of a grimace, he went to fetch a glass.

~

I decided to give them Flora's tower. Louise took Flora's rooms, for which she was charmingly grateful, while Peter was consigned to Mrs Northcutt's old room upstairs. By the time breakfast was done, Mrs Felton and the new maid, Mellor, had finished making the beds, and Peter staggered off to his, smelling of whisky.

"I'll let you have some peace and quiet before lunch," I said to Louise at the door.

"Thank you so much, Thomas," she said. "I really didn't want us to impose ourselves on you like this, and I would have utterly refused had I known..."

"It's quite all right," I said. "There's plenty of space here, as you can see, and my wife is perfectly capable of ignoring everything else that's going on. You may not see much of her, I'm afraid."

For a moment, I considered how strange it was that Louise McNulty stood before me as a guest, no longer aloof as she appeared in the old days, and with her plump, youthful features transformed by time. Yet there was the mole on her cheek that had always fascinated me, and the Roman nose she shared with her brother. Her once untidy mousy hair was now tamed in a bun; the lips that had stirred strange feelings were quite as full, while her slender fingers now fiddled with a fossil brooch. I recalled that she had always been obsessed by these echoes of ancient life. She had been a bookish child, while her older brother and I had played with lead soldiers or made mischief amongst the London traders. And often it had been with reluctance that I followed Peter on some game or other, glancing back at this quiet, detached girl, curious to find out more, wanting to reach a hand out and touch...

She smiled, as if reading my thoughts. "What could you have thought of me when we were all young? I must have been a dull, shy girl."

"Not at all," I said. "You intrigued me. I regretted not talking to you properly and discovering what interested you. I might have learned something. I was equally shy, especially around girls."

"And I'm afraid a fossilised shark's tooth was far more compelling to me than any boy," she said. "Well, most boys," she added.

"I must leave you in peace," I repeated. "You can find me or Mrs Felton, or Shipley, if you need anything. Fox will be wanting his walk."

"Thank you, Thomas," she said. "You have been so kind to us."

~

I peeked into the library, not wanting to disturb Phyllis, but keen to discuss our new guests.

She was at the table. "Come in," she said, sensing the open door despite my best efforts at stealth. "I need a break. I've done quite well." She stood up, went to the window, and stretched.

I joined her at the window and clasped her hand. "I'm sorry about this," I said. "It's really extraordinary. I don't believe he wrote any letter to us, for fear of being rebuffed.

And so soon in our marriage! The man's a boor."

"It's not your fault," she said. "Did they say how long they want to stay?"

"A few days, Peter said. But that could mean anything."

"I see. Well, we'll take him at his word and give it a few days before dropping any hints. Has Peter always been like this?"

"Now I come to think of it," I said, "he did take liberties. He used to borrow my clothes, and I would get them back dirty or ripped, for which I would get the blame. And one time he delighted in tearing the cover off a treasured book. I've no idea why I put up with him. But our fathers were friends, supposedly. And he could often be amusing company, I'll give him that."

"His poor sister," Phyllis said. "I can only imagine what it's like for her. I assume she has to accompany him for reasons of economy?"

"I would think so," I said. "I can't imagine it's for sentimental reasons."

"At least one of them seems bearable. Unless her respectability is all an act, and they mean to rob us blind in the night!"

"Oh, surely not," I said, but realised it had been naive of me not to have at least considered this possibility. "My instincts tell me that Louise is genuine, and you didn't see how embarrassed she was about her brother bringing her here. That would have to be part of a very cunning strategy. And she admires your work, which makes her a woman of taste."

"I defer to your judgement," Phyllis said, "as you have more knowledge of the McNultys than I. We shall draw them out at lunch. Oh," she added, dropping my hand. "She's not one of your conquests, is she?"

"Far from it," I said, embracing her and kissing her on the lips. "You're one of only two women in this house to see me naked."

"I beg your pardon?"

"Mrs Felton, I'm ashamed to say," I said. "On my first day here, I was so tired I just collapsed on the bed in my natural state. And she brought me breakfast."

"Lucky her," Phyllis said, "but luckier me," and she drew her fingers through my hair.

"I suppose there isn't time to...?"

"Certainly not," Phyllis said, cruelly planting a lingering kiss on my neck to magnify my frustration. "You will have to wait."

~

"So, Louise," Phyllis said as we ate lunch, "what are your interests? Are you still collecting fossils?"

"The ladies have to keep themselves occupied, naturally," Peter cut in, "and if it's not needlepoint or scrapbooking, it's wallowing in the mud looking for old bones. Undignified, I say. Why not just sit and read a book if you don't have duties to perform? Leave science to men who know about these things."

Peter's ruddy face and the empty decanter betrayed an excess of whisky consumption.

"Mrs Rufford asked me, Peter, so I shall answer," said Louise. "I do like reading – including your excellent novels, Mrs Rufford – but I confess my main interest is indeed as a muddy fossil-hunter. The field of palaeontology, that is. I hope to write a book for children on the subject."

Peter snorted. "That I would like to see," he muttered.

"Very well, then; I shall not disappoint you," Louise said with spirit. "I believe the coastline here is quite fertile with fossils."

"How interesting," said Phyllis. "Then we shall make sure

we find transport for you, and get you to the cliffs with sturdy boots. Do you have equipment?"

"I have a little bag of things that I carry with me, just in case," Louise said. "A hammer and chisel, a brush, some linen bags, and a notebook. So you see I have come prepared – I even have the boots."

"Wonderful!" said Phyllis. "Perhaps we should all have an expedition. Who knows, I might find some inspiration."

"Let me think," I said. "A feisty lady fossil-hunter meets a rugged local, and an unlikely friendship develops over a shared interest in ancient beasts."

"Something like that," said Phyllis. "Throw in a murderous cleric determined to disprove the existence of dinosaurs, perhaps. Oh, sorry – this wasn't meant in a mocking way, my dear Miss McNulty!"

"Of course not!" said Louise. "I'm all for a novel that commends the subject to the public."

"Count me out of your expedition," said Peter. "I can't imagine what the appeal is. All that dirt and weather just for a few bones."

Phyllis turned to Peter and gave him a penetrating look. "Tell me, Mr McNulty, what are your interests, if I may be so bold?"

"Oh, this and that," he said dismissively. "I dabble in investments. I read a bit. I like to go to the races. The usual sort of thing."

It was a thin list. What happened to the Peter McNulty who was going to be an engineer, and then a lawyer, and at one point, a Member of Parliament? Probably drink had overtaken him, and a loss of respectability that made it hard to climb either a social or a professional ladder. And now he was desperate enough to seek shelter from friends, or former friends. It was pathetic. And poor Louise had been dragged down with him.

"Your parents, Peter," I said. "Are they living still?"

"Alas, no," he said. "They died some years ago. Consumption got both of them."

No doubt, I thought, Peter had then quickly run through his inheritance, and anything that Louise had been given. I felt little sympathy for Peter, but Louise did not deserve this. At least she had the distraction and challenge of her fossils.

"Any more of that whisky?" Peter said, clutching his empty glass.

"No more, Peter," Louise said. "You've had quite enough, and it's making you crotchety. Perhaps some water?"

"To blazes with water!" Peter erupted, standing up. "Typical female response. I'm going to see what Hawksbridge has to offer. Tom, can you get your man to find me a carriage?"

Shipley cleared his throat. "I can get old Howard to take you down in the trap, sir, but I'm afraid you'll have to make your own way back."

"Oh, fine, fine," Peter said. "If necessary I'll stay over. You'll all enjoy yourselves better without me anyway, I'll be bound."

~

Phyllis went back to her work, and I found myself in the drawing room drinking coffee with Louise. She was looking vexed.

"Is he safe on his own, in town?" I asked.

"Probably not," Louise said. "But what can I do? Where he's going won't be fit for ladies."

"Quite," I said. "It must be extremely hard for you."

"Somewhat," she said. "And it's sad watching the decline of one's own brother. I live on tenterhooks waiting for something awful to happen."

"I'm sure he'll be back tonight in one piece. He's made it this far. Do you have plans?"

"That's the most terrifying thing," she said, turning her coffee cup absently in its saucer. "I confess we have none. The money is almost spent – I'm sure you will have guessed this already – on drink, horses, and unprofitable ventures."

"If I may ask – you have no independent means?"

She shook her head. "All gone, save my mother's jewellery, which he's been pawning. I tried to dissuade Peter from coming here, but we were thrown out of our lodgings, and I had little choice but to come with him. This is why I need to publish."

"Quite so," I said. "And for that, you need a conducive atmosphere in which to write."

She shook her head. "A desperate dream. I don't know what to do." She sighed, and added, "I'm so sorry to burden you with this – with us. We must leave in the morning."

"To go where?" I said.

"I have no idea," she said.

"Then you must stay until the future is clearer," I said, regretting it almost immediately, but knowing that I could not possibly throw her onto the street – although her brother was a different matter.

"That's kind of you," she said with a short-lived smile, "but it would be absurd. How long have you been married?"

"A month or so," I said.

Louise closed her eyes. "Oh, Lord. I'm so embarrassed."

"Don't be," I said. "Such a predicament could happen to anyone. Fortunes shift. I cannot deny the sheer luck that has brought me to this point – luck that could just as easily have turned against me."

"Thank you," she said. "Let's not talk about me and my brother any longer. I'd like to hear about your life. Have you got to know interesting people here?"

"I have indeed," I said, pouring us both more coffee. "Let

me tell you all about the remarkable Mrs Francesca Campbell, and her theatre."

~

Dinner without Peter was an enjoyable affair, and the two women warmed to one another. Phyllis was happy to field Louise's questions about her books, and we were engaged in such an intense discussion about the nature of prehistoric life on Earth that we quite forgot to worry about Peter's continued absence.

CHAPTER THREE

IN THE morning, Peter had not returned, but we reassured each other that he was sleeping off a sore head in one of the town's less savoury inns. We were about to retire after breakfast when there came the sound of brisk hooves on gravel.

I went outside to greet Francesca as she was dismounting. She seemed to be in a state of excitement.

"Thomas! You'll never guess what we've found at the inn!"

"Oh? We? What have you found?"

"Well, John and his men. Writing. A message from the past!"

She pulled a piece of paper from her sleeve. "Here, I've written it down. What do you make of that?"

I read while Francesca looked expectantly at me, catching her breath.

I read the strange words in Francesca's handwriting, and then re-read them.

> GOD FORGIVE ME, FOR BY MY COWARDLY SILENCE I HAVE IMPERILLED MY MORTAL SOUL. RIP C. AND A., SWEETEST OF BEINGS, WHOM I INTERRED IN THEIR ... GRAVE WITH NO ... SAVE THE LORD'S PRAYER. DEATH IS MY PENANCE AND MY RELEASE.
> R.M.

The last line sent a shiver down my spine.

"Good God," I said. "The last words of some poor wretch."

"Precisely," Francesca said. "Chilling, but fascinating. I couldn't make all of it out, but the gist is clear."

"Where was this message?"

"In one of the guest rooms in the old part of the inn. It was on the wall under the wainscoting – it's being replaced."

"A deathbed confession," I said. "'Penance' implies his or her death is a self-imposed punishment. If this was a long time ago, I don't suppose we'll ever know who it was."

"Oh, Thomas, you disappoint me!" said Francesca, taking back the note. "We have three sets of initials. Are you not intrigued?"

"Well, yes, but..." I had the disagreeable sensation of now possessing knowledge that would torment me if I did not try to make sense of it.

"You know perfectly well that a mystery such as this cannot just be put aside. We must know what it's about. A horrible crime must have taken place, presumably in Hawksbridge! And then the poor devil..."

I sighed. "I suppose so. Shall I come and look at it? I don't have any other plans today."

Francesca smiled, and then turned to see who was trudging wearily up the path. It was Peter, dishevelled and bleary; he must have walked from town. He grunted as he passed us and sloped into the house, and I felt disinclined to make introductions.

"Goodness!" said Francesca. "Who on earth is he?"

"A rather unwelcome house guest. Peter McNulty. I have mentioned him concerning..."

"That unpleasant business in your youth, of course. He's not here to make trouble, is he?"

"I hope not. He seems more of a danger to himself than to us. His sister is more charming, though. Louise."

"Two guests? How inconvenient for you – you have my sympathies."

"Thank you. Phyllis is being surprisingly patient about it. Let me fetch Celeste, and we'll go and take a look at this confession."

~

"It could be a hoax, of course," I said, staring at the faded scribble on the wall while a frowning John Hutton turned a piece of the freed, crumbling wainscoting over in his hands. "A bored guest may have decided to play a prank."

Francesca looked disappointed. "Really? Oh, how annoying that would be. How could we begin to tell?"

"Still," I said, "even the existence of a prank is a story. You might find the publicity helpful in any case."

"Don't you think there's something about the writing, though?" Francesca said. "It seems... fraught."

Hutton looked up. "Written with a nail dipped in ink, I reckon," he said.

I got closer and peered at the wall. Francesca was right: there was a crookedness in the strokes of the letters, and deep, uneven depressions in the plaster that spoke of a frantic state of mind rather than someone carefully constructing a deception.

"The word before 'grave'," I said. "Is that an 'F' or an 'E' at the beginning? Do you have a candle?"

"I'll get one," Francesca said.

I observed a brief twitch of a smile on Hutton's face as he watched Francesca get to her feet and leave the room.

He turned to me. "Seems the ghosts are coming back to haunt the place after all," he said. "Has Mrs Campbell told you the story of the Veiled Sisters yet?"

"No," I said. "I quite forgot to ask."

"Ah, well, she'll enjoy telling you it herself when she's in the mood. I won't spoil it. When this gets out, more superstitious folks than me will say the building's cursed."

"You're not troubled by such notions?"

He chuckled. "Not me. Too busy for fancies. Never seen a spirit myself, but I keep an open mind. You?"

"Likewise," I said.

"An admirable woman, Mrs Campbell," Hutton said. "I mean, to take this on, ghosties and all, on her own." He shot a glance at the empty doorway before adding, "She *is* on her own?"

"As far as I know, yes," I replied, and he shook his head and tutted.

"It's not right," he said. "A woman like her."

"I was thinking that myself," I said. "But she does enjoy her freedom. Marriage didn't agree with her."

"Oh, aye, I can fathom that," Hutton said. "What fellow could measure up to her?" He put the wainscoting carefully aside where no one would trip over it.

"Still," I said, not wanting him to be discouraged, "she's also a passionate woman who values noble qualities over worldliness."

He nodded. "Rare, she is," he said. "Rare indeed."

Francesca appeared with a candlestick and a lucifer match. "What's rare?" she asked.

"Discovering a mystery such as this," I said to spare Hutton's blushes.

I held the lit candle up to the wall and moved it around, and the shadows in the depressions made it a little easier to read the scribble where the pigment had faded.

"R, perhaps," I said. "The last letter is D or O. Not many words end with O, so let's say D."

"Frigid!" Francesca said. "Could it be that?"

I squinted. "Yes, I think you're right. 'Frigid grave' – that makes sense."

"Oh, goodness," said Francesca, shivering. "That's even grimmer."

Moving the candle some more, I read the second faint word as 'comforts'.

"'No comforts save the Lord's prayer'," repeated Francesca.

The three of us fell silent, pitying the distressed soul who had scrawled such a tortured admission.

After a minute, Francesca sighed and said, "But who is this message for?"

"Everyone and no one," Hutton said.

"I suppose he had to unburden himself," I said, "even to an audience not yet born."

"Assuming it's a 'he'," Francesca said.

"Burying two people requires considerable muscle strength," I said. "It seems more likely to be a man."

Hutton nodded in agreement, and Francesca winced. "Yes, you're probably right. And who were C. and A.? His victims?"

"Well, he displays considerable guilt – enough to end his own life. And we might assume that the use of 'sweetest' implies the two to be female, unless..."

"Unless?"

I hesitated. "Unless they were children, which would discount my theory about strength."

Hutton swore under his breath.

Francesca shook her head and knelt on the floor by the wall. "It's horrible, yet fascinating. I'm sorry. Who were you?" She slowly moved her fingers over the writing as if this would reveal its secrets.

"If you've no use for me here, ma'am, I'll get on with my duties," Hutton said, moving towards the door.

"Yes... yes, of course," Francesca said distractedly. Hutton smiled at me and left me to await my friend's wakening from her reverie.

~

Although it was not the day for men to be allowed into Myrtle's, Bess had made a permanent exception for me, due not least to my position as investor in the coffee shop.

"You're an honorary female!" Francesca said after a little small talk with Bess.

"An honour indeed," I said. "Now – are you going to enlighten me about the Veiled Sisters? Hutton said you would enjoy telling the tale."

"How thoughtful he is," Francesca said. "Very well. This is what John told me, from local folklore. Did I mention that the inn is built on the grounds of an old nunnery?"

"You did not. But I think I can see where this is leading."

"Don't spoil it for me, Thomas. Well, apparently there was a bout of cholera that wiped out many of the nunnery's inhabitants – perhaps that was why it was abandoned. The story goes that shortly after the inn was built – using some of the stone from the nunnery – a guest had a strange experience. As the clock in the hall struck midnight, his room became chilly and shrouded with mist, and he heard the sound of women whispering close by. Terrified, he hid his head under the blanket."

The image this produced in my mind was disquieting, despite my scepticism.

"After a minute," Francesca said, "he plucked up courage to peep out from under the blanket, and to his horror, he could just see two veiled figures standing at the end of his bed. The mist cleared, and he could tell they were women, staring at him – and yet they wore kind expressions. They both smiled, and then faded away. And he was only the first to see the figures in that particular room."

"Remarkable," I said, taking some coffee. "I would imagine that would not be good for business."

"On the contrary," Francesca said. "If a guest saw the Veiled Sisters, it was said that good fortune would follow. So for a long time, the inn was popular for this reason, and the proprietor even charged more for the haunted room."

"That would be excellent for those wishing to assure creditors of their financial soundness," I said. "They would only have to claim to have seen the Veiled Sisters, and they would be a good bet."

"Exactly," Francesca said. "And apparently plenty of people did profess to see them."

A peal of laughter interrupted our conversation. At a nearby table, a young woman with copper hair, perhaps nineteen or twenty years of age, was having an animated conversation with her friend.

"So Mr Lilley comes up to me and says, 'What a *pleasure* to meet such a *charming* employee!'" The young woman enacted both Mr Lilley's role and her own, in exaggerated style. "'Oh, thank you, sir, thank you!' says I, and he looks me up and down for a while with a twisted smile – ugh! – puts his hand on my head, and says, 'Delightful, to be sure, Miss Gardner, delightful! You must come to my office if you have anything you want to talk about with me. Think of me as a wise old uncle.' And he walks away."

"No!" her horrified companion breathed. "How odious, Rosabel!"

"That's the word, Mabel, that's the word. I wanted to go and scrub myself."

I looked at Francesca, who was clearly fascinated by the young woman.

I bent forward. "Mr Lilley," I whispered, "is the managing director at the Pottery. Never took to him."

"The poor thing!" Francesca whispered back. "Would she

not make a wonderful actress, though?"

I stole another glance at Rosabel. She positively glowed with youthful energy and beauty. I looked away, not wanting to risk any comparison with Mr Lilley.

"You're right," I said. "And she might like a break from the Pottery, judging from her story."

"Indeed," Francesca said. "We know where to find her. I'm sorry – what were we saying?"

"The Veiled Sisters – not birth sisters, then, but sisters in Christ," I said.

"I suppose so," she said.

"And do you believe this to be history, or fable?"

"I don't know. How could we ever know?"

"Doesn't it terrify you that you might see the Sisters yourself?" I asked.

"Not if it brings good fortune! And it would be fascinating. I rather hope to see them."

"All very engaging," I said, biting into a scone. "So why, then, will you change the inn's name to the 'Angel Arms'?"

"Oh, just an instinct," she said, "that I must break with the past and establish a new association – ministering angels rather than misty, whispering spirits. My more timid customers might be put off by the prospect of being haunted at midnight."

"And it doesn't do any harm to publicise your own role as model for the Town Hall's mother angel."

"None at all," she said, smiling. "I think it all works quite well." She became more serious. "And yet... we now have a graver mystery than the Sisters. I need to know who died in my inn."

"John didn't have any further myths for you that could shed any light?"

She shook her head.

"Then I'll do some reading," I said, wondering if my library might reveal any 'R.M.s' of old.

"Oh, would you, Thomas? I would be so grateful," Francesca said, putting her hand on mine. "And we must find a director for the theatre! That will be quite a task."

CHAPTER FOUR

FOR some time, I had been looking forward to the first dinner party of our married life. But it was hardly possible to exclude our house guests, and the prospect of Peter shaming us now cast a shadow over our plans.

"Louise will handle him," Phyllis had said, as we dressed for dinner. It was two days after the discovery of the writing on the wall. "She has obviously had plenty of practice. If he misbehaves, we'll send him straight to bed."

"And if the damage to our reputations has been done by then?"

"We'll be amongst friends," Phyllis had said. "They will understand."

But my misgivings remained as we took our seats for dinner.

"My dear Phyllis," said Olivia Harris, "how are you finding your new home? To us it looks heavenly, of course, but I realise that visiting a house and living in it are two quite different things. Do you miss your old place? If this isn't a little too personal, that is!"

Phyllis smiled. "Not at all, Olivia. Fortunately, I can report that I have very few quibbles with Ramsburgh. I have a library to write in, wonderful staff, and an amusing husband. Yes, I miss my old home now and again, though mainly for my father rather than the house."

"Oh, poor, dear Anthony – how is he?"

"In decent spirits, thank you. The rheumatism is tiresome, but he bears it well."

"Bless him. He has always been so kind to us. Now, Francesca," Mrs Harris continued, "what's all this about an inn? Or was it a theatre? I hear confusing things about your latest adventure!"

"I know it sounds extravagant and silly," said Francesca, "but I've bought an inn with a theatre attached."

"Really?" said Mrs Harris. "How extraordinary! Tell us more."

"It's not a theatre yet," Francesca said. "It's a chapel. But I'm converting it into a theatre."

"You do surprise me, my dear!" said Mrs Harris. She turned to her husband. "But then, I shouldn't be surprised to be surprised, should I, David, where Francesca is concerned?"

"Paradoxically so," Mr Harris said. "You are reliably interesting, Francesca."

Peter put down his glass of wine and opened his mouth, and I steeled myself for his contribution to the conversation.

"Oh dear," he said. "I heard in town that some foolish woman was trying to revive a haunted inn with no prospects. I do hope they weren't referring to you, ma'am."

"Peter!" Louise cried. "That's a horrible thing to say. Apologise at once."

"There's no need to get agitated," said Peter, languidly sitting back in his chair as if unfazed by the criticism. "I was merely reporting what the natives told me. That's all."

"They may be quite right," said Francesca. "It may be entirely foolish. But I have set myself this challenge, and I intend to see it through."

"And so you shall!" said Mr Harris, glancing contemptuously at Peter. "Some people create, and some people carp. I could never be so brave as to do what you're doing, Francesca. But we shall be loyal patrons of both your tap room and your theatre. You may count on it."

"I can't wait," Mrs Harris agreed. "And is it really haunted?"

Francesca looked at me. "In a manner of speaking," she said. "That is, I haven't seen the resident ghosts, but I've made a strange discovery. In fact, it's a case Thomas has promised to help me solve."

At that moment, the first course arrived, and Francesca sat sipping her wine and smiling.

"Well, my dears?" said Mrs Harris after we had all been served, looking first to Francesca and then to me. "What did you discover?" Francesca seemed inclined to let me tell the tale, and I obliged.

"My Lord!" said Mrs Harris. "What a terrible thing. And you have no notion at all of who these initials might belong to?"

"None," I replied. "But I'll make inquiries. There must surely be historical records of suicides, and since the inn was first opened in the late sixteen-hundreds, and the writing looks to be several decades old at least, we have about a hundred years of history to scour."

"Not Thomas' usual kind of case," Phyllis said. "Which is a relief, since there is no danger in it for a change."

"Not unless he awakens the spirits of the dead!" said Mr Harris dramatically, placing a candle under his chin for ghoulish effect.

"Oh, hush now, David," said Mrs Harris. "You'll set yourself on fire. Let's change the subject – I'm getting goose-bumps. Miss McNulty, do tell us all about yourself! I gather you're interested in fossils. They seem just as much of a mystery to me as ghosts."

Louise ignored her brother's groan. "I suppose that's what they are, in a way," she said. "Each is the trace of a former life from millions of years ago. That's part of the fascination – looking back such a long time, to when the world was utterly different. There are tiny fragments left for us to find and piece together an inkling about what life was like."

"So you're a detective, like Thomas?" Francesca said.

"You might say that," Louise said. "Except this puzzle can never really be solved entirely. The record is always going to be incomplete, and our interpretation subject to error."

"That must be frustrating to know," said Mrs Harris.

Louise shrugged. "I rarely think about it – only about what can be learned. Just as science is never complete."

"You would get on so well with my son!" said Mrs Harris. "Wouldn't she, my dear?" she added, turning to her husband and sighing. "I wish he were here."

"Certainly," said Mr Harris. "Victor hopes to find the mechanisms behind the creation of species, and he would undoubtedly be fascinated to hear your opinions on the subject."

"I assure you, Mr Harris," Peter said, "my sister has no pretensions to answer such weighty questions. And with the greatest respect to your son, I very much doubt that nature will yield its secrets to our generation, if indeed any."

"How can you be so sure, Mr McNulty?" said Mrs Harris. "Surprising advances are made by our scientists all the time. Just look at the progress in medicine, and the miracle of daguerreotypes!"

"Quackery and parlour tricks, I'm afraid," said Peter. "Of which I expect the town's new attraction will be full."

"What, Mrs Campbell's theatre?" said Mr Harris, who looked poised to rise and punch Peter in the head.

"I think he refers to Tanner's Wonderland, David," Phyllis said hastily.

"Ah yes," I said, "Tanner's *Magnificent* Wonderland, no less. It opens on Saturday – does anyone fancy going?"

"Certainly," said Francesca. "I'm intrigued to see what depths of vulgarity Mr Tanner is prepared to plumb."

"Then I'll go too, if I may," said Louise.

Her brother scowled, but Mrs Harris said, "That's settled! Those of us who wish to go shall make a day of it. What fun!"

I glanced at Phyllis, and she smiled and nodded.

"It'll be overrun with filthy navvies," Peter said. "You're welcome to it."

~

By the time Catherine came in with a fruit tart, Peter's face was red from the wine, and I wondered what would be next to set off his irritability. We were obviously a sore trial for him when he would rather be in a drinking establishment giving the locals the benefit of his wisdom.

"Thomas," Francesca said, "I believe I may have found my theatre director. A Mr Walter Jenrick. Is anyone familiar with him? He appears to have some experience in London."

"Ah, yes," said Mr Harris. "The story-teller. I gather he's quite popular. If he has a background in the theatre, then I suppose he must be filling in time with his stories. Have you interviewed him?"

"Not yet," Francesca said. "I'd like Thomas to be there. But he's been recommended to me, and I doubt there are many others with the appropriate experience in Hawksbridge."

"What sort of stories, may I ask?" said Mrs Harris.

"Fairy tales, apparently," said Mr Harris. "Is it just me, or are fairies and myths growing in popularity? I have to say I find it a trifle immature. Hunter's seems full of the stuff, and our great painters are turning to the likes of Robin Hood instead of Christian or historical themes."

"A passing fad, no doubt," said Peter.

"I confess I welcome it," Francesca said. "It's harmless, and some of it is rather charming."

"I'm sure you're right," said Mr Harris, never one to contradict Francesca for long. "I believe one of Jenrick's stories was about some kind of local beast."

"The Hawksbridge Worm!" said Francesca. "My housekeeper told me the story. May I repeat it? But it is quite gruesome, Olivia, so I wonder –"

"Oh, no, don't hold back on my account," Mrs Harris said. "I am now fortified by wine and the most glorious food."

"Very well," said Francesca. She thought for a moment, and then began: "A long time ago, before the town had its walls, Hawksbridge was plagued by a large serpent or basilisk. It would slither out of the river into the back streets and snatch unsuspecting townsfolk with its fearsome jaws. The beast was so stealthy that often relatives would only know their loved one had been taken when they didn't turn up for their next meal. Bones and clothes would be found on the shore soon after."

Mrs Harris grimaced, and looked at the piece of strawberry tart on her fork with unease.

"The Hawksbridge Worm, as it became known, plagued the town for some decades until a compromise was found. Every month, a maiden was chosen by a grim lottery, and the loser would be tied to a post by the shore. She would be naked to save the Worm the trouble of spitting out her clothes. After several years of this, the population of tasty morsels were so depleted that an old woman volunteered herself. The Worm was so enraged at the substitution that it spat the poor woman out half-eaten and went on a rampage, killing several townsfolk. And so they had to go back to their earlier scheme."

Francesca paused for a draught of the coffee that had been provided by Mrs Felton, before continuing.

"One day, a man named – oh, I forget. Let's call him John. One day John's fiancée lost the lottery, but his beloved sister decided to sacrifice herself in her place. As she was taken from their home, his sister's last words were, 'I die so that you and your sweetheart may live. Remember me, darling brother!' Utterly distraught, he vowed that whatever it took, he would do it in order to destroy the foul Worm. At that moment, a fairy appeared, and asked him to repeat his vow. When he had done so, the fairy cackled and said, 'We shall destroy the beast reviled – our reward shall be your first-born child!'"

Francesca's menacing tone for the fairy was good, and the

diners – even Peter – were listening intently.

"John groaned, and yet he realised that this was a fair price to save the town from the Worm for evermore. The fairy was as good as his word, giving the next maiden a potion that poisoned the beast after only consuming one arm. The maiden survived, and the beast's head was paraded through the town with great joy and celebration.

"John was shortly married, and his bride fell pregnant. He could not bear to tell her of the dreadful pact he had made. He cursed himself for it, and one night, he finally confessed to her. After they had both shed many tears, they stole off and rode as far as they could to escape the fairies. They made it to Edinburgh, and stayed until she had had her baby. But soon after, the same fairy as before appeared in the night and demanded the child. 'Your promise to us you shall keep, or Hawksbridge town shall never sleep!'

"John did not doubt that if the fairies had the power to vanquish the Worm, they could easily enough visit some other evil upon the town, perhaps worse than the beast itself. So he offered himself to the fairy in place of the baby. The fairy vanished, and returned with his ageing, wrinkled queen, her face almost hidden under long grey hair. She looked John up and down before saying, 'Baby's fair, but small and weak. A husband strong is what I seek!' And she took him by the hand and led him out of his humble quarters. Mother and baby were left in peace, but John was never seen again."

Francesca paused. "And there you have it!" she said. "The story of the Hawksbridge Worm, which is apparently now to be exploited by Mr Tanner and his gymnasium."

"Bravo, Francesca!" Mr Harris said. "A fearful tale, well told! Mr Jenrick has lost some of his audience now, I think."

"I'm sure he does it much better," Francesca said. "At least I hope so, if he will be overseeing drama at the Angel Arms Theatre."

"Poor devil," said Peter. "Spending the rest of his life

with a fairy hag. Mind you, some men like an older woman. I'd sooner leap into the jaws of a basilisk."

"If you are ever lucky enough to marry," Louise said briskly, "you will have to accept that your wife will age just as you will."

"Not necessarily," he said.

"You intend to follow Henry VIII and dispose of your wives?" said Mr Harris.

"There are alternatives to that," Peter replied.

Louise shook her head, and Mrs Harris, momentarily wide-eyed with shock at the scandalous implication, said, "Well, I think we've all finished our tart. Ladies, why don't we withdraw and leave the men to their own devices? I'm sure they'll want to talk about manly things. Oh – but I forget myself! It's not my party. Forgive me, Phyllis!"

Phyllis smiled indulgently and the ladies retired to the drawing room, leaving me solely responsible for preventing a conflagration between Peter and Mr Harris.

~

Mr Harris tried valiantly to be polite to Peter. "And how did you both come to be acquainted, if I may ask?"

"Didn't Tom tell you? We're old school friends. Got up to plenty of merry mischief, didn't we, Tom? Some of which we would never dream of divulging to our nearest and dearest!"

"I see," said Mr Harris. "I confess I never kept up with my friends from so long ago, but it must be a fine thing to be able to discuss the old times."

"Oh, indeed," said Peter. "Mrs Richmond and Bertie! Now there's an interesting memory. Bertie was an extremely naughty boy, and we were all envious of him. And yet... the affair got us all into huge trouble, didn't it?"

I tried to smile, and shuffled my foot on the floor with discomfort. I was acutely aware that I had not shared every aspect of my past with Phyllis.

"Don't worry," Peter said with a smirk, "I'm not going to spill the beans. Speaking of telling tales, that was a daft one from Mrs Campbell. So maidenhood qualified a girl for sacrifice! All it would take, then, is a young man with a business head and reasonable vigour to set up a practice saving lives. What might his slogan be? Perhaps 'Better a little worm than a big one!' Ha!"

He stood up unsteadily. "Right, I'm going outside for a cheroot. I've been told off for smoking in the house. Fussy lot, the Ruffords!"

When he had gone, Mr Harris said under his breath, "How can you bear it?"

"With difficulty," I said. "I hope to be rid of him soon. But I feel for Louise."

"Can't she get away?"

"The prospect of hardship ties her to him – or perhaps the other way around. But I'll try to persuade her."

"We must do something," said Mr Harris. "She's a fine young woman, and she must be free to pursue her scientific interests. Or to find a husband."

I sighed. "Yes. I'm sorry. This is not how I wanted my first married party to be."

Mr Harris smiled reassuringly at me. "It's not been so bad," he said. "My hosts are charming. Francesca is on fine form, and I've enjoyed meeting Miss McNulty. And of course, Catherine's cooking is always worth coming for."

"True. More port?"

~

"What did you talk about?"

Phyllis looked up from her book and watched me undress. "Oh, all sorts of things. I like Louise. She's rather intense, but she has a keen sense of humour too. She's quite set on writing her book on fossils. You should take her to the cliffs so she can add to her collection."

"Really? On my own? Isn't that a little improper?"

"I trust you," Phyllis said. "I need to get on with my book, and she'll be far too excited about her specimens to bother you. Come here."

I obliged, and she tutted over a missing button in my night-shirt before running her hand over my thigh. "Get in and warm me up, then. It's turning chilly."

I climbed over her, taking the opportunity to kiss her on the way.

"Francesca is a natural story-teller," I said. "I wonder if we'll have nightmares about the Hawksbridge Worm."

"I expect you'll be happy to dream of naked maidens," she said.

Titian, Flora's cat, jumped onto the bed and curled up by my feet.

"He's becoming very loyal to you," Phyllis said. "It's a good thing Fox likes to sleep in the kitchen, or there would be no room left for me."

"I assure you I would favour you over any animal," I said, wrapping my arm around her.

"How could any woman ask for more than such gallantry?" she said, rolling on her side and yawning. "I'm sorry, I'm very tired. Good night!"

I lay awake for some time, disturbed not by the prospect of any ancient monster lurking outside, but by a threat within my own castle. I turned Peter's words over in my mind. He seemed to know exactly what would make me uncomfortable – no, terrified would be closer to the truth.

I had told Francesca all about it: the affair between my

friend Bertram Mercer and Mrs Fanny Richmond, and how my first love, Mrs Richmond's maid Hazel, was molested by John Oliphant, the butler. How thanks to my anger, Oliphant was subsequently dismissed, and out of revenge tried to blackmail Bertram and Mrs Richmond with stolen love letters. How in our youthful stupidity, my friends and I tried to steal back the letters, happening upon the ailing Oliphant; how I left behind a blood-stained handkerchief that would implicate poor innocent Hazel, and lead to her untimely death in jail.

Though Mr Oliphant's death was purely coincidental with our presence, this ill chance could still be used powerfully against us. I had not told Phyllis. She had given up many secrets to me, including her anonymous authorship of the notorious book 'Malamor', and yet I had not fully reciprocated.

Was it Peter's intention to spoil our marriage and our lives in a fit of jealousy? Or to exact a payment, as Hazel's brother, Alan Sharpe, had tried to do previously? I tried to tell myself that I was exaggerating the danger, that Peter might be ungentlemanly in many ways, but he would not betray a youthful confidence. I was not comforted, but exhaustion and wine eventually drew a welcome veil of sleep over me.

CHAPTER FIVE

THE chapel was now wrapped in scaffolding, both inside and out. On entering the building, I found Francesca with a man of muscular build and an excess of curling black hair that swept about his shoulders as he looked around the chapel and gesticulated confidently.

Examining rafters at the top of a platform was John Hutton, in a perfect position – by accident or design – to keep an eye on the proceedings. He saw me and smiled and nodded, but not before I caught his wary scrutiny of the stranger.

"Thomas!" Francesca said when she caught sight of me. "Good morning. Let me introduce you. Mr Thomas Rufford, Mr Walter Jenrick. Mr Jenrick has been describing some of the theatrical machinery we'll need for scene changes and so forth. I had no idea it was so complicated!"

Jenrick bowed and said, "Very pleased to meet you, sir. Naturally I'm familiar with your name from the newspapers." He turned back to Francesca. "I trust I haven't discouraged you, ma'am. Not all of it is strictly necessary, but to build a reputation –"

"Of course, of course," said Francesca, dismissing her own doubts with a wave of her hand. "We'll do this properly, or not at all! Now, please will you repeat what you told me of your experience, Mr Jenrick, for the benefit of my business partner?"

"Certainly, ma'am, sir." Jenrick folded his arms, and Hutton chose that moment to start hammering at a rafter.

Francesca tutted and called, "John! Please let us have some peace and quiet, just for a moment!"

Hutton gave her a look of innocent surprise. "Of course,

ma'am," he said, and put down his mallet with a show of forbearance.

Jenrick continued. "I have played many of the important dramatic roles in London – Shylock, Hamlet, King Lear, and so on – in addition to my capacity as director and manager at The King's Theatre in Richmond for three years."

"Impressive," I said. "I imagine that would give you a broad perspective of the theatrical business."

He nodded, his single gold earring glinting in a shaft of light. "I don't wish to brag, but what I don't know about the trade isn't worth knowing!"

Out of the corner of my eye I could see Hutton shaking his head.

"If I might ask," I said as mildly as I could, "what brings you back to Hawksbridge, and to the pursuit of storytelling?"

He smiled. "Unfortunately the theatre was defrauded by the company treasurer, and went to the wall a couple of years ago. It was an uncomfortable time, and I decided I needed to get out of London. So I've been happy to tread water instead of the boards, until an opportunity arises. Besides, there's an appetite for stories, and being my own master for a time isn't so bad."

"But you would welcome a new challenge?" I prompted.

"Precisely, sir. I can't think of a better one – a brand new theatre and company. To pull it all together and make a programme that will get the town talking – and establish a reputation far beyond Hawksbridge – well, you need a veritable wizard, sir. It's no small task, but I humbly present myself as that wizard."

Jenrick bowed and I looked at Francesca, who smiled and raised her eyebrows to signal her approval. There was no doubting the confidence of this fellow, and he apparently had the credentials. We were unlikely to find a better candidate; indeed, we were lucky to have a candidate at all.

"And you would be able to find suitable players?" I said.

"Certainly," Jenrick said. "I've a keen nose for talent. Some of the local amateurs can be knocked into shape, and I know travelling players who would be glad to settle for a while."

"Well, Mr Jenrick," said Francesca, "you have much to recommend you, but Mr Rufford and I will have to discuss the matter – we'll send you a letter soon."

"Thank you, ma'am," said Jenrick. "You'll have no cause for complaint if you should honour me with this opportunity. It's been a pleasure meeting you both – Mrs Campbell, Mr Rufford."

I glanced up at Hutton, whose gaze followed Jenrick out of the chapel. When Jenrick was out of earshot, Francesca said, "Well? What do you think?"

"If he's all he says he is, he sounds the ideal man," I said. "I take it he gave a reference?"

"Yes, I shall write forthwith," Francesca said. "But I think we have our manager! How exciting!"

There was a snort from the top of the scaffolding. Francesca looked up. "Yes? You have something to say, John?"

"No, no, ma'am. It isn't my place."

Francesca put her hands on her hips and sighed. "Out with it," she said. "You didn't like him."

"Neither here nor there, ma'am."

"Oh, John! You're infuriating," Francesca said. "What's wrong with Mr Jenrick?"

Hutton shrugged. "I'm sure he's able. Just seemed a bit full of himself, ma'am, that's all."

"He was being interviewed for a job," Francesca said. "Of course he would put his best foot forward."

"As you like, ma'am. I'm sure he'll do."

"Thank you, John. Now feel free to make as much noise as you like."

Hutton scowled and took up his mallet, while Francesca

and I went out into the sunshine.

"How endearing," I said as the banging sounds commenced.

"Endearing? How so?"

"Mr Hutton being so protective of you," I said.

"Well, he has no right," Francesca said. "It's annoying." Then she smiled and added, "Although it is kind of him to take an interest, I suppose. Now – there's no time to lose, given I need theatre design advice immediately. I intend to write to Mr Jenrick today and offer him the position on a month's trial, by which time I hope that his referee will have sung his praises. Agreed?"

"Agreed," I said. Although Jenrick seemed knowledgeable and competent, Hutton's suspicion of him was understandable. Hutton was, I postulated, a man under the potent influence of love.

~

My letter to Mr Leonardo Fountain, a retired tutor and the most respected antiquarian in Hawksbridge, had received a heartening reply. He wrote that he would be happy to apply his knowledge to the task in question, and even if he could not shed light, it would give him an excuse to open a specially precious bottle of port that he had been saving.

And so it was with the prospect of an agreeable afternoon improving my mind and my palate that I rang the bell of Mr Fountain's unassuming home: like its owner, it was tall and thin, and only a little older. Clad in roughly finished stone, with a steep roof swelling its attic space, it had more the appearance of a tradesman's house than that of a successful merchant or professional, which would have boasted a more manicured frontage. The windows failed to line up vertically, giving it the look of a house thrown together rather than designed; but for all that, it possessed an idiosyncratic charm well suited to its owner.

While I waited at the door under a disintegrating sandstone pediment – the building's one, grudging concession to classical form – I glanced through the only window on the ground floor. Books lined the walls, and overflowed into precarious piles rising from the floor. It embarrassed me to think what a luxurious library I had at Ramsburgh, and how few volumes I had so far read or indeed had much interest in reading.

I was ushered in by Spade, Mr Fountain's manservant, who was of a similar vintage to his master and in no hurry to climb the stairs to the drawing room.

"Mr Rufford! How good to see you. Please make yourself comfortable – oh, you will need to move Tacitus from his favourite chair."

I carefully deposited the cat on the floor; Tacitus gave me a dirty look and fled.

"We haven't spoken properly since that awful business..." He shook his head. "I confess I miss poor Ambrose, flawed creature that he was. Anyway," he said, brightening, "we need not dwell on that. Spade, pour Mr Rufford a glass of the Ferreira, and leave the bottle next to me. I confess I've had a glass already, and it's quite as good as I hoped."

He was right, and I settled into my chair. "I'm honoured, Mr Fountain," I said. "I'm no expert, but this is exceptional."

Mr Fountain smiled and said, "The honour is mine, Mr Rufford. How are you enjoying married life? I hope you are leaving your beautiful wife alone just enough for her to write her books." There was an unexpected twinkle in his eye.

"She is indeed finding time, and I would prevent her at my peril!" I said. "I'm finding that marriage very much agrees with me."

"I'm sure, I'm sure," he said. "So, despite pleasurable

distractions at home, you have found yourself another mystery! You have a confession and some initials, I think you wrote? That does sound like a challenge."

To spare Mr Fountain a shock, I had not gone into details in my letter. "Please brace yourself," I said, handing him a copy of the bleak message. "It makes for unpleasant reading."

Having put on his spectacles, Mr Fountain sat reading it several times, frowning.

"'R.M.'," he murmured. "It is distressing, isn't it? And this was found where?"

"On a wall in The Veiled Sisters, an inn on the south side of town. Mrs Campbell is reviving it, under a different name."

Mr Fountain chuckled at the mention of Francesca's name. "A delightful and capable lady, although as you know, we had our doubts – the Antiquarian Society, that is."

He took another sip of port and let out a satisfied sigh. "But she has proved herself an asset to the town, while her portrait keeps watch over the council. And now she has a new interest – inn-keeping! I admire her, I truly do. Now, The Veiled Sisters..."

Mr Fountain put down his empty glass and pressed his fingertips together, staring at the ceiling. "Built on the site of – let me think – St Cecilia's Abbey. How wonderful it would be had the abbey survived. But the inn is an attractive building, and its neglect has disturbed me. I've spoken to the Mayor several times about it, to no avail."

"You're aware of the ghost story attached to the inn?" I said.

He nodded and refilled both of our glasses. "Naturally. There was a time when I used to frequent the place. That was many years ago now. I never saw the fabled nuns, but then I never stayed overnight. This disturbing message – I take it there was no date?"

I shook my head. "No such luck," I said. "But the writing looks as though it's been there a long time, and the wainscoting that covered it is certainly old. So I would be surprised if it had been written in this century."

A strange look came over Mr Fountain's face, as though the nuns themselves had appeared before him, and he spluttered some of his precious port onto the floorboards. His complexion took on a sickly pallor, and for a ghastly moment I thought he was having a fit, and called for Spade. But in a moment Mr Fountain had stood up and held up his hand to refuse assistance from his manservant.

"I'm perfectly all right, just breathed in at the wrong moment!" he said, coughing and extracting a handkerchief from his pocket. He fumbled and dropped it; bending stiffly down and sweeping his hand across the floor to retrieve it, he winced.

"Damned nail," he said, looking at the blood oozing from his hand before wrapping it in the handkerchief. "What a stupid old fool I am. And Spade, I've told you about this loose board before – please see to it today. Excuse me a moment." He left the room with Spade and, disconcerted, I took my seat again and hoped I had not been the cause of Mr Fountain's indisposition.

After a minute, I heard footsteps on the stairs, followed by shuffling about in the room below. Tacitus wandered in to see whether his spot was free, and being foiled, wandered off again. A good ten minutes later, Mr Fountain came back upstairs, a bandage around his hand, and placed a slender book on the side table next to him without comment. I could not make out the title.

He took his chair and sighed. "I'm sorry for leaving you on your own. I had to attend to my hand." He refilled our glasses once again, took a sip, and then looked at me with a serious demeanour.

"I must also apologise that I cannot help you with your mystery. Do you not think, Mr Rufford, that you might best serve these poor people by leaving their fate in the past? You don't know who you might hurt with your investigations. And your time might be better spent with your new wife."

I was surprised at this apparent change of tone. "But surely this fellow wanted his story to come out! Otherwise, why would he have gone to the trouble of scratching his last words on the wall?"

Mr Fountain shrugged. "A last cry of pain, I suppose. It's very sad, but nothing can be done for him – for them – now. Perhaps you should put aside your curiosity."

"But your life's work has surely been spurred by curiosity!" I said with some warmth. "Is it not the basis for civilisation itself?"

He smiled. "You're quite correct." He rubbed his face with unbandaged hand and then sighed. "I'm a man of faith, Mr Rufford," he said, "and I like to think I'm also a man of honour. So I'm not always free to..." He trailed off and took some port.

"I'm afraid I don't understand," I said, and he looked genuinely pained at my bafflement.

"Oh dear," he said. "Let me change the subject, if you will permit me." He picked up the book and got up. "I've been meaning to give you and your wife a wedding gift. I am an old man, and the sentiments expressed in these pages are for those with youthful blood in their veins." I stood up and he handed me the book, which I took with care as the edges of the leather binding were crumbling.

"That's extremely kind, sir!" I said, touched and humbled by his sincerity.

"It's my pleasure. Forgive the strangeness of this gift – you may find the contents improper or offensive, in which case feel free to dispose of it as you see fit. But a young married couple will not offend God by reading these reflections on His gifts. And the author has a beautiful style. Well, in my opinion. Being a man of Hawksbridge, he may already be known to you."

I shook his hand, unable to think of a sufficient response to this unexpected act of generosity. "Thank you," I said. "I shall read it with great interest."

He nodded. "It's all I can do, I'm afraid. Sometimes we must leave things to a higher power."

~

In the street, I tried to make sense of Mr Fountain's remarks. Leave what to a higher power? I had expected him to consult at least one of his many historical tomes for the possible identity of R.M. Instead, he had handed me a mysterious wedding gift and sent me on my way, mildly giddy from the port.

With some apprehension, I opened the book and read:

THE POEMS

OF

ALLAN LAWRENCE

VOL. I: 'LOVE UNDYING'

FOURTH EDITION, 1752

CHAPTER SIX

"I MUST say," said Phyllis, "I'd never have expected Mr Fountain to have a book of this kind. It's quite a comical thought!"

We had been left blissfully alone: Peter had gone into town to debauch himself, while Louise was sequestered in her room with a book containing terrifying illustrations of prehistoric reptiles.

"I'd rather not dwell on his private tastes, if you don't mind," I said.

"I recognise the name. My older friends used to giggle over illicit copies of his poetry at school. But I was a good girl."

There was a pause as Phyllis read one of the poems. "Oh dear," she said. "Quite unfair. And he doesn't answer her question properly."

I put down the Hawksbridge Herald, which was exhaustively listing the types and quantities of materials going into the new railway bridge. "Very well. Let's hear it."

Phyllis began to read.

On the Virtues of Ignorance

Do not ask, my sweet, the history of my loving heart
Nor count the maidens' hearts that lie in shards
For want of sense to see the lover's art
And wisely flee from me, the knave of bards.

Nor shall I demand to know the ardour of your past
Your girlish dreams of shining knight, his jousting pole in hand
Or half-cloth'd sailor storm-tied to his mast
Or gentle shepherd poet; or player in a roving band.

"Fie!" – you cry – "why must you weigh my dreams against your sin?
Mere wraiths of fancy next to fleshly deeds!"
But lust is lust, my love, and human will is thin
And quickly breaks when tried by carnal needs.

So let us wash our wits and paint our pasts with lime
And vow to love until the day we die
Ne'er mastered by the shades of perished time.
Come, my love, and cast off all, and sweetly lie.

"You're right," I said, after a moment's consideration. "The scales don't balance. Still, at least he acknowledges his own flawed nature." Given the ghosts of my own past, the verse made me uncomfortable, but also stirred warmer feelings. "Is it too early for us to cast off all, and...?"

Phyllis ignored this. "The foreword says he was a recluse,

and his life was a mystery. I don't think Mr Lawrence is known much outside Hawksbridge. I've certainly never heard him mentioned in the same breath as his contemporaries."

"For every Andrew Marvell, there must be twenty men like him – decent enough, though not brilliant, and doomed to obscurity," I said.

"Indecent, rather," she said, leafing through the book. "That was not the frankest of his poems. Oh my!"

She snapped it shut. "This belongs in the bedroom. We can read it to each other if you wish, and then if old schoolmaster Fountain tests you on it, you may impress him!"

"Not a pleasant prospect," I said, shuddering at the thought of such an exchange. I got up and stared out of the drawing room window at the deepening blue of the evening sky. "It was a strange conversation today. I thought the poor fellow was having a fit at one point."

"Oh?"

"Yes," I continued, "we were discussing the possible date of the message, when his colour changed and he choked on his port. I was convinced he was going to have a stroke and die right in front of me."

"Goodness! How awful."

"But he recovered soon enough, and then went to fetch our book."

"Do you think it's significant?"

I frowned. "What do you mean?"

"That Mr Lawrence's poetry is in some way related to the message," Phyllis said, taking up a piece of needlework from a basket next to her chair. It was a habit that she insisted was helpful in ordering her thoughts.

"That seems unlikely," I said. "He said he'd been wanting to give us a wedding gift for some time."

"Ah, but he might not have chosen one yet."

I rubbed at a mark on the window that turned out to be a bubble in the glass. "That would be an absurd thing to do, wouldn't it? Why not just tell me straight what he's thinking?"

Phyllis shrugged. "I've no idea, but let's assume he has his reasons, having had a moment of inspiration. Then it's likely that this book is some kind of clue. Surely?"

"Well, that's damned inconvenient of him, I must say," I said. "So we have to trawl through every poem trying to imagine what it could possibly tell us about R.M.? Does he suppose I've nothing better to do? Besides, he encouraged me to give up on it. So why bother giving me any clues at all?"

Phyllis frowned and said a little testily, "Don't ask me. I'm only making suggestions."

"I'm sorry," I said, going over to her and massaging her shoulders. "I didn't mean to be peevish. It's simply a little frustrating."

She looked up at me and smiled. "I know," she said. "But you'll get to the bottom of it, I'm sure." She yawned and put her needlework in her basket. "Shall we take Mr Lawrence upstairs?"

~

Having left our conveyances at Francesca's inn, our little party of amusement-seekers arrived at Tanner's Wonderland – less than ten minutes' walk away – to find that seemingly half of Hawksbridge's residents had been similarly minded.

Mr Tanner's enterprise, in what used to be sheep-filled pasture, was encircled by high railings painted in black and gold, festooned in bunting and broken by a large entrance gate. On a board above the entrance, the words 'TANNER'S MAGNIFICENT WONDERLAND' were ornately painted, flanked by two half-naked, winged females portrayed in a naive and sentimental style. On either side, illustrations of the attractions were accompanied by showman's hyperbole.

“Fairies,” said Louise, pointing upwards, “or angels?”

“How vulgar,” said Mrs Harris, raising her voice above the excited hubbub. “Perhaps it’s an impertinent reference to the Town Hall.”

“I shall try to be patient, and reserve judgement,” said Francesca. “But so far it’s quite as I expected!”

We paid our tuppences at the booth by the gate, and as we squeezed through the entrance, jostled by the crowd, the sound of a band grew louder. A signpost indicated the way to various districts, including the zoo, the Hawksbridge Worm, the gymnasium, the fair, and refreshments.

We decided to try the zoo first, and found the exotic birds and monkeys amusing enough. Most visitors’ attention, however, was on Tanner’s tiger, lavishly advertised on hoardings as a ferocious and proud creature brought from India at great trouble and expense. Alas, while the animal may have had these qualities in his native habitat, they seemed to have been lost on the return voyage. A worryingly thin specimen, Hercules constantly paced up and down his small enclosure, occasionally staring at the onlookers with soulful eyes.

“The poor creature,” said Louise. “He looks utterly miserable.”

“Pitiful,” said Phyllis. “I’m afraid I’ve taken a dislike to Mr Tanner already. The wretched thing looks half-starved.”

“He’s probably lost his appetite,” said Mr Harris, “having been torn from his homeland.”

“I can’t bear it,” said Mrs Harris. “Let’s go and find the Worm, shall we?”

This contraption consisted of a pond some eighty feet in diameter on which floated a series of canoes, connected in a circle to each other and also to rods joining an axle at the centre of the pond. The front canoe was decorated with a carved dragon-like head with bulging eyes, while the rear one provided a tail. A party of men – navvies, by the look of them

– were rowing energetically and with evident enjoyment, propelling the beast swiftly through the water. Some motivation was provided by a speed indicator on the central shaft, with a dial and a pointer. (The latter was moved by a mechanism similar to a steam engine's fly-ball governor, as I was later informed by my knowledgeable colleague at the Pottery, Mr McPhee.) A sign by the pond's dock indicated the speed that would result in a prize for the rowers – tokens for free refreshments – and a rowdy cheer went up from crew and onlookers when the required speed was easily achieved by the muscular participants.

"Extraordinary," said Mr Harris. "Not the worst way to take exercise, for those of a suitable disposition."

"Ah, you're tempted, my dear!" said Mrs Harris. "Perhaps we should form a crew ourselves?"

"This is not for ladies, Olivia," said Mr Harris, "and we don't have the numbers. I shall stick to golf, I think."

"Or you could develop your muscles in there," Mrs Harris teased, pointing to a large hut bearing the sign, 'TANNER'S INDOOR GYMNASIUM: ALL THE MODERN METHODS OF PHYSICAL IMPROVEMENT. LIFT, VAULT, ROW, AND JUMP!'

Mr Harris frowned. "I can't think of anything worse than being in the midst of a crowd of sweating, grunting strangers trying to impress their womenfolk. No, thank you, my dear. Shall we move on?"

We wandered through the 'Wonderland Fair', a gaudy collection of the usual fairground attractions and booths selling cheap goods.

"Ah! Louise," Francesca said, pointing to a hut decorated with outlandish beasts, "you'll be interested in this."

"SEE TERRIFYING CREATURES FROM ANCIENT TIMES," Mrs Harris read aloud. "RARE FOSSIL REMAINS FROM A GODLESS ERA. ENTRY 2D. Let me treat everyone. How wonderful – we have our own expert guide!"

While the exhibits did not live up to the chilling paintings, they were nevertheless intriguing. Skulls, vertebrae and other bones of various reptiles gave an indication of the size and ferocity of these odd residents of an ancient Earth, with accompanying placards that made dubiously specific statements about the appearance of their original owners.

"The scholarship could be improved," said Louise, gazing at a Megalosaurus femur, "and of course I would rather see these in a proper museum, but I suppose it could be worse."

"I shall have the signage updated forthwith," said a baritone voice behind us. "'It Could Be Worse', it will say – high praise from an esteemed visitor."

We turned to see who was speaking. A tall, thick-set man stood with his arms folded and a smile on his face. "Philip Tanner at your service, ladies and gentlemen. I'm glad to see you're enjoying yourselves."

"Oh," said Louise, flushing crimson, "I'm so sorry – I didn't mean..."

"That's all right, ma'am, I know my limits. I'm just a showman. But I do confess a childlike enthusiasm for fossils, and I was offered some nice bones. We live in an age of science, which I've tried to represent on these premises. And the dinosaur skeleton provides us with a felicitous blend of titillation and scientific enlightenment, would you not agree? Did I rightly understand you have a special interest in these matters, ma'am?"

"I have an amateur interest, yes."

"Oh, Louise," Francesca said, "you're too modest! It's a little more than that – my friend is planning a book for children on the subject of fossils, Mr Tanner."

"Indeed?" said Mr Tanner. "Admirable – in which case, you may be able to help me improve my humble display."

Louise smiled and said, "Perhaps. And your collection is most satisfying, despite my unforgivable rudeness."

"Capital," said Mr Tanner, beaming. "And there's nothing

to forgive. Come back when it's quieter. Now, I must continue my tour to see how everyone else is enjoying themselves. Don't forget the Mayor's speech at eleven-thirty!"

He left, and Louise covered her mouth with her hand. "Oh dear, what an idiot I am!" she muttered.

"Not at all," I said. "It gave Mr Tanner a way to introduce himself, and you have made your talents known to him, which may or may not prove useful."

We retired to the coffee shop that Mr Tanner had shrewdly organised with the North British Railway Company, and which was situated in one of their luxurious coaches. Standing on its own fragment of railway adjoining an imitation of a station platform, it was both a pleasing novelty for Mr Tanner's business and an effective propaganda device for North British.

The comfortable upholstering and polished panelling were at odds with the tone of cheerful cheapness exuded by the rest of Tanner's business, and we felt pleasantly insulated from the vulgarity of the teeming Wonderland.

"I'm almost disappointed," Francesca said when we had settled at a table with a view of the Worm. "Mr Tanner is not entirely the brute I assumed he would be. One really should try to avoid meeting those one intends to hate."

"I can't entirely forgive him for Hercules," said Phyllis, after a sip of coffee. "But yes, a whiff of the enemy's humanity can sap the will. I once had a dreadful anonymous review from a London newspaper, and I wrote furiously to the editor to protest, which of course I shouldn't have done. But I received an apologetic reply from the editor, telling me that the reviewer was an unsuccessful, impoverished author nursing her aged mother. Naturally my anger evaporated."

"Who could blame you, though?" said Louise. "An unfair review must be hard to bear. And the newspaper should not have published it when it was obviously motivated by envy."

"I'm glad for her sake that they did – she needed the

money. And I should be hardened to it," said Phyllis, "but when I'm accused of failing to breathe life into my characters, it hurts. I don't particularly mind what they say about the implausibility of my plots – I know that reality is often far stranger."

"No sane person who reads your books could possibly accuse you of either of those things!" said Louise with passion.

"Thank you," Phyllis said, and touched her arm. "Oh – I've managed to turn the conversation to myself. Thomas, if I make a habit of it, feel free to berate me."

"I shall, sternly," I said, looking towards the opposite side of the carriage where a gathering crowd could be seen through the window. "It must be nearly eleven-thirty – the Mayor has arrived."

"I'm afraid I'm going to sit tight and finish my cake and coffee," said Francesca. "I expect we'll hear his speech through the window."

Tanner was visibly swelling with pride as he introduced Mr Gillis, the Mayor. The latter fiddled nervously with his chains, no doubt aware that it was not the most salubrious enterprise for him to endorse, but he valiantly highlighted the potential advantages of the Wonderland to the town and the prospects for improvements in citizens' physical health as well as their amusement and a little scientific education.

"Education!" spat a man at the front of the audience. "It's a joke, sir! This damned" – he waved a beer bottle in the general direction of Tanner's attractions – "fairyland, is only about gold, sir." To my horror, I recognised the speaker, and exchanged a glance with Francesca. "It's a vulgar tinker's tray of baubles and swindles, sir," he continued. "A filthy stain on Hawksbridge."

"Jenrick!" I said. "Good Lord."

Tanner flushed red. "Now, now, Walter, you can't be interrupting the good Mayor – if you want an argument, have it out with me after."

The poor Mayor had flinched and taken a step back, but he attempted to compose himself and finish his speech. He cleared his throat. "As I said, an inventive collection of devices and entertainments to –"

"Hubris is what it is!" Jenrick shouted, taking a swig from his bottle. "Bloody hubris and flimflam. Don't trust the chiselling charlatan. Especially not with your women. You know what I'm talking about, you..." At this point two of Tanner's men grabbed hold of him and started to drag him towards the gate, while Tanner stood with a fixed grin on his face as the cursing grew fainter.

"I apologise, ladies and gentlemen," he eventually said, "for this unseemly interruption. But what better example of a man who should spend more time grasping an oar and improving his body, and less time grasping a bottle and destroying his mind. Mr Mayor, pray do continue your excellent speech."

When the Mayor had finished – with obvious relief – Mr Tanner shook his hand ostentatiously, thanked him, and exhorted the throng to enjoy themselves. The crowd broke up with much gossiping, and it seemed to me the added drama of the heckler would not do any harm to Tanner's business.

"Well!" said Mrs Harris. "I'm glad we stayed inside. What an awful man."

Francesca grimaced. "That awful man is supposed to be managing my theatre and directing my plays," she said. "Jenrick's only on trial – we shall have to reconsider, Thomas. Bother." She sighed and polished off her cake.

"That's awkward," I said. "What can have possessed him? But we have no one else. Can he be chastised into improving his behaviour? He won't want to lose his position, surely?"

"We shall haul him across the coals," Francesca said. "We can't have a drunk in charge – our reputation would be sunk before the first performance."

~

On the following Monday, it was a transformed Mr Jenrick who stood in the newly plastered office at the inn, holding his hat in place of a beer bottle. His hair was kempt and his cheeks smooth, and his expression was one of carefully contrived contrition.

"You may be sure that this won't happen again, ma'am, sir," he said. "I'm deeply sorry for my behaviour. Tanner and I go back a long time, and I didn't want to think anyone else might be taken in by him. There was a young woman – but I shall keep my opinions about him to myself in future."

"I see," I said. "You fell out over a woman, and it still rankles?"

Jenrick frowned, apparently now regretful about mentioning it. "Mr Tanner is not an honourable man, and not above physical violence. That's all I shall say. But that doesn't excuse my behaviour on Saturday."

"Mr Jenrick," Francesca said in a stern tone, "the question is, do you think you will be able to perform your duties here without disgracing yourself, and us?" This chastisement represented a side of my friend I had rarely seen.

"I do, ma'am," he said. "I shall not let the drink, or anything else, get the better of me in future. This position is one I fervently desire, and therefore I shall take myself in hand."

"Then I shall give you another chance, if Mr Rufford is agreeable," Francesca said, and I nodded.

Mr Jenrick bowed and said, "Thank you, ma'am, sir. If you will excuse me, I shall make a start on recruitment for the company."

"Please do, Mr Jenrick," said Francesca, allowing herself a slight smile. "Oh – I believe I have a possibility for you. Rosabel Gardner, working at the Pottery – I saw her perform an impromptu impression of her employer in Myrtle's and she had a natural talent. She must be suited to a minor role, at least. I'll try to talk to her again to see if my impression is confirmed."

"Intriguing, ma'am," he said, registering surprise at the name. "I believe I know of her – I shall also have a word."

CHAPTER SEVEN

NO SOONER had I settled myself in the drawing room after breakfast with coffee and a book – a too-frequent indulgence – than Peter appeared, pale and dishevelled. It was all I could do to stop myself angrily exhorting him to leave me alone. Instead, I managed an unenthusiastic "Good morning."

"I'm famished," he said. "Have I missed breakfast?"

"I'm afraid so," I said, "but if you go to the kitchen, you'll find some bread and cheese. If you ask nicely, Catherine might do you a plate of bacon."

"Headache," he groaned, sinking into a chair and holding his hand to his head. "And nightmares. Dreadful nightmares. Usually the same one. Don't you have it too?"

"I doubt it," I said. "What nightmare?"

"The police," he said. "Knocking at my door and telling me they know I was at Oliphant's. And John Oliphant's there too, smirking at me and saying, 'That's one of 'em! Killed me stone dead, the little bugger.' And the police put a noose around my neck, and start to tighten it until I can't breathe any more, and then I wake up in a dreadful sweat."

"I'm sorry to hear that," I said, attempting a tone of sympathy.

"Yes, well, it's all your fault, isn't it? That's why I'm in this... position."

"I beg your pardon?"

"If you hadn't inveigled me into that stupid wild goose chase, I wouldn't have been haunted by that reprobate, and then I probably wouldn't have been on the sauce as much." Peter was working himself up, despite his headache. "You have a lot to answer for, do you realise? A lot."

I was almost too astonished to answer, but after staring at him for a moment I said, "I grant you that Bertram and I came to you for help, but then we were all as stupid about it as each other. In fact, I seem to remember you becoming the most enthusiastic. What was it you said? 'Brothers in vengeance', I think."

He waved his hand dismissively. "It was mostly in jest. You know what I used to be like – prone to drama, I dare say. You didn't discourage me. You were supposed to be the sensible one, out of us all."

"Which you always found boring."

"Be that as it may – you should have been true to yourself, Tom, and stopped us."

Perhaps there was a grain of truth in this, I thought. I often wondered if I would have been able to dissuade the others – I had had misgivings, but I was also drawn to the idea of an adventure with a righteous objective. The mentality of the mob was in play, forming an intelligence – or foolishness – of its own. Admittedly, our luck had been wanting in the execution of our plan, but, more to the point, the sin of blackmail had not justified unlawful intimidation.

"Once the idea had been discussed, I doubt I could have stopped it, even if I had wanted to," I said. "And had we been more successful, you would remember the moment with satisfaction instead of regret, I imagine."

"Damn you!" Peter said, putting both hands to his forehead. "How can you be so bloody phlegmatic about it? Sitting here so smugly in your fancy house – which you only procured through your father's adulterous lusts – with your precious wife and your precious dog, without a care in the world, looking down your nose at everyone else. But I know what you're like, Tom Rufford, and you're as much of a sinner as the next man, for all your airs and graces."

I stood up and looked down at him in anger and pity, my fists clenched. "You will blame anyone but yourself for your own misfortunes," I said. "I'm sorry about what happened all those years ago – I do think about it, and I was nearly killed for it, after all – but we can't let it rule us. You're responsible for your own destiny, and you need to pull yourself together and find a way to support yourself. What other choice do you have? You'll soon be dead if you carry on like this."

"Damn you to Hell," Peter muttered.

"And you can't stay here much longer. Please make other arrangements as soon as possible."

"You would throw Louise out too, like a street bitch?"

"She can stay as long as she likes," I said. "She needn't suffer for your fecklessness."

"That will look very fine," he snorted. "Your reputation will be ruined."

"I think my reputation can take it," I replied.

"We'll see," he said, getting out of his chair, and he threw me a hostile look before stomping out of the room.

~

I knew it was hazardous to provoke Peter, but he could not be appeased forever. Were his nightmares entirely due to Oliphant, or did the dead man perhaps stand in for other of his sins? I did not care to delve into his night-time occupations, but for my own peace of mind, I would have to assume they were on the right side of the law, if not moral convention. Still, as regards reputation, it was certainly not safe for us to be associated with him. He would have to be coaxed out of the house, somehow.

To take my mind off my anger with him, I went to my private study at the top of the house to read Allan Lawrence's verse. I searched for anything that might stand out as a clue, as Phyllis' instincts were frequently correct.

In amongst the erotica was more serious writing, in which the Church was often cast in an unflattering light. One such was 'Man of God'.

I shudder as this scabrous wretch, ungodly man of God,
Mounts his twisting pulpit with unblinking impure gaze
That deems his female flock unlatched, unfrock'd, unshod
And darkly dreams an endless realm of sinful days.

'A Love Renounced' displayed similar contempt.

How shall I convince thee? my love for her was mere mishap
Borne of lust; and vain and false as any vulgar Bishop.

Was is it simply that Allan Lawrence was an atheist, I wondered, or did he have a more personal animosity against the Church, or certain employees of it?

I noted another Lawrence obsession in 'Facets'.

I dreamt my folded arms comprised the golden mount
That held the diamond of your bliss to me.
The facets of your love, too great to count,
Blazed and blinded, so that I might see.

And likewise in 'To Gemma':

My em'rald fury splinters at your sapphire stare
That strays to his fool's gold. Pray, let your jaded heart
Gently rock by mine in polished quartz of love; your hair:
Amber veins I'd brush from ruby bluffs I cleave apart.

My mortality briefly troubled me. How fiercely this man's passions burned, so many years ago: and now they were simply words on a page. The warm, sensual women who inspired him had returned to dust long since, perhaps one day to be formed into gemstones of the far-distant future. At least, I mused, he was one of the few of us whose thoughts and loves were preserved, albeit imperfectly and for a diminishing audience.

But having got to the end of the book, I felt no closer to unlocking the identity of 'R.M.', so I took my book and leave of my industrious wife, and headed to Halfpenny House.

~

Francesca was at home, and she was not alone. Sitting nervously in her drawing room, cheeks charmingly flushed, was Rosabel Gardner, who immediately stood and shook my hand as I offered it. "Miss Gardner, I'm delighted to meet you," I said.

Francesca also stood and held her hand out for a kiss.

"What a lovely surprise, Thomas," she said, indicating to her maid to bring more tea. "I was discussing fairies with Miss Gardner. She was wondering whether she could join our theatre company and continue to work at the Pottery."

"I don't see why not, Miss Gardner," I said. "I'll discuss it with Mr McPhee, but we should be able to allow you a little time off when you need it. Then you can see whether the acting life is for you."

"Thank you, Mr Rufford!" Miss Gardner said, taking her seat again. "It's so exciting – Mrs Campbell has been telling me all about her plans, and I would like to play a fairy – if Mr Jenrick thinks I'm suitable, of course."

"Do you have a play in mind already, Francesca?" I said.

"Indeed – Mr Jenrick has suggested that we adapt the story of the Hawksbridge Worm, which I thought would be an intriguing challenge! Do you approve?"

I smiled. "Good Lord. It's rather – frank, perhaps?" I glanced at Miss Gardner, who had turned a deeper shade of pink.

"Oh no, we'll do it tastefully, of course!" Francesca said. "I've appointed myself chief playwright, and I'm making small adjustments for modesty while elaborating the story with some ideas of my own."

"I see it more as an opera, or a ballet," I said, "but I'm sure you'll make a wonderful play from it."

"I hope so," said Francesca, "though I have none of your wife's experience and sophistication in these matters. I'll ask her advice, of course – and yours. And I have just the part for Miss Gardner – a wayward fairy who seduces our hero!"

"If you employ the dramatic skill you displayed in the coffee shop, Miss Gardner," I said, "you will be a success indeed."

My compliment made her squirm a little. "Thank you, sir, but what I said about Mr Lilley –"

"Was simply the truth, and I would be grateful if you and your colleagues could alert me if anything untoward happens at work. I apologise on behalf of Mr Lilley."

"Thank you, sir," she said. "But it's all right really – I'm sure it's only his way."

"Nevertheless," I began, and then saw Francesca turn and her face light up.

"John!" she said. "We are having quite a party this morning! How lovely."

"I'm sorry," John Hutton said, hanging back in the doorway and looking at us doubtfully. "I'll return when it's more convenient. I just wanted to discuss the proscenium arch with you. Mr Jenrick said –"

"Oh, come and sit down, John," Francesca said, patting a spot on the sofa next to her. "We can talk business in a while, but let's have tea first. Let me introduce you to Miss Gardner – she will be joining us as an actress! Miss Gardner, this is John Hutton, my exceptional builder."

"How do you do, miss?" Hutton said, shaking Miss Gardner's hand, and he nodded and smiled at me.

Slightly reluctantly, he took his place on the sofa, and Francesca beamed at him.

"Now, Thomas," Francesca said, turning back to me, "do you come bearing news, or is this purely a social call?"

I hesitated. "I wanted your advice, but –"

"Wonderful! Even better. Concerning...?"

I took Lawrence's book of verse from my coat pocket. "I have a possible clue about the writing in the inn, and yet... it's not even a clue, in fact, it's simply a book of poems. Mr Fountain gave it to me when I saw him."

"How interesting!" Francesca said, holding out her hand.

I frowned and looked around, keeping hold of the book. "I'm afraid it's quite... well, forthright on the subject of human relations."

"Oh, I see," Francesca said, laughing. "In that case, let's have a little stroll together, and we'll leave Miss Gardner and Mr Hutton to get acquainted."

As we left the room, Miss Gardner said to Hutton, "May I ask – what writing is this?" and I heard Hutton begin to explain.

In the garden, I showed Francesca the book and gave her my scant observations on it. She stopped under the shade of a tree, absorbed in one of the poems.

"My word," she muttered. "This man is a veritable goat. But what has it to do with R.M., or those poor women?"

"I was hoping you might have some ideas," I said.

"I shall try," she said. "Poor Mr Fountain. We may not be able to ask him what he meant, if indeed he meant anything by it."

"Oh? Why not?" I asked.

"Haven't you heard? No, I suppose you won't have – I've only just had it from my maid, whose uncle is a friend of Mr Fountain's manservant. The poor man has a bad fever from an infected cut. And he was so kind to me after the Hawksbridge Castle affair, when he had every right – Thomas? What's wrong?"

I had put my hand over my mouth. "It may be my fault," I said, a sense of dread creeping over me. "What have I done? What am I doing, pursuing these dead people?"

"Your fault?" said Francesca, closing the book. "How could it be?"

"When I was talking to Mr Fountain, he had some kind of a turn, and then he grazed himself on an exposed nail after he dropped his handkerchief. If it hadn't been for my curiosity, none of that would have happened."

"Oh, Thomas, that's nonsense – bad luck might happen at any time, but that doesn't make it anyone's fault, necessarily! Why – I could be struck by lightning right this moment, and you would take the blame for luring me into the garden with sensual poetry!"

I closed my eyes and took a deep breath, wanting to be reassured by her. "I just might," I said. "Why must I always interfere?"

"If it's anyone's fault, it's mine," Francesca said, "for setting you on this path. I'm sorry. You're absolved from any more investigations. Why don't you leave the book with me? Then you won't have to think about it, and I can see if anything occurs to me."

"If you would," I said, relieved. "Forgive me; it was a shock."

~

Returning to the drawing room, we could hear a peal of girlish laughter. Hutton had evidently found how to render Miss Gardner helpless, and she struggled to regain her composure as we came in.

"Goodness," said Francesca, with the hint of an uncharacteristic brittleness. "Have we been so long that you're best friends now? Perhaps promises have already been exchanged! Do let us in on the joke, John."

"It was nothing, ma'am," Hutton said. "I was just doing a poor imitation of Mr Jenrick at Tanner's Wonderland."

"Oh, you were there?" Francesca said, frowning. "Yes, that was an unfortunate display, but the man is contrite, so there is no need to dwell on his mistake. You really do find any opportunity to throw scorn on him, John – it's neither helpful nor kind."

"Sorry, ma'am, I'm sure," Hutton said coolly. "Well, I've finished my tea, and you're busy, so I'll talk to you about the arch another time. Good day, ma'am – miss, sir." He stood up and walked briskly across the room.

"John –" Francesca began, and then gave up. "Oh, bother."

"I'm very sorry, ma'am," Miss Gardner said meekly, standing up to leave.

Francesca bit her lip, and then smiled and said, "Oh, my dear, there's nothing to be sorry about. You're delightful, and I know you'll be a shining jewel in our theatre company." She held Miss Gardner's hands for a moment. "I'm so glad you came. And Thomas, I would ask you to stay for lunch, but I'm afraid I feel one of my headaches coming on."

~

Unpleasant news and an equally unpleasant display of petulance from my host had made for an unsatisfactory encounter. However, a certain informality was revealed in Francesca's and Hutton's dealings, and a fragile affection.

As I waited outside for Celeste to be brought around, I saw Hutton successfully persuading Miss Gardner to return to town with him instead of using Francesca's carriage. I had to admit that Miss Gardner might be a better match for him than Francesca, despite the former's youth. And poor Francesca had seen it.

CHAPTER EIGHT

Louise had asked me, with some tentativeness, if I might help to take her to the cliffs to hunt for fossils, and I readily agreed, if only to avoid encounters with her brother. We took the pony trap, with a picnic prepared by Catherine and Mrs Felton, and Louise's bag of tools and a map she had purchased in town.

It was a fine day; I felt a small pang of guilt leaving Phyllis behind in the library, but I knew she was never happier than when pulling the strings of her literary marionettes, and the sunshine soon dissolved any misgivings.

"I may be able to sell some of my finds," Louise said as we trotted eastward to the coast. "I have done before, like poor Mary Anning."

"Ah – the palaeontologist from Dorset. I believe I saw a mention of her death a while back."

"Yes. She's one of my heroes. I was heartbroken when she died. She found a Pterosaur, and a Plesiosaurus, and others besides. Imagine! One day, perhaps, I might be as fortunate. After all, it's a young science, and such discoveries are still possible." She laughed. "But that would be like an archaeologist who only wants to find gold coins and palaces. I am quite content with lesser treasures."

"And why 'poor' Miss Anning?" I asked.

"She lost her savings to a failed business scheme, and then she succumbed to illness before her time."

"I'm sorry to hear it," I said, and we fell silent.

"But the writing on the wall – how are your investigations progressing?" she said after a minute.

"They're not," I said. "All I have is a book of passionate

verse given to me by Mr Fountain, an authority on local history, on whom I had set my hopes to tell me instantly who 'R.M.' might be. The poetry may or not be a clue, but I'm jiggered if I can extract anything of use from it."

Louise looked mystified. "But why would he give you a clue, rather than simply telling you, if he knew?"

"A very good question – I've no idea. Perhaps the fellow is a little confused. Or perhaps it isn't a clue at all."

"Could you not go and talk to him again?"

"Unfortunately not," I said. "He's suffering from a bad fever from which he might never recover."

"Oh dear," she said.

"Indeed," I said. "Anyway, this obscure poet liked women and lapidarian metaphor, but was repeatedly cynical about the Church. It's not much help. What would you do with this information?"

"Me?" Louise said, and laughed. "Oh, I only have an instinct where to dig. Where there is favourable geology, and there are reports of previous finds, that's where I go. And of course I've learned to recognise what finds may be significant, and what might be assembled according to anatomical principles."

I closed my eyes in search of inspiration from this. "So to apply that to my case, I might dig where my poet is supposedly indicating. Perhaps I should concentrate on a Church connection."

"Indeed," Louise said. "Find out what churchmen he might have been referring to. I think you said he was a local poet? So you can start in Hawksbridge. Perhaps he had fights with the Church that are documented by local historians."

"Yes, of course – that is somewhere to start. Thank you."

"My pleasure," Louise said, as a sign came into view. "Castle Newton! That didn't take too long."

~

We left the trap at a local inn, and walked along the cliff path for half an hour before scrambling down to a small bay that Louise had identified on her map.

There was no one around, and the only sounds were the waves and the gulls. I felt Louise's vulnerability and was glad she had not needed to ask for anyone else's protection. On the other hand, she was the one wielding a hammer.

I sat on a rock, watching her methodically examine the bay, occasionally tapping with her hammer and turning objects over in her hand. Most she threw away, but some she placed in linen bags.

When she got to the far reaches of the bay and could go no further, she returned and sat down, her knapsack between her knees.

"How did you do?" I asked.

"Nothing that will make my name," she said, "but I have some pretty things to sell." She brought out a couple of bags. "This ammonite has marble in it, and here's another with an iron pyrite layer."

"Very nice," I said.

"Plus some fern and half a trilobite," she said. "I'm absolutely famished."

I extracted the picnic and we munched on our beef sandwiches, watching the white foam endlessly rearrange itself.

"So why this bay in particular?" I asked.

"A few interesting bones have been found here," she said. "And part of a footprint of something large, probably a Megalosaurus."

"Surely everything would have been discovered here by now?"

"Not at all," Louise said. "The sea is always eroding the cliffs and rocks, turning up new things. Look at that part of the cliff," she said, pointing at fissured rocks and a perilous overhang I had not noticed. "It looks as though it'll peel away soon, and who knows what might be revealed."

"Then we shall come back again soon," I said, "when the ocean has done some of your work for you."

"Thank you," she said, smiling and taking a swig of ginger beer.

This was her native habitat, I realised. In Ramsburgh, she was a sister, a spinster, a constrained female of no consequence. Her clothes, her movements and even her expression were domesticated, measured and polite. Yet here, the loose strands of her hair blowing carelessly in the wind, a jaw set in scholarly determination, and an honest practicality in her dress, she was transformed. On this beach, she was mistress of her domain and emancipated by nature.

Had I possessed the freedom, I might have revelled in all the qualities before me that had the potential for an unconventional and stimulating marriage, including her unshowy beauty. Instead, I took pleasure in her obvious happiness to be doing entirely what she loved, in a temporary reprieve from the sordid realities of her position.

"I thought I might write some poems for my book on dinosaurs," Louise said. "I don't recall them being the subject of verse, yet, although of course there might be a valid literary reason for it!"

"That's an excellent idea," I said. "You might well achieve fame."

"Or notoriety," she said, "as a presumptuous, silly woman writing silly poems."

"I don't think so," I said. "Things are changing. And in any case, notoriety might be better than anonymity."

"If it puts food on my table – our table – then I welcome it." She sighed.

"You surely don't have to continue keeping company with your brother, and funding his excesses?" I said.

"I don't know," she said, looking up at me. "I can't just leave him to rot, can I?"

"You must protect yourself. He will drag you down with him. And he needs to be jolted into action." I kicked at the sand. "I'm sorry – that must seem disloyal. I know he was my friend... but that was a long time ago."

"It is I who should apologise on his behalf, for our presence here," she said. "We are entirely out of place. And yet..."

"Yes?"

She smiled briefly at me and then looked away, out to sea. "Is that a seal?"

I shaded my eyes and scanned the choppy waters. "It might be. It usually turns out to be a rock in my experience. Oh – it's moving. Definitely a seal."

"They always look as though they're enjoying the water, don't you think?" she said. "Aren't you envious of them? I am – desperately."

"Off you go, then," I said. "I'll avert my gaze."

"Oh, I wish I could." She looked from the sea, to me, and back again. "Could I? There's no one else about, and I know you to be a perfect gentleman."

She laughed nervously. "I can't believe I even thought about it – with no swimming costume! How ridiculous."

"Not at all," I said, "if it would make you happy. Heaven knows you've been long enough in Peter's shadow. You deserve it."

"You know, I think I shall," Louise said. "I could be dead tomorrow. Perhaps you would like to read my book." She removed her palaeontology book from her bag.

"With pleasure," I said, taking the book and turning on the rock so my back was to the sea. "Don't go too far – there may be rip tides!"

"I won't," she said, and I heard her undressing before crunching quickly down to the shore in her chemise. She exclaimed as the cold water hit her legs, and instinctively I turned to check on her. I quickly went back to studying the Iguanodon, guiltily enjoying the forbidden glimpse of her wet, clinging chemise. It amused me to think how my younger self would never have believed such a day possible.

I checked a few times thereafter, ensuring I could still see her bobbing head, but all was well, and she waved to me.

When I arrived back, panting, I said, "I only wanted to ensure you hadn't drowned. And that you hadn't attracted the attention of a giant maiden-eating serpent."

"Of course," she said. "Thank you. But I think that was a freshwater creature." Out of the corner of my eye, I could see that she had sat down on a nearby rock.

"I'll need to sit and dry off for a few minutes," she said. "I take it you didn't bring a towel with you."

"Alas, no," I said.

"Well, next time you can. Perhaps two towels. It really is most invigorating."

There was a mischievous note in her voice. She was clearly enjoying not only the hunt, the water and the sun, but the strangeness of being nearly naked on a beach with a man and breaking all the rules.

"You know," I said, "I had no idea you were such a Bohemian."

"Nor me," she said. "It must be the ginger beer."

~

"Perhaps you can read to me from Mr Lawrence's book," Phyllis said as we lay in the gloaming. "There's just enough candle left if you need more light."

"Ah – I'm afraid I left it with Francesca," I said. "I grew frustrated with it. Perhaps she will see something we don't."

"In that case, you can tell me all about your fossil-hunting expedition," she said. "Did Louise find anything?"

"Just a few things that she can sell – unfortunately nothing novel. But she was in her element, and it was the first time I've seen her truly happy since she came here."

"How sweet," Phyllis said, kissing my shoulder. "Are you sure her happiness was due to the fossils, and not you?"

I decided it would not be productive to tell her about Louise's impromptu dip. "Not me, and not just the fossils," I said, "but the freedom, and nature generally. It really was beautiful. I must take you there! It's not good for you to work so hard. You must have some sun and air."

"I suppose you're right," she said. "It's so hard to stop in mid-flow – and when I come back to the real world, for a moment it feels so..."

I half sat up, resting on my forearm. "Dull? Is your world of fictional heroes better than reality with me?"

"No, no, that's not what I'm saying," Phyllis said. "As I said – just for a moment, I have this feeling of dread when I have to stop writing. Confusion, even. And then I get used to the world again, and all is well."

"It's not the best compliment I've had," I said, as lightly as I could. But I was stung. It was as though she had not tried to make the adjustment from unmarried life, where most hours were hers to dispose of as she wished. Or – worse – she had tried, and decided it could not be done. I realised that I had been happy to go along with it from force of habit.

"Oh – I didn't mean that I find you or Ramsburgh dull, truly!" she said. "But you have your distractions, don't you? And besides, you know how much pressure my publisher puts on me. I'm terrified of letting him down – of him losing interest in me. And I have younger authors snapping at my heels."

"Yes, but..." I struggled to counter this. "Your work is important, I realise, but I think we should try to do more together – that's all."

"Of course, my sweet," Phyllis said. "Perhaps we could do something together now."

"If it's not going to fill you with dread?"

"I give you my word it won't," she said, and wrapped herself around me, having first removed the cat from the bed.

CHAPTER NINE

WHETHER my attendance at church the following day was prompted by an interest in Allan Lawrence's clerical animosity, or remorse at the previous day's events and a wish to redress the balance with a little easy conformity, I cannot recall. Perhaps something of both. In any case, as the Rector's droning voice became mercifully attenuated by my own thoughts, it gave me the time and tranquillity to review several recent complications.

The increasing separateness of my life with Phyllis was a risk to the understanding that must underpin a healthy marriage, to be sure, but with an effort to plan joint endeavours, I supposed that might not be difficult to rectify. A picnic trip to the Devil's Teeth might be just the thing – not the bay at Castle Newton, on reflection, with its recent improper associations. Legends of the standing stones and their mystical properties were back in common circulation with the new interest in mythology; I thought of the scandalous tale of Bess Shannon's conception within the ancient circle. It would make an amusing day, although poignant too: the stones would be haunted by the memories of our visit there with our lost friend Victoria.

Francesca's theatre: it was an exciting venture, but was its joy about to be marred by strains between Francesca and her builder? And while I had given the nod to Jenrick's employment, his good behaviour was not guaranteed. This might, however, be the price to pay for artistic brilliance. I would have to keep my eye on the business side, especially as I had invested a tidy sum of money into it, albeit one I could afford to lose.

The strange message at the inn had already caused indirect trouble – poor Mr Fountain's dangerous illness. On the other hand, I knew neither Francesca nor I could rest easy with this macabre mystery unsolved. And an injustice in the past was still an injustice.

Another pressing problem was the question of how to oust Peter. I could physically throw him out, but this would surely rebound on me one way or another. I could find alternative accommodation for him – even a subsidy might be worthwhile, although it could lead to an unpalatable longer term obligation. I would look into cheap lodgings. Perhaps he could be found employment, if he were not too proud to accept it. But Louise... that was another matter. I could not countenance ejecting her and leaving her to her brother's mercy. I seemed to have taken on a role of protector. It was to be hoped she would soon be able to make her own way in the world, but she needed time. Meanwhile, as my enjoyment of her unusual company grew, I would need to resist further intimacy. It would not do for Louise to become too attached.

All the while I had been staring at the board listing previous rectors, without seeing it at all. A sudden inflection in the Rector's voice derailed my train of thought, and the board came into focus, with the carefully painted strokes and serifs of its gold letters. My eyes automatically followed them: Mark Nisbet, 1634. Andrew Gittings, 1663. Richard Manners, 1689.

I had stared at this board countless times, and the names had had no significance at all. Now, my heart jumped and I let out an involuntary 'Good Lord' that had my neighbours turning in their pews. The initials could be mere coincidence. Or it was possible that the Reverend Mr Richard Manners was a desperate suicide, implicated in the deaths and illegal burial of two innocent souls.

~

After the service, it took me a few minutes to find the rector's grave. His lichen-covered headstone was a simple rectangular one. The only decoration was a depiction of a winged cherub on an open book, and under it, the inscription read:

HERE LIES RICHARD MANNERS
BELOVED RECTOR OF HAWKSBRIDGE 1689
TO 1717
MOURNED BY HIS DAUGHTER JULIA AND
ALL HIS FLOCK
DIED 5TH AUGUST 1717 AGED 41 YEARS

THE CHAPTERS OF MY LIFE ARE WRIT
MY SINS ARE PLAIN TO SEE
READ ME, LORD, AND JUDGE ME FIT
TO DWELL FORE'ER WITH THEE

I had a curious urge to look up. Was he watching me now, wondering whether I would unlock his secrets? His sins were by no means plain for me to see, yet, but I was making progress.

~

I came home to the sight of Louise weeping among the roses, gasping with fury and misery.

"Ignore me," she said as I approached. "I'm all right."

"Clearly you are not," I said. "Please tell me what's wrong, and how I can help."

She sniffed into a handkerchief. "Oh, it's so silly. A trifle."

"Yes?"

"My fossil brooch – it's gone. It's not worth much, but it was from my dear father. He was so delighted with my interest in palaeontology, especially after the disappointment my brother turned out to be. He encouraged me, and gave me..."

She paused while she struggled to control herself.

"He gave me the brooch for my nineteenth birthday," she continued. "I could not have been happier. It's my most precious possession, a kind of talisman – it's all I have left from my father, save a few letters."

"Surely it can't have gone far? You weren't wearing it on our trip, I think."

"No, I was afraid of losing it. I put it in the little drawer in the dressing table the day before the trip. I wouldn't have been careless with it. And since your staff are beyond suspicion, there is only one person who could have taken it."

"Peter? What would he have wanted with it?"

"Oh, the usual. To pawn it for drink, no doubt. And to spite me."

"Good Lord. Have you asked him about it?" I said.

"He won't answer. He's either in a drunken stupor or pretending to be in one."

"We'll see about that," I said, starting to stride towards the house.

"No, Thomas! Please don't! It's not worth it," Louise implored.

I stopped. "But he mustn't get away with this thieving," I said.

"He won't admit it," she said, "so there's no use. It'll only be deeply unpleasant for everyone, and so embarrassing."

"Very well," I said. "I'll check the pawn shops in Hawksbridge tomorrow."

"Thank you," she said, managing a smile. "What rotten trouble we are!"

"You aren't," I said. "I wonder if we might find your brother accommodation in town? Nothing fancy. But I don't mind funding it for a limited time."

"Which will become forever," she sighed, "knowing him. That's so kind of you. It's tempting."

I smiled and turned towards the house, and then turned back. "Oh – I nearly forgot. I've found a candidate for my 'R.M.' – Richard Manners, a former rector from 1689."

"That's wonderful! Do you know anything about him?"

"No," I said, "but I'm about to scour my library for local histories, assuming my wife isn't too deep in work there."

"She went for a walk not long ago," Louise said. "To clear her head."

"I'm glad she's getting some fresh air," I said. "She becomes so engrossed in her work that sometimes I think she forgets to breathe properly. Would you care to help me excavate for clues?"

"With pleasure," she said. "It'll be a good distraction."

~

The following day I rode into town with the only book of relevance we had managed to turn up in my predecessor's collection. I found Francesca and Hutton leaning over drawings in the inn's office, which now had new windows and was freshly painted in a pleasing light blue.

They had their backs to the open door and were so absorbed that when I hesitated in the doorway, they were oblivious of my presence, and I was able to observe how, as Francesca emphasised a point about the proscenium arch design, she touched Hutton's back, her hand lingering. Clearly they had overcome their previous difficulties.

I cleared my throat and said, "Good morning!"

Francesca jumped a little and moved her hand. "Oh! Thomas, you startled me. Good morning to you! John, do you have enough from me?"

"Certainly, ma'am, for the time being," Hutton said, gathering up the drawings, and he smiled at me as he left the room. "I may have something for you to look at later, ma'am," he called from the hall.

Francesca turned back to the now empty table, her hand to her mouth, apparently to stifle a laugh.

"I'm pleased you two have made up," I said. "I like him."

She turned to me again. "Do you?" she said. "I'm so glad. He's an excellent man. I'm afraid if you're wondering whether I've deduced something from the poems, I have nothing to report. Except that I rather enjoyed them."

I was tempted to ask if Hutton had enjoyed them too, but refrained.

"No, that's not why I came," I said. "I've made some progress. I believe our man may be Richard Manners, a rector at St Ninian's at the end of the seventeenth century. He's listed at the church."

"Goodness!" said Francesca, her eyes widening. "Clever you."

I took a seat, and opened Henry Kitchen's 'A Recent History of Hawksbridge'. "Louise helped me find this book in my library, which sheds a little light on him. But there's nothing about a suicide."

I handed her the book, and she read the passage I indicated.

> In 1689, the Rev. Mr Andrew Gittings was most unfortunately killed by a wagon on the Old Bridge, and was replaced by a young curate, Richard Manners. Handsome in feature and prone to an unbecoming weakness for females, he nevertheless established a reputation for kindness and sympathy for his parishioners, many of whom suffered dreadful hardship. Amongst many eccentricities, he had a habit of visiting the sick and reading them poetry, as well as paying for their treatment out of his own pocket. He was a good friend of that notorious

writer of passionate verse, Allan Lawrence; he also wrote a little himself, but of no particular distinction.

Manners is probably best remembered for having inherited a magnificent jewel from his adventurer father: the 'Manners Ruby', also known as the 'Anaukpetlun Ruby', uncut and weighing nearly an ounce. The story goes that his grandfather, Oliver Manners, worked for the East India Company and was sent to Burma to investigate expansion into that territory. Once there, he was caught up in a war and ended up spying on the Portuguese for King Anaukpetlun. His reward for this service was one of the gems for which Burma is famous. It was eventually inherited by the young Richard Manners. However, Manners lost the jewel to his friend Nathaniel Whickham, apparently in a wager, and it has remained in that family ever since.

Manners never married, although he had an adopted daughter named Julia, rumoured to be his natural child. He died in 1717 to a considerable outpouring of grief in the parish.

"Well!" Francesca said. "How interesting – and yet this man is depicted as having a generous nature, and surely not someone who could be involved in the deaths of two people? Do you really think this could be the same man?"

"I think it's about the right period," I said, "and there is the poetry connection."

"But plenty of people like poetry," she said.

"True," I said. "I just have an instinct he was the sort of person who might have got himself into trouble – after all, he loved women, and his judgement was obviously not impeccable if he managed to lose the ruby to his friend."

"Some friend," Francesca said. "What friend would insist he honour such an outrageous wager?"

"I hope to find out," I said. "It might have a bearing on the tragedy."

"So Louise is making herself useful," Francesca said. "Please thank her for her help. And what of your other lodger?"

I grimaced. "It gets worse. Louise suspects him of stealing a treasured brooch."

"Oh no," said Francesca. "What on earth will you do about him?"

"Find him alternative lodgings, probably," I said.

"And Louise?"

"She may stay as long as she likes."

"With Phyllis' blessing?"

I rubbed my face. "I hope so. I haven't really talked about that... Louise and I went to Castle Newton last week, to look for fossils. She..." I hesitated, but I felt a strange need to confess.

"Yes?"

"She went for a swim. In her chemise."

Francesca looked slightly shocked. "I see," she said. "Well, how nice that she trusted you. You may need to be careful, though, Thomas."

"Yes. I like her too much to allow her to be hurt. But she's good company, and I believe she has a promising future."

"We must see if we can find her a good man," Francesca said. She then laughed. "Do you know, I felt a pang of jealousy to think of you and her cavorting on the beach! How ridiculous of me."

"Hardly cavorting," I said, a little flattered by this. "And I believe your affections are well engaged already."

"Oh dear," she said. "Is it so obvious?"

"Somewhat," I said. "If he gives you any trouble, I'll come and whip him."

"Thank you!" she said. "But it makes him sound like an unruly horse."

"I'm sure you have him broken in by now," I said.

"Well, I've left some wildness in him," she said with a sly look. "At least I hope so."

Not wishing to give her a chance to betray any more

embarrassing confidences, I got up from my chair.

"I must scour the pawnbrokers of Hawksbridge, a task I don't relish," I said. "How is the theatre coming along?"

"Splendidly," Francesca said. "I'll show you the next time you're here. However, it won't be ready for rehearsals yet, so we'll use the Town Hall in the meantime."

"You have your company already?"

"A good part of it," she said. "Jenrick has been working hard. And my play is progressing wonderfully too – I'm rather proud of it. Will you come to our first rehearsal on Wednesday afternoon?"

"Most certainly," I said. "When does The Angel Arms open?"

"Oh, in about a month," she said. "I have a lot of furnishings yet to choose, and staff to recruit."

"I'm impressed. This business seems to come naturally to you," I said, and she smiled happily.

~

It must be galling, I thought, as I stood before Bailey's Antiques and Pawnbrokers, to see your own goods displayed in the window in a ritual of public humiliation. Several paintings, a fancily carved chair, some silver candlesticks – they were probably all associated with stories of financial embarrassment.

Mr Bailey, as I assumed him to be, was reading the Hawksbridge Herald, and got up to greet me.

"Good morning, sir," he said, putting his folded newspaper next to a silver teapot on the counter and removing his spectacles. "How may I help?"

"I'm looking for a brooch –"

"Ah, you've come to the right place," he said, turning

towards the chest of drawers behind him. "I have a wide selection –"

"Sorry, no, that's not what I meant," I said. "I mean a specific brooch that may have been deposited here a few days ago."

Mr Bailey turned back and frowned. "Then it won't be for sale yet, I'm afraid, sir. I need to give my clients a chance to raise the money, so I put items aside for a while."

"I fear this particular item is stolen," I said, "and your client is unlikely to be back for it. It's a fossil brooch with an ornate silver mount. Does this sound familiar?"

I could tell that it did, as he looked alarmed and said, "Stolen? Lord, I hope not." He went to his cabinet of drawers, pulled one out, and removed a small box, which he then placed on the counter. Opening it, he said, "Is this it?"

"That's the one," I said. "I'm afraid Mr McNulty was not entitled to bring it here. It belongs to his sister."

"That's bad news, I must say, sir," Mr Bailey said. "As you can imagine, I have to be totally above board with anything that comes across this counter. I'm not sure what to do about this, to be frank, sir." He scratched his head. "I'll make a loss on this. Do you think McNulty can be persuaded to return my money? Should I go to the police?"

"I have a better idea," I said. "I'll buy it from you to spare the McNultys' blushes, and you won't be out of pocket. I can guarantee you that Mr McNulty would not be in a position to buy back the brooch, even if he were the owner."

"Thank you, sir, I would be much obliged." He shook his head, donned his spectacles and carefully wrapped the brooch up in paper. "I gave him ten shillings, I'm afraid."

I extracted the necessary coins and Mr Bailey wrote out a receipt. "Thank you, sir," he said. "It's very generous of you."

"Thank you, Mr Bailey," I said, taking the box. "The owner will be overjoyed to have it back."

I turned to leave, but on a whim stopped and said, "I

realise this may sound strange, but given that you deal in ancient artefacts: have you heard of something called the Manners Ruby?"

Mr Bailey puffed out his cheeks as he considered this. "That rings a bell, yes. Indian, wasn't it?" He chuckled. "I'm afraid no one's come in with that, sir. I would hardly be their first choice."

"Burmese," I said. "Richard Manners apparently lost it in a wager."

"The silly bugger – pardon my language, sir! What's your interest in it, if I may ask?"

"I'm looking into Manners' life. He was a rector here a hundred and fifty years ago; but I can't find much about him, aside from this ruby of his."

"Ah well, that's the capricious sieve of history for you, sir. Depends on people being interested in an individual, doesn't it? A person may have achieved much in his life, but no one bothers to write about him, or he falls out favour."

"True," I said. "And I suppose the reverse can be the case."

"Oh, most certainly," he said. "Take Johnny Speed."

"Johnny Speed?" I asked.

"Have you not heard? He's to have a statue made of him, by public subscription. And who's going to bother with that? He was a smuggler in the last century, who used to evade the custom officers with prodigious turns of speed, by foot, boat, or horse. He also liked to play the penny whistle – not especially well, by all accounts."

"I see," I said. "A notable eccentric."

"You could call him that. To be honest, sir," he said, looking around him conspiratorially and lowering his voice although there was no else in the shop, "I don't give a rat's tail about him, and I dare say this subscription will fail just like so many others in this town. But then I'm an old cynic."

"Interesting," I said, hoping I would not be asked to

contribute. "So, as you say, Manners may have been all but obliterated by your sieve of history."

"Perhaps – but not necessarily, sir," he said. "You can try to find surviving family – though I don't know any people by that name hereabouts – and there's also a type of person who collects the scribbles of dead men. Personally, I think it's gossip-mongering, and what a man writes in a personal letter is no business of anyone else's. I'm old-fashioned like that. But as I say, there are people who like to collect these things, and it's just possible that someone has a relevant scrap. Mr Blackwood traded in private items, I do know that, but of course we can't ask him."

He scratched his head. "I know Mr Tambard used to collect pretty much anything, including local mementoes. Mr Tambard is sadly –"

"Deceased, indeed, but his widow is not," I said. "Thank you, Mr Bailey. I'll talk to her, slim chance that it may be. And I shall try to find the remnants of the Manners family, if there are any."

"You do that, sir. I'm glad to have been of service."

~

I knocked on the door to Louise's rooms and presented her with the box, for which I received a grateful embrace.

"Please let me pay," she said, wiping her watering eyes.

"Entirely unnecessary," I said. "I'm just glad I found it."

"You're too good," she said, and then gave the box back. "Could you possibly keep it for me? Do you have a safe?"

"Certainly," I said.

"It would be less complicated than if he finds it again," she said. "He would either get angry – not that he's remotely entitled to – or put it entirely out of my reach."

"It will be secure, I assure you. Are you feeling better today?"

"Now I am," she said, smiling. "A thousand times better. I've been trying to think about my book, without much luck – but now I think I might be calm and productive."

"Good," I said. "I shall take Fox for a walk. I have to amuse myself somehow while the women of the house stock the libraries of Britain."

CHAPTER TEN

WITH the theatre renovations still incomplete, the first rehearsal of 'The Fairies' Revenge' took place in the Town Hall. When I came in, a little knot of actors were looking at their hand-written scripts while Jenrick spoke to Francesca. One of the actors was looking from Francesca to the mural and back again with wonder, trying to reconcile his employer with her sensual depiction as a mother angel, scooping human souls from a burning mill. As she gesticulated to Jenrick, it was easy to see how the artist had been inspired to transfer her natural energy to the dramatic scene.

Seeing me, she came over, and yawned. "I'm sorry – I was up late making changes and copying out the parts again. I hope they can read my handwriting – it got distinctly crabby in the candlelight. They've had a draft already, so they should be au fait with most of it."

"I'm looking forward to your creation," I said.

She looked around her. "That's strange," she said. "Have you seen Rosabel? I would have expected her to be prompt."

"I haven't see her," I said. "I made sure she would have the time off from the Pottery – I'll be cross if she's been denied it. She's probably just nervously titivating herself. It's all going to be new to her – or does she have some experience?"

"A couple of plays at school," she said, "and a small part in an amateur performance of 'A Midsummer Night's Dream'. So she's not a complete novice."

Jenrick cleared his throat and said, "Welcome, everyone, to the first rehearsal of Mrs Campbell's play, 'The Fairies' Revenge'. I trust everyone now has the latest manuscript. You may refer to it this time, of course, but in future rehearsals you'll be expected to know your lines."

He looked about him. "Has anyone seen Miss Gardner?" he said. There were blank looks and shaking heads, and Jenrick said, "For heaven's sake! Is a little professionalism too much to ask? Well, let's hope she's here for her entrance in Act II. Let's make a start. Act I, Scene I: the council is meeting to decide what to do about the Worm. We are sombre, as the beast has been ripping the townsfolk apart for some months."

He arranged the actors in a semi-circle, with himself in the centre since he was playing the King of Greater Hawksbridge.

"The curtain rises," he said.

KING

The attacks are getting more frequent and the Worm easily evades our warriors. There is much fear and our citizens demand an end to it. I demand an end to it. What say you all?

COUNCILLOR 1

If you would permit me, sire. A net made from a stronger rope -

KING

We have already tried it. The Worm can bite through anything we make in an instant.

COUNCILLOR 2

My suggestion, sire, is a hundred archers at the side of the river, waiting -

KING (*waving dismissively*)

Arrows have no effect on its scaly hide.

WISE MAN (*standing*)

Hear me, sire, and let your anger subside when you have listened to my words. For you will all be filled with foreboding - yet it may be the only path.

KING

Very well. We shall listen.

WISE MAN

We cannot stop the beast from taking our citizens. But we can appease it. We must feed it.

COUNCILLOR 1

Feed it! It has been happily feeding itself.

WISE MAN

Indeed. So we must give it what it wants, in order that it never comes into town. You have seen the corpses. It rarely consumes an entire person, leaving many dead. The answer appeared in a dream, which has filled me with horror but which I know to be an instruction from God Himself.

KING

And what exactly would God have us do?

WISE MAN

Each month, we must offer a morsel so tender and enticing that the beast will gorge himself and then rest. God commands that it be a maiden, to be offered up in her natural state. Only then will the beast leave our town in peace. Many shall be spared in exchange for the few.

KING

God asks too much, old man. How may we do this without an insurrection?

WISE MAN

We must, if the kingdom is to be saved from utter desolation.

COUNCILLOR 2

God save our immortal souls!

(the monster howls)

WISE MAN

Make haste! The maidens of this kingdom must draw straws. There is no other way.

KING

Never have I ruled with a heavier heart, but it shall be done.

The second scene depicted the first such maiden being offered up, and Francesca whispered to me that the actress would go behind a screen, cast her robe to one side, and then disappear down steps into the stage to the roars of an invisible but hungry Worm. Today, a shawl did service as the discarded robe, picked up by her young man who wept inconsolably over it.

The first act ended, and Jenrick became more agitated than the King of Greater Hawksbridge.

"Where the devil is she?" he barked. "We need her for the next scene."

"Oh, the silly girl," Francesca said, getting up and going to the front of the hall. "She had better have a good excuse! Never mind: I shall take the role of Veldra for now."

Francesca sat on the floor by the actor playing John, and adopted a seductive pose.

VELDRA

But my love, can it be that your passion cools for me? You told me only yesterday that you would carry me far away where we would only have one another to care for. Do you not like to caress my hair? Do you not yearn for the cool breeze of my trembling wings?

JOHN

Of course, Veldra, you inflame me as much as ever, though I cannot tell whether it is truly my honest heart or your sly magic that rules over me. But my father forbids it, and I must return to the woman I once loved, before you cruelly ensnared me.

VELDRA

Oh! That mortal lump, Margaret. She is fat and old. How can you even compare us? Can you give your whole life to a mere human? A wife without wings, who cannot do this...?

JOHN

Stop it, Veldra, cease your fluttering. I know it is part of your witchcraft. And Margaret is neither fat nor old. A union of man and fairy could never be: you must find yourself one of your own kind. Oh - hide yourself, my sister approaches!

FRANCES

John? I thought I might find you here - this glade reminds you of... her. But you have put her aside now, haven't you, John? Please tell me you have! Margaret loves you so much, I think she will die without you. Can you love her again as you once did, before you were bewitched?

JOHN

I have put Veldra aside, Frances. I have been foolish. Let us go back and I will pledge myself to Margaret. By leaving this place, I renounce Veldra forever!

(Veldra appears from behind a tree)

VELDRA (grabbing John)

You are mine! You love only me - you said so! And once betrothed to a fairy, you are forever bound to her!

FRANCES (wresting John from her)

He has chosen Margaret, Veldra! I feel pity for you, for to lose a man as fine as my brother is lamentable indeed. But your hold over him is over. John, we must go.

VELDRA (screeching)

You hateful scrap, you harpy! Margaret may have her fool - I am well rid of the faithless wretch. But I know you have poisoned him against me. And you shall receive poison in return. From now until your mortal doom, you'll grow no baby in your womb!

(she casts a spell at Frances and leaves)

FRANCES (clutching her belly)

Oh! John! I burn - what has she done? She has cursed me - I shall never be a mother! I am a woman destroyed!

(John comforts his sister)

"Very good, ma'am," said Jenrick. "John is torn between two women and wracked with guilt, so we need to see more of that torment in his face and gestures. And Frances could take the last line more slowly, as she gradually realises what's happening to her. Other than that – quite acceptable. Next scene, please."

I was curious to know how Francesca's expansion of the Worm legend would play out, and the actors, despite needing to refer to their manuscripts, were not unskilled. Frances' woes continued when Margaret was nominated to be a feast for the Worm; Frances heroically volunteered to go in her place since her future as a mother, and therefore her chance of married happiness, had been wrecked by Veldra.

After the consumption of Frances, John was maddened with grief and in the name of the fairies, cried that he would give anything for the Worm to be defeated. And so, with some elaborations, the story continued much as Francesca had originally told it, but with a hopeful ending: a faithful friend is entrusted with Margaret's welfare when John departs to live out his life with the fairy queen.

Despite the absurdities of the plot, I was nevertheless moved by the themes of human frailty, love and sacrifice – earnestly depicted – and so when a triumphant Francesca finally collapsed into the chair next to mine, her face shiny with perspiration, I could congratulate her with sincerity.

"I'm so glad you enjoyed it," she said. "To think I'll soon be performing in my own play, in my own theatre! I feel I'm twenty-five again."

"Some people have the talent of a youthful heart all of their lives," I said. "You're fortunate."

Francesca smiled broadly, but only momentarily, and she shook her head. "Rosabel – I was so convinced she would be perfect, and she's let us all down. What *can* have happened to her?"

~

"I have to say," I said as Catherine put a plate of chicken in front of me that evening, "Francesca did a decent job with the play. It engaged my emotions, which I had not expected at all."

"Good for her!" Phyllis said. "I sometimes wonder if what writers do is altogether fair."

"Whatever can you mean?" Louise asked.

"Well – it seems to me that humans are so prone to react

to the feelings of their fellows, that it's far too easy to write stories that exploit this reaction. It's like seeing a face in a potato – we simply can't help it. If a completely ridiculous story can make us cry... then I worry that my occupation is too easy, if not even a little questionable."

"I wouldn't worry about it," I said. "What you do is far more than simply prodding our heart strings. You wouldn't say the same thing about art, surely?"

"Oh, no," Phyllis said. "But then I think of artists as having real skill."

"As opposed to your own talentless scribblings?" I said. "You must see how silly that is."

"Thomas is quite right," Louise said. "And if you bring joy to many, then that is the proof that what you're doing is worthwhile, surely?"

Phyllis smiled. "Yes, yes, of course. It's simply a tiny pinprick of doubt that I feel now and again."

Peter had been picking at his chicken, and had barely uttered a word all evening. He put down his cutlery and I dreaded to think what he would add to the debate. But I was surprised to see his lower lip tremble.

"You should be glad of your skills, Mrs Rufford," he said hoarsely. "It must be gratifying to have any talent, for anything. I..."

To our consternation, he burst into tears, wracked with sobs that seemed to have been building for some time.

"I'm useless," he managed to say. "Worse than useless. I might as well be dead."

"Oh, Peter!" Louise said, going to his side and putting her arm around him. "You mustn't say that! You can still find something to occupy you."

He shook his head and whispered, "I have done such things..." His broke into sobs once more.

To see Peter's bluster disintegrate was worse than enduring his customary arrogance. I wondered what might have set this off.

"Let's get you to bed," Louise said, and she and Peter left.

Phyllis and I looked at each other.

"Oh dear," she said. "That's a side of him I didn't expect to see. I feel sorry for him."

"It is rather ghastly," I said. "But perhaps a breakdown was inevitable."

"Should we fetch a doctor?"

"I think that's premature," I said. "He's likely to be back to his obnoxious self in the morning."

"Very well," Phyllis said. "Should we still go on our picnic?"

We had finally got around to planning a day out at the Devil's Teeth.

"If the weather is fine, I don't see why not. Louise can look after her brother, and the staff are on hand if anything untoward happens."

"She's too patient with him. After the matter of the brooch..!"

"Poor specimen that he is, Peter is all the family she has," I said. "But yes, it does her credit."

~

The morning ushered in blue skies. Feeling only a small pang of guilt to be leaving the house during a minor crisis, I loaded the picnic basket into the pony cart and took the reins, and once more, Phyllis and I were – for the day – carefree lovers.

"I'm glad I prised you from your desk, my dear barnacle," I said.

"So am I," she said, "my sweet chisel." She adjusted her hat to keep off the strong sunshine. "I'm bound to have an idea or two anyway, so it's barely time off at all."

“I suppose it’s quite dangerous, you and I going to the stones,” I said.

“Why? Oh, I see,” she said. “In case mystical forces overpower us, and... Well, perhaps it wouldn’t be so terrible.”

“Really?” I said. “Do you think you’re ready to...?”

“I like children. And we would have plenty of help, so I dare say it wouldn’t hurt my work too much. Now, if we had a child like Felicity...”

“That would be extremely pleasant,” I said. “Pet squirrel and all.”

“I think I would prefer her to have a kitten.”

“Or him, to have a spaniel.”

“We’ll let them choose,” she said, “and no doubt they will make a delightful portrait.”

“I’ll write to Mr Millais at once,” I said, squeezing her hand, “and warn him that his services will be needed in due course.”

~

When we reached the path approaching the Devil’s Teeth, the sky had darkened and we felt a few drops of rain. Hitching the pony to a post, we hauled the basket out and carried it between us up the path. As we reached the stones, the shower had turned into a deluge, and we sheltered as best we could by one of the stones, laughing at the absurdity of it.

On a soggy rug, with a second rug thrown over us, I embraced Phyllis and then kissed her, both of us giving in to the nature around and within us. But out of the corner of my eye, I noticed something almost hidden from view behind our stone that made my blood run cold. It was a pale, lifeless, human hand.

CHAPTER ELEVEN

PHYLLIS could see the look of horror in my eyes, and turned to see what had caused it.

"Oh my Lord," she said, covering her mouth. My arms were still around her and I could feel her tremble.

Wiping the rain from my eyelashes, I turned Phyllis away and crept around the stone. The body lay on its front, without clothing, and I immediately knew from the hair and figure that it was a woman.

I needed to ascertain, quickly, whether she was still alive, but I had never touched a potentially dead person and I had to gather my courage before turning her head. It was clear from her colour, coldness and lifeless eyes that she was gone, but not only that: my suspicions as to her identity – having been aroused as the rain washed the mud from her copper-coloured hair – were confirmed. I also noticed what looked like bruise marks on her neck. I forced myself to look at the rest of her, and found some further marks on her wrists. I staggered up and was violently sick.

"Thomas, tell me!" Phyllis cried. "What did you find?"

Panting, I spat, and went over to her.

"I'm sorry – it's – she's – dead. We must leave at once and get the police. It's Francesca's protégée – Rosabel Gardner."

"Oh, dear God, no," Phyllis said. "Are you sure?"

I nodded.

Phyllis stood frozen to the spot, trying to make sense of this information. "We can't just leave her here like that," she said after a moment. "Let's at least cover her up."

We gathered the sodden rugs and laid them over Rosabel.

Then we hauled the picnic basket back to the trap as quickly as we could. The very idea of a picnic now seemed incongruous. We travelled back to Hawksbridge in grim silence and went directly to the police station.

"This is extremely disturbing news," said Inspector Simmons. "Taylor! I need you now. You're sure she was dead, sir?"

"Perfectly sure, Inspector," I said, wiping dirt from my shaking hands with my handkerchief. "From the bruises on her neck, I'd say from strangling. And I'm afraid she was naked. Naturally we covered her up."

"And you say you recognised her?"

"I believe so. Miss Rosabel Gardner. She was missing from the rehearsal I attended yesterday, but I had no conception..." Phyllis squeezed my arm.

"Of course not, sir. It must be a great shock. You may rest here as long as you like, but I'll have to go to the stones. I would be grateful if you could leave an account with Constable Gawley – as much detail as you can, if you please."

I nodded, and Simmons left.

I vividly remembered Rosabel's enthusiasm in Francesca's drawing room, and thought about the promising life that had been cruelly cut short. The terrible sight of her dead eyes gripped me and it was a while before I could bring myself to write my account. Knowing that the Inspector would be curious about my movements in the last couple of days, I added these details.

Finally we made the journey back to Ramsburgh, which seemed interminable.

"I'm sorry," I said as we turned into the drive. "This started out such a wonderful day."

"The poor, poor girl," said Phyllis, shaking her head.

"If I ever know who did this," I said, "I'll rip them limb from limb, I swear it."

"Hush, dearest," Phyllis said. "Of course you will feel like that now. But the perpetrator will be dealt with, by the law."

"By God and all that's holy," I said, gripping the reins tightly in my fist, "there is no punishment – not even hanging – that could remotely do justice to this."

~

It was obvious to Mrs Felton and Catherine when we arrived with our uneaten picnic and grim faces that something had happened, and so I gave as brief and gentle an explanation as I could.

"Merciful heavens!" Mrs Felton said, steadying herself on the hall table. "Who would do such a devilish thing? Catherine, was it not Miss Gardner you said you were talking to in Myrtle's, about the fairy play?"

Catherine had her hand to her mouth, and she nodded before excusing herself and quickly leaving.

Phyllis went upstairs, and Mrs Felton stared at me, wide-eyed.

"What do the police think?" she asked.

"I don't know yet," I said. "Mr Simmons went off to attend the scene, and I haven't seen him since. In this weather, it may be hard to tell exactly what happened. But someone will know something."

"Oh, it breaks my heart, sir, it truly does. Poor Catherine was just getting to know her, and she sounded such a clever, beautiful young woman."

"Yes," I said, "I met her a few days ago, and she was charming. I can't comprehend that she..."

"No, indeed. And the person who did this thing is still free to terrorise us all!"

"I fear so, Mrs Felton – but we must hope that it's an isolated crime, and that he will be caught soon. He's likely to brag about it to someone, and ensnare himself."

"Oh, do you think so, sir?" Mrs Felton said.

"I'll be praying for it – and for her."

"I too, sir. You had better go and comfort your poor wife – what a shock she's had!"

~

Phyllis was bathing, perhaps hoping to scrub her memory as well as her mud-spattered body. I came and sat next to the bath, reflecting on the vulnerability of the naked human.

"Someone must tell Francesca," she said, soaping her neck. "Or perhaps the police will speak to her?"

"Yes, I expect they'll want to interview everyone who knows her – knew her. At the Pottery too. Perhaps even Catherine."

"Oh, it's so cruel – not just for Rosabel, but for so many others. And imagine all the people who would have known and loved her, had she lived. They too are victims, strangely, though they'll never even realise it. And perhaps there are many children who will never now be born..."

"What an unhappy thought," I said, "but you're right. This evil spreads far and wide, and into the future."

"What will you do?"

I shrugged. "Leave it to the police."

"Not even help them a little? Can you bear it?"

"I might damage their investigations at this stage. But rest assured, my dear, if they fail, I'll be ready to try my best."

She nodded, and then screwed her eyes up. "That dead hand keeps coming back to me. It will haunt me, won't it?"

"For a while, I'm afraid so," I said.

"And of course it will be far worse for you. You actually saw her face."

"Let's try not to dwell on that," I said, flinching at the memory.

Phyllis hauled herself out of the bath – a sight my senses could thankfully still appreciate, with heightened gratitude – and I wrapped her in a towel. Then, silently, we held each other tight.

~

I left Phyllis to her needlework and went up to my little study where I indulged myself in a steadying glass of port. I went to the window and stared at the west lawn and the hills and trees beyond. These simple but inestimable pleasures of nature were now denied to young Rosabel. It seemed as though I could only see the world through the lens of this dreadful event.

Although I had just now confidently dismissed the possibility of interference in Mr Simmons' investigation, I felt the sheer brutality of the crime burn into my resolve. The perpetrator was no doubt crowing about being undetected – yet. Could it be anyone I knew in Hawksbridge, however slightly? I had only briefly been acquainted with Rosabel, so I was largely ignorant of her social circle.

And it could equally have been a stranger – there were many at large, thanks to the construction of the railway and its impressive bridge. Any of the boisterous navvies I had seen at Tanner's Wonderland might be a potential suspect, known as they were for their insobriety and brash behaviour. I did not envy Simmons his task.

I realised that Louise should be told – and warned – so I went downstairs and knocked on her door.

"Do you have a few minutes?" I asked.

"But of course! Come in. How was your picnic? Cup of tea?"

"No, thank you. I'm afraid I have some rather grim news to share."

"Oh – oh dear," she said, ushering me into the chair that used to be Flora's favourite. "I hope no one is unwell – not Phyllis, I trust?"

"No, it's not that," I said. "It's about young Rosabel Gardner – an actress Francesca hired for her play. I don't suppose you ever met her."

"I haven't had that pleasure. What's happened?"

"I'm afraid she's been found dead. Most likely as a result of foul play."

"Oh goodness, no!" Louise said. "The poor woman – and her family! If I may ask, what were the circumstances?"

I sighed. "Phyllis and I found her by the Devil's Teeth this morning. She was unclothed. It wasn't entirely clear how she died, but I suspect the marks on her neck indicate strangulation."

Louise whitened. "Oh!"

"I know. It's horrible. But we must trust that the police uncover the perpetrator quickly. I wanted to warn you to take extra care, given this maniac is still at large."

"Thank you," Louise said. "I shall indeed. How awful."

"I'm sorry, I forgot to ask," I said. "How's Peter?"

"Still wallowing in bed, I'm afraid. I took him some food. He does suffer from occasional melancholia, but he seems particularly agitated this time."

"Do you think something happened in town to push him into this state?" I said, and as I did, I made a terrible connection.

"I think it's simply the realisation of his folly and lack of prospects," Louise said.

And yet the few words he had spoken last night at dinner troubled me greatly. "I have done such things..." As far as I knew, there was no link between Peter and Rosabel. But it was not impossible that he had accidentally encountered her in town, and something had happened he now regretted. On the other hand, it was easy to form groundless suspicions – and for all his sins, I doubted Peter had this crime in him.

~

Francesca was not at home the next morning, so I took Celeste down to The Angel Arms. The weather had cleared, but the sunshine only made it harder to comprehend this wanton act of murder. We are born an extraordinary world, I mused, and yet there are those who are not content with this gift, but want to gratify themselves with the misery of others. Sometimes, it was hard not to despise the human race.

As I approached the inn, I encountered Inspector Simmons and Constable Taylor coming out.

"Good morning, Mr Rufford," Simmons said. "Thank you for your comprehensive report, sir. Might I trouble you with a visit in the next day or so? I would like to talk to your cook, Mrs Wakeley. I believe she was an acquaintance of Miss Gardner's."

"Please do, Inspector," I said. "I hope Catherine will be able to shed some light on this atrocity. Do you have any leads yet?"

"We have precious little yet, I'm afraid, sir, except our determination and patience. But Miss Gardner was well liked, and the town's outrage will be helpful in flushing out the perpetrator. Or perpetrators. Good day, sir."

I found Francesca and Hutton in the office, sitting in sombre silence.

"Oh, my dear Thomas – the Inspector said you and Phyllis found her! It's too awful. And I was so cross with her in the rehearsal, while she was lying there, with no one to... oh!"

Hutton placed a large hand on her shoulder to reassure her.

Hutton looked up at me. "What fiend would want to harm that beautiful creature?" he said. He shook his head. "To think I was in the trap with her only the other day, yapping about nothing in particular, and neither of us could know..." He stopped. "The Inspector took an interest in that – an innocent drive in a carriage, and that makes me a suspect!"

Francesca reached out and squeezed his other hand. "What nonsense. You have the best heart anyone could have."

"Her poor family," I said. "They will be in despair."

"It's just her father," Francesca said, "and now he's alone."

"Should we go and pay our respects to Mr Gardner?" I said.

"What a good idea – yes, Thomas, I think we should," she said. "It will be difficult, of course."

"Jenrick knows?" I said.

Francesca nodded. "The Inspector has already seen him. He was devastated, naturally."

"Will you continue with the play?"

"I think so," Francesca said. "But I'll need some time."

~

I was required to look in on the Pottery and give my approval to a new line in Marbleware – a depiction of Venus drying herself that I would normally have found charming. However, the mood was necessarily sombre, compounded by an unspoken feeling of queasiness that we intended to profit, it might be said, from female vulnerability. I passed my condolences on to the Pottery's employees, and discussed with McPhee the ways in which the company might honour and remember Miss Gardner.

When I returned to Ramsburgh, the Inspector had already come and gone. I met Shipley in the hall.

"Mr Simmons wanted to talk to Mr McNulty, sir, as well as Catherine," said Shipley, "but he's finally out of bed and off away."

"I wonder what Simmons wanted with him," I said.

Shipley shrugged. "New fellow in town, getting a bit of a reputation for a drunkard, then there's a murder... Had a chat with me as well, but I couldn't give him anything useful."

"Any idea where he went?" I said. "I wanted to have a word with him myself."

"He didn't say, of course," said Shipley, "but I'll bet a shilling he's at The Hare and Hounds. Perhaps with one of his fancy new friends," he said with a snort, "such as dainty Miss Buxton."

"A new friend? Interesting," I said.

"Oh yes, sir. I heard they were quite cosy. Someone should warn him."

"Warn him? Why would that be necessary?"

Shipley smiled. "Lucy Buxton is a sweet little whore, sir, begging your pardon. I'm sure your friend isn't dim enough not to know that, but she's a crafty one and will milk him dry telling him she's the first man she's really fallen in love with! That's Lucy's way."

"I see," I said. "Then Peter's even more of a fool than I imagined."

Shipley looked around and then said in a lowered voice, "Have to confess, sir – I've nearly been caught out myself. She's a witch, that one – as comely as you like" – he cupped both of his hands before him by way of illustration – "and when she smiles at you – well, she can make a fool out of any man, sir."

"Thank you, Shipley – useful to know. I shall have to warn Peter off."

"I don't envy you, sir. Once Lucy gets her hooks into a man... she's a good listener, and damnably good company, curse her."

Shipley really had been bitten, I thought. "Then we shall have to ensure he's fully informed of the dangers of Miss Buxton," I said. "Although I agree, that will be hard if she's taken on the role of confessor and friend, which no doubt Peter badly needs. On the other hand, Peter will soon run out of money, and then she may run out of patience."

"Yes, sir, and then woe betide the next man if Mr McNulty is the jealous sort!"

CHAPTER TWELVE

When Mr Gardner opened the door of his cottage to us, the grief on his thin, stubbled face was so painfully apparent that I felt a pang of shame for intruding. But it was too late to withdraw now.

"Francesca Campbell," my companion said, extending her hand, which Mr Gardner shook limply. "I was privileged to know your beautiful daughter, all too briefly – I'm so terribly sorry."

Mr Gardner nodded. "Thank you," he said quietly.

I introduced myself. "We wanted to pay our respects," I said, "and ask if you have all that you need, at this difficult time."

"Thank you," he said again. "It's kind of you. Please come in."

Mr Gardner showed us into a sparsely furnished parlour and said, "I'll make some tea," before disappearing into his kitchen.

Avoiding the one upholstered armchair that was obviously his favourite, we sat on a couple of battered country chairs in awkward silence until Mr Gardner came in with the tea.

"I took an instant liking to Rosabel," Francesca said. "A charming, talented young woman – she was so keen to be in our play. You must have been extremely proud of her."

"Aye," he said. "I loved her as well as any father could." His tears were visibly welling up. I could not decide if we were inflicting torture on him, or whether it would be good for him to talk about Rosabel. "She were the best daughter any..." He stopped and blew his nose.

"I suppose the police haven't informed you of any progress...?" I said.

"Nay," he said. "But I have precious little faith in them. There's a monster about – probably a cleverer creature than Mr Simmons. He may be far away by now." He shrugged. "And in case, nothing will bring back my Rosabel."

Mr Gardner was displaying a disturbing fatalism. I tried to imagine how I would react in his place. I would, I thought, have had an uncontainable rage at the perpetrator.

Francesca shot me a glance. "Well," she said, "we must hope the police make progress and prevent this happening to anyone else."

He looked up at her. "Oh, aye. I pray no other father in Hawksbridge buries a murdered daughter."

Francesca poured the tea, and I said, "I take it Rosabel lived with you?"

"Of course," he said.

"She was missing during the rehearsal on Wednesday, so perhaps something happened on the Tuesday. If I may ask, when was the last time you saw her?"

Mr Gardner looked puzzled at my questioning, but said, "Tuesday afternoon, it were."

"Did she leave here in the afternoon?"

Mr Gardner slowly sipped his tea. "Aye. She went out. Didn't tell me where."

"Oh, I see," I said. "Was this common?"

He shrugged. "Maybe. Not really. She can do as she pleases. I mean, she could."

"It must have been worrying when she didn't come back that night. I suppose you went to the police that evening, or in the morning?"

"As I say, Mr Rufford, she could come and go as she pleased. I'm not the kind of father to breathe down her neck. I weren't going to bother the police because my daughter were gabbing to a friend, as she likes to do."

"Ah – so the first you knew about it was being told by the police?"

He nodded, and blew his nose again. "On Thursday."

"And you have no idea what might have happened to her?"

He shook his head. "Must have been walking back and some monster took a liking to her. Like as not one of those navvies – rough lot. That's what I told Mr Simmons."

Standing up and going to the fireplace, he picked up a small painting of a beautiful young woman, and gazed at it morosely.

"If you see Mr Simmons," he said, touching the glass, "be sure to ask whether he's talked to the navvies yet."

"I will," I said. "May I ask if that is your daughter?"

"Nay, my wife, Helen," he said. "Rosabel was the spit of her. When Helen died... it was as though she were still here. It were a comfort – and a torment."

"I'm deeply sorry," I said. "This must be hard to bear."

"Aye," he said, "but bear it I must, mustn't I? When God and me are talking again, I'll ask Him how I am to live. If that is even His will."

"Is there anything we can do?" said Francesca. "Anything you need?"

Mr Gardner shook his head. "Nay," he said. "All I needed is gone." He put the picture down carefully, and turned back to us with a look of exhaustion and resignation. "I've been judged and punished by a higher power. That's the long and the short of it."

~

"Oh, heavens," Francesca said as she climbed into the trap. "That was even harder than I expected. The poor, poor fellow."

"You don't think I was impertinent with my questions?" I said.

"Not at all," she said. "But wasn't it strange? He seemed too... accepting, somehow."

"I agree. And what did he think he was being punished for? I didn't like to ask."

"Original sin, or something he did? If the latter, is that why he was so resigned to his daughter's death? Surely you don't think he would harm her? Oh, this business is twisting our minds. I need to think of normal things. Thomas, would you mind taking me to Ramsburgh for a strong cup of Mrs Felton's coffee? I don't want to go home just yet, and I haven't spoken to Phyllis in ages."

"Of course," I said, "so long as you don't mind the risk of seeing Peter."

"I'll take that risk," she said. "I can deal with bluster."

~

"I'm glad you gave Catherine some time off, my dear," Mrs Felton said to me as she brought in a tray. "She was that upset – Miss Gardner fairly haunted Myrtle's." She froze, horrified at herself. "Oh! I'm so sorry – what a terrible turn of phrase I have."

"Don't worry," I said. "We know what you mean. I haven't dared speak to Bess Shannon yet."

"How was Mr Gardner bearing up?" asked Louise.

"Grief-stricken, naturally," I said, "although not raging as I might be. Everyone reacts differently, I suppose, and he may have no energy left for anger."

Mrs Felton was about to leave when Catherine appeared.

"My dear! But you're supposed to be resting!" she said.

"What are you doing here?"

"I have something I want to say to Mr Rufford," Catherine said. "Something I didn't tell the police."

"About Miss Gardner?" I said. "Would you like to speak in private?"

"No," she said, "I've been too private about it already."

Mrs Felton thoughtfully moved a chair from the window, and Catherine sat down.

"It was something that Rosabel didn't want anyone to know," Catherine continued. "And it's unkind to Mrs Campbell. I should have told Mr Simmons, but... it didn't seem my place to hurt anyone."

"I have a remarkably thick hide, Catherine," said Francesca. "Don't mind me."

"And I didn't want to tell tales on Mr Tanner," Catherine continued, "if he's done nothing wrong. But now, at least the truth can't hurt Rosabel."

"No, indeed," I said. "When you've told us, do please go and tell the Inspector. I'll take you."

Catherine nodded and sighed. "Rosabel told me that Mr Tanner had asked her to audition for a show at his Wonderland. He was offering good money – to entice her away from your play, Mrs Campbell."

"Oh! I see," said Francesca, putting a brave face on the revelation. "How funny! Well, it was canny of her to seek out the highest bidder. She clearly had talent, and I'm flattered to have had my opinion of her confirmed. Had she been to the audition?"

"It was supposed to be last Wednesday," Catherine said. "So I don't know."

"Do you know what the role would have been?" I said.

Catherine frowned. "It was a show about ghosts, I think. Two famous ghosts?"

"Oh, no!" said Francesca. "Not The Veiled Sisters?"

"Yes, ma'am – that was it, exactly. The Veiled Sisters."

"Good Lord," I said.

"How *dare* he!" Francesca said, now shaking with rage. "To steal my Veldra is one thing, but to steal my ghosts! Well!"

"Ma'am?" Catherine said, looking to her and the others for an explanation. "I'm sorry, I..."

"It's all right, Catherine," said Phyllis. "Mrs Campbell is cross with Mr Tanner, not you, and you were perfectly right to tell us. Tanner is making mischief, I think."

"You did take on the Hawksbridge Worm, Francesca," I said, "after he had used it for his gymnasium. So perhaps this is tit-for-tat. Or simply a business opportunity. Unfortunately – or fortunately – neither of you owns exclusive rights to these legends."

"Whose side are you on, Thomas?" Francesca said. "Really!"

"Always yours," I said. "But I'm also your business partner, and I try to be objective once in a while."

Francesca pursed her lips and fumed silently, and it was almost a relief when Peter appeared, staggering slightly and spilling a few drops of the brandy he was holding.

"Hey ho!" he said. "I heard raised voices and thought I'd join in the fun. Budge over, Lou." He sank into the sofa next to his sister and took a sip of brandy, sighing with satisfaction.

"I'm glad to see you in a more cheerful mood," I said.

"Oh, well, there's nothing a good Cognac can't cure," Peter said. "Now, what are we all talking about? Ah – that dead actress, I expect. It's the talk of the town. Have they got the blighter yet?"

Catherine stood and walked with dignity across the room. "Good evening," she said, and left.

"No," I said, "and that dead actress was a friend of Catherine's."

"Oh dear," Peter said, putting his hand over his mouth in mock mortification. "How like me to put my foot in it. Anyway, I know what you're all thinking, and I had absolutely nothing to do with it."

Met with a stony silence, he adopted a comic voice and said, "No, Peter, of course not, Peter, we never thought you had! Good God, people, I'm a drunk, not a killer! Anyway, if you don't believe me, I can tell you who I was talking to every night last week."

"I fear no one who could be described as a reliable witness," I said.

"Don't you speak about Lucy like that," Peter said, and then giggled. "I find she's reliable as..." He searched for an appropriate simile. "A steam engine. And as noisy!" He laughed hysterically. "Wump... wump... wump... wheeee!"

"Peter!" Louise said severely, digging her elbow into his arm. "That's quite enough. You're making a complete exhibition of yourself. You need to go to your room and have a rest. Let me help you."

He shrugged her off and rose unsteadily to his feet. "Bed-ho!" he said. "You win, Lou. But I do love my bed. Also extremely reliable. Always there when I need it. Unlike most people. Except Lucy. Wump... wump... wheeee!"

Peter and Louise left, leaving us speechless for a moment.

"What an unusual friend you have, Thomas," Francesca said, finally smiling. "Quite a clown. He should look to Mr Tanner for employment."

"Ugh," I said. "I offer unlimited apologies for him."

"At least he was in a congenial frame of mind tonight," Phyllis said. "From what Louise has said, this is not always the case."

"A disturbing thought," Francesca said, rising. "Well, I must beg a ride home – perhaps Mr Shipley would be so kind as to arrange one. I have to go and recover from today's odd events – a long, hot bath is what I shall have, followed by a cup of chocolate."

~

I had, following my visit to Mr Bailey's shop, written to Mrs Tambard enquiring into the possibility of her late husband's collection containing letters by the Richard Manners. My increasing sense of futility of this search – now put into perspective by the horror of Rosabel's demise – was slightly alleviated by Mrs Tambard's enthusiastic and rapid reply, and her promise to have an answer by the time of my visit. The following Monday, it was a pleasure to see her magnificent Gothic house again, stuffed to the gunwales with her husband's treasures.

"Mr dear Mr Rufford," said Mrs Tambard, getting up from her sofa to greet me. "It's been far too long! You have been remiss and neglectful, but I shall not hold it against you."

I held my hand out but she ignored it and instead embraced me warmly.

"I apologise," I said. "You're very kind. I won't leave it so long again, Mrs Tambard, with or without a pretext!"

"Well, it couldn't really be helped," Mrs Tambard said, leading me by the hand to her sofa. "I do realise you have been kept occupied by members of my own sex, one way or another." She signalled to her housekeeper to bring coffee. "Now, you're a charming young man, but even I would hesitate to lock you in my cellar! Whatever would the neighbours say?"

She looked me up and down as if I were a new horse that pleased her. "And my dear boy, call me Florence, and I shall call you Thomas, if you have no objection."

"None at all," I said. It was strange to think of her as Florence, let alone address her so informally.

"So you're married now!" she said, again taking my hands and squeezing them. I was close enough to smell the lily scent she was wearing. "How glorious! I always thought you would make an extraordinary couple. You're perfect for one another. Of course, you dashed the hopes of many young women in Hawksbridge, and I dare say" – she looked pointedly at the ceiling in mock nonchalance – "a few of us more mature ladies."

I smiled, unsure how to respond to this compliment.

"We are not all dried up old husks, contrary to common opinion," she continued. "Now. Let me pour you a little glass of sherry while we wait for our coffee."

I consented, and leant back in the sofa listening to Mrs Tambard and nodding as she spoke of a picture gallery she had visited the week before. I was happy to leave the business of my visit for a while.

"My husband would have loved the Gainsborough," she was saying. "The subject's beautiful complexion, and the folds of her dress – quite extraordinary." She took a sip of sherry, and then said in a conspiratorial tone, placing her hand on my knee as was her tactile habit, "Oh, he would have *adored* the Boucher. Goodness me. I'm surprised they had the courage to display it. The shepherd girl was so obviously recovering from the delicious effects of..."

She giggled and tapped my knee. "Well, you can guess." She then sighed, and said, "How blissful to be young and in the throes of such passion. But you don't want to hear such talk from an old woman – let me show you what I found."

She got up with a waft of lily and fetched a leather bag sitting on a table in the window. She placed it between us and before opening it, said, "I was rather pleased with the results of my hunt! And all it will cost you is a little kiss, if this is what you were looking for."

"A reasonable bargain," I said. "I confess I wasn't holding out much hope."

"O ye of little faith," Mrs Tambard said, opening the bag. "My husband was absurdly obsessive in his collecting, and at last it may have borne fruit! But first, you must tell me what this is all about. Are you writing a book on Richard Manners?"

"No," I said. "I'm sorry I didn't explain, but it's quite complicated."

"Oh, good gracious," said Mrs Tambard when I had given her the full story. "What a terrible thing Mrs Campbell has uncovered. And yet how exciting."

"Perhaps it seems strange, even distasteful, to pursue it in the light of recent events, but –"

"Not at all," said Mrs Tambard. "The truth must be found and told. Now I'm agog about the contents of these letters!"

I took out the first yellowing letter and carefully unfolded it.

"Fortunately this little trove was neatly labelled in my husband's hand," she added, "as my eyesight isn't up to deciphering ancient signatures."

"It's addressed to a Reverend Mr Marshall – July 5th, 1712," I said, and began to read the letter aloud.

Dear Philip,

Pray excuse my tardiness in replying to your most recent letter, which I read with great satisfaction at your glorious news. The precious addition of a son to your family will bring you both the greatest joy.

I, alas, have not contrived to combine passion with the matrimonial blessings of God. My heart has been captured, but there are certain obstacles in the way of our union. Nevertheless, I am content enough, and I have Julia to chase away the raven of melancholy when it descends.

My friend of old, Allan, continues his ascent into poetic infamy, inspired by all manner of natural instincts, leaving any such toil of mine in the dust. But I am sanguine, and I have taken to reading a selection of Allan's verses on my pastoral visits, at least to those who raise no objection. I find the rhythm soothes the sick, whether or not the meaning is clear to them.

I stopped. "Allan is Allan Lawrence, I take it."

"Ah," Mrs Tambard said, smiling. "The risqué poet. What could his sick parishioners have thought? A distraction from pain, to be sure! My husband gave me a volume of his during our courtship. I seem to recall the one that particularly made me blush rhymed hips with lips. Are you an avid reader of his? I can well imagine it."

"Not exactly," I said, "but I possess a volume. I suspected an association with Manners and this confirms it."

"Well – read on, please, Thomas! This is fine gossip, if strictly speaking a little stale."

I scanned the rest of the letter. "I'm afraid the rest comprises rather mundane parish observations, and Manners trying to raise a subscription for the poor."

"Oh, how dull," said Mrs Tambard. "But we have learned he has a lover – one who is reluctant to say yes to him. Obstacles... what could they be? Perhaps she's not healthy. Or he's not healthy. Or the parents don't approve."

I shrugged.

"Oh!" said Mrs Tambard, wrapping her shawl tightly around herself. "I just felt a cold shiver – we're looking back in time, and observing the events prior to a crime we can do nothing about. It's a little frightening. No matter, more sherry will warm us up."

She filled our glasses again. "So – let's try another letter, shall we? David will have put them in date order, so we'll be travelling forward in time."

"Very well," I said, extracting the next letter. "To Philip Marshall again. October 14th, 1712."

> *Dear Philip,*
>
> *Your kind concern has done much for my peace of mind.*
>
> *I ofttimes wonder why I entertain Allan as a friend when he has caused me such anguish. He continues his attacks on the Church, with ever greater ferocity. I abhor his crude passions, and yet I have become envious of his work and success. My heart aches secretly for an impossible love, while he is able to express the grossest lusts and be lauded for it.*
>
> *And yet - this is as nothing against the needs and pain of my parishioners, who for the most part live in wretched conditions and have scant comforts beyond their faith. They look to me, and I can do so little. But I shall persist with my representations to the Freemen and the Council, and try what else I may.*
>
> *I should, of course, sell that confounded trinket and give the proceeds to the needy - but my sinful soul*

does not allow it. Philip, I have an odd terror that when it leaves my possession, I shall die. One day I shall be tempted, I know, to take that leap and find out the truth of it once and for all. But while God has work for me, and Julia is in my care, I dare not risk my life.

Your respectful friend,

Richard Manners

"What a tortured soul," Mrs Tambard said. "A friend who he has grown to despise, and an object he mustn't part with. A trinket, he said?"

"It's a Burmese ruby he inherited from his family," I said. "An extremely valuable one, apparently. I can understand a reluctance to part with it; but to imagine that one's life depends on it..."

"I fear our Mr Manners may not be entirely of sound mind," Mrs Tambard said. "How horrible for him – and his sweetheart."

"And yet," I said, "is the fear of a ruby worse than many sanctioned superstitions? I find it almost more plausible that, say, wine turning into blood."

"Quite possibly it is," she said, "but a superstition espoused by many becomes a hallowed belief. A superstition held by one man is less kindly regarded."

She smiled at my reaction. "Are you shocked? David was that unusual and discomfiting creature, an atheist, and I picked up a certain scepticism from him. Oh, I still have some faith in the love of God. Yet, against all reason, I have a greater faith – or at least hope – in finding earthly love once more. But how pitiful that sounds when said aloud!"

"Not at all," I said. "You deserve the devotion of an exceptional man."

"How sweet of you," she said. "While such an exemplar eludes me, I will at least claim my reward for the Reverend's letters." She leant towards me, closed her eyes and briefly locked her sherry-sweetened lips with mine. I had expected that only a peck on the cheek would be required of me, but I had the presence of mind not to recoil in surprise.

"My goodness," she said, leaning back and touching her lips. "What a fortunate woman your wife is. Well, young man, you had better leave before I make even more of a fool of myself, and scandalise my staff. A mouthful of sherry and I lose my head!"

She put the letters back in the bag and pressed it into my hands. "Do let me know what you find, my dear. I'll drink tea and quite behave myself the next time you come!"

CHAPTER THIRTEEN

I FELT it was safe to tell my wife about the minor indiscretion of a mature widow.

"Oh!" Phyllis said as we walked Fox in the last of the day's sunshine. "I shouldn't let you out of my sight! The poor woman. What can you have said to encourage her?"

"Nothing," I said. "But I confess I had unwisely agreed to the bargain, thinking it perfectly innocent. I hardly expected her to take a pound of flesh, of course."

"I like Mrs Tambard," Phyllis said. "She's a cultured and amusing woman. She should moderate her sherry consumption, but I can't fault her taste in men."

"Thank you. But more importantly," I said, "the letters are rather extraordinary. I've just read the last of them. I can't wait to tell Francesca."

"Well, you can tell us all at the Harrises tomorrow. We need a distraction." She sighed. "Catherine is still miserable. I foolishly told her that if the police don't find the perpetrator, you would not let it rest! Do you mind?"

I stopped and kissed her with passion. "How lucky I am to have a wife who believes in me," I said. "No, I don't mind at all."

Supportive as she was, I had not expected Phyllis to encourage my hazardous investigative efforts. Her pride in my abilities was touching, and I only hoped that I could live up to that faith.

~

"How wonderful to have you all here again," said Mrs Harris as we drew our chairs up to the table. Louise had been invited, but had made her excuses for the sake of her brother.

"Now, I wish poor Miss Gardner no disrespect," Mrs Harris continued, "but might we have any discussion of her first so we can move on to happier topics? Does that sound too callous? I've been dreading having it hang over us while we all skirt around it."

"Not at all callous," I said. "I'll declare my hand. Francesca and I went to see Mr Gardner, who as you can imagine is distraught, and yet strangely resigned. He imagines some fault of his own."

"Oh?" said Mr Harris. "Are you sure it's entirely imagined?"

"My dear," said Mrs Harris, "what a hideous aspersion. Her own father!"

"We can't be entirely sure," said Francesca, "but my intuition is that his guilt simply comes from the notion that he could have persuaded Rosabel to stay at home, or protected her in some other way."

"Yes, that would be natural," said Mr Harris, as he carved the woodcock. "I felt quite the same when Euphemia became ill. I'm still queasy about her travelling all over the world for her music."

"And not Victor?" said Mrs Harris. "He deliberately goes to some stupidly dangerous places. It makes me feel faint to think of it. Lands with huge biting insects, terrible diseases – and cannibals!"

"Naturally, I worry about Victor too," said Mr Harris. "But his sex and experience afford him some protection."

"As does Flora," said Francesca, smiling. "She's indomitable."

I felt a pang of sadness. I felt I had only just begun to know my half-sister. Still, her alliance with Victor and adventures abroad gathering knowledge of the natural world had given her an astonishing new life of which she could not previously have dreamed.

"Miss Gardner was strangled, according to The Herald," Mr Harris said. "Perhaps our children are safer abroad after all. Who do you favour for the perpetrator, Thomas?"

"I'm afraid I've no idea," I said. "But Catherine told us a rum thing – that Rosabel was being recruited by Mr Tanner for a show about the Veiled Sisters. So it does throw some suspicion in his direction."

"Before anyone else points it out," said Francesca, "Mr Jenrick was acquainted with Rosabel. And John Hutton gave her a drive in his carriage. Is every man who ever had contact with the poor girl to have their character questioned?"

"You may as well add Peter to the mix," I said, "since he has few moral scruples."

"Which leads us precisely nowhere," said Mr Harris. "And from what I hear from my golfing friends, the great Inspector Simmons is similarly confounded."

I looked at Phyllis, and she smiled at me sweetly. "We must hope that Mr Simmons has luck, or help," she said.

"I'll speak to Tanner," I said. "I want to find out what he knows about the Veiled Sisters, since he's putting them in some kind of exhibit. And Francesca, I have some significant news about our minister."

"Really?" Francesca said. "Oh, bravo! What have you found? That is, if it's not too bleak for dinner, Olivia."

"I'm sure it won't be," said Mrs Harris. "And it's all in the past. Do tell. Phyllis said Florence found something for you – oh, I should have invited her!"

I was relieved that she had not, as it might have been awkward so soon after my visit. I described the two letters I had read to Mrs Tambard.

"Fancy that," said Mrs Harris. "A cursed jewel and a hopeless romance! But does that get you any closer to understanding the message, Thomas?"

"Well," I said, pulling a page of notes out of my waistcoat pocket, "the next few letters are even more interesting. The Reverend Mr Philip Marshall was a relatively new friend, and Manners wrote to him giving an account of his earlier life, and to explain how he came to the area. These are the essentials." I took a draught of wine, and cleared my throat.

"Manners, by his own admission, was a free-thinking fellow at Cambridge, destined for the Church but writing frankly about his experiences of love. At university, he befriended one Nathaniel Whickham whom he found of like mind, and the pair became almost inseparable, developing a shared taste for the dramatic, whether in poetry, art, or theatre.

"Now Nathaniel's father owned an inn called The Priory, built from the remnants of an old lodge where nuns used to give out hospitality to travellers. When the nunnery was dissolved, a chapel became part of the inn property – it was stripped of its fittings and used for storage."

"Oh!" said Francesca, her eyes widening.

"Old Mr Whickham," I continued, "had succumbed to strict puritanism at the outbreak of the civil war. He formed an alternative congregation in the old chapel. Here, he and his flock prayed to be spared the end times, which they thought were imminent.

"Nathaniel reacted violently against this. He fell in with the pro-Royalist, Anglican sect that was in the ascendant when Charles II returned to the throne, and of which Manners was a member.

"When his father died, Nathaniel Whickham returned to the inn and successfully lobbied for his friend Richard to be given the living at St Ninian's after the death of the incumbent.

"And so they continued their intense friendship, writing – so Manners says – rather passionate poetry and plays." I paused. "But here it gets slightly uncanny. Where do you think they put on their productions?"

"Surely not my chapel," Francesca said, staring intently at

me.

"Your chapel," I said. "According to Manners, Nathaniel spent a fortune turning it into a little jewel box. But then things went wrong. Manners came to dislike Nathaniel's plays, while Nathaniel accused Manners of becoming a prig. Manners formed a new friendship with the poet Allan Lawrence, and apparently this was the cause of jealousy on Nathaniel's part. Nathaniel also developed a severe drink habit; and so the friendship became strained, although not extinguished. Their theatrical plans came to nothing, and the chapel reverted once more to a mere storage room."

"Oh, no," said Francesca. "How terribly sad. I don't know what to think. Is this a good or a bad omen?"

"Whatever the case, it's quite a tale," said Mr Harris. "Does Manners say any more?"

"There's one more detail worth mentioning," I said. "Living and working at the inn were Nathaniel's two sisters."

~

"Are we to suppose," Mr Harris said as we settled ourselves for coffee in the drawing room, "that one of the sisters is the lover that Manners speaks of? It seems entirely plausible that he would fall in love with the sister of his friend."

"And that the rift between friends would be the obstacle to his marriage?" said Francesca.

"It's possible, but alas, without further information, we can only speculate," I said.

"Oh, please let's speculate," said Mrs Harris. "It can't do any harm, surely?"

"In which case," said Phyllis, "as Manners has not yet mentioned the wager over the ruby, as described in the local history, it must have happened some time after. Therefore their friendship existed long enough for them to play silly games. So why should his marriage be impeded?"

I shrugged, and poured myself more coffee. "Let's go back to the message on the wall," I said. "After all, it was written in a convulsion of torment – have we missed some hidden meaning? He interred them in a 'frigid grave'. Does that have any significance?"

"Simply a poetic flourish?" said Mr Harris. "I have been guilty of the promiscuous use of adjectives in my own humble efforts."

Mrs Harris frowned at her husband. "Oh, it surely refers to the coldness of death, and the earth, I imagine," she said.

"That's what I assumed," I said, and Francesca nodded.

"Or perhaps it was snowing," Phyllis said, "although I do like the idea of promiscuous adjectives." She pressed a finger against her lips, deep in thought. "As a writer, I find it too simplistic – almost tautological – unless he had a specific meaning in mind beyond the obvious."

I picked up my coffee cup, but it did not reach my mouth. Instead, I let out a cry that made Mrs Harris jump. "Oh Lord," I said, feeling a shiver go through my body. "The ice house."

"The ice house?" Francesca repeated with a horrified look. "Do you think...?"

"Can you get Hutton to excavate there?" I said.

"Oh, heavens," said Mrs Harris. "I feel faint. Please, my dear – do fetch my smelling salts. They're in my dressing table."

"Of course, of course," Mr Harris said and hurried out of the room.

"John won't like it, but he'll do it," said Francesca, her face drained of colour. "I pray to God we find nothing."

~

Frustratingly, John Hutton was visiting relatives in Perthshire for the next week; I would have to find other matters with which to occupy myself, although the grisly implications of my conjecture haunted my dreams and waking hours. It must have been even more disturbing for Francesca, working in sight of the old ice house when she was not at rehearsals.

"Louise – may I use you as bait?" I said at breakfast the following day.

"Oh, Thomas!" said Phyllis. Louise looked questioningly at me.

"Well, not bait, exactly – more of a pretext," I said, wiping toast crumbs from my mouth with my napkin. "I want to talk to Tanner and see how he reacts when I mention Miss Gardner. But I don't want to arouse his suspicions, so I wondered if I could enlist you to talk to him about fossils. He clearly wanted to discuss them with you further."

"Yes, of course," said Louise. "Most people are indifferent to the topic – oh, not you two! – and if he has a genuine interest, which I think he does..."

"Thank you," I said. "I'll write to him."

"What a strange fellow Tanner seems," said Phyllis. "I hope he's managed to fatten Hercules up by now." Louise nodded. "I wonder what made him pounce on the story of the Veiled Sisters?" Phyllis continued. "And to try to poach Miss Gardner like that."

I considered this. "With Jenrick making such a fool of himself, it may have drawn Tanner's attention to Francesca and her new business ventures. And he obviously has a sharp eye for a novelty – no doubt he's itching to try out some trickery for the ghost show."

"Don't you think it's odd," said Louise, "that two sisters lived at the inn – and there's a myth about two spectral sisters?"

"I did wonder about that," said Phyllis. "But the story is about nuns, not siblings. So it must be a coincidence."

"Yes, of course," Louise said, but she still shuddered.

~

The Angel Inn had not yet opened officially, but barrels had been delivered, staff were settling in, and Francesca had let Jenrick bring in some friends by way of a trial.

"I didn't feel a grand opening was appropriate," she said. "Not with everything that's been happening. Perhaps later in the year."

"Understandable," I said, observing that her theatre manager was in jovial spirits. "I hope Jenrick will moderate his beer intake."

"I'll keep an eye on him," Francesca said, as a waitress handed me a glass of ale.

Jenrick came over, a small knot of acquaintances following. "Mr Rufford!" he said enthusiastically. "I'm pleased to see you, sir. Perhaps I could introduce you to some of my friends. This is Joe Tufnall – the watchmaker." I inclined my head suitably at the balding, spectacled artisan. "And Jacob Whickham. The... connoisseur of fine wines, shall we say?"

He grinned and bowed. "And of fine ladies," he said, looking at Francesca, who chose not to react.

Jacob Whickham was in his mid-forties, with a stout physique and a nose reddened and veined from – I assumed – too much connoisseurship. He breathed with an unhealthy wheeze.

"Whickham?" I said. "Are you descended from a Nathaniel, by any chance?"

"Indeed I am," he said. "Proudly so, although we have improved ourselves since then. To the tune of four hundred acres, a healthy stock portfolio, and three fine homes, I'm happy to say."

"What became of the famous ruby, if I may ask?"

Whickham laughed loudly, before coughing. "Good man. Straight to the point, as I like it." He tapped his red nose. "It's quite safe, and that's all I can tell you." He stepped closer and lowered his voice. "Has Walter tried to recruit you yet?"

"It's more the other way around," I said, mystified.

"I doubt Mr Rufford would be interested in our little club," said Jenrick. "We talk about local folklore, and our members give readings. A bit dull for a busy gent, really."

"Ah," I said, "hence your storytelling. What do you call yourselves?"

"Wormers," said Whickham, "or if you want to be formal about it, 'The Hawksbridge Folklore Society'. I'd call it just bloody good grounds to get stewed!"

Jenrick smiled and said, "Steady on, Jacob. Remember who my employers are!" Becoming more serious, he added, "I'm sorry about poor Rosabel Gardner, sir – to be laid in the ground tomorrow, I hear. It's a sad loss, not least to the company. She was most promising. I believe Mr Tanner may have been one of the last to see her."

I nodded, and Whickham's jovial expression changed in an instant to one of anger.

"Damn it, Walter, did you have to remind us all?" he said. "I'd just drunk enough to put that evil out of my head. If Tanner was the wretch that did this, I'll wring his neck, even if I put my own on the line! God burn him in Hell!"

Cursing and wheezing, he stomped off to find another drink.

I glanced at Jenrick, who looked sympathetically at his friend, and then apologetically at me.

"He may not always look it," he said, "but Jacob is a sensitive fellow. He feels the shadow of his own mortality, and hates to discuss such topics. It was insensitive of me."

"It's to his credit," I said. "The crime is so senseless and dispiriting. Do you really think Tanner might have been involved?"

Jenrick drained his cup. "I wouldn't put it past him, sir, I really wouldn't. I know there's bad blood between us, but I assure you, no self-respecting woman should ever be left alone with him."

~

"Wormers?" I exclaimed to Francesca in her private parlour. "Did you know about this?"

"Not until today," said Francesca. "Perhaps it's a secret society. Well, semi-secret. As Whickham said, it's probably an excuse for male company and a lot of drink."

"Not bad for trade, if they meet here," I said, "so long as it doesn't get out of hand."

"A balancing act for any proprietor," said Francesca. "I may need to find a burly fellow to help keep order."

"Just keep John Hutton on a leash," I said.

She grimaced at me. "I doubt John would give up his building business for that, unfortunately. Not even for me. And I wouldn't exactly call him burly. But perhaps a dog is the answer."

"Maybe," I said. "Or a tame tiger. I'm going to see Tanner, if he's willing, and taking Louise. Anything you'd like me to say to him?"

"Plenty that's not genteel. But please ask him about the Veiled Sisters, would you? Was Rosabel really going to work for him? And does he know any more about the myth than I do? Oh – his show seems so... so tasteless now, and I can't put my finger on why. And there I am with my play about monsters and dead maidens, so I can't talk."

She wiped a tear from her cheek. "Sorry. I'm so tired that reality and fantasy are all mixed up. And my head is pounding."

She looked up at me with a pleading look, and I nodded. I took up my position behind her armchair, and then hesitated. "Perhaps this is more for John to –"

She waved her hand dismissively. "He's not here. And you're better at it. Please, Thomas."

~

I was determined to experience no guilt at applying my amateur healing skills. A doctor is sanctioned to brush aside social norms to a far greater extent. If the sensation of Francesca's elegant skull under my hands gave me any satisfaction, that was irrelevant to the objective of easing her pain, and immaterial to the attention I gave my wife. Phyllis could have no cause for complaint.

Nevertheless, when I returned home to Phyllis, who was working in the library, I found myself balancing an imaginary ledger of favours, and she did not object.

"Ah! My reward for writing nearly a whole chapter," she said, leaning back in her chair and unpinning her hair.

"And what will mine be?" I said, dragging my fingertips over her temples.

"Have you done anything to deserve a reward?"

"Yes – I've endured the company of Jenrick and some of his tiresome friends. They call themselves the Wormers and read each other fairy stories."

Phyllis giggled. "How funny! But I thought you approved of Mr Jenrick, at least – apart from his outburst at Tanner's. Enough to keep him on, at any rate."

"I respect him as a director and theatre manager. He's entirely competent. But I respect him less when he's in his cups. Still – he did introduce me to a descendant of Nathaniel

Whickham."

"Really? That's interesting. What's he like?"

"Brash," I said. "I'd rather not think about him while I'm doing this."

"As bad as that?" Phyllis said.

"Well, he was upset about Rosabel Gardner, so perhaps he's not all bad," I said. "Oh, and he hinted that he still has the Manners jewel!"

~

Being a woman who seldom let tradition stand in her way, Francesca insisted on coming to the funeral, and I fetched her in the pony trap. It was a pity that convention kept away Rosabel's friends, leaving a circle consisting almost entirely of dour-faced men. Perhaps it was pure sentiment, but I imagined that a phalanx of her dearest female associates guarding her vulnerable body might have been some comfort. To whom, exactly, I was not sure.

Mr Gardner stood opposite me, his face screwed up in misery, and in a touching gesture, I saw Jenrick pressing his arm to comfort him, which seemed if anything to solicit more tears from the bereaved father.

Seeing this, Francesca whispered, "Oh, Thomas," and took my hand briefly. It was hard to bear, and however much the Rector's words were meant to soothe, to me they were a conspicuously hopeless attempt at dispensing solace where none could truly be found. Nor did the grey, sunless sky mitigate the mood of desolation.

After the service had ended, Mr Gardner left as soon as decency allowed, and Jenrick came over to pay his respects.

"How unspeakable to see a promising, beautiful young woman's life snuffed out," he said, shaking his head. "I sincerely hope it was mercifully quick and without pain, although I'm afraid sometimes with strangulation..."

Seeing Francesca's expression, he said, "Oh, forgive me, that is too grim." He sighed. "After Mark's wife died, I hoped never to witness such misery in him again."

"You've known Mr Gardner a long time?" I said.

"Yes, indeed," Jenrick said, "we were at school together. And I had the honour of introducing him to his wife. His happiness was something to behold!"

"It's too cruel," Francesca said. "Why must such a glorious example of womanhood be crushed? No punishment is too great for whoever did this."

"We can only pray for the wisdom of the police," Jenrick said, "although they sometimes fall short of our expectations."

"They must not fail in this case!" Francesca said fiercely. "They cannot fail Rosabel."

Jenrick nodded and excused himself.

"Not the most tactful fellow," I said.

"No," Francesca said, "but he means well. I would suggest coffee at Myrtle's, but since that's where we first..."

"I'll take you home," I said. "We shall light a fire to help banish the gloom, and drink a toast to Rosabel."

CHAPTER FOURTEEN

Not even Philip Tanner's eloquence could persuade the town to allow his attraction to open on a Sunday, but it afforded him the opportunity to do necessary maintenance, and us the chance to visit without the usual crowds. He had been effusive in his response to my letter, to the extent that I worried about taking Louise, but she attributed his manner to his energetic personality and showmanship.

"Mr Rufford, and Miss McNulty! I'm doubly honoured," he said when we were shown to his office. This was in a sturdy clapperboard hut, and was adorned with sketches and plans of his kingdom. He got up and shook our hands vigorously before indicating seats and ordering coffee. "What a great pleasure to host not only a distinguished citizen, but the most charming palaeontologist of my acquaintance. I'm glad you returned, even if it's with a different mission this time."

It was evident from his emphasis of the word 'mission', and his intense look in my direction, that he was perfectly aware of my interest in him.

"Thank you, Mr Tanner," I said. "It's good of you to see us."

"Nonsense," said Tanner. "I'll be in your debt, Miss McNulty, for any light you may shine on my humble business. While we wait for refreshments, why don't I show you one or two little changes I've made here?"

He first led us to the tiger enclosure, and Louise and I looked at each other with some anxiety: not fearing we were about to become cat breakfast, but because Hercules' less than god-like physique was fresh in our memories.

"I'm mindful," said Mr Tanner as we approached the iron

fence that surrounded the enclosure, "that Hercules was not in prime condition when we first opened, and there has been some concern about him. There! Has he not made strides, as it were? And literally, as I've increased the size of his enclosure."

Hercules padded over to us, his demeanour visibly more relaxed and his ribs no longer alarmingly visible.

"Oh yes!" said Louise. "He looks very healthy. He has adapted, then, to his new home."

"Indeed you have, haven't you, my dear Hercules?" Tanner said to his animal, who was rubbing his head against the bars. I winced as he put his hand through the gap and petted the tiger, who responded with affectionate nuzzles.

"He and I have become firm friends," he said. "Anyway, I wanted to dispel any impression that I'm a monster who mistreats his faithful employees – human or otherwise."

"Do think he craves company of his own species?" Louise ventured.

"Quite possibly," said Tanner. "I'm trying to get him a female. It does add some complication and expense, of course. We give him lots of attention, but yes, yes – you're perfectly right. Hercules may yet have his Hera."

He stared at the animal as it padded around the enclosure. "I spend far too much time with him, and neglect my business. But he mesmerises me with his beauty, and nobility. Anyway," he added, turning sharply, "let me show you a little something I've been developing. Can you both keep a secret?"

We nodded. "Then I'll let you have a peek at the Veiled Sisters."

Again we exchanged looks, and followed Tanner to another hut, unpainted but no doubt soon to be daubed in gaudy illustrations.

Inside was a corridor, about a quarter of which contained a window into a dark room inside the hut.

"You will stand here," Tanner said, "and watch a short play. A man sitting innocently in his bed will suddenly be visited by two apparitions! He will try to touch them, but his hands will pass straight through them. They disappear, and he tries vainly to sleep, closing his eyes lest he see them again. And as he takes his hands from his face, the dreadful sisters appear gradually again, slowly removing their veils to reveal deathly white faces and sunken eyes!"

"Goodness," said Louise. "How terrifying."

"Indeed it will be – I just hope I don't inadvertently kill any poor visitor who might have a weak heart!" he said, laughing grimly. "But there will be plenty of stern warnings, which will make it all the more attractive to those with a stronger constitution."

"I assume it's done by a kind of projection?" I said.

"Trade secret, I'm afraid," he said, "and one I paid a good deal to use in advance of most of my competitors. But of course all three personages will be quite real. It's a matter of great regret..." He fell silent.

"Were you about to employ Miss Gardner?" I asked.

"As a matter of fact, I wasn't," Tanner said, removing a large splinter from a wooden post, "on account of the fact that she turned me down. I thought she had the perfect face and bearing for one of the sisters... but although she was kind enough to audition, at the end of it, she apologised and said she couldn't let Mrs Campbell down, even though I offered twice what Mrs Campbell was promising her."

"I see," I said. "And she went home immediately?"

"She left," Tanner said, "although I couldn't say if she went home. I suppose she didn't, sadly."

"It must have been a shock when you heard about her death," I said.

He nodded. "It was. I went straight to the police station to give what information I could. Which was precious little, really, besides my alibi. I was working late on that day, as my men can verify. Oh – there's evil about, Mr Rufford, to be sure, and horror far worse than anything my little shows can create. I'll gladly attend the hanging when they find the animal that did this. No – that's insulting to the likes of Hercules, who would only kill to eat. Rather, the soulless devil that did this wicked thing."

He sighed. "But let's console ourselves with coffee. It will be growing cold."

~

"Did you know the Veiled Sisters were supposed to bring good luck?" I said when we were back in the office.

"Excellent cake," said Mr Tanner, with his mouth full. "Mrs Tanner made it." He took a swig of coffee, and added, "Yes, so the tale goes, but I won't be including that part. I hope Mrs Campbell doesn't mind me using the story – I've been meaning to put on a ghost show for some time. It's a perfect fit, even if it does involve the extra cost of two apparitions instead of one."

"Mrs Campbell was curious about it," I said, tactfully. "She wondered if you had more information about the story than she knows."

"That depends on what she's already heard," Tanner said, "but I only know what's in common circulation. Dead nuns appearing at the end of a bed, and good luck following. It may just be my line of work, but I'd say it's a clever way to attract custom to the inn, wouldn't you?"

"You mean the story was invented by the inn owner purely for financial gain?" said Louise. "Oh, how unromantic. Still, perhaps that would be a comfort to Francesca."

"That's my way of thinking," said Mr Tanner. "But how amusing would it be if my audience were to see four apparitions in the show, and only two of them were mine!"

Louise grimaced and said, "That would be most

disquieting."

"I fear this is a sensitive topic, Mr Tanner," I said with trepidation, "but may I ask you about a mutual acquaintance – Walter Jenrick?"

"Ah," Tanner said with a wry grin. "Walter. Aren't we both blessed? What would you like to know, Mr Rufford?"

I hesitated. "This is rather embarrassing, but I wondered about his outburst, and..."

"You want to know if there's any truth to what he said? That I'm a womaniser and all-round scoundrel? Well, fair enough, I'll satisfy your curiosity."

"I'm sure he must have exaggerated," I said. "Especially when he referred to a supposed danger to women."

Tanner let out a derisive snort, refilled our coffee cups and took a swig. "Walter and I have always been rivals, ever since school. He always had to be better at everything than everyone else, especially me, and have the last word. He took the lead in the school plays, and even wrote one of his own. I admit I was envious of that, and was determined that one day, I would outshine him and put on a show even he couldn't conceive of.

"Anyway, I was a shy boy with the opposite sex, although you may not believe that now. When I finally managed to catch the eye of a girl, after we left school, he couldn't stand it, and had to take her from me. She threw him over before long, but I'm not sure he cared – he just wanted the conquest and triumph over me."

"But that's not the woman he was referring to?" I said.

"Oh, no. That was many years ago. Eventually he went away to London, and I didn't see him for some years, though I heard he was doing well for himself in the theatre. But perhaps he made a mess of things – why else would you return to Hawksbridge from a successful career in London? – and I found myself once again competing with him for a woman's attention."

He sighed and pushed some cake crumbs around his plate. Glancing up at Louise, he continued, "I'm ashamed of my behaviour – it's difficult to speak of this in front of a woman – but any suggestion of battery is utter slander. Two years ago, I was engaged to Mrs Tanner, but fell under the spell of a certain female, having more beauty and charm than such a vixen has a right to possess. It does me no credit at all. I saw her a few times, and I enjoyed being with her, but one day she appeared with bruises on her arms and legs, and cuts on her face. I was appalled and tried to comfort her, but then to my surprise, she recoiled from me and accused me of being responsible for these injuries. When I denied it, she said I had been too drunk to remember, and she said she would go to the police if I didn't pay her the amount of... well, a considerable sum. I was astonished. I said I had no intention of paying her a penny, and then she said she would tell my fiancée. I said to please do so, so long as I never saw her again."

"And did she?"

"No, it was all bluff. But I saw her with Walter a few days after. I reckon they cooked it up between them, though whether her injuries were genuine or inflicted purely for show, I have no idea. Nor how long Walter had been seeing her." He sighed again. "I told Mrs Tanner all about it, although I was a coward and left it until after we were wed. She forgave me. She's far too good for me." His eyes glistened. "And I'm only telling you this, Mr Rufford, because I know you're persistent when the police fail in their duties. It's better you know the truth than have Walter's accusations fester in your mind. I assure you I'm not in the habit of confessing my darkest secrets to anybody."

"Thank you, Mr Tanner," I said. "I'm grateful for your frankness."

"Aye, well, I'm sorry we had to discuss it. Now, Miss McNulty. May we talk fossils?"

~

Mrs Tanner had briefly appeared, and her presence gave me sufficient confidence to excuse myself and wander around the attractions, trying to make sense of the showman's account. While Walter Jenrick did not come out of it well, it was entirely possible he had also been deceived, and that the woman had dreamed up her blackmail scheme on her own, having been beaten by some unknown man and spotting an opportunity. This enchantress sounded all too familiar; indeed, she put me in mind of Peter's infatuation.

Alternatively, of course, Mr Tanner could be lying, and had beaten his mistress, who had tried to get justified compensation from him but had her own reasons for avoiding the police. In this light, he might be a danger to women, while presenting a genial front to most. I had learned by now that liking a person was no guarantee of their trustworthiness. And Tanner's men could have been persuaded to provide an alibi.

I came to Hercules' cage. He was lying outside the den that had been constructed for him, and he stared at me for a moment before looking away, almost as if to allow me to admire his magnificent profile. He seemed docile enough now, but given the right circumstances, such as hunger or provocation, I imagined his wildness could easily return, with gruesome results. And likewise, a smiling murderer was going about his business in Hawksbridge, the people around him unaware that his true, primitive nature had become unshackled from all moral restraint.

~

I had left Mr Tanner in sombre mood, but on returning to his office to collect Louise I found his spirits had entirely reversed. Smiling broadly and with shining eyes, he shook my hand energetically and implored Louise to return for further scientific discussions.

"You seem to have been the antidote to my prying," I said on the journey home. "He was entirely charmed."

"I'm not sure about that, but I did make one particular suggestion he was pleased with."

"Yes?"

"You'll laugh," she said.

"I promise I won't. Tell me."

"Very well – I thought a display of dinosaurs would be interesting, at their natural size. In the manner of a sculpture garden. Is that quite mad?"

I stared at her. "No, it's brilliant. But how?"

"Painted plaster. Mr Tanner wants me to help with the designs, since interpretation and guesswork will be involved."

"Good Lord! So he's already decided he wants to do it?"

"Yes – he was tremendously excited about it. He couldn't believe he hadn't thought of it himself."

I shook my head. "You amaze me. It's no small thing to be invited to advise on a scientific matter. Congratulations!"

"Thank you. It does give me some hope for the future. But..." Her pleased look gave way to seriousness, and she hesitated. "You don't think he can have had anything to do with Rosabel's death, do you? I couldn't go back if you had the slightest doubt. Were you convinced by his story?"

"He was certainly convincing, which is not quite the same thing," I said. "I think it unlikely he was lying; but I have no real evidence to go on, simply his word and intuitions about his character. And an alibi. A person is innocent until proven guilty, and I think you should assume the former for now – while being sensible about your dealings with him, of course."

~

"So now Louise is entangled with a person you suspect of a cruel and gruesome murder," said Phyllis when we had settled ourselves in bed. "Is that a good idea?"

"Hardly entangled," I said, "and to be truthful, I have no more hard evidence against Mr Tanner than I have against, say, Francesca's Mr Hutton."

"Ah yes," said Phyllis. "What news of that strange match?"

I shrugged. "I think they have reached some kind of understanding, although there are ebbs and flows."

"Poor Francesca," said Phyllis. "She has such romantic notions – it must be exhausting. And the world always finds a way to foil them. First Mr Manners writes her a distressing note from the past, and then this awful business with Miss Gardner. The least she deserves is someone to confide in – besides you, of course. I hope Mr Hutton is an honourable man."

Before I could muse more on the matter of Francesca's liaison with her builder, there were sounds of a commotion – hammering on the door, then raised voices.

"What on earth?" said Phyllis, alarmed.

"Oh, God," I said. "I expect it's Peter. I'll go and check."

I donned my dressing gown and went downstairs, where Peter had collapsed on the hall floor. Shipley and another man were bending over him, trying to get him on his feet. The other man looked up at me – it was Walter Jenrick.

"Your friend had more than's good for him," he said, yanking at his arm. "Come on now, Peter. Let's get you to bed, shall we?"

Reluctantly and unsteadily, Peter got to his feet, at which point Louise appeared in her dressing gown.

"Good evening, ma'am," Jenrick said, grinning at Louise. "This is your brother, I take it? Perhaps you'd be so good as to direct us to his quarters."

Mortified, she nodded and said, "Thank you. I'm sorry to

inconvenience you."

"No trouble, ma'am," Jenrick said, again smiling toothily at her. "It was lucky I happened to be in the same drinking establishment. He told me where he lived before becoming... indisposed."

The three of them bundled Peter up the stairs, and I followed, ready to catch whoever might topple down. It was laborious getting him up the tower to his rooms, but finally Peter was laid out snoring in his bed.

It was a distinctly awkward way to introduce Jenrick to my home. I found myself alone in the hall with him.

"I'm in your debt, Mr Jenrick," I said. "I apologise for my guest's behaviour. He has an unfortunate habit, as you can see. His sister is long-suffering."

He nodded. "His sister is a fine woman," he said. "What a pity she must waste her life tending to him. Oh, Mr Rufford," he added, looking about and lowering his voice. "I must warn you that Mr McNulty is not the most discreet fellow. He has something of an obsession about events that occurred earlier in his life... well, you know what I mean. I trust he doesn't make things awkward for you."

That Jenrick knew as much as this about my life was a blow. "I understand," I said, "although I don't think anyone will stop him talking nonsense when he's in his cups."

"Perhaps he's all talked out now. Naturally I shan't breathe a word, sir."

I tried not to show how infuriating this concession was. "Thank you, Mr Jenrick. I dare say his drunken babble has little grounding in reality."

"Ah, well, I expect not," he said. "In which case, he's a talented storyteller. I had better not keep my cab waiting. Good night, sir! My best to Miss McNulty."

CHAPTER FIFTEEN

THE Angel Arms was shrouded in mist, which did not bode well for the day's excavations, and the ice house was barely visible from the back of the inn.

"It was supremely awkward," I said to Francesca as we waited in the parlour for Hutton to arrive, "bordering on impertinence. To find Jenrick in my hall with Peter at ten o'clock at night, like two stray revellers – and for him to mention my personal business as well! How dare he?"

"I think you're being quite unreasonable, Thomas," Francesca said. "Walter was helping – what else would you have had him do? Leave Peter to be thrown unconscious into the street?"

"He should have learned to look after himself by now. This is just pandering."

"Oh, you can't mean that," said Francesca. "You're out of sorts. Let me pour you some coffee."

"And what was Jenrick doing there in the first place? Did that trollop Lucy tell him Peter was there? I have to tell Peter he's no longer welcome – he's used us long enough."

Francesca sighed heavily and put a hand on my arm. "Please, Thomas. I'm trying to stay calm about today. I don't think I could bear to fall out with you."

"Yes, of course," I said. "I'm sorry."

Francesca smiled to indicate I was forgiven. "So Mr Tanner thinks the myth of the sisters was simply a business ruse? Either he's a cynic, or I'm hopelessly naive. Do you think Mr Manners' friend Nathaniel was responsible?"

"I suspect so. He seems to have been in charge of the inn when its name was changed from The Priory. I expect we'll find that the story has its origins at that time."

"What a strange man Nathaniel must have been," Francesca said. "Passionate and theatrical, yet cynical and grasping, if the story about the ruby is true. Perhaps disillusionment with his friend did that."

"Well, he certainly got his revenge on Manners. And Manners even ended his life in his inn, it seems, though it may have had a different owner at that point."

We lapsed into silence and drank our coffee.

"Good morning, John," said Francesca after a minute or two, as Hutton appeared in the doorway.

"Morning, Franny," said Hutton warmly, and then he noticed me. "Ma'am, sir," he corrected himself.

"Let's get this horrible thing over with, shall we?" Francesca said.

"I don't expect to find anything," Hutton said. "Not on account of a word on a wall. Still, I'll start at the entrance – the chamber is full of rubbish, and then there's the brick lining, so not the best place for a grave dug in haste. But the entrance is just soil, I think."

We went out to the ice house, where a couple of Hutton's men were waiting, having opened the rotten door to the entrance, which was a passage some eight feet in length leading to the conical ice chamber. Hutton pointed at the entrance floor near the door. "Here?" he said, and Francesca nodded. She stood with arms folded and lips grimly pursed as the men dug, while Hutton shovelled the spoil into a bucket and emptied it in a heap next to the ice house.

For a few minutes, only soil and pebbles went into Hutton's bucket. Francesca's expression softened with relief, but it was short-lived. One of the men stopped shovelling, and picked up a small object. "Bone?" he said.

Hutton took it, brushed the soil off carefully, and turned it over in his hands. He looked at Francesca and me, and said quietly, "Finger bone, I think."

"Oh Lord, no," Francesca said, her hand over her mouth. "Please let it not be."

"Human?" I said.

He nodded. "I'm no expert, Mr Rufford, but it looks human to me."

"Why don't you go back in?" I suggested to Francesca. "We can let you know what we find."

She shook her head. "I have to know. It will be worse waiting inside."

"Very well," said Hutton. "I'll take over, boys."

He took up a trowel and started to carefully dig again. "More, I'm afraid," he said, putting several objects aside. "Depending on how it's lying, I might find..." He widened his search and his trowel hit something hard. "As I thought," he said, and slowly removed the soil from what soon revealed itself as a cranium. He continued to scrape away in the vicinity, and made another, similar find.

"Oh, heavens," Francesca said, her voice trembling.

"I think that's enough, Mr Hutton," I said. "The authorities will have to do the rest."

"Indeed, Mr Rufford. I'll gladly leave it. It looks as though you were right."

"I wish I hadn't been," I said.

"I'm sorry, I really am," said Hutton, emerging from the tunnel and wiping the soil from his hands. He turned to face the entrance, and removed his cap. "The Lord rest their souls," he murmured, before turning and heading towards the inn with his men.

Francesca stared bleakly at the skulls, and I squeezed her arm. "At least they can be buried properly now," I said.

"But we don't even know who they are," she said.

"We have their initials, and their association with Manners," I said. "We shall restore their names and dignity to them – you can depend upon it."

~

"Let me get this straight," said Inspector Simmons, scratching his head and forcibly underlining something in his notebook. "You found some writing on a wall, and this led you to dig up the ice house and find two bodies?"

"That's correct, Inspector," said Francesca. "As you can see, the words are suggestive of foul play, and Mr Rufford thought the ice house a likely grave for the two people mentioned."

"Did he now? What a lucky guess, sir," Simmons said coolly, glancing at me. "That would make two unpleasant discoveries in only a few weeks, would it not, Mr Rufford? Three if you count individual persons."

"I'm afraid so, Mr Simmons," I said. "But no killer is at large here. We believe the crime – if there was one – was committed over a century ago."

"I see," he said. "Well, I don't entirely, but I would be grateful if you could each submit a statement to the police office. Meanwhile, we'll take the remains away for examination and burial. We'll have to make do with their initials on their headstones, if that's all you have. I'm afraid our time doesn't permit a wild goose chase on behalf of long-dead people."

He got up, and hesitated. "That is," he added, "if they *are* long-dead. We'll have to be sure of that, especially in the present circumstances. You won't be going anywhere for a while, I take it, Mr Rufford?"

Francesca's eyes widened at the implication, and I smiled. "No, Inspector. I have nothing planned. Can I ask – is there any progress in the Rosabel Gardner case?"

"You can ask, Mr Rufford, you can ask. However, I'm not at liberty to give details, as I'm sure you must appreciate. Suffice it to say, no arrests have yet been made."

"But you have some suspects?" Francesca said.

He rolled his eyes almost imperceptibly, and ignored her question. "We shall continue our work outside. Dreary weather for it. Perhaps it would be best if you confined digging of any kind to your own estate, Mr Rufford. We have quite enough on our plate as it is." He turned to go. "Good morning, ma'am, sir."

Francesca waited for a few moments until the Inspector was out of earshot, and then said, "The cheek! To think you might have had anything to do with it!"

"Well, I don't blame him," I said. "For all he knows, this happened recently. I could be a monster."

"If you turned out to be a monster," Francesca said, "I should lose every shred of faith I have in humanity. Fortunately, I know you're anything but."

"After my unkind words about Jenrick and Peter, I'm not so sure," I said.

"No one else needs to know," she said. "And Peter is highly provoking."

"Perhaps that is the pertinent question here," I said.

"Meaning...?"

"What provoked someone to kill two people? Passion? Madness? Cruelty? Because if they were natural deaths, they would surely have received lawful burials. We must find all of the possible players in this drama, and see how their minds were working."

"You could talk to Mr Fountain again," Francesca said. "Apparently he's recovering well."

"Oh, thank God!" I said with feeling. "I was convinced my visit had killed him. Perhaps he'll be more candid with me now, if he's up to hearing our grim news."

~

That evening, I nearly tore up my letter to Mr Fountain, not wishing to impose myself further on the poor man, but curiosity got the better of me, and I went to leave it in the hall for Shipley to post. Catherine was passing with a hot chocolate on her way to the library, where an inspired Phyllis was in full flow.

"How are you?" I said. "I take it you're not back at Myrtle's yet?"

She shook her head. "I don't want to let them down," she said, "but..."

"I understand perfectly," I said, "and so will Mrs Shannon. Meanwhile, we are the beneficiaries – although I've no wish to take advantage!"

"That's quite all right, sir," Catherine said. "I feel safe here. Do you know if the police have made any progress?"

"Not as far as I know," I said. "But there may be plenty Mr Simmons isn't telling me. By the way, I did speak to Mr Tanner after what you told me."

"Yes?"

"Rosabel turned down the position he was offering. I didn't find him to be troubling, but of course, appearances can be deceptive."

"They can indeed, sir," she said. I knew how hard this knowledge had been won. She turned towards the stairs with her tray, and then turned back. "There's something else, sir. I got to know a Mrs Paxton in Myrtle's. She wouldn't like me mentioning it, because her husband has a... a dislike for the police, and I don't want to get either of them into trouble, which is why I didn't mention it before, but..."

"Yes? You can speak plainly to me, Catherine. You think it might be important, don't you?"

She nodded. "It might be. Mrs Paxton lives near the Gardners – her husband is a tailor."

"Ah, yes," I said. "I commissioned a coat from him."

"Well, she said she saw something that puzzled her, on

the day Rosabel disappeared."

"Really? What was that?"

"She wouldn't tell me, sir," she said. "But you could ask her, couldn't you? If you said you wouldn't tell the police."

I sighed. "I don't like to make such a pact, but I may have no choice. Every lead must be followed. Very well; can you write a short note for me to show Mrs Paxton? Something to reassure her and press on her the importance of speaking up? It'll give me a better chance of earning her trust."

"Yes, of course, sir. I'll do it directly I've taken this to Mrs Rufford, and I'll leave it on the hall table."

Fox had come to insist on his walk, and was waiting expectantly at the front door, tail wagging frantically. "Thank you, Catherine," I said, putting on my coat. "And please remind Mrs Rufford not to make herself ill with work!"

~

A light rain shower refreshed me as I stood in the street opposite Mr Gardner's home. As I had hoped, Mr Paxton was in his shop, leaving Mrs Paxton alone with her small daughter. She opened the door to me herself, looking as puzzled by my presence as I had expected.

"Good morning – Mrs Paxton? My name is Thomas Rufford – I'm a friend of Catherine Wakeley's. Might I have a word? I come with a reference."

I handed her the note, and Mrs Paxton read it a couple of times, frowning. She looked up at me and said, "Oh! Well, aye, I suppose so." Reluctantly, she led me to the parlour.

"I'm sorry to say it, sir," she said in a strong Scottish accent, "but Mr Paxton wouldn't like this at all. With all respect, sir. I shouldn't have said anything to Catherine."

"I realise this may seem intrusive, Mrs Paxton, but I

wouldn't be here if I didn't think it was important. I imagine you knew Rosabel, and want to see her murderer caught and punished?"

"Yes, of course, sir," she said, fiddling with Catherine's note. "Everyone wants that. Rosabel was such a bonnie girl. It's just that... my husband doesn't trust the police. Doesn't like any kind of attention that way – not that he's done anything! You do see that, don't you?"

"Yes, yes, I understand," I said. "Sometimes the police get the wrong end of the stick. But in finding justice for Rosabel, a tiny scrap of information may be of crucial importance. Depending on what your information is, it may at some point become inevitable to speak to the police, but then again, it may not. Do you feel able to tell me?"

"Oh, Lord. I'll be in trouble, but for Rosabel... I'll tell you what I ken. It may be nothing at all."

"Thank you," I said.

"Well, on the Tuesday before she went missing, I was playing with Annie in the front garden, and I saw Rosabel return home in the afternoon."

"I see – what sort of time would this have been?"

"Around four o'clock, or thereabouts. And then I was looking out the window in the evening, around seven o'clock or a little before, and I saw them leaving."

I sat up in my chair. "Them?"

"Aye, Rosabel and Mr Gardner. She seemed in a bad mood with him."

"Interesting," I said. "Did you notice which direction they went in?"

She shook her head. "Sorry, Mr Rufford. I felt I was being nosey, so I stopped looking after they came out."

"That's still useful information. I don't suppose you saw anyone return?"

Again she shook her head. "No, but Rosabel can't have come back, since..."

"So her father returned and didn't report her missing," I said. "He only found out on Thursday, so it would seem he knew where she was."

"It's not right, Mr Rufford," Mrs Paxton said. "For a father not to care where his daughter was? Or worse, to ken, and not tell a soul?"

"Quite," I said. "It's worrying. Thank you, Mrs Paxton. I realise you've been put in a difficult position. I'll speak to Mr Gardner, and if I don't have a satisfactory explanation, we may have to persuade your husband that the police need to know about this. I'm sure he'll understand."

"I'm not sure he will, but if you think it's best, Mr Rufford."

I got up. "I appreciate your frankness sharing what you know. And in normal circumstances, I would say send my compliments to your husband – a very fine tailor, in my opinion."

She smiled, and pressed Catherine's note into my hand. "You'd better take this," she said. "I don't want him finding it."

~

The sun had come out, and with it, several of the neighbourhood children. Two girls were playing a skipping game, and I stopped to listen to their chanting.

Seven bonnie maidens go to church and pray
Ne'er to pick the short straw and wait on Tribute Bay.
Six bonnie maidens...

The words were repeated with only numerical variation until the last verse.

One bonnie maiden goes to church to pray
For Jesu's hand upon the sand of lonely Tribute Bay.

CHAPTER SIXTEEN

Mr Gardner was not at home, so with the grim chant echoing in my head – made starker by the girls' innocent pleasure – I called at The Angel Arms. I was worried about Francesca's state of mind.

"Thank you, Thomas," she said, staring out of the parlour window. There was only a trace of the soil heap left, most having been shovelled back into the unhallowed grave.

"I confess I'm not quite myself at present," she continued. "I'm delaying opening the inn, and putting the play on ice – oh heavens, a poor choice of words! – for a short while at least. I hate to let people down, but I can't contemplate any of it. I'm weaker than I supposed."

"You're not weak!" I said. "Far from it. But this discovery is a huge shock. Of course you must allow yourself a little time, and there is no shame in that. If anything, it's my fault for suggesting an excavation. It would perhaps have been better to let those poor souls rest in peace."

She shook her head. "One can't deny the truth. And how could I put my favourite bloodhound on the scent, only to tug back on his leash at the critical moment?" She smiled at me.

"The highest compliment," I said, touched. "Anyway, I'm glad Mr Hutton will be a comfort."

She frowned. "Oh," she said. "I don't know. I haven't spoken to him since... the excavation."

"You've fallen out? I'm sorry to hear that."

"No, we haven't argued," she said. "I just fear I'll associate him with that awful discovery. And the work is nearly finished on the inn and the theatre – he's already busy repairing a mill."

"You need some time," I said. "It's only been a few days. Other things will intervene and occupy your mind."

She nodded, evidently forcing back tears of frustration. She reached in her sleeve for a handkerchief and dabbed her eyes.

"I'm sorry. It's not only... that" – she waved her hand in the direction of the ice house – "but everything. It's been draining getting this place straight, and then the play, which I was so hopeful for... and having to appear so stoic and unflappable..."

"I can imagine," I said. "I don't know how you do it."

She managed a smile. "I feel a little better already. But I haven't asked about you – how selfish!"

"Not at all," I said. "But I'd like to discuss Mr Gardner with you, if you don't mind."

"Please do!" she said. "Just let me make some tea first."

~

"Highly suspicious," Francesca said, putting down the teapot. "You must speak to him as soon as possible. He hasn't been straight with us. And you say his neighbour forbids you to report Mr Gardner to the police?"

"I might have to, and I've prepared Mrs Paxton for it. There is the distinct prospect of damage to the Paxton's marriage, so I need to establish as far as I can whether Mr Simmons needs to take an interest. That is not a decision I relish, of course."

"Indeed not," said Francesca. "But you cannot be held responsible if Mr Paxton has an unreasonable objection to officers of the law."

"Perhaps," I said, and took a sip of tea before getting up and pacing around the room. "But trust within marriage is a hard thing to mend, once broken. A fact of which I'm all too aware." I sat down again and held my head in my hands.

"Thomas? Whatever have you done?" said Francesca, alarmed.

"Nothing lately," I said, wondering whether admiring a barely-dressed Louise on the beach counted. "Just my sins of old. Peter has already blabbed to Jenrick, and it's only a matter of time before Phyllis finds out."

"Then you must tell her," Francesca said. "She will believe you that you did nothing to that sick man."

"It's not what I did, or didn't do, so much as the fact that I haven't told her. I don't know why I haven't – surely I trusted her to trust me? Or was I too ashamed? I think I was protecting her from having to keep my secret. And now I've made it worse."

"Promise me you'll tell her," Francesca said earnestly. "It would be so much better coming from you than Peter."

"I'll try to find the right moment."

"Good," said Francesca. "I'm afraid I shall nag you dreadfully until you do."

~

Given the urgency of it, I went back to Mr Gardner's house the same evening. He was surprised to see me, and regarded me with as much suspicion as I felt for him.

"I'm sorry to disturb you at this hour, Mr Gardner," I said, "but might I have a word?"

He grunted and led me to the parlour, gesturing for me to sit. However, he stood by the fireplace, nudging the poker with his foot and avoiding my gaze, as if he knew the precise subject of my visit.

I was suddenly struck by the impertinence of what I was

about to ask. Nevertheless, I cleared my throat and said, "It's just that when Mrs Campbell and I called before, and I asked you about Rosabel, I think you had perhaps forgotten an aspect of it – of what you and she were doing on the Tuesday afternoon and evening."

"I didn't forget a thing," he said. "And what business is it of yours anyway? I've told the police what they wanted to know."

"But did you tell them you went out with Rosabel on Tuesday evening?"

He stopped kicking the poker, drew himself up and glared at me. "Who says I did?"

I shrugged. "Someone noticed."

"Well, whoever it were, they were lying. Like I told you, she went out in the afternoon. That were the last time I saw her."

"But I have information that she came back in the afternoon, and then you and she went out in the evening, at around seven."

"Someone spying on me, is there?" he muttered, going to the window and peering out. "Bloody neighbours. Bet it's that Paxton woman. Always out in the street with her squealing child."

"So you're saying that a neighbour might have seen you and Rosabel go out in the evening, Mr Gardner?"

"I'm not saying any such thing, Mr Rufford. You can make up any lies you want. And if you're thinking of taking your story to the police, I'll say exactly what I told you. They'll believe a grieving father over a daft woman. Anyway, I know what happened to her."

"You do?"

"Fairies," he said simply.

"Fairies?" I repeated. "What do you mean?"

"Just that," he said. "Everyone knows they have a liking for the Devil's Teeth. Must have dragged her off there."

"But for what reason?"

"Do fairies need a reason? It's just their evil nature. And they don't like us humans, and what we're doing to the world."

I was stunned into silence for a moment, marvelling that such a tradition had survived for so long.

"But I thought you said it was likely to be a navvy, when we spoke last," I said.

He shrugged. "Thought about it more," he said. "Too diabolical for the work of a man. But of course you don't believe me. Too clever, I expect. Coming here from a fancy city, living in your big fancy house. But mark my words, Mr Rufford, where there are old stones like that, there are fairies. And Mr Simmons won't find any human hereabouts wicked enough to... to do that to Rosabel. I'll show you out."

On the doorstep, I turned and said, "I'm truly sorry for what happened to your daughter. I can't imagine what it would do to a man. But you must tell the truth if her killer is to be found. Please, Mr Gardner!"

He glowered at me, but his scowl gave way to an expression of despondency, and he sighed. "I've said all I'll say," he murmured, and shut the door, leaving me to wonder what was left unsaid, and why.

~

I was in a bad enough mood after this unproductive interview, but worse was to come. When I returned home, a tearful Louise was returning to her rooms, saying simply, "He's gone," before hurrying off.

Phyllis was at the south window in the drawing room, staring into the gloom. "You'd think she'd be grateful," she said, turning to me.

"About what?" I said.

"Peter leaving. He said if I lent him a little money, and took him into town, we would never see him again. At fifty pounds, it seemed an excellent bargain."

"Fifty...?" I said, aghast. "Did he say why he was leaving, and without Louise?"

"He was agitated," she said. "He was worried the police wanted to talk to him again. He had a haunted look, really. He was extremely insistent – I don't think I had any choice about it."

"So you helped a man evade the police?"

"Thomas, that's not fair!" she said, her hand tightly gripping the back of a chair. "Mr Simmons has already spoken to him. I don't see they would get anything new from him."

"That's hardly for you to say. Now we're on the hook for aiding and abetting a possible criminal."

"Nonsense," Phyllis said. "You're only cross because I took some initiative this time, and not you."

"This isn't initiative, this is more like perverting the course of justice." She snorted at this. "You could at least have waited for me to get home."

"There, it's just as I said," she said triumphantly. "Your pride is on full show. Well, I'm afraid the world doesn't stop when the great Thomas Rufford is away. I can manage things very well on my own."

"Be my guest," I said, knowing I was crossing a line, but unable to stop myself. "After all, you love your own company above any other."

She shot me a shocked, wounded look that cut me dreadfully and marched to the door. She stopped for a moment. "Why did he ask me if you told me everything? He seemed to think the police might want to speak to you too. Was he warning me about something, Thomas?"

"He talks drivel, as you well know. I assure you the police have no business with me."

She paused, and then left without another word.

~

My limbs felt like lead as I mounted the stairs to my small refuge, in search of some solace. This was the worst argument I had yet had with Phyllis, and I was surprised at my own vehemence. Could she be right, and I felt my role had been threatened? It was unfortunate that Mr Gardner had already put me in a poor frame of mind. But the prospect of being accused of helping a criminal was a real one. Had Phyllis persuaded him to stay for another hour or so until my return, I might have been able get some sense of out him, and even summon the police if this had been warranted. Rosabel deserved better than this.

And yet... perhaps Phyllis was right. It was unlikely she could have stopped him leaving, and Peter would not have revealed anything. If he had committed some horrible crime, was it not far better to have him out of the house? Even Mr Simmons might have advised it. It was a crumb of comfort, at least.

I turned over Peter's remarks to Phyllis about me. Evidently the past had been on his mind, and the police might have wanted to talk about that rather than about Rosabel. Had his drunken candour caught up with him? Jenrick had learned more of the truth than I was comfortable with, and so could anyone in earshot, in the inns he frequented. And the police would undoubtedly be interested in getting to the bottom of our sordid tale, since Peter could easily have been lying about our innocence, as far as anyone knew. It could have been taken for the brag of a killer, the kind of verbal incontinence that has ended the life of many a miscreant.

I sat and closed my eyes for a few minutes, as if that could banish all the unpleasantness. My emotions had exhausted me, and slipping into sleep, I started dreaming strangely. Like an angel of truth, Francesca appeared before me. "I shall nag you forever! Why did you not tell her? She's your wife!"

She turned into my poor, murdered Hazel, holding on to her prison bars. "Tell her, Thomas! Tell her how much you love me. Kiss me!"

I drew close, and as I was about to kiss her, she became Peter, who shouted in my face, "We're all going to swing for it! Run!"

Terror overcame me, and I tried to run, but could not, and some shapes I took to be the police were quickly approaching. But as they neared, I saw it was two cloaked women, lifting their veils to reveal hollow eyes and sad smiles. "You have found us, Thomas," they whispered. "Now we are yours."

As they stretched their bony arms out to me, I awoke with a tremendous start and a cry. I realised I was sweating profusely.

It was dark outside, and I made my way down to the marital bedroom with apprehension. Phyllis was coming out holding some clothes. "I'll be in the nursery tonight," she said, avoiding my gaze, and disappeared in the direction of the room we had earmarked for our future children. That happy possibility seemed remote now.

CHAPTER SEVENTEEN

"How is your injury?" I said to Mr Fountain. He was sitting in his favourite chair, with a glass of port in his left hand. He still had a bandage on his right hand. "I'm sorry – if I hadn't visited, then..."

"Oh, don't trouble yourself about it, my dear fellow!" Mr Fountain said. "That nail had it in for me, and would have attacked me sooner or later. It's much better. Now, how is Mrs Rufford?"

"She's well," I said, but I looked away.

"Are you sure?" I nodded. "Well, something isn't right. I hope my gift didn't cause offence."

"No, that was very welcome," I said. "Another matter entirely is causing some difficulty. But it will pass."

"Dear, dear, what a shame," he said. "I sincerely hope it does pass, and soon. Anyway – I expect you have some questions for me."

"Yes," I said. "We have discovered that Richard Manners was the most probable author of the message on the wall. I think you knew that, didn't you? And that's why you gave me a book by his friend."

Mr Fountain took a sip of port and sighed. "Indeed, indeed. It's all extremely distressing. I'm sorry if I was a little... indirect. I'm in a difficult position. I have a great love of the Church, and do not betray its confidences readily – even after all this time."

"Its confidences?" I queried.

He swept his bandaged hand through the air to signify this was a topic he would not discuss. However, he said, "I confess that in my indecision, I proposed that God choose –

may He forgive me. If it was His will that you know the truth, then I supposed He would reveal it by leading you from Allan Lawrence to Richard Manners."

"It was a kind of confirmation, certainly," I said, "although the name Manners first came to me in church."

Mr Fountain nodded. "Of course, of course," he said. "And now this message – and perhaps the Lord himself – has steered you to a grim discovery."

"The remains at Mrs Campbell's inn – yes. Do you know who they are?"

He shook her head. "But..." He hesitated and emptied his port glass.

"Yes?"

After a moment, Mr Fountain fixed me with an intense look, his blue eyes wide and glistening. "Since the Lord has revealed this much, I feel justified in being more frank than previously. I shall give you the name of a person who may be helpful to you."

He paused and wiped his eyes. I detected a faint tremor in his voice.

"Miss Ruth Wooler. She's Richard Manners' last surviving descendant, so far as I'm aware."

"Good Lord," I said, without thinking. "Oh – please excuse me!"

"Don't mention it," he said. "That makes two of us who are shocked to be speaking of Ruth. For once, you know, she was simply 'Ruth' to me!"

At this point he buried his face in a voluminous handkerchief and blew his nose.

"I apologise," he said after a moment. "Pure sentiment and nostalgia – where does it get us? Now. Miss Wooler is a spinster in her early seventies; she's the daughter of – let me see – Max Wooler. Max Wooler was the son of Andrew Wooler, who married Julia Manners. Julia was Richard's adopted daughter."

"Ah, yes," I said, "I heard about Julia from some letters of Mrs Tambard's."

"Mrs Tambard!" Mr Fountain said, with a smile. "An excellent and most diverting woman, but you must be careful. Rumour has it that she has a robust taste for" – he leant forward and lowered his voice – "handsome young men!"

"I'll be on my guard," I said, remembering the scent of lily as she claimed her reward. "But her husband's collection of letters has been extremely helpful in getting to know Mr Manners. Still, what happened in his last years remains a mystery. Do you really think Miss Wooler might be able to assist?"

Again he paused, evidently thinking deeply. "It's possible," he said. "Mr Rufford, I've decided to tell you a story that does not reflect well on me, but which must now be told. I owe it to Ruth."

He poured himself more port, which I declined.

"A few years ago, I had a visit from a solicitor, named Mr Andrew Barrowman. His clerks had been clearing out a cellar room where they stored clients' records, stretching back to – oh, as early as the sixteenth century, I think. He wanted my opinion about a particular box. A box that had been sealed with a peculiar instruction: that it should be opened only by kin, and not less than a hundred years after the owner's death."

"Really?" I said. "But why not simply destroy it?"

"A sense of history, or justice, perhaps," said Mr Fountain. "Something was important to the owner, but it was also – I imagine – highly sensational, or embarrassing."

"Do you know who the owner was?"

"Yes," said Mr Fountain. "It was none other than Richard Manners. Mr Barrowman thought that with my knowledge of local history, I would be able to identify Manners' descendants, to whom the box should be given."

"And you directed him to Miss Wooler?"

He sighed. "Miss Wooler is a very private person. She's

shy about her lineage, and so it's not generally known. I was tempted to feign ignorance to protect her feelings. However, a little diligence would have enabled Mr Barrowman to discover the truth, so I told him about Ruth. I also advised him not to give her the box yet because the contents might be a mortal shock for her. I said I thought it likely that other relatives might be found, so to wait a while, and if no descendants should be living in a few years' time, that it was my strong opinion that the box should be burned."

"Burned?" I said. "But why?"

"Because what is in that box may bring unnecessary harm," Mr Fountain said. "It may throw unwanted light on certain people and certain institutions."

"By 'institutions', I take it you mean the Church?"

He hesitated for a moment, and then said, "Yes, the Church. I know all this is a long time past, but we live in an age when doubt is being thrown on our cherished beliefs. The Church is not only a touchstone for our morals but an inspiration for our greatest works, and I fear what will happen if the people lose respect for it. Will we build cathedrals, with no dread of judgement or hope of salvation? Will our love for our fellow man burn as brightly, when we are not bound by the same convictions? Where will our energies go, if not to a common cause?"

I found the depth of Mr Fountain's feelings on this subject moving, and disconcerting.

"When our religion falls away," he continued, "we may be divided, and false, dangerous beliefs may creep into our minds. I fear for the future, although it will not be a future I shall have to endure. But please forgive my diatribe. The point is that Richard Manners was buried in the churchyard, not as a suicide. The Church must have known, and they may also have seen the message and ordered its erasure – which was certainly not done properly!"

"I see," I said. "The Church has looked the other way, to

avoid embarrassment."

"Indeed," he said, shaking his head. "It's perfectly shameful, although understandable. But my respect for the truth is starting to get the upper hand over expedience. The earnestness of your investigations has reminded me of my obligations as a historian, and not only as a Christian. I may yet be damned for it, of course, and I still fear for the effect on poor Ruth."

"So what should we do? Does Barrowman still have the box?"

"I leave it in your hands, my dear fellow. Yes, as far as I know, the box lies unopened in the vaults of Mr Barrowman's office. I suggest you go and see Miss Wooler, and ask whether she wishes to take possession of it. What she does with it must be her decision alone. If Mr Barrowman makes any objection, send him to me."

"I will," I said. "Thank you."

"She lives in the village of Conundrum, a few miles south of Hawksbridge – Honey Farm Lane. Number five. She moved there after we – well, many years ago. I have never been."

"May I convey a message?"

He considered this and again pressed into service his increasingly damp handkerchief. "Please give her my sincerest respects. No – my fondest regards. And my everlasting regrets."

~

I realised I had been giving too much time to Richard Manners, and not enough to poor Rosabel. The police did not seem to be making much headway, having – according to Mr Harris – arrested two of the railway navvies, who had apparently made some offensive remarks about the case. They had, however, been released without charge, and their accuser suspected of malice.

So after my visit to Mr Fountain, I looked in on McPhee at the Pottery.

"I wonder if I might speak to Rosabel's friend, Mabel," I said. "I think she's one of ours?"

"Ah, yes – a fine worker, if understandably glum at present. Different department from Rosabel. Rosabel painted crockery, while Mabel reviews our pieces before packing. Let me fetch her for you."

"One thing, Frederick – Rosabel complained about Mr Lilley making rather unctuous remarks to her. That's nothing we should be looking into, is it?"

McPhee stopped at the door and smiled. "I don't think so. I know what you mean, and I don't particularly like it. I'll have a quiet word, if you like. But he's harmless. He has a weak arm, sustained in a fall from his horse. So I can't believe he could drag a heavy object to the Devil's Teeth, and it's unlikely he would have compelled her to go with him."

I nodded, and McPhee soon returned with Mabel and directed her to a seat. She still bore a look of misery.

"You were close to Rosabel, weren't you, Mabel?"

"Yes, sir. I loved her like a sister. Well, more than my own sister! But that's family for you, they can be... Sorry, sir, I don't know what I'm saying! I'm that upset. She was the best friend I ever had, funny as you like, and generous."

"Indeed," I said. "I met her briefly, and her personality shone brightly. You have my sincere condolences."

"Thank you, sir," she said quietly. "What did you want to ask me?"

"I wondered if there was anything she did or said prior to her death that might shed light on it. Can you think of anything at all, however small or seemingly insignificant?"

Mabel considered my question, gazing out of the window

with furrowed brows.

"I don't know, sir. She did say her father had been morose lately. But why wouldn't he be? He must miss Rosabel's mother terribly. And now Rosabel..."

"That's an interesting observation, thank you," I said. "Did she also tell you about her forthcoming interview with Mr Tanner?"

"No, sir," she said. "I was shocked to find out about it afterwards. She usually tells me everything. I suppose she was ashamed, after Mrs Campbell was so kind to her. But I don't know what I'd do if I was offered a lot of money."

"She seemed happy about the play?"

"Oh, yes, sir, she was so excited, and I was excited for her. I couldn't wait to see her in it!"

At this point she broke down, and I waited for her to compose herself.

"I'm sorry, sir. It's just so... horrible and unfair. Do you think they'll catch whoever did this?"

"I hope so – I expect so," I said. "Especially if everyone who knew her reports every tiny detail they can recall."

"I'll try to think," she said, "but that's everything I can remember at the moment. Oh – one thing, I suppose." She looked at the floor and coloured slightly.

"Yes?"

"Someone sent her a book of poems a couple of weeks ago. A secret admirer, I suppose."

McPhee and I exchanged glances.

"Ah. So you don't know who it was from?"

"No, sir. It was a bit... well, rude. She lent it to me."

I smiled. "Was it any good?"

Her blush deepened. "It was silly. I don't know why I read any of it. A lot of nonsense about love and monsters."

"Might you lend it to me?" I said.

"Yes, of course," she said. "You can have it. I don't want to be reminded..."

"Of course. I'll hand it to the police when I'm done with it, in case it's relevant. Thank you, Mabel," I said. "That's all for now."

"Did that help?" McPhee asked when Mabel had gone. "If we can find out who sent the book..."

"I suspect no one is likely to admit that," I said. "But perhaps something about it will be identifiable. She really should have told the police about it."

"I expect she forgot," McPhee said, "or she was embarrassed."

"Indeed," I said. "As far as Mr Gardner is concerned, he's being coy about something. If Rosabel mentioned her father's mood, it may be pertinent. I wish I could get Simmons to question him properly."

~

I had longed for the moment of Peter's departure, so that the Ramsburgh household might once again fall into that state of order and bliss that every married couple desires, and which once we knew.

But it was not to be. Mealtimes were awkward and as short as possible. Louise increasingly took her meals in her rooms to avoid the tension. Why could I not simply apologise and make things right? Perhaps because it would be a sham of an apology without the full truth. And I could still not bring myself to have that conversation, and admit to Phyllis that I had hidden my past from her. It might mark the end of our already fragile marriage.

Phyllis could resort to her work, and at least that was an excuse for our separateness to use in front of the staff. But the sorrowful and sympathetic looks I received from Mrs Felton indicated she was not fooled. Even Fox seemed agitated at the change of tone in the house.

A few days after my conversations with Mr Fountain and Mabel, a letter arrived that was addressed in a feminine hand – a fact not lost on Phyllis.

"An admirer?" she said, pointing to the hall table on her way up to the library after breakfast. "How sweet!"

Her lack of concern was pointed and hit its target. I took the letter into my study to read. It was from Mrs Paxton, and it was brief and to the point.

> Dear Mr Rufford,
>
> *I have further important information about Mr Gardner you will find interesting. Please meet me at Holden's Mill on Tuesday morning at ten.*
>
> Mrs Luke Paxton

I preferred to be out of the house as much as possible, so this suited me; and Holden's Mill was on the south side of town, convenient for a trip to Conundrum. The fact that I would be with a married woman, unchaperoned, did not unduly concern me. Finding Rosabel's killer was far more important than keeping to every rule, and besides, my present bitter state was making me reckless.

I found that Holden's Mill was an old brick ruin by the river, gradually and picturesquely disappearing under an assault of trees and other vegetation. No doubt it had been the place of many a furtive assignation. I sat in a small clearing next to a scattering of timber and roof tiles that were too broken for looters to bother with, and began to forget my troubles at Ramsburgh. I thought instead of Rosabel and girls like her, wandering along the river bank while laughing with their paramours and talking pleasant nonsense.

Eventually the mill would disintegrate entirely, all signs of it buried, but couples would still walk this way, hoping for the same things, chasing the butterflies, picking the blackberries... These cracked bricks and twisted remnants of water wheel were once part of a proud, energetic factory feeding swathes of townsfolk. It occurred to me that our continued vigour and sense of purpose is dependent on forgetting how easily our efforts crumble into dust as fine as the miller's best flour.

"Hello, Mr Rufford."

I looked up to see Moira Paxton standing awkwardly in front me, a patterned cotton scarf around her neck and a covered basket in her hand.

"Good morning, Mrs Paxton," I said, scrambling to my feet. "Thank you for your letter. Do you frequent this place much? It's a beautiful spot."

"I suppose so. I..."

"Yes?"

"I lied, Mr Rufford. I don't have any new information. I'm sorry. But I do have this."

She untied the scarf to reveal several dark blue marks on her neck, and I noticed a shadow under her left eye.

"Good God – who did this?" I said.

"It's like I told you," she said. "Mr Paxton don't like people poking their nebs into our business. Mr Gardner came around all steamed up, demanding to ken if we'd clyped about him. I said no, but Mr Gardner was sure it was me, and Mr Paxton..." She sniffed.

"Your husband had no right to do that," I said. "I didn't say it was you who told me, but Mr Gardner guessed. What can I do?"

"What you can do, Mr Rufford, is not go clyping to the police like you were saying. You mustn't, or I'll get worse than this."

"But Rosabel..."

"I don't care! She's dead, isn't she? And I don't want to

join her. I'll do anything, but just don't get me into bother! I've a bairn to think of, too."

I was silent for a moment, wondering what I could promise. Surely I could not let Paxton – evidently a brute, however talented a tailor he was – impede the pursuit of justice.

"Very well," I said, "but I'm not happy about it. You won't consider at least going to the police about your bruises? Mr Paxton shouldn't think he can get away with knocking you about like that."

"No," she said firmly, "I've told you – it'll make it far worse. I love my Luke, even if he isn't perfect. I don't want to rile him up. God knows what would happen. You promise?"

I sighed. "I promise."

Mrs Paxton smiled broadly. "Thank you, Mr Rufford. I've brought something for you." She put her hand in her basket and withdrew a jar. "Bramble jelly. I hope you like it. My mother's recipe."

~

I soon stood in front of a wisteria-laden cottage in Conundrum. The name of the village hardly augured well, and I doubted the occupant was even in: most of the shutters were closed. Perhaps Mr Fountain's information was out of date, and Miss Wooler was no longer of this world, let alone this address.

But a second, louder rap of the lion door knocker bore fruit. A slightly bent woman with white hair stood blinking in the doorway, like a mole disturbed in its burrow.

"Yes? Do I know you?"

"Good morning – Miss Wooler?" She nodded. "No, you don't know me – my name is Thomas Rufford. I'm in search of information, and I've been directed to you by an old friend of yours."

"Friend?" she said, chuckling. "That I doubt, these days. Whoever could it be?"

"A Mr Leonardo Fountain."

"Oh!" It was as though I had struck her, and she put her hand over her mouth. "Leo! Did you say Leo sent you?"

"Yes, Miss Wooler. Would you mind if I came in?"

"But of course. You must excuse the mess. I so rarely have visitors, you see." She led me through a low door into the gloomy parlour, and went to open a shutter.

"I don't mind at all," I said, and took a seat after carefully moving a pile of wool and a book from it and onto a table. On the walls, white crystals told of endemic damp, and the discoloured ceiling was buckled and cracked.

It took a while for her to make tea, and the milk looked well past its prime so I only poured myself a drop, but it was nevertheless a welcome refreshment.

"Now then," Miss Wooler said, having deposited herself with a hissing sound into a threadbare armchair. "Why, pray, has Leo sent you to me? And please speak up, young man! My hearing is not as good as it was. Oh, I'm not the pretty thing Leo used to know, that's for sure!" And she chuckled again. "But I expect he's as handsome as ever. Isn't that the way with men?"

"Forgive me, Miss Wooler, but I'm looking for information about Richard Manners. Mr Fountain mentioned that you're his last surviving descendant."

"Oh! He did, did he? Why would he say that?"

"Because I need to know the circumstances of Manners' death, and he thought you might be able to help."

Miss Wooler frowned. "Why do you need to know that?"

"Because..." I hesitated. "Because I believe something terrible happened to him, on the premises of an inn that my friend has bought. And she needs to get to the bottom of it, for her peace of mind."

"Indeed? How strange," she said. "I wasn't aware that there was anything unusual about Richard's death. Heart failure, I think it was. Tragic, but nothing for anyone to get themselves worked up over now."

It seemed unkind to inflict my grim knowledge on her, but I pressed on. "Richard Manners left a message on a wall in the inn. It indicated that he had buried two people nearby, and that he was about to join them, seemingly by his own hand."

Miss Wooler stared at me. "Why would you say such a horrible thing?"

"I'm sorry," I said. "But this is what we have discovered, and we need to understand what happened. Whether Richard did some terrible thing, or whether he was somehow a victim himself."

"No, Mr..."

"Rufford."

"No, Mr Rufford, I don't believe any of this, and there is certainly no need for you to go prying into the Manners' affairs. I'm afraid I shall have to see you out after you have finished your tea."

I nodded. "Of course. By the way, I asked Mr Fountain if he wanted to convey a message to you."

"Yes?" she said.

"He told me to give you his fondest regards, and his everlasting regrets. I could see that he meant it, Miss Wooler. It was said with some... intensity."

She was silent, staring at the window and evidently struggling to compose herself.

"How kind," she eventually said in a quiet, quavery voice. "You must stay, Mr Rufford. Forgive my rudeness. Tell me about him. Is he well? Is he still writing his historical pamphlets?"

~

I gave as full a description of Mr Fountain's present life as I could, including his role in the events surrounding the transformation of Hawksbridge Castle. She was entertained by my sketch of its former owner, Mrs Campbell – "oh, what an interesting woman!" – and suitably horrified by the fate of Fountain's friend Ambrose. It seemed that she had been blissfully ignorant of many of the recent incidents that had consumed my energies in Hawksbridge.

"Well!" she said when I had at last exhausted every tidbit of information I possessed that was vaguely associated with Mr Fountain. "What a tremendous storyteller you are!"

"Thank you," I said. "It's been an interesting time, to say the least. And I've been privileged to know such a generous and knowledgeable man as Mr Fountain."

"Well said. Perhaps I misjudged you, Mr Rufford. I thought you had come for tittle-tattle – that some lurid tale about my ancestor would be printed for all to see. One has to be careful." She sighed. "If what you say about Richard Manners is true... It does seem strange, but then, I always knew there was something different about him. Do you know about the ruby?"

I nodded. "Yes, and that he lost it in a wager."

"Ridiculous!" she said. "How could that be? I've never believed he lost it fair and square. It should still be in this family. I should have it around my neck this very moment!"

"You may be right," I said. "I've seen letters from Richard in which he expresses terror at losing it – that it would be awful luck to do so."

"Letters? Can I see them?"

"I shall lend them to you with their owner's permission," I said. "But they don't tell the whole story. I believe that may be contained in a box at a solicitor's office."

I related what Mr Fountain had told me, to her astonishment.

"And Leo wanted to protect me from them? He had no right! But I expect he had the best intentions."

She rubbed her hands together and stared into the distance, lost in thought.

"If I take the box, and show you whatever might be inside," she said at length, "Richard could be destroyed. His memory, his reputation for good works. Our whole family could be vilified forever. I would like to trust you, Mr Rufford. But how can I? The consequences might very well finish me off."

"Whatever is in that box is entirely yours to do what you want with," I said. "You would have the final say in what I might reveal to anyone else."

"So you say, Mr Rufford, and perhaps you believe it – at this moment. But I'm a suspicious woman. I have been ever since... Life has not been easy. I would need to know I could trust you. Mr Rufford, you would need to prove that to me. Do you understand?"

I nodded. "I think so. But how can I prove myself? What could I possibly do to persuade you?"

"I don't know, my dear, I really don't. But if this knowledge is so important to you, and to your friend, you must find a way."

CHAPTER EIGHTEEN

I HAD lunch in The Duke's Head, picking over a plate of gristly lamb and the morning's events. It was grindingly disappointing that Miss Wooler was reluctant to exercise her power to reveal the information I craved, but perhaps I had expected too much. If Richard Manners had put a century-long embargo on it, then the knowledge contained in the box almost certainly had the ability to cause discomfort – at least to Miss Wooler. Her life had not fulfilled her hopes; what remained should at least be free from the humiliation that past sins of the family might bring.

Still, she had not ruled out the opening of this Pandora's box. I merely had to find a way to demonstrate, beyond a shadow of a doubt, that I could be trusted with the ensuing spill of knowledge. But how?

As I was leaving The Duke's Head, two men I recognised were coming through the door.

"Mr Rufford, isn't it? Yes!" said Jacob Whickham, nearly crushing my hand with his greeting. "Come to escape the missus? Of course you have!"

"Good afternoon, Mr Rufford," said Mr Jenrick, touching his hat. "I trust you're well? It's a pity Mrs Campbell felt the need to suspend our production, but I can understand it after that shocking discovery."

"Thank you, Mr Jenrick," I said. "I'm sure she'll be back in harness soon enough, when she has recovered her nerve." I immediately regretted my choice of metaphor.

"Oh, Lord," Whickham said. "There's a thought! Mrs Campbell restrained. You have a wicked imagination, Mr Rufford, and so do I. By God, so do I!"

"It is you who should restrain yourself, Jacob," Mr Jenrick said, smiling. "Mrs Campbell deserves our respect."

"Naturally, naturally, I beg your pardons," Whickham said with an exaggerated bow. "But those bones! What a fascinating discovery! Mr Rufford, did you not take an interest in my great-grandfather, Nathaniel? Is all this related?"

"I believe it might be," I said. The fellow made my flesh crawl, but it had to be done. "I've been meaning to talk to you about Nathaniel. May I come and see you?"

"But of course, my dear chap! I'd be delighted to have a chin-wag – and the excuse to share a bottle of something amusing. I'm not otherwise engaged tomorrow evening. Shall I see you at seven?"

"That's very good of you," I said.

"Don't mention it," he said, beaming. "Capital, capital!"

~

My hand still aching from Whickham's greeting, I rode up the drive to Ramsburgh to find a carriage painted with a familiar livery. Having stabled Celeste, I found Mr Simmons and Constable Taylor waiting for me in the drawing room.

"Ah, Mr Simmons," I said, putting out my hand and wincing in anticipation of his grasp. "I'm afraid you've missed Peter. He left a few days ago without leaving an address."

Simmons shook my hand, and said, "So I've been told, Mr Rufford. That's a pity. But I would like to speak to you, please, sir. Somewhere private."

With a feeling of foreboding, I led him into my study where we took the comfortable chairs by the west-facing window.

"This isn't the principal reason I'm here, sir, but you may be interested to know we had a report from Dr Weldon about the two bodies."

"Oh yes?"

"Two adult females, in their twenties or early thirties, he thought."

"I see," I said, absorbing this disturbing information. "Any signs of how they died?"

"None, sir, I'm afraid," said Simmons. "Unless there was bone trauma – and there wasn't, as far as we could tell – it really could have been anything. Except old age, sadly. I'm afraid we won't be spending any more time on the case – we also found a penny from 1698 amongst the bones, so it seems likely they died not too long after. We have an active murderer on the loose, and as you can imagine, it takes precedence over the long dead."

"Quite," I said. "Do you have any suspects for Miss Gardner's murder?"

"I can't say, Mr Rufford. I'm sure you understand."

"I think it may be useful for you to speak to Mr Gardner again, Mr Simmons."

"Oh? And why is that? Do you know something?"

"I just have a feeling he knows more than he's letting on."

"A feeling. I see, sir. Well, I'm afraid we won't be disturbing a grieving father over one of your feelings."

I remembered Mrs Paxton's bruises, and dared not say more.

He opened his notebook. "Magnificent view you have," he said. "Somewhere to contemplate the balance of things. The good, the bad. And times past, perhaps," he added, with a glance at me.

"I suppose so," I said, as innocently as I could. "Although one should always be forward-looking, in my opinion. Nostalgia is a drug to be taken in small doses."

"Indeed, sir. But sometimes one's past has a habit of intruding on the present, however much you want to be rid of it."

"I think you have a point in mind, Mr Simmons," I said. "I would be grateful if you could make it."

"Of course, sir. I refer to the John Oliphant case. I was disappointed to learn – from whom need not concern you – that you were not entirely honest with me last year. When we discussed your intruder, Mr Sharpe."

"I wasn't?"

"No, sir. You never mentioned an important fact: that you and two others were present in Mr Oliphant's house shortly before he died. Had this been known to the authorities, things might have been quite different. And it puts Mr Sharpe's death in a different light, too. I'm sure you'll appreciate the concerns I have."

There was nothing for it but for me to come clean.

"Yes, you're perfectly correct, I haven't laid out the full story, because it was bound to be misinterpreted. It's a complete red herring, I assure you. We had nothing to do with Mr Oliphant's death – he was a sick man. But I'm sorry I was not entirely plain with you."

"Well, at least we are seeing the whole picture now," Mr Simmons said, writing in his notebook. "At least I hope so. Might you describe in your own words what happened?"

"Certainly. As you know, my friend Bertram was having an affair with Hazel's mistress, Mrs Richmond, who was also Oliphant's employer. Bertram and I contrived to get Mr Oliphant dismissed for his molestation of Hazel, and Mr Oliphant subsequently took revenge on Bertram by blackmailing him with stolen love letters by Mrs Richmond. Bertram, Peter and I planned to remove the letters from Oliphant's possession, given that the consequences of publicising them might be the end of the Richmonds' marriage, and Bertram's ruin."

"So you conspired to break into Mr Oliphant's house and threaten him? Is that it?"

"Not threaten him, Mr Simmons, but persuade him to do

the right thing."

"That could be interpreted as threatening, couldn't it, sir? Especially with three of you on his premises without invitation."

"Quite possibly, but don't forget that the man was a blackmailer!"

"But not a convicted one, sir. And two wrongs don't make a right – not in law, and not in life."

"I take your point, Inspector. But we were young and foolish, and burning with righteous indignation."

He nodded. "So you broke into Oliphant's house?"

"Not at all. We knocked, and when we didn't get an answer, we opened the door, which was unlocked. There we found him at the bottom of his stairs, bruised and bloody. We got him onto his sofa, tended to his wounds, and gave him brandy. It was a rather strange situation. Bertram searched the house for letters, but finding nothing, asked Oliphant if he might have the letters back. After some hesitation, Oliphant told us their location – under a loose floorboard in the bedroom. He didn't want us to fetch a doctor, so we left with the letters. Of course, not all of them, since Sharpe eventually found the others. And we left Hazel's bloody handkerchief, which I stupidly dropped and which ended in Hazel's unjust arrest, and her murder in jail."

Mr Simmons scribbled furiously in his notebook. "I see," he said after a moment. "As you say, a strange situation. You come to this man's house in anger, and you end up ministering to him. But you got what you came for, as far as you knew. This may still be seen as coercion, at the very least. And that's if you're to be believed."

"I assure you –"

He raised his hand. "I'm not saying I don't believe you, Mr Rufford, although you have previously been sparing with the truth, which is regrettable. But you must see that this information should rightly have been considered at the time, and must be considered now, by the proper authorities."

My hands were becoming sticky with sweat, and I felt dizzy. My worst fears were being realised.

"Tell me, Mr Rufford. Why did you not come forward about the handkerchief? You could have absolved Hazel. After all, you were greatly in love with her, I believe."

"I would gladly have sacrificed myself for her," I said. "But by the time I found out she had been arrested, she had been beaten to death. And I did not have only myself to consider. It would have been pointless to put the three of us at risk of a miscarriage of justice."

"I see. I must say, sir, the death of Hazel's brother, Sharpe, is a most unfortunate facet to this case. You must see that you now have a strong motivation for killing him, to cover up your presence in Oliphant's house – whether or not you were responsible for Oliphant's death. Indeed, were it not for Sharpe's accident, the full story might well have emerged last year."

"From the mouth of a desperate criminal? Perhaps not the strongest witness."

"Maybe not," Simmons said, "but some of his evidence might have been corroborated by your friends, Bertram and Peter. And you might well have admitted it yourself."

"Why are you doing this?" I asked. "What will anyone gain from it?"

"The truth, God willing," he said. "You can't expect me to turn a blind eye, can you, sir? Put yourself in my shoes. If I were to ignore the evidence of a possible crime – and murder at that – how could anyone expect justice from me, and my colleagues, again? And how could I respect myself?"

"But you have the truth, Mr Simmons. The legal process will simply distort it."

"The truth is not a plaything of mine, sir. The truth is for society to determine. It may not be a perfect apparatus – I fear it is not. But it's the only one we have. You're free to suggest a better one. In the meantime..."

"What will happen, Mr Simmons? Are you arresting me?"

"No, sir, if you agree to confinement within this area. I shall write to my colleagues in London, where the incident took place, and they will determine what is to be done. That is the extent of my role. You're likely to be summoned by the magistrates there. What happens next is up to them."

I shut my eyes, unable to accept the reality of the situation and hoping to wake up from a bad dream. But Simmons was still there when I opened my eyes again, observing me with a hint of pity.

"I'm sorry, sir. I know this must be difficult for you, and for your wife."

"Thank you, Inspector."

"I forgot to ask, sir – where might I find your friend Bertram?"

"Nowhere. He's dead, Mr Simmons. He was shot by a jealous husband, having become accustomed to spending time with other people's wives. I assure you I was nowhere in the vicinity – not that my word is worth anything now."

"I'm sorry about your friend, sir. And you have no idea where Peter is?"

"I'm afraid not."

"Thank you, sir. I have no other questions." He rose and walked towards the door. As he reached for the door handle, he said, "I suppose there's no point in me advising you to stay out of trouble?"

I stood up and summoned some defiance. "None whatsoever, Inspector."

He shook his head. "Thought not," he said. "I expect you'll hear from the London Metropolitan Police within a couple of weeks. Good day, sir."

~

With shaking hands, I reached into a cabinet in my study and poured myself a brandy. Peter's nightmares were not pure fantasy: they were premonitions. I had been too complacent. Now I hardly dared imagine the possibilities. The circumstantial evidence could easily persuade a jury to convict me and Peter (were he to be found). I might even be tried for Sharpe's murder into the bargain.

How I wished I could seek refuge in Phyllis' arms and tell her everything. With her affection and esteem, almost anything could be endured. But I had neither. The first had inexplicably faded, and I had made the second impossible. For what could she think of me, if I told her I was a murder suspect with the expectation of trial and the possible extinction of my life? How could I expect her admiration when I was about to destroy her own hard-won reputation?

Who else could I tell? Francesca would only berate me for not having told Phyllis sooner. Had I done so, today's blow might have been softened. But if I ran to Phyllis now and expected forgiveness, I would be seen as insincere as the playground bully who is only sorry to be found out.

If only Flora had been at Ramsburgh still. The ties of blood would oblige her to take my side. Had it come to this? Had I so few allies in my time of need?

Louise. Louise might listen, since it was her devil brother who had opened up these wounds. I downed another two brandies, and made my way unsteadily up the several flights of stairs to her rooms, thankfully encountering no one on the way.

"Thomas! What did the police want? Are you all right?"

She looked horrified at my demeanour. "May I come in?" I said, aware I was slurring my words.

"Of course," she said. She directed me to her sofa and went to make a pot of coffee while my churning thoughts crashed into my skull likes waves in a storm.

"So – what did the police have to say?" she said, pouring

the coffee.

"A lot," I said. "Mr Simmons wants to put me in jail, and perhaps on the end of a rope."

"I beg your pardon?" Louise said, dropping the coffee pot heavily on the table. "Whatever can you mean?"

"Just that," I said, taking a grim satisfaction in her reaction. "You know more about our Oliphant disaster than Phyllis. Sharpe is getting his revenge from the grave, and everything will be considered by magistrates in London. Then – who knows what."

"Oh, Thomas, that is awful! Surely it cannot be as bad as that? Whatever can I do?"

"I assure you it is, and I would be glad if you could take my hand for a moment."

She offered it, and I greedily held it in both of mine. "Thank you," I said, tears welling in my eyes; but I was determined not to break down, despite the effects of the brandy.

"You poor thing," she said, touching my shoulder with her free hand. "You'll beat this – the magistrates, Simmons, all the insinuations, everything."

I heard a floorboard creak, and then: "Insinuations? Magistrates? What is this?"

Phyllis had come into the room, her expression a mixture of horror, revulsion and betrayal, the like of which I pray never to behold again.

Louise dropped my hand and moved away. "I'm sorry. Thomas is in a bad way. I do hope you can both..."

"What is this?" demanded Phyllis again. "How dare you come into my home, Louise, and carry on with my husband like this? Were you about to give me instructions as to how I should behave with my husband? The nerve! And what is it that I don't know, and you apparently do?"

I stood up, a little unsteadily. "It's not Louise's fault. Everything is my fault. I should have told you. I was afraid to."

"You should have told me what?"

"That I entered that damn butler's home with my friends. That he was bleeding at the bottom of his stairs. That we nursed him, got the dirty letters and ran. Then he had the effrontery to drop dead, and we would have got the blame if poor Hazel hadn't got it instead."

"Oh, for goodness' sake. You nitwit. But this was years ago. What do the police want with you now? And why the talk of magistrates?"

"That numskull Simmons has heard about it, presumably from Peter, and is now intending to make a song and dance about it. It may end badly for me."

"End badly?" Phyllis said. "Is that all you can say about it?"

I shrugged. "What do you expect me to say or do? Everything is ruined. Now you know you married an unworthy dolt, you may as well call it quits."

"Oh, Thomas!" Louise said. "Please don't say that."

Phyllis stood still for a moment, unable to form words. Then she marched from the room and slammed the door.

The world was spinning, and I sank down into the sofa again. I closed my eyes and gratefully fell into oblivion.

~

I woke in my bed, having presumably been put there by my staff on Louise's instruction. There was an abundance of light showing through the gaps in the curtains: how long had I been sleeping?

Worse than my headache, the miserable facts of the day before came back to me in a sickening gush. Terror pinned me to the bed, and I felt myself grow unpleasantly hot. I suddenly felt an impulse to be forgiven, to throw myself at Phyllis' mercy, to prostrate myself and admit anything and everything. An image formed in my mind of a tender, tearful reunion, of my head on her breast, being forgiven and comforted. "We'll get through this terrible thing together," she would say, and all I had to do was give up my pride and repair my fractured vows to her.

I leapt out of bed and, still in my nightshirt, ran down the corridor to the nursery, like a child scurrying to his mother after a bad dream. But I found an empty room, and an ominous letter on the patchwork counterpane. My delirious moment of optimism and longing was dashed to pieces.

Blinking in the harsh light, I took up the letter, knowing full well it would extinguish all remnants of hope.

> Dear Thomas,
>
> *I do not seem to please you enough as a wife for you to confide in me. Although I am sure you are not capable of the murder of which you are suspected, you are not entirely the man you presented to me - you have a darker history, which now threatens to choke both of us. You must realise the unfairness of this misrepresentation.*
>
> *I do not know if our life together is reparable, but I must take some time to think things over. My father is not well, and the recent disturbances in our household have made concentration on my work more difficult. So I am going back to live with him, giving us both time to contemplate the future.*

Please convey my apologies to Louise for my harsh words. As you said, none of this is her fault. She may stay for as long as she wishes until she finds somewhere else to stay, but do have the wit to avoid causing a scandal with her. I do not have to tell you what further misery that would heap on all concerned, yourself included.

Naturally I fervently hope you are not subjected to any legal discomfort. I would be glad to know of any developments on that front.

Yours,

Phyllis

P.S. I will send for more of my things today.

A fog of unreality had descended and I felt numb. Having dressed, I knocked on Louise's door; she let me in, and I saw she was packing.

"I'm sorry about last night," I said. "I have a habit of making a bad situation worse."

"That's all right," she said. "Phyllis was within her rights, and it was quite wrong of me to encroach on her territory. But I shall be leaving you both in peace shortly. Might you drive me into town, Thomas?"

"You're not going, surely? Where to?"

"Of course I'm going. What alternative do I have? I'll put up at an inn for a while."

"But you can't afford to do that!" I said.

She closed her suitcase. "I have some money from selling

my fossils. And there's always my brooch. Would you mind fetching it for me from your safe?"

"Louise, please let's talk about this. Let's sit down and talk. Just for a minute?"

She hesitated, and then sat, fiddling nervously with her cuffs and looking down at her shoes.

"Phyllis left this morning," I said.

Louise looked up, startled. "You mean, she has left you? Oh no! I've ruined your marriage. I knew it. I'm perfectly hateful." She started to get up again, and I signalled her to sit down again.

"It may not be forever," I said. "It's too early to tell. Anyway, she told me to say sorry for what she said to you. She knows this isn't your fault. Can you understand that? It's the truth."

She sighed. "I don't know..."

"Please believe it. There is no point in you tormenting yourself about something you're not responsible for. God knows there's enough misery as it is."

"Thank you, Thomas. But in any case, I can hardly stay here. People will talk."

"Let them, if they enjoy it. Phyllis said in her letter that you can stay as long as you like."

She stared at me again. "She really said that? How can she? What an extraordinary woman. I really don't know..."

"Please stay," I said. "I know it's not your burden to carry, but I don't think I could stand it if you left too. It will sound pitiful, but I need a friend."

She wiped away a stray tear and smiled. "Well, if you put it like that. Perhaps I will stay a few days longer, if I may."

"Thank God!" I said. "Have you had breakfast?"

"No," she said. "I didn't dare face anyone. I am rather hungry."

"Me too," I said. "Let's see what Mrs Felton can do for us."

CHAPTER NINETEEN

I was surprised at my appetite. Mrs Felton did her best to hide her curiosity and distress at recent events, but her resolve crumbled as she took up a tray of dirty crockery. She put it down again, and turned to me.

"I'm sorry, my dear," she said. "I know it's none of my business, but will Mrs Rufford be returning soon? I do hope nothing's wrong."

"I'm afraid I don't know when she'll be back," I said. "We have had a small misunderstanding."

Mrs Felton looked pointedly at Louise, and Louise, mortified, busied herself with gathering toast crumbs on the tablecloth.

"It's nothing to do with Louise, I assure you, Mrs Felton," I said. "I should have mentioned something in my past, but didn't; and now Mr Simmons is taking an interest."

"Lord! So that's what he was about yesterday," she said. "I'm sure you can't have done anything wrong! I won't believe it."

"Thank you, Mrs Felton. The only thing I did wrong was omit some details in my testimony to the police – both then and last year – but otherwise, I'm glad to say I'm innocent. Not that that will protect me, necessarily."

"Oh, Mr Rufford! When everything seemed to be going so well for you both! It's not fair, really it's not."

"Well, quite," I said. "Miss McNulty will be staying until she can make arrangements."

"Very good, my dear," Mrs Felton said, and left the room, but I could see from her pursed lips that she had some private opinions about it.

"This is awkward," Louise said. "Are you sure...?"

"Perfectly sure," I said. "This is my house, and I decide how it's run. Don't worry about Mrs Felton. She likes you, and she will get used to the situation."

"I hope so. How are you feeling?"

"About Phyllis, or what Simmons said?"

"Both."

I sighed. "Slightly better for a full stomach, but still like a condemned man. I shall try to occupy myself. I can make myself useful for a little while, at least."

"Thomas, this is utterly selfish, but..."

"Yes?"

"The cliffs at Castle Newton. Do you remember the fissure?" I nodded. "There was some bad weather the other night, and that part might have fallen by now. Might we venture out again? Or is that in awful taste, given...?"

"Well, I'm afraid I'm not good company, so it may be a miserable trip for you. But yes, of course. In the next few days, if you wish."

"Oh, thank you! I've been subduing the urge to ask you."

"You should have said earlier," I said, finishing my coffee.

"But it will be even less appropriate now than before!"

I considered that Castle Newton was local enough not to antagonize Inspector Simmons, and besides, he did not have the men to keep a close watch on me. "Scientific curiosity is entirely appropriate," I said. "And there's no time for such scruples. I've squandered so much – let me not waste time too."

~

Mr Whickham's latest house lay in generous grounds to the east of Hawksbridge. It was a modern and inoffensive stone affair in a symmetrical, classical style, and I wondered whether a far more interesting and ancient farmhouse had been razed to accommodate it. But modern life, I conceded, had new requirements, and it was natural to value comfort over antiquity. Nathaniel would have been astonished at the advancement in the Whickham family's fortune, and all, it would seem, without having to sell the famous ruby.

"Welcome, Mr Rufford!" Jacob Whickham said as I entered the large hall, hung with stag's heads and the expected parade of faintly pompous family portraits. "Welcome to my humble abode. I have champagne at the ready, and we shall natter like a couple of old spinsters. Come and see my drawing room. I'd value your opinion!"

The redness of his cheeks indicated that he had already started on the champagne, and there was a slightly alarming wheeze in his breath that I had not noticed previously.

I handed my coat to the footman, and followed him into the drawing room. It was immediately obvious that the room was dedicated to the naked female. Curvaceous bodies writhed at either side of the fireplace; huge paintings of classical and mythological women adorned the walls; and the ceiling seemed to take its fleshy inspiration from a Florentine palace. The Three Graces had been arranged in front of a mirror to offer the greatest possible enjoyment of their virtues, and in one corner of the room there was a statue of a white slave girl in chains, looking mortified at her own nakedness. It was a theme I had always detested.

"Good Lord," I said. "It's breathtaking."

"I'm glad you approve," Whickham said, taking a glass from the tray offered by the butler. "Paid for by some pleasingly well-performing mining stocks. Don't think I would have been allowed this if I'd been hampered with a wife. Not that I've anything against the institution, by and large," he added, as I took my own glass. "I've heard your missus is a fine specimen, and brings home the bacon to boot. But it wouldn't suit me. Too limiting."

I smiled politely, feeling a stab of pain at the thought of how badly I had handled my own marriage.

Whickham continued: "So tell me, Mr Rufford – where are you in your investigations? I always thought Richard Manners cut a rather pathetic figure, with his adopted daughter and an untimely death. It's such a shame he fell out with my great-grandfather."

"Ah, so you know all about that?"

"Yes, and how the Manners Ruby came into our possession. It's the main reason Manners is remembered at all."

We sat, on ugly upholstered chairs in a French style, with frothy gold decoration. Glassy eyes stared at us from a tiger-skin rug by the fireplace.

"From some letters I've had access to," I said, "I gather there were differences over their writing. And perhaps Richard's ecclesiastical career conflicted with the philosophy of freedom and permissiveness that they once shared."

"Interesting, interesting," said Whickham, coughing. "Yes, that may well be. Nathaniel was quite advanced in his thinking, I believe, and so friendship with a clergyman would have its difficulties."

"And no doubt the matter of the ruby didn't help."

"Oh, undoubtedly! What a terrible thing for Richard! A blow to his pride, as much as anything, that he could be quite so foolish." He stopped to cough again, which turned into a fit that lasted for an uncomfortable minute. "My asthma playing up," he gasped. "I'll be fine in a moment."

"What do you make of the myth of the Veiled Sisters, if I may ask?" I said when I judged he was able to answer.

Whickham took a swig of champagne and said, "Ah yes – poor show that Mrs Campbell is changing the name of the inn. Trying not to scare the patrons, is she? If they don't know about it, it'll only make those lasses a darn sight more frightening when they appear!"

"So you believe in them?"

"Of course, of course! Not that I've seen them myself. But why wouldn't they be real? Who would make a thing like that up?"

"It's been suggested that a landlord might, to drum up trade."

"What rogue said that? That'd be a villainous thing to do, and certainly not Nathaniel's style. No, they're at the inn, all right. All that history – nuns and rituals, and who knows what goings on – it's bound to spill over into our world, so to speak."

He looked around him to see that the butler was not in earshot, and spoke conspiratorially. "Truth to tell, the story has given me a weakness for nuns – toying with the idea of commissioning a painting. A pair of 'em being friendly to one another. Spirited, not spirit, of course!" He wheezily guffawed at his own joke, and managed to hold back a coughing fit.

"What about the Hawksbridge Worm – do you believe in that too?"

"Ah, that's a question, Mr Rufford, one that I leave open. As a Wormer, I find the story of enormous fascination. It's survived and grown over the centuries, like some knobbly old oak. The tale is tragic and gruesome, and yet do you not find a soupçon of titillation in it? A chained, disrobed maiden waiting for the fatal embrace of a powerful beast? Is that not savagely erotic?"

"I hadn't really thought of it in those terms," I said, searching my own conscience. It was possible the idea had stimulated my imagination for a brief moment before I was overwhelmed by the horror of it.

"Oh, come now," Whickham said with a smirk. "A red-blooded young man like you, who affirms his virility in so many interesting ways? I find this hard to believe, given what the less respectable papers have printed about you. When you were sequestered in that cellar and brought out to stud, was that altogether unpleasant? I find a compelling correspondence with the myth, only in reverse, and with a harpy as your nemesis."

It was utterly intolerable, but if I wanted further information, I knew I had to be patient. "It's an episode I try to recall as little as possible, Mr Whickham. I'm sorry."

He held up hand, his glass still in it. "Understood, my dear fellow, understood. My fault entirely – shouldn't have brought it up. Bad form. But it was the talk of Hawksbridge at the time. Well, on the matter of the Worm, I might show you something interesting later, and I'll ask you the question again. Then we'll see. Would you like to see around the house? You would oblige me with your impressions of it."

~

Whickham's house was luxurious, but sacrificed decorative warmth for showiness. There was much tedious talk of the architect's failure to adhere exactly to Whickham's specifications, including mouldings that were insufficiently grand.

When we got to Whickham's bedroom door, he smiled and said, "Now – could you have imagined that I'm allowed to see your delightful friend Mrs Campbell in a state of undress every night?"

I was mystified, and appalled at the vision this evoked. He led me in and gestured to a table behind the door, opposite the bed. There, a Marbleware statue from the Pottery had been given pride of place: the Hawksbridge Angels.

"Ah!" I said. "That is a surprise."

"Yes," he said, staring at the mother angel's scantily-clad form. "What an exquisite, callipygian model she made. Some may gravitate towards the younger, slimmer female, but I must say, her voluptuousness does her credit. I often sit in bed admiring her. May I congratulate your Pottery for its good taste!"

The butler had been trained to follow us around ensuring our glasses were topped up, so by the time we returned to the drawing room, we were both a little unsteady.

"What congenial company," he said, beaming at me. "We could be good friends, you and I – though I may have to loosen you up a tad. Joining the Wormers would be a good start. Or is that too advanced?" He laughed.

"Perhaps there's a prospectus," I said, not wishing to seem completely resistant to the idea.

"Ha! Prospectus! Excellent," Whickham said, and offered me a cigar, which I decided it would be politic to accept. "No, there's no prospectus. It would be most amusing to write one, though. Now, if you have sharp eyes, you may have noticed that there was a room I didn't show you. The best room! Let me have a smoke and then you will have a rare privilege, because I've taken a liking to you. Yes, sir. Damn fine company, you are!"

I supposed that what he liked in me was the ability to listen. He lit up and puffed with a satisfied sigh, although it was rewarded with a small coughing fit.

"Shouldn't really," he said, gazing at the cheroot. "Not according to Dr Weldon. Said I need to eat less and better, too. Told him my pleasures are not up for negotiation. Gave me a very sour look."

Despite the fog in my brain, I realised I had not asked all the questions I had come to ask.

"Do you know anything about Nathaniel's sisters?" I said.

"You mean Caroline and Anne? Not much."

I inhaled sharply, unfortunately with the cheroot still between my lips, and it set off my own coughing fit.

"Not you too, dear boy? What cripples we are. Yes, there

was a cholera epidemic, so off they went."

"You mean it killed them?"

"No, not at all. They took off to America, like a lot of people. They were do-gooders in Hawksbridge, so I dare say they went to do their good in America."

"Any idea what kind of good works?" I said.

"Don't recall, I'm afraid. But they strike me as a bit cold and dull to me."

"So you don't think it possible that it's their remains that were found in the ice house?"

"Well, they would be cold, then, wouldn't they!" he said, guffawing. "No, it's quite out of the question. Went to America. No idea who the bones belong to. Probably some poor buggers who got cholera."

"Even though Manners' note spoke of burying 'C' and 'A'?"

He turned to look at me. "Did it, by Jove? Good Lord. Well, it must be a coincidence. Can't possibly be them – I'd know about it. Now then, enough shilly-shallying. I'm itching to show you the Gallery."

He gave me a glance that suggested that he expected me to be impressed, if not shocked.

~

A small hall contained two doors: one to Whickham's study, which I had already seen, and a second that he now unlocked. As I stepped inside, I could sense his eyes on me, waiting for my reaction.

"The Gallery," he announced.

Like a convention of ghosts, a multitude of white marble figures posed, embraced, bathed, stretched, and bent around the perimeter of the room. Classical and mythological themes mixed together; no excuse was too flimsy for robes to slide off hips or breasts to be gratuitously bared.

The walls were plastered with the fanciful representation of human skin, portrayed in oil – fauns frolicked with nymphs; Sappho blissfully held her buxom lover; and a hitherto innocent shepherdess slept under a tree, ravished and dishevelled, her exhausted and exhilarated Lothario looking on.

My gaze rested, however, on a huge, garish and frightening statue in the centre of the opposite wall, between two barred windows. It was a larger than life depiction of a young woman with an immense serpent coiled about her, rearing above her with open jaws, and staring down at her terrified, upturned face. She had been left white except for her copper hair, and the serpent was painted a deep blue, with shining red eyes and a black forked tongue. Small, spiky wings sprouted from the beast, and it had a spine dotted with sharp quills. The maiden's flesh was visible between the serpent's coils, and there was a visceral sense of the awful compression squeezing the breath out of her body, and the creature's claws tearing into her skin.

"My God!" I whispered, entranced and horrified. The woman's face seemed dimly familiar, but I could not place it.

Whickham approached the statue, which was labelled 'The Worm and the Maiden', and ran his hand slowly over beast and victim. "Isn't it magnificent?" he said. "A masterpiece. The only plaster in the room, but it makes no odds. Come closer, Rufford! It won't bite. Although it might give you nightmares!"

I obeyed, and stared up at the monstrous, gleaming eyes, more sinister for having no pupils.

"Quite extraordinary," I said.

"You don't know quite *how* extraordinary, my dear fellow. Can I take you into my confidence?"

I assumed this question was rhetorical, so looked at him

enquiringly but said nothing. He stood looking at me, before saying, "Of course I can! You're an honourable fellow. I'm sure you're curious about the ruby, and its fate."

I nodded. "Extremely. But I suspect it's another myth, disappearing like mist when you reach for it."

He smiled and said, "On the contrary. You're looking at it. I hide it in plain sight. In a secure room, of course."

I looked again at the ruby red eyes of the monster.

"The worm's right eye. The left is a paste copy. Mr Belford did well, though he tends towards insolence."

I shook my head in disbelief. "Surely not. The Manners Ruby?"

In answer, he dragged a chair over and, with much grunting and wobbling, climbed up and plucked the oval jewel from the creature's right eye socket.

"Here," he said, and I gingerly took the jewel, weighing it in my hand. It was not cut, but it had been polished and had a beguiling lustre that the paste left eye did a creditable job of matching. The ruby's mount incorporated a metal clip that evidently snapped into an aperture in the eye socket.

"Seven eighths of an ounce," he said. "Worth a decent fortune!"

I passed the object back to him, glad to be rid of the responsibility, and he restored the beast's sight before getting down from the chair heavily with a groan.

"Poor old Manners," he said, looking again with satisfaction at the ruby. "I do feel slightly sorry for him. Nathaniel was being a tad mischievous."

"How so?" I asked.

"Wrote to a cousin boasting of an ingenious wager to get the jewel. Letter came back into my possession, fortunately."

"Are you suggesting the wager wasn't straight?"

Whickham laughed. "Oh, what a natural, innocent fellow you are. Don't look so shocked! It happens. I'm sure Nathaniel had his reasons. And Manners was a fool to risk it, so he learned his lesson."

"May I see the letter?"

"Alas no. Burned it, in case of any tedious legal complications. Nathaniel didn't explain himself, but he did rather crow about it."

He stared at me earnestly. "On another matter," he said. "Do you know if Mr Simmons and his men are any closer to finding whoever killed Miss Gardner? I expect you keep a close watch on that, don't you?"

"I believe they've had little luck, unfortunately," I said.

"I see, I see. Poor show, poor show indeed. Not even with you to help them?"

"They haven't asked me," I said. "Of course, it has greatly occupied my thoughts, especially as my wife and I discovered her body."

"God Almighty," he said, his hands curling into fists. "If I only knew his name, then...."

I was curious. "Did you know Miss Gardner, Mr Whickham?"

He shook his head. "No. I did not have that pleasure. But by all accounts, she was a beautiful and charming girl. She might have done great things. Her death is a... a disaster."

He went into a kind of reverie, his gaze resting on the statue that was his pride and joy. I realized who the maiden reminded me of – was I imagining it, or was there an infinitesimal hint of Rosabel Gardner in that upturned face?

CHAPTER TWENTY

I WAS in the drawing room nursing a headache from my odd evening with Whickham, with most of the shutters closed to the painful morning sunshine, when I heard the clatter of hooves outside. The rider was in a hurry – was I about to be arrested? But I had no urge to open a shutter to find out.

In a moment, there were raised voices in the hall, before Francesca burst in, followed by Shipley who gave an apologetic shrug and then left.

"What's all this, Thomas?" she demanded, unbuttoning her coat and throwing her riding crop on a chair. "My housekeeper says Phyllis has left and gone back to her father! Did you not take my advice? And why are you in the gloom? Let me give us some light." She busied herself with the shutters.

I closed my eyes. "Please, Francesca. I have a terrible headache. Yes, Phyllis has left."

"Oh, Thomas, what have you done? How long has she gone for?"

"I don't know," I said. "That's not even the worst of it. I assure you I'm being abundantly punished for my stupidity."

"What in heaven's name do you mean?" she said, standing over me.

"Please sit," I said. "This may take some time."

Reluctantly, she sat, still glaring at me.

"Well?"

I sighed. "Must you be so cross with me? In a few weeks, I may be in jail, charged with murder. Perhaps two murders."

"Don't joke about such a thing," she said. "I can't help being furious at you. What did you do to drive your lovely wife away? And what do you mean, charged with murder?"

"Exactly that." I attempted to deflect her censure. "Did you know Jacob Whickham is leering at your bosom every night? And that the Worm has a ruby eye?"

"Thomas, you're worrying me! You're talking gibberish. Should I call Dr Weldon?"

I looked up at Francesca, who was staring at me as though I had taken leave of my senses.

"I'm sorry. I'll explain myself."

I described Inspector Simmons' interview as well I could. She was silenced for a while, her eyes widening.

"God in heaven," she whispered. "Has it really come to this?"

"It seems so. And my wife hates me."

"I'm sure she doesn't But why didn't you come and talk to me?"

"I was ashamed. As you say, I didn't take your advice and come clean. Had I done so..."

"Have you tried to talking to her again? She may have cooled off."

"There hasn't been time," I said, lamely. In truth, I could not find any words that would mollify Phyllis. It would be like using a bandage to repair a holed warship, and our marriage appeared to be thoroughly breached below the waterline.

"Then you must make time, surely! What have you been doing that's more important than your marriage?"

"Oh – befriending a rich reprobate, and visiting a descendant of Richard Manners."

"Befriending who?"

"Jacob Whickham. It was a degrading task. He has the Hawksbridge Angels in his bedroom and he likes to stare at you – her – from his bed."

"Oh, good Lord," she said. "How disgusting. How can I look him in the eye now? I regret I ever sat for it, putting myself on display for all time."

"Aha!" I said. "So you make mistakes too."

She grimaced at me, got up and paced the room. "I need something bracing. May I ring for coffee? I feel I've wandered into a mad-house."

I nodded. "Please go ahead. I could do with some more."

~

Mrs Felton was pleased to see Francesca, and she introduced an air of normality and order that calmed my friend down a little.

"I'll bring you some coffee, my dear," Mrs Felton said. "Would you like to try a treacle scone with Mrs Paxton's lovely bramble jelly?"

"I recommend the combination," I said.

"Then yes, please!" Francesca said. "It sounds delightful."

"Oh, Thomas," she said when Mrs Felton had left. "What are we to do with you?"

"Well, in the absence of a solution for me, may I tell you what I've found out?"

"Of course," she said.

"According to Whickham, Nathaniel may well have obtained the Manners Ruby by deception, although how is unknown."

"Oh! And that tells us...?"

"It reflects badly on Nathaniel's character," I said. "And that might swing the scales of blame for the deaths of the two sisters from Richard to Nathaniel. That is, if we are to speculate that one or other is responsible, given they were at one time so close."

"Or it gives Manners more motive for revenge after the disaster of losing his ruby, depending on the order of events. Oh – you said sisters! How do you know that?"

"Whickham told me that Nathaniel's sisters were called Caroline and Anne," I said. "Surely the 'C' and 'A' of the message! It's possible, anyway."

Francesca looked at me. "Of course! But how desperately tragic. The more we find out, the closer I feel to them, and the more ghastly it becomes. Did Whickham know they were buried in the ice house?"

"That's the odd thing. He thinks they went to America during a cholera epidemic, to continue their good works."

"That would be a highly convenient explanation for their disappearance," said Francesca.

"Indeed it would," I said.

Francesca's coffee and scone arrived. "Oh, that is delicious," Francesca said after biting into her scone and licking bramble jelly from her lips. "What was that you said about the Worm's eye?"

"Ah – I held the Manners Ruby in my hand yesterday."

"No!"

"Yes, it's lodged in the eye of a plaster sculpture of the Hawksbridge Worm. Spectacularly grim and in the worst taste, but Whickham was immensely proud of it."

Francesca shook her head. "And he let you into his confidence? Isn't he worried the jewel might be stolen?"

"The room is perfectly secure. But yes, I think the wine was probably responsible for his openness – that and loneliness. He has chosen to be without a wife, in the pursuit of more transitory pleasures."

"What wife would put up with him?" Francesca said.

"I suppose some women will endure a lot for a luxurious way of life," I said.

"True. I was a little like that myself. Happily, I've grown to value more precious commodities than mere riches."

"You can afford to now, of course, if I may say so!"

"I know, I know," she said. "What else have you discovered, Inspector Rufford?"

"I think the key to the whole Manners affair may be in sight," I said, "but frustratingly just out of reach. There's a box of Manners family documents held by a solicitor, which I'm trying to persuade a Miss Ruth Wooler to share with me."

"And who is Miss Wooler?"

"Richard Manners' great-granddaughter, via his adopted daughter Julia."

"Remarkable," she said, and drained her coffee cup. "I wonder why you can't solve your own life so efficiently."

"The cobbler always wears the worst shoes," I said. "Would you care for a walk?"

~

The leaves were starting to turn, and a brisk gust of autumnal wind made Francesca button up her coat.

"How simple nature seems," Francesca said, surveying the garden, "compared with the muddles we get into."

"Flora and Victor might disagree," I said. "They must see great complexity when they observe nature closely. Every discovery seems to beget more questions, and I suspect the microscope powerful enough to uncover the fundamental material of life has yet to be invented."

"I suppose so," Francesca said. "But you must allow me my romantic notions."

"Speaking of which," I said, turning to her, "how is Mr Hutton?"

She smiled. "He's in good health. He came to Halfpenny House a few days ago, with his children. We had a very pleasant time."

"His children? I didn't know. I take it he's a widower?"

"Yes, since last year. His sister is looking after the children – a boy and a girl. Six and eight."

"And did you and the children get on?"

"I believe we did! Robert brought a set of building blocks and set about constructing a creditable house. I think he'll be a builder too – or perhaps an architect."

"And the girl?"

"May is delightful, and an avid reader. Fortunately I had a book of fairy tales, which she buried herself in."

"Nothing too frightening, I hope?" I said.

"Nothing to compare with Mr Whickham's Worm."

I tried to keep a straight face, but the comic vulgarity of the phrase was too much and I let out a loud snort, for which she gently slapped me.

"That doesn't bear thinking of," she said with amusement.

"But Jacob is a strange one," I said after a moment. "Such are his proclivities – one might say obsessions – that it makes me wonder if he's not capable of molestation and worse, as in Rosabel's case. He might have had access to her via his friendship with Jenrick."

"It's worth considering," she said. "And yet if one is to be condemned by one's tastes in art, what does my Wicked Cassone say about me?"

"It's a matter of degree," I said. "In Whickham's case, it's rather extreme. And it's reflected in the way he talks about women – with respect only for their fitness for his fantasies. There was a sickening gleefulness about how he looked at his terrified maiden. And the rest of his art isn't much better, captivity and violence being recurring themes."

"But nothing concrete would lead you to believe...?"

"No, nothing," I said. "I suppose I could go back and ask him directly! I might see the truth in his eyes."

"Please be careful," Francesca said. "You're in trouble enough as it is. More subtle questions to begin with, I think!"

"Yes, quite," I said. I was beginning to form an idea for how Whickham could be of use to me, in the matter of

Richard Manners; but it was a plan I could not possibly share with Francesca.

~

I spent an evening writing to Phyllis to tell her how miserable I was without her, and how foolish I had been. It was the fourth attempt that I finally sent, the sentences in my previous attempts having seemed inert and inadequate.

I hoped that by making myself useful in the pursuit of science, I would be removed from the reminders of my wounded marriage. As Louise and I made our way to Castle Newton on a bright, crisp, October day, I astonished her with an account of my visit to Jacob Whickham. In return, she read out a letter she had unexpectedly received from her brother.

> *My dear Sister,*
>
> *I hardly know how to begin this letter, except to acknowledge the pain I have inflicted on you. But please be assured that you no longer have to concern yourself about me. I have found a measure of contentment! I cannot tell you where I am, nor what I am doing, but finally I know peace through using my body, wretched thing that it is after my abuse of it.*
>
> *When my day ends, I am tired and fulfilled, and have no need of my former demeaning pursuits. I know you will be surprised at this; sceptical, even.*

But I have learned much recently, not least from friendships – if they can be called that – hatched in the Hell of my own weakness. I had imagined Hawksbridge to be a genteel place, albeit with the usual harmless diversions, but I found more depravity than even I can stomach. It makes me fear for the young women of Hawksbridge. Please be vigilant, Louise!

It was to escape these circumstances and temptations, as well as suspicions of the police in several regards, that I fled – ever the coward – and came by accident to my present life. It is best for both of us that we remain apart, for now. I shall try to repay Tom's kindness and expense in due course, although my debt to you for your care and forbearance I will never be able to return.

I hope you are in good health.

Yours affectionately,

Peter

Louise folded the letter up, sniffed, and said, "What do you make of that?"

"Extraordinary. What a change! Could it be a forgery?"

"It's his hand," she said.

"But what happened?" I said. "Did someone hold up a mirror to him?"

"He must have fallen into bad company," Louise said. "And it gave him a shock. Perhaps it's for the best."

"Why didn't he tell us more about the danger he mentions? I wonder if we could find him."

She shrugged. "There was no return address – he could be anywhere. It's disturbing. Have you found out anything more?"

"Not really. My witness to Mr Gardner's activities refuses to speak to the police, in case she gets a beating from her husband. Mr Gardner is definitely hiding something, and yet he seems to believe that her death was not caused by human hand. I must speak to him again."

"Could you bribe him into speaking up?"

I laughed. "Do you know, I hadn't thought of that! I was so convinced a father would naturally want justice for his daughter. I could try it, and risk being unceremoniously chucked out of his home."

"So there is no sign of the police arresting anyone yet?"

"Apparently they arrested and then released a couple of navvies," I said. "A false alarm. It must be frustrating for the police."

"I have no sympathy for Mr Simmons," Louise said, "given what he's doing to you."

"Perhaps he really has no choice," I said. "I'm not sure what I would do in his place. After all, he couldn't be sure of my innocence. And for all I know, we gave Oliphant a shock that hastened his death. Then perhaps I really am a murderer."

"Thomas, no!" Louise said, touching my arm. "You mustn't think like that. You couldn't deliberately hurt anyone – it's not in your nature."

I wondered what I would do if confronted with the fiend that murdered Rosabel. Then my good nature would surely be tested to the limit. And had I not hurt my wife dreadfully?

"Thank you," I said. "Perhaps." I was happily prevented from further brooding with our arrival in Castle Newton.

~

Louise had been right. A large pile of debris on the beach indicated that the weather and waves had done their work on the cliff. As before, I sat on the beach, rather chillier now, while she examined the newly exposed rock.

I was lost in my own thoughts for an hour so. I observed a parallel between Louise's concentration now, and her brother's new-found satisfaction. The sweet distraction of a productive task – indeed, my own investigations were all that were keeping me going after recent bitter blows. I might at least retrieve some honour if the capricious fates were to –

"Thomas!"

I started and looked up. Louise had climbed up a ridge in the cliff and stood precariously, waving her hammer at me.

"Thomas, come quickly!"

I picked my way carefully to the spot where Louise stood gently prising rock from an object embedded in the cliff. "Careful," she said as I balanced on the ridge, about ten feet from the ground.

"What have you found?" I said, peering at the rock.

"I don't know," she said, "but the skeleton of some creature, I think!"

I could make out a pattern of closely-spaced corrugations, the whole object being nearly two feet in width, and about four feet in length. It appeared to be comprised of three segmented strands – thick in the middle, and thinner portions at either side.

"There may be more," she said, chipping gently at the sandstone at either end. More ridges appeared, and where they stopped at one end, the middle portion ended in what looked a little like a helmet, a foot wide.

"The head?" Louise said.

"I dread to think what of," I said. "It's huge."

"And I don't think we've uncovered all of it yet," she said.

"Any idea what it is?"

She put down her hammer and chisel on a ledge, and cocked her head to one side. "I've seen something like it before."

"You have?"

"But not a fossil. I hope you're not feeling squeamish, Thomas."

"I'll manage," I said.

"There are plenty in your garden," she said, "and occasionally in your house. It looks like a millipede to me."

"Oh, good God," I said.

"If it's anything like today's millipedes," she said, "then judging from the thickness of its body, I'd say..."

She thought for a moment. "Eight, perhaps nine feet in length. Maybe more."

"Horrific," I said, shivering. "Let's hope it's thoroughly extinct."

"Oh yes," Louise said with a smile. "I would think so. Can you imagine that slithering through Hawksbridge today?" She put down her tools and extracted a sketch book from her bag.

I stared at the fossil, shaking my head. "Louise, I do believe you have found the Hawksbridge Worm!"

~

"I'll write to the Natural History Society in Newcastle," Louise said on the way home. "I shall ask them to urgently excavate the fossil before the weather and looters get to it. It's far too large a task for me."

"Do you think it might be discovered and carried away?

There must be a good market for it."

"Mr Tanner, for one," Louise said. "But it's at a sufficient height for most people not to notice it. It's probably safe for a few days at least."

"Do you know of any similar discovery?"

She shook her head. "No, although there might be."

"Then it will make you a celebrity, will it not?"

"I doubt it," she said, smiling. "I'm just a humble amateur, and I'll probably be an embarrassment to the Natural History Society."

"Nonsense," I said. "I'll make damn sure you're credited properly. They should name it after you."

"Thank you," she said. "Alas, my name is too ungainly for that."

"Is it possible," I said, "that there really is any connection between this and the Hawksbridge Worm? It's terrifying enough. Even more so than the usual depiction."

"It's conceivable that someone found a similar specimen a long time ago," Louise said. "Perhaps even better preserved. And that could easily have given rise to a myth."

"In that case, I have to concede that Jacob Whickham's beliefs are not entirely ridiculous."

"Naturally, these millipedes wouldn't have been slithering around eating humans," Louise said. "But the idea of enormous, peculiar creatures wandering the earth is awe-inspiring. How natural it is to imagine vulnerable humans confronting them – hence Mr Tanner's reaction to my sculpture garden suggestion."

"I can't help imagining Whickham's statue with this monster wrapped around its prey, and not the basilisk," I said. "It might be too horrifying for even Jacob Whickham to get any sensual enjoyment from the piece."

"Could my brother have been referring to Mr Whickham?" Louise said.

"I'm beginning to think he might. Peter might have been

introduced to the Wormers, and it seems reading folk tales and drinking may not be all they get up to."

CHAPTER TWENTY-ONE

When we reached Ramsburgh, Louise was in an endearing state of excitement with her discovery, but not so much that she forgot about my predicaments. Like Francesca, she urged me to talk to Phyllis. "You must have her beside you if you should be summoned to London," she had said. "Apart from anything else, won't it look bad that your own wife has given up on you?" And she had apologised for being so brutally frank, but she had a point, one that I had not yet considered.

So the following day I stood outside the Drummond house, trying to think what I might say to melt Phyllis' frosty heart. The front door opened, and my pulse quickened; but it was only Mrs Harris, who smiled sadly at me, closed the door behind her, and came to embrace me.

"My dear Thomas, what times! How unbearable that you and Phyllis..."

"I came to speak with her. Do you think she's amenable?"

"Oh, my dear boy – not yet, I fear. She's still furious and distressed. Of course, I don't know the full circumstances... but I cannot imagine you would deliberately hurt her. Time will surely heal... so perhaps if you return in a week, she might have wept out her anger. If you see her now, you and she may lash out, and make everything worse."

"Thank you," I said. "I shall take your advice. Though I never imagined a time that my wife would not..." I could not continue.

"I know, I know," Mrs Harris said softly. "It will all be better soon, I promise. The pair of you are too well suited and too intelligent to let this – whatever it is – defeat you. Don't despair! And please come and call on Mr Harris and myself whenever you wish. We shall not take sides!"

"Thank you," I said again. "You're far too kind to me."

She pressed my hand, smiled encouragingly, and left. I stood for a moment, trying to spot figures moving about inside the house, hoping against hope that Phyllis would see me and suddenly rush out to fling herself into my arms. Realising the folly of such thoughts, I walked miserably on. I had a second destination in mind, one that might yield more satisfactory results.

~

Mr Belford, a man who smiled perhaps three or four times a day, honoured me with a broad grin.

"Mr Rufford, you're most welcome in my shop. What brings you in today?"

"Good morning, Mr Belford. Mostly to gossip, I'm afraid. How is business? And how is your daughter? And little Moira?"

"As good as can be expected, all of them, sir. Well, I'm nearly as happy to gossip as I am to sell a pretty ring. And if I can do both, then praise be! Now – do you have gossip for me, or I for you?"

"I wanted to talk about a Mr Jacob Whickham. I think the name will be familiar to you."

His face darkened. "Now why would you be interested in him, sir? A more odious reprobate I have never had the displeasure to do business with. Can't abide the man."

His brow furrowed and he added, "So you know what business he had with me? Who would be telling tales like that?"

"Mr Whickham himself, actually," I said.

"Hmph!" said Mr Belford. "Was he drunk?"

"Extremely," I said.

"What a fool. He's going to get himself burgled if he carries on like that. And he'd better not be blaming me."

"He said – and please forgive me for repeating it – that you 'tended towards insolence'. Did you fall out about something?"

"Oh, yes, sir, we fell out. Well, you would if your daughter had been propositioned, wouldn't you?"

"Propositioned?"

"Lillian was helping me when Whickham was here. The foul man – devil, I should say – leered at Lillian, and when she went to the back, he offered me money for a night with her! Can you believe it?"

"Oh, Lord. Unfortunately, having some knowledge of him, yes, I can believe it."

"I wanted to thrash him, but – well, I've learned my lesson there, haven't I, Mr Rufford? So I took a deep breath, and said the only things for sale were my skills, and what's in my cabinets. He took offence."

I shook my head. "It seems you managed to conclude your business, though."

"Just about," he said. "He didn't complain about my work in the end. So you know exactly what that was?"

"I do," I said. "I find it fascinating."

"Well," he said, hesitantly, "since you're in the know already, I don't suppose there's any harm in showing you something. Wait a moment, sir, and I'll find it."

~

I had held out a faint hope that Simmons' approach to the London Metropolitan Police would be lost in bureaucracy and deficiencies in manpower. This weak flame was instantly snuffed out when I returned to find, once more, the police carriage outside my door, and two unfamiliar faces accompanying Simmons.

"Good afternoon, sir," said the taller officer, who sported an impressively groomed moustache. "Detective Inspector Armstrong at your service, and this is Sergeant Pattison." Pattison, who seemed to be compensating for youthful looks with an excess of ginger facial hair, nodded unsmilingly. "Where might we have a little talk, sir?"

I led them into the dining room, where Armstrong and Pattison positioned themselves to face me across the table, and Simmons took up a pensive, observational role at one end.

The silence as they settled themselves was painful and I felt compelled to break it. "You are efficient, gentlemen," I said. "I wasn't expecting a visit for a while." I immediately realised that my small talk sounded defensive.

Armstrong looked up at me as if he were gaining an insight from every word I uttered. "Indeed, sir? Well, the element of surprise is often useful, I find! And yes, we pride ourselves on our efficiency. The felons of London don't let up, and neither can we."

He carefully smoothed down a blank page in his notebook in a way I found strangely intimidating.

"Inspector Simmons has outlined the facts, sir. I believe the incident in question took place in 1837?" I nodded. "I would be grateful if you could describe the circumstances to us."

This I did, aware again how suspicious it must appear that we were present so soon before Oliphant's demise. Armstrong's smoothed pages filled with copious notes and observations, and Pattison solemnly did likewise.

"I see," Armstrong said when I had finished, reviewing his notes. "Thank you, sir. I will now ask you a few questions. When you planned to enter Mr Oliphant's house, did you intend to break in?"

"To be frank, Inspector," I said, "I don't think we had planned exactly what we intended to do if he hadn't answered the door. But we didn't bring any tools to do that, and I don't recall planning to break a window or some such."

"And you didn't receive an invitation from Mr Oliphant to come in?"

"No. We knocked, but there was no answer. So we let ourselves in."

"And you found Oliphant at the foot of the stairs. Did you have the impression he might have been assaulted?"

"No, I assumed he had simply fallen down the stairs. I was never suspicious of an assault. I thought he might have had some sort of attack – of a medical nature, that is – but there was nothing to indicate it, and I probably wouldn't have been aware of the signs."

"And as to the blood, you cleaned up his injuries with a handkerchief that your – how shall we describe her, sir? – your sweetheart had given you, with her initials."

He pulled a pile of documents towards him and leafed through them.

"The coroner's report concluded with the opinion that he died from an assault by person or persons unknown, given that sadly Miss Sharpe did not survive to be tried. I take it you disagree with this conclusion?"

"Wholeheartedly, Inspector," I said. "Hazel had nothing to do with it, and I know we weren't responsible for it either."

"But you were perhaps lucky that the ownership of the handkerchief wasn't pursued further, given that the authorities no longer had a suspect to try. If there had been someone to link the handkerchief to you – and there were probably several people in the know – then you would certainly have been arrested."

"I imagine so," I said.

"Do you regret not coming forward, sir?"

"Well, obviously not, since I would have been arrested."

Armstrong glanced at Pattison and Simmons.

"So you had a guilty conscience?"

"Not at all, Inspector, only the rational fear of being convicted for something I didn't do."

"And yet you did do something, Mr Rufford. You entered someone's home without their permission, and then you withheld important information from the authorities."

"Yes, Inspector, I know we shouldn't have taken the law into our hands and entered Oliphant's house. However, that is not a capital offence, and I believe we prolonged Oliphant's life, albeit for a short duration until he succumbed to natural processes."

"Let us turn to Mr Alan Sharpe. He arrived at your house last year with the intention of extracting money from you, correct?"

"Yes."

"He wrote to you in advance of his arrival?"

"He did."

"And do you still have that correspondence?"

"Unfortunately not, Inspector. I destroyed it."

"That is indeed unfortunate," Armstrong said. "So from what I gather from Inspector Simmons, he climbed a scaffold up to your room, and entered your bedroom?"

"Correct. He threatened me with an iron bar. My butler Shipley gave chase, and Sharpe fled through the window, falling from the scaffold."

"Now, a court might well believe that you had a compelling motive to silence Sharpe, even if you had nothing to do with Oliphant's death. What would you say to that?"

"The truth – only that yes, he was an embarrassment to me, but no, I didn't kill him. As you know, I was arrested and freed."

"But had Inspector Simmons been in possession of all the facts," Armstrong said, "he might have thought twice about releasing you."

"I can't answer for Inspector Simmons." I glanced at Simmons, but he was maintaining a studiedly impassive demeanour.

"But the problem is, sir, the two incidents reinforce a certain impression."

"I'm afraid I can't help that," I said. "All I can say is, it may be human nature to make such connections and draw erroneous conclusions, but I have killed or injured no one."

Armstrong breathed out noisily and smoothed a new page in his notebook.

"You take a particular interest in crime, Mr Rufford. Is that an accurate characterisation? This hobby of yours has attracted some renown. Indeed, I've read about your exploits myself."

"It's more that crime takes an interest in me, Inspector. If I receive a request to exercise my meagre talents for the good of an individual, I'm obliged to honour it. I would not say that I seek out such pursuits."

"And yet you appear to derive some satisfaction from an association with criminal activity. And perhaps also gratification from the resulting attention, might one say?"

"You make it sound like a crime in itself, Inspector," I said. "I take no more satisfaction in it than you do, or when I solve any other problem in my life."

"Ah. And Mrs Rufford – I take it she supports your position? I'm sorry not to have had the pleasure of meeting her."

"She believes me, of course. She's – indisposed at present."

"I'm sorry to hear that, sir."

Armstrong scribbled some more, put his pencil down, and looked at me. "Very well, sir. Thank you. Unless Sergeant Pattison has further points?"

Pattison cleared his throat and said, "Only to request, Mr

Rufford, that you kindly stay within the parish for the time being."

"Of course," I said. I noticed Mr Simmons looking at me a little anxiously; presumably it would be on his head if I absconded.

"Then that concludes our interview," said Armstrong, closing his notebook and getting to his feet.

"What happens next, Inspector?" I asked.

"I shall prepare a report, and submit it to the magistrates. They will decide whether to summon you."

"And if they do?"

"Then it will be advisable to see that your affairs are in order, sir, in case they send you for trial."

~

Louise shook her head in disbelief. "What an awful travesty. I'm so sorry."

The police had gone, and I had gone up to Louise's tower to describe my inquisition.

"Well," I said, "at least they haven't clapped me in jail in the meantime. So they must think I can be trusted not to run away. My activities have won me that concession!"

"Oh, Thomas. If you are called to London, would you like me to come with you? After all, I'm partly responsible for all this!"

"You're not in the least responsible. And while I'm greatly touched by your offer, it would make less trouble for everyone if I go alone. But I may ask Francesca, since she and I are established friends and business associates."

I sensed she was hiding disappointment. "Of course," she said. "Francesca will be a wonderful support. You wouldn't consider asking Phyllis?"

I shook my head. "Impossible, at present. Things may change."

"I do hope so."

"Have you written to the Natural History Society?"

"Yes, enclosing copies of my drawings," she said, pointing to a sketch on the table. "I confess I'm dreadfully anxious about it – something or someone might get at the fossil. Or they may decline to send anyone. Oh, how foolish, though – this is nothing compared with..."

"You don't have to draw comparisons," I said, smiling. "You're perfectly entitled to your own anxieties. But you've done all you can for now, and you've made a record of the beast, whatever happens to it."

"Yes, yes, that's true," she said, relaxing a little. "Did I tell you? I had a letter from Mr Tanner. He would like me to come and discuss the sculpture garden with him on Tuesday."

"Excellent! Alone?"

"Apparently a sculptor will also be there. So I believe it will be safe, and my cab driver will be waiting for me."

"I'm more than happy to accompany you."

"Thank you!" she said. "But I'll try to be independent."

"Will you tell Tanner about your discovery? He may well wish to commission a model of it."

"I'll see," Louise said. "Perhaps if it's been removed by then. Otherwise it's too much of a temptation."

"Yes," I said. "While Tanner delights in the trappings of tradition and learning, my instincts tell me a certain wildness lurks within, ready to burst through a thin shell of restraint. Still – I could be maligning him, and unfairly ascribing to him a general human condition."

"That might be a sketch of Rosabel's attacker," Louise said.

"Perhaps the magistrates in London will think that of me," I said. "And that all my endeavours here are a frantic attempt to absolve and hide my inner fiend."

"You would make a poor fiend," Louise said with feeling, "when you're a kind and true friend."

~

On Sunday afternoon, Louise joined me for tea in the drawing room. She brought in a package that had arrived, and I recognised McPhee's hand.

"Ah – Rosabel's poetry book, I presume," I said. "By rights, this should be with Simmons, but I'll pass it on. If I can bear to enter the police office."

Louise watched me open the package with anticipation. "What is it?" she said when I tore open the brown paper and smiled in recognition at the name on the binding.

"Mr Lawrence, again," I said, turning to the title page. "His books seem to make popular presents, at least in Hawksbridge. 'The Poems of Allan Lawrence, Vol. III: Man and Beast, Eighth Edition, 1809.'"

Flipping through its pages, the subjects appeared to be mainly legend, interspersed with reflections on love. The story of Hawksbridge's basilisk was represented, and I began reading aloud.

The Feeding of the Worm

The river spits its torrent to the sea,
Chafing headlands where strange creatures rise
To stuff their dripping maws – one such is me:
A cunning, stealthy, brute that never dies.

Patrons of my belly meet to groan and give
Their best to dodge the fate they darkly dread
The withered, lean and dry conspire to live
While luscious meat quakes in my jaws instead.

Once a year, the frighted corps of males
Tie twice the bounty to the blood-stained stake.
And wreath'd with ice about my chilly scales,
With joy, a double fill of flesh I take.

Louise wrinkled her nose. The association with poor Rosabel was too vivid to stomach reading more, and I put the book down and pushed away half a slice of uneaten cake.

"I hope Mrs Felton isn't insulted," I said, "but it can't be helped."

"Can I have a look?" Louise said and I nodded. She picked up the book gingerly to avoid more damage to the worn leather cover, and leafed through the pages. "Perhaps this will be less grim. 'Twice Damned'," she read.

Twice Damned

For me, my Eves have bitten through a shield of fruit
To let me slither 'round their hearts and try my double suit
They give their love beneath the tree, on tender mossy bed
And I, writhing, not my skin but Heav'nly favour shed.

Twice the sins of Adam damn my errant, forfeit soul
Yet I chance the flames for joy upon our am'rous knoll
Lips, and lips again press me to my Cupid's task
My days are bliss, my Eves are fill'd with all they ask.

"I wonder what he – oh!" she said, and turned pink, snapping the book shut without her former care. "Good heavens. And someone gave this to Rosabel? How very indelicate." She put it back on the table.

I laughed, before checking myself. "I'm sorry. The way your expression changed..."

"Thomas, I'm surprised at you," Louise said, standing up. "And I thought you were a gentleman!" But then she smiled at my mortification, and sat down again. "There! We're even. But what a wicked poem – a man not content with merely one lover!"

"Probably an empty boast," I said. "Invention was his

livelihood, after all. It's an impractical fantasy that some men indulge in."

Louise looked at me pointedly. "Yes?"

"Well, anyway," I said, feeling my own cheeks burning. "The point is, could this book have anything to do Rosabel's death?"

"If you could find the original owner..." Louise said.

I examined the book again. "There's nothing I can see."

"Try Hunter's, in case he sold it recently?"

"Good idea," I said. "I wonder if Rosabel even knew who her admirer was?"

"Some poor devil," she said. "Or perhaps – a devil indeed."

CHAPTER TWENTY-TWO

But this copy of Lawrence's poems had not passed through Mr Hunter's hands, as far as he could recall, and I could find nothing of interest in its pages besides a dreamer's fancies.

"Thank you, Mr Rufford," said Mr Simmons, taking the volume and opening it up. "That's decent of you, especially considering you might be feeling – well, a little sore about things."

"I hope I would try not to let that interfere with the pursuit of justice," I said, though feeling this was slightly prim given my previous reluctance to be entirely forthright.

"Quite so, sir," he said, and looked thoughtful for a moment. "Forgive me, Mr Rufford, but we have been busy of late, and... Would you wait in the interview room for one minute?"

"Of course, Inspector," I said, mystified. Simmons led me to the room and gestured for me to sit at the table, before leaving with the book. For what would I now have to forgive Simmons, other than the utter ruination of my life?

When Simmons returned, he was carrying a small box, which he placed on the table before – to my surprise – taking a chair next to me, instead of his customary position opposite. He placed his hand on the box.

"These were discovered at the grave site in Mrs Campbell's ice house. It didn't seem fitting to discuss them when we had the... the other matter to discuss, and I didn't have them with me. But since you're here, I thought you should see them."

He opened the box, took out two blackened oval objects and placed them on the table.

"Silver," he said, as I picked one of them up. "Quite old."

"A locket," I said. "And two similar ones, in the same place – interesting."

"Yes, sir," Simmons said. "I would imagine they belonged to those two poor souls."

"Have you tried...?" I said as I picked at the edge.

"Yes, sir, they both open up, with effort. Constable Taylor greased the hinges."

I managed to get my nail into the gap and prise it apart, revealing an exquisite miniature portrait of a man.

"It was filthy," said Simmons, "but Taylor gave it a good clean."

"Good Lord," I whispered, entranced by the painting. It showed a clean-shaven man in perhaps his late thirties, with a full, shoulder-length head of hair and a duck egg blue coat. He calmly returned my stare, a handsome fellow with a hint of compassion – or was it love? – in his eyes, holding one hand to his heart in an obvious declaration of his feelings.

I looked up at Simmons, who was watching for my reaction.

"Nice, isn't it, sir?" he said.

"Superb," I said. "Congratulations to your constables for finding these."

I picked open the lid of the second locket, and found a similar portrait, but this time a three-quarter profile view, so that instead of facing the viewer, the subject seemed to be yearning for a world beyond his oval confinement.

"The same man, do you think, Inspector?" I said.

"The same man courting two ladies?" said Simmons, evidently shocked at the idea. "Well, it's possible, I suppose, sir, but is it likely?"

"Or the artist had a particular style," I said. "I do find some portraits by the same artist uncannily similar; although kinship and national characteristics might partly account for it."

"And hair fashion, and so forth," said Simmons.

"Indeed. Mrs Campbell will be fascinated by these."

"She's more than welcome to come in and examine them," said Simmons. "I'm afraid I'm not at liberty to let them out of the office at present. I suppose it might give you an idea of the identity of the women, which is something we don't have time to pursue, regrettably."

"Are you suggesting, Inspector, that I indulge in some detective work?" I said.

"I wouldn't exactly put it that way, sir, no. But I can't stop you doing your own personal research, can I?"

"Thank you, Inspector," I said. "I'm glad to have seen these."

"No trouble, sir. It's a pity about... the other thing."

I nodded. Could I be witnessing a glimmer of remorse? "Ah well, Inspector," I said. "We all have our jobs to do."

This was, of course, more generous than I felt, but the moment had the faint feeling of an amnesty about it.

~

Francesca had invited me for dinner to get to know John Hutton. Going without Phyllis felt strange. It was almost unbearable waiting for her anger to subside as Mrs Harris had advised, but I told myself that timing was everything. Might she be ready to forgive me in a few days' time, once more ready to share the intimate conversations, comforts and pleasures that only a marriage can supply? There was the unpleasant alternative that her heart would have had time to harden as she contemplated my shortcomings. And she might be getting used to a relatively solitary life again: ensconced with her beloved old father, managing a simpler household, and avoiding the danger of pregnancy.

At the dinner table, Francesca smiled at me sympathetically as the wine was poured.

"How is Louise? Has she been fossil-hunting recently?"

"Indeed – she's in a state of excitement," I said, "having discovered something significant on the shore. Alas, I can't say any more! She's worried – quite rightly – that it'll be plundered before it can be claimed by science. But I'm sure she'll be able to reveal all shortly."

"Oh, how delightful!" said Francesca. "And so well deserved. Please congratulate her for us. I can't wait to hear more!"

I glanced at Hutton, whose expression indicated that he was unused to being part of Francesca's 'us'.

"I haven't met the lady," he said, "but she sounds a determined lass. Not unlike this one." He gestured at Francesca with his wine glass. "She's driven me hard, this last few months!"

"And you wouldn't have it any other way," said Francesca. "Far better a client who knows what she wants, than a total ditherer!"

"Oh aye," he said, grinning. "You know what you want, to be sure."

"Although I've faltered lately," she said, sighing, "but I'm summoning my energy again."

"Hardly surprising in the circumstances," I said. "And I have news about our ice house... what should I call them?"

"Guests?" Francesca offered. "It's too awful to call them bodies when I see them in my mind as breathing, loving people."

"Our guests," I said, "who we assume are Caroline and Anne. I went to see Inspector Simmons, and he showed me two objects they found in the ice house."

"Yes?"

"Well, loving people they certainly were – they found two lockets, containing paintings of two handsome men. Or perhaps, man."

"Lockets?" said Francesca. "How wonderful! But what do you mean, 'man'?"

"The two portraits are of individuals that bear a striking similarity to one another," I said.

"Twins, like?" said Hutton, his interest piqued. "They could play some tasty games, those lads."

"Oh, John, you're disgusting," Francesca said, poking his arm. "Not everything is about... that."

Hutton shrugged and sliced into his chicken breast.

"Tell me more, Thomas," she said. "Can you tell when they were painted? Oh, I must see them! How tantalising."

"From the clothes and hair, they seem about the right period – seventeenth century, or early eighteenth."

"Goodness! How extraordinary that you have looked Caroline and Anne's lovers in the eye."

"Or lover, singular," I said.

"Good lad!" said Hutton enthusiastically, drawing an amused glare from Francesca.

Allan Lawrence's poetic self-condemnation came to mind. "And perhaps killer," I added.

~

"Since the weather is foul, gentlemen, you may smoke in the drawing room, for once," said Francesca.

"Thank you," I said, "but I'm content with my port."

"I will, if you don't mind, Mr Rufford," Hutton said, opening a box of cigars. "Present from Fr– ...from Mrs Campbell."

"A little something for his diligence," Francesca said, holding a glass of wine. "Although my scintillating company should be reward enough."

Hutton lit his cigar, took a puff, and said, "You have a high opinion of yourself, ma'am. One that is altogether justified."

Francesca gave him an affectionate smile. "Flatterer."

Turning to me, she said, "You said you went to see Simmons about something? To dissuade him...?"

"No," I said, "nothing like that. All the wheels are in motion now, and my fate is in the hands of the authorities in London."

"Oh, I'm so sorry, Thomas. Then what...?"

"To give Simmons a piece of evidence. I found out from Rosabel's friend – Mabel, who we saw with her in Myrtle's – that someone gave her a poetry book two weeks or so before her death. Presumably an admirer."

"Really?" Francesca said. "That's worrying. There's no indication of who the admirer might be?"

"None, unfortunately," I said. "I've scoured the book, but I couldn't find anything of interest. So I went in to give it to Simmons. You'll never guess who the author was."

"Not our Allan Lawrence, surely?"

"The same. Volume three, this time, and full of legends. One of which he supposes to be himself. And to the extent that his books are in demand here, perhaps he's right."

"You're speaking in riddles!" Francesca said, pouring herself another glass. "Legend in what way?"

"Mr Hutton would approve," I said, and Hutton raised his eyebrows questioningly. "He writes of taking his pleasure with two women."

"Oh, honestly!" said Francesca. "Is there perhaps something in the River Gill that does this to the men of Hawksbridge?"

"What's in the Gill comes out to bite the lasses, not the men!" said Hutton.

"Very good, John," said Francesca.

"Well, I'll say it if neither of you will," said Hutton. "This

Lawrence fellow has been having his wicked way with your Caroline and Anne! And then he got bored, or they fell out or some such, and he killed 'em."

"But it was Manners who was on the scene. Perhaps he was envious of his friend's happiness," I said, "and killed them himself. His message is dripping with guilt."

"Or Caroline and Anne killed each other in a fit of jealousy," said Francesca. "Oh, but I wish I hadn't thought of that. It's worse than them being murdered by someone else – at least I could imagine them dying together, united."

I nodded.

"Anyway, that's quite a book to give a young lady," Hutton observed. "To Rosabel, I mean. Full of smut. From a possible murderer, by a possible murderer."

"It's not exactly wholesome fare, no," I said. "It's more the kind of thing the Wormers would like!"

Hutton nodded at me. "You think on that, Mr Rufford. I won't say more, for someone here will box my ears, but you know my opinions on certain Wormers!"

~

It became hard to distinguish between the haze of smoke, and the fog in my head due to Francesca's excellent port. I found myself silent, content to watch them talk. They seemed comfortable with each other, but what was the prognosis for the future association between Francesca and a builder, albeit one with uncommon intelligence and charm?

Hutton could be the sustaining pillar that Francesca needed, or he could be the misguided addition that threw the original edifice out of balance. How could two such dissimilar materials be lastingly bonded together? Had they sketched out a plan? But for now, they were building a warm friendship, and perhaps that was all that mattered.

"This is one of the few poems by Lawrence I like," Francesca was saying, opening the volume Mr Fountain had given me. "No monsters or romantic adventures here."

She began to read aloud, her soothing voice fading as drowsiness prevailed.

Opus Interruptus

Precious muse, that bears a torch to light my barren gloom
Also wakes the brute that loots the stillness from my room.
No sooner does my wingèd god of hope descend
Than stretches Bram, who mews and begs my art to end.

My thoughts, though forced in line like soldiers in the morn
Are once more scattered, from their posts now torn
By greater might than muses can supply.
Claws are drawn – and blood, if long I shun his cry.

Later will this creature seek a flash of wing
Or trembling tail and to my study bring
A prize to pay me back for scaring off my words
Which alight, then flap away like mobs of skittish birds.

But haste – at last, the weary hunter naps for now
On his cushioned throne, while poet prays for no miaow
Until the verse is poured upon the waiting leaf:
A modest haul of treasure safe from hirsute stanza thief.

CHAPTER TWENTY-THREE

I WAS surprised to receive a warmly-worded letter from Jacob Whickham, who had apparently enjoyed our evening together greatly and was anxious to discuss an artistic matter with the potential for 'fruitful collaboration'. I had no idea what he meant, but his approach was fortunate, as I was searching for an excuse to impose on him again and extract what further information I could.

John Hutton's antipathy to Jenrick had reminded me that I had not sufficiently considered the Hawksbridge Folklore Society, or Wormers, in relation to Rosabel's death. While our culture had a certain tolerance for representations of suffering with erotic connotations, what I had seen at Whickham's home, especially his prurient interest in damsels in distress, pushed strongly at the boundaries of propriety. Might this be an indication, or the cause, of a disturbing excess of passion?

To my alarm, when I was shown into Whickham's drawing room, my host was engulfed by a long coughing fit as he rose to greet me. He was wearing a silk dressing gown, and his pallid face was wet with perspiration. I was shocked by his condition.

As he controlled his coughing, he smiled, held his hand up, and gasped for air. "What a welcome for my new friend," he wheezed. He nodded to the concerned footman, who poured me a glass of red wine – Whickham's was already full – and left the room.

"Come, take a seat," he said, sitting and gesturing to the chair opposite his. "Excuse me putting my feet up, but my legs are two fat mutineers." He placed his feet on a gout stool and raised his glass. "To friendship, and artistic collaboration!"

I raised mine and took a sip. "You intrigue me," I said. "What kind of collaboration do you have in mind?"

My host beamed. "It's all a matter of being unselfish," he said. "The more I take pleasure in my Worm and the Maiden, the more I feel regret to be keeping it all to myself. After all, I have so much. And the public are generally provided with such insipid, lacklustre offerings in comparison, that have no blood and no – well, bite!"

"I see," I said. "An exhibition, then. I would imagine a tour of the cities? Would you not be afraid of letting the ruby out of your sight?"

Whickham chuckled. "Dear boy, you have quite the wrong end of the stick. How could we possibly collaborate on such a thing? No, my notion is for the public to be able to possess my maiden, to be able to touch her, and carry her home, to be on display forever in her ecstasy of mortal apprehension."

With a heavy heart, I understood the nature of his plan, which was, of course, out of the question. Whickham was looking at me expectantly.

"Then I take it," I said, "you're speaking of a commercial reproduction?"

"You've got it, sir!" Whickham said. "As you know, I'm tremendously fond of Mrs Campbell's angels, as manufactured by your splendid factory. So as I was contemplating it the other night, the idea came to me! Why not a statue of my Maiden? I shouldn't be hiding this light under a bushel. She'd make a splendid piece of Marbleware, would she not? I have absolute faith in your ability to do her justice!"

I had a strong instinct to immediately stamp out all hope in such an endeavour. But I did not want our interview terminated so abruptly.

"An interesting thought, Mr Whickham," I said levelly, rapidly concocting some non-committal blether. "Obviously the reduction in size would reduce the impact of the piece. On the other hand, it would also reduce the resistance of family members who might object to the presence of a life-size monster in their home!"

"Quite, quite!" said Whickham, shifting his legs and wincing. "But given your firm's admirable attention to detail, I'm sure it'll still convey the essence of the scene. Now, now, Thomas, don't be shy – you may recognise my genius and congratulate me! Is this not the most splendid idea you've heard this year?"

"It's certainly a – a unique proposition," I said. "Congratulations." I raised my glass again and managed a smile.

"That's the spirit!" he said, raising his and draining it. "Well, we can discuss the details anon, but I shan't be greedy with the rights fee. I consider it an act of philanthropy to encourage the dissemination of such enlightening art for a modest outlay. Naturally, a man can't be blamed for taking a modest profit, but this will be a happy conjunction of art and commerce."

It appeared that Whickham had taken my responses as acquiescence. However, I could let him down gently another time, with apologies for the proposal's rejection by my colleagues at the Pottery. It was almost a shame to spoil his child-like enjoyment of his idea. I wondered if the project was meant as a distraction from his physical pain as much as a burning desire to enlighten the multitude.

He became lost in contemplation for a moment. "And," he said, "it will be my modest tribute..." He rubbed his eyes.

"Tribute?" I enquired.

He shrugged, and the butler came in to enquire if anything was needed.

"Another bottle," Whickham said.

The butler bit his lip. "Are you sure, sir?" he said. "The doctor was exceedingly concerned about your gout, and also –"

"Are you my nanny, man?" Whickham retorted. The butler shook his head. "Then get me another bloody bottle, and I'll deal with the consequences!"

Whickham rolled his eyes. "We shall go to the Gallery in a minute and take another look at my maiden, but I need another glass. Tell me, Thomas, what have you been up to, eh? What gossip do you have? What news of the murder investigation?"

"Nothing of note," I said. "It's frustrating."

"Damn scandal is what it is," Whickham said. "Has Mr Tanner not been arrested? Was he not the last to see her?"

"Unfortunately he has an alibi for his whereabouts. His men will vouch for him."

"Of course they will, of course they will!" he said. "Proves nothing at all."

He shook his head. "I know you're supposed to be good at this sort of thing. If the police are too dull-witted, you must apply your mind, Mr Rufford! Will you do it?"

I was surprised at his imploring tone. "I'll do what I can," I said, "but alas, I don't have the authority to conduct a proper enquiry."

He nodded, and I stared into the fireplace, embarrassed at his evident disappointment in me.

"Is there something different about the hearth?" I said. "Something seems missing."

"Ah, sharp eyes, sharp eyes," he said. "Walter came and borrowed my tiger. Using it for a play or some such. Damn well hope he takes care of it – shot by my father!"

His butler refilled our glasses, and Whickham folded his hands and set his gaze on me before reciting:

Tyger Tyger burning bright,
In the forests of the night:
What immortal hand or eye,
Dare frame thy fearful symmetry?

"Red-blooded fellow, Mr Blake," Whickham said. "And prodigiously talented. Who made the tigers, Thomas – and who made the monsters? That is the question. Who would make a creature so adept at destroying men and women? Oh, you may dismiss the great Worm as pure fantasy, of course. But it comes from the certain knowledge that there *are* terrible monsters abroad, chewing up our feeble human flesh. And I for one welcome them, whether they're for the Creator's amusement, or to keep us on our toes, or simply to be admired for their sheer, ruthless power."

I was tempted to mention Louise's millipede, but I was sworn to secrecy. I knew Whickham's eyes would have lit up had I been at liberty to describe it. Instead, I tried a different topic.

"I concede that terrible power can have a sort of beauty," I said. "And I agree about Blake's genius, although not with all his beliefs. Tell me, is poetry important to you – and to your fellow Wormers? For example, Allan Lawrence?"

"Oh, definitely it is," Whickham said, "and yes, Lawrence is absolutely an inspiration to us. For example, 'The Feeding of the Worm' –"

"Yes, indeed," I said, heading off another recitation. "I recently came across it. I assume you have that volume?"

"Naturally!" he said, heaving himself off his chair with a groan. "Let me find it. I don't trust my staff with it."

He shuffled back in a few minutes, empty-handed. "Must

have forgotten I lent it to someone. I fear I've done my mind no favours, and not only my body! Oh well," he said, and picked up his glass. "Too late to worry about that now."

I noted the missing book for later consideration. "Would it be fair to say you and your colleagues in the Society are interested in... how shall I put it... the idea of restraining women?" I said. "And perhaps an interest in the idea of their suffering?"

"Hm!" said Whickham. "What a question. If you put it like that, and in that tone, it might appear a little... crass, perhaps. An appreciation of the Worm does imply taking an interest in these things, yes. But we are talking fantasy, my dear boy, fantasy."

"Blake was of the opinion, as you know," I said, "that humans have two parts to their character – one half good, and one half evil. Then there must inevitably be a struggle between these halves. Sometimes one will win, and a person will do good. And sometimes the other part will win."

"Agreed," said Whickham. "What is your point?"

"If I may be so bold as to ask," I said, and took a sip of wine before continuing.

"Yes? Out with it, my dear fellow!"

"Might one not ask – and I apologise if this seems impertinent – whether this interest in particular myths might, when indulged by the wrong sort of person, encourage the bad part of his character and spill over into actual harm?"

"Oh, not a bit of it, sir, not a bit of it!" he said. "No more than reading the Bible induces a man to sack a city or stone an ox. We would have to burn a great deal of books, dear Rufford, starting with the Bible, if we were to assume that terrible tales were to prompt terrible deeds. Credit a man with the ability to distinguish between fact and fiction!"

"That is generally the case, of course," I said, "but I wonder whether sometimes there might be an association – very rarely, that is, and for those with a mental weakness of some kind."

He frowned. "I see what you're getting at it, but you're barking up the wrong tree. There are no members of our Society that don't know the line between play and reality. I can vouch for them all."

"I'm sure," I said. "It was only a passing thought."

He smiled indulgently. "And so of course you should have such thoughts, shouldn't you, seeing that justice is an interest of yours! Well, I can understand your curiosity. After all, when we play, we do it properly."

"Properly?"

He looked around. "Not supposed to say, strictly speaking, but we enlist the help of an actress to play the part of the maiden in our celebrations of the Worm. She knows perfectly well what she's getting into. Gets paid handsomely."

"Ah. An actress?" I said.

"Well, a professional, then, if you know what I mean."

"And she plays the maiden?"

"Oh, yes."

"Without clothing?"

He shrugged and smiled. "Perhaps."

"And she's tied up, and...?"

"And, my good fellow, if you're not joining the Society, it's time for me to shut my trap and for us both to admire my maiden in the Gallery. You can tell me how hard it might be to make a facsimile in your Marbleware."

Wheezing, he got laboriously to his feet, and we walked over to the Gallery, his gait alarmingly unsteady – whether from drink or illness, I could not tell. He removed his necklace and unlocked the door with a key that was attached to it.

"Can't be too careful," he said, and gestured for me to step into the room.

Again I stood before the plaster monster, or rather, monstrosity, its ruby and glass eyes glowing.

I was entranced by the horror of the embracing pair, so

unsuitable for an ornament in a respectable home. Had I been wrong about the resemblance I saw? Something in the eyes, and the dimples in her cheeks...

After a moment I heard Whickham's wheeze turn into a gasp, and I turned to see that he was leaning against a window frame, struggling for breath.

The attack was severe, and his eyes, fixed on me, bulged in fear. I shouted for assistance, and the footman and butler came running. A maid brought laudanum in brandy, but he was unable to drink much of it, and there was also now fear in the eyes of his helpers.

"Let's get him to bed," the butler said, and they bundled him out of the room, leaving me staring after them in horror.

~

I had been left in the Gallery on my own. After a minute of contemplation, I closed the door and turned the key, which had been left in the lock still attached to the necklace, and made my way to the drawing room where I placed the key on the table by Whickham's chair. I waited for some forty minutes, and finally, Whickham's butler came to inform me that his master was now comfortable and sleeping. Relieved, and having conveyed my concern and good wishes to my host, I requested my horse be brought around; I had not drunk as much as Whickham and felt able to ride.

I mulled over the encounter. I felt some pity for Whickham, although he exhibited attitudes and predilections that appalled me. I suspected that his bachelorhood was not as voluntary as he maintained, and perhaps that deficiency had contributed to the indulgence that now devastated his health. A reasonably cultured man, despite a tendency to the grotesque and vulgar, he evidently now desired the distraction of congenial company, knowing his days of amorous encounters were behind him.

The missing book was troubling. Had he sent it to Rosabel, and why? Surely he could not have hoped to woo her? And yet when he had spoken of her, there was a passion that I could not explain. Had she rejected him, and evoked a rage that led to her death? It was not hard to imagine Whickham, with time on his hands, becoming unnaturally preoccupied with the girl, who, after all, had a mesmerising beauty and character. He had denied meeting her, but he must surely have admired her from afar, at least.

Then there was the matter of his frailty. Whickham's health had deteriorated markedly since her death, and it was possible that he had originally possessed sufficient strength to overpower her.

Supposing he had not done it. He had been emphatic that none of his fellow Wormers could be capable of a barbaric act. How much store could I put by that? But the revelation of the Society's celebrations of the Worm myth was highly troubling. Evidently the legend had excited thoroughly unscholarly behaviour in the Society's members.

CHAPTER TWENTY-FOUR

IT WAS time to face Phyllis, and my heart was pounding as I stood once more in front of the Drummond house. Its immaculate and elegant façade was a bulwark against the disorder of the world: seemingly, this now included myself.

The maid who answered the door looked surprised, and asked me to wait a moment. After some discussion that I could not make out, I was ushered into Dr Drummond's study. I hoped I would not have to face the shame of receiving her father's admonishments.

But I did not have to wait long before Phyllis came in and shut the door. It was strange to meet so formally.

"Hello, Thomas," she said. "How have you been?"

Her politeness cut through me. "Holding up," I said. "I've been missing you most dreadfully."

"Have you?" she said.

"Yes. I suppose you've had more time to write," I said.

She shrugged. "I haven't felt much like it. I'm not sure what the purpose is any more."

"There is plenty of purpose!" I said. "Your admirers are waiting to be diverted."

"Ah," she said. "Diversion. I suppose that's all it is, like a cheap circus trick, distracting the world from its woes. How depressing."

"Not at all," I said. "Entertainment is tremendously important, and I didn't mean it was only diversion. Your novels are..." I searched for the right words.

She dismissed my attempt with a wave of her hand. "Don't worry, I know what my books are and what they are not. I have no illusions they will exist in a thousand years' time.

Maybe not even a hundred. But that is all beside the point." She sighed and added. "Please enlighten me."

I ran my hand through my hair. "The point of my visit? To tell you I was wrong not to be entirely truthful about my past. To tell you I still love you fiercely. To ask you to come back to Ramsburgh, where you belong, and be my wife again. To ask for your forgiveness. In short, to ask the impossible of you."

She smiled for the first time. "I would have to trust you again. Could you assure me of that?"

"Yes, I could," I said, "but it's not only a matter of trust. You would have to love me again. That might be far harder."

Her carefully-maintained composure suddenly cracked, and tears ran down her cheeks. "Of course I love you, Thomas. How could I not? But love is the easy part – either it's there or it isn't, and it overwhelms and confuses everything. I cannot let myself be hurt again. I must be practical. Can't you see that?"

"Surely it's quite the reverse," I said. "Love is a great clarifier! All the rest is secondary – negotiation, accommodation, mistakes, penance – but love rides above all that. Love marks out the road for us, and we must stagger down it, in the sun or rain, and whatever the obstacles and trenches in the way."

"Whatever the cost?" Phyllis said, wiping her face.

"I think that perhaps you exaggerate the cost," I said, "compared with the enormous advantages."

"Do you?" she said. "You think I'm exaggerating the pain of your betrayal? Yes, betrayal, that you didn't see fit to tell me what you told others, actions of yours that may have the direst consequences. Even Louise! Your new friend, or rather, your old friend with goodness knows what shared history. How can I not be devastated to find you intimately exchanging confidences when –"

"Hardly intimately," I said. "I was just keeping her

informed."

"That's not what it looked like to me! She was comforting you, rather warmly."

"That's simply what humans do," I said. "Kind ones, that is." I regretted the barb instantly.

"Oh!" she cried. "How dare you come into my house, the home of my sick father, and accuse me of being unkind! If I'm so awful, you may leave right now."

"Phyllis, I'm sorry –"

"Please leave."

I had no choice. I had not gone ten yards from the house when I turned into a narrow lane, clung to a young oak tree, and wept as long and bitterly as I can remember.

~

Fate has a habit of kicking a man when he is down. Waiting for me at Ramsburgh was a stern summons to Blackheath Magistrates' Court on November 7th, and I fell into a pit of despair, slumped in a chair in the drawing room.

Louise came in and saw me staring into the grate. "Are you all right?" she said. I handed her the letter without a word.

"Oh no!" she said. "How miserable."

"And I went to see Phyllis today," I said.

Louise took a seat near me and said, "Will she go with you to...?"

I shook my head. "I insulted her work, then I insulted her. So all I have left to do in my bid for reconciliation is dance on her ancestors' graves."

"Oh, I'm sure you can't have insulted her," she said. "Aren't you overstating it?"

"Unfortunately not," I said. "I was trying to compliment her work, in my usual clumsy fashion, and then... well, what's done is done."

"Bad luck," she said. "But you will try again?"

I sighed and closed my eyes. "I suppose I will, in a few days. I'm exhausted. I don't know what to say or think any more." I tried to empty my crowded, aching mind.

~

"Tea and seed cake, my dear," said Mrs Felton. "You need to build up your strength!"

I opened my eyes. "Oh! How long have I been asleep?"

"Just an hour or so," said Louise. "It's about four o'clock. Feeling better?"

"Slightly," I said, reaching for my tea.

"Then I'll tell you my news," she said, "if you don't mind."

"Of course not," I said.

"Well, firstly, I had a highly enjoyable talk with Mr Tanner and Mr Griffin – that's the sculptor he has in mind. I suggested what creatures they might like to do, and to my surprise, they took me seriously."

"As they should," I said, earnestly. "I'm very glad. And secondly?"

She smiled at me a little nervously, as if unsure whether she could fully enjoy the moment, given my own predicament.

"The Natural History Society have written to say that not only have they sent a team to remove the fossil, they congratulate me for a 'potentially significant discovery'. And the director has invited me to Newcastle to stay with him and his wife for a few days, and discuss the find, and have a tour of the museum!" She handed me the letter.

I scanned the letter: in marked contrast with my summons, it was warm in tone.

"Oh, my dear Louise," I said, excited for her. "This is marvellous! I knew you would be famous." I reached out for her hand and squeezed it. "We must celebrate."

"Thank you!" she said. "But – I can't possibly celebrate anything. Not at the moment."

"Nonsense," I said. "Now is an excellent time. It will distract me." I got up to ring the bell.

~

I began to feel more sanguine after a couple of glasses of wine, and listened to Louise describe her ideas for the sculpture garden. Her enthusiasm was touching.

"And your own creature?" I said. "Then surely Tanner will recruit you to open the garden."

"I wonder if Millie would really work as a sculpture," Louise said. "She's somewhat flat and long."

"How about as a mosaic? Perhaps on a path leading up to the sculpture garden. You look down, and you find you're walking on something terrifying."

"An excellent idea!" she said. "I'll suggest it, now it's no longer a secret."

"If I may change the subject," I said, "I suppose there's no more from your brother?"

"No. But we have to assume from his letter that he's happy – and that's more than I had hoped for."

"True. Whickham has been hinting at a beastly sort of ritual at the Wormers – in both senses of the word. I wonder if that can be what Peter was referring to, or something even worse."

"Perhaps you should speak to Walter Jenrick," Louise said. "After all, he's the one who dragged Peter in that night. He rather leered at me, I thought. We may have to be grateful that he helped Peter, but I'm not sure I like him."

"Yes," I said, "I suppose I've been avoiding any suspicions about Jenrick out of respect for Francesca, who won't have a word said against him. She doesn't like Hutton criticising him. Certainly, Jenrick seemed to recognise Rosabel's name when Francesca first mentioned her, and he had presumably already spoken to Rosabel before the first rehearsal, since he said he would. But why would he do away with a promising young actress, when it obviously caused him so much professional frustration? It doesn't make sense."

"Quite," she said.

"No – it's more logical that Whickham is involved," I said, "given his preoccupation with her and the fact that the same volume of poetry that Rosabel was sent seems to have gone missing from Whickham's library."

"Goodness! I take it he denies sending it himself?"

"Yes. But he said he's becoming forgetful, so didn't absolve himself completely."

"Which rather indicates," Louise said, fondling the stem of her wine glass, "that he was unaware of your suspicions."

"Or," I said, "that he's adept at covering his tracks – a kind of double-bluff to persuade us of his naivety and innocence."

"Is he as clever as all that?"

"I don't know," I said. "He can't be entirely stupid, having accumulated so much wealth. And there's something I really don't like."

"Yes?"

"His maiden sculpture. It seems to remind me of... but that's ridiculous. Could he have destroyed a living person and substituted a plaster reproduction, knowing he would never possess the original?"

Louise shuddered. "What a ghastly thought. But I know that some men are proprietorial to the point of violence. And from all you say about his interests, I'm afraid it doesn't seem so unlikely."

~

I went into my office to write a letter to Mr Simmons to inform him of my fears regarding Whickham, but after some deliberation, I put it aside. I had my reasons for not wanting a police invasion of Whickham's house, not least because it would be the end of cordial relations and opportunities to learn more from him. And I had in the past contributed to the unjust arrest of Mr Belford, although it had been resolved and forgiven in due course. Could I be sure this would not be a similar case?

Besides, given Whickham's poor state of health, a raid, based on slender evidence, might well precipitate his early demise. If he was indeed the culprit, it was inconceivable that he presented any further danger to the women of Hawksbridge.

CHAPTER TWENTY-FIVE

Francesca's confidence was returning. She was determined to pick up the reins at the inn and revive it from its sleep, and she had written to me to ask for some moral support. So on a fresh autumnal morning, I rode into Hawksbridge.

The cool air was bracing on my face, and I lost myself in Celeste's rhythmic breathing. Hers was a steadfast, simple companionship that drew me a little out of my melancholy.

As I passed the churchyard, I heard a commotion coming from the churchyard. I tied Celeste up and followed the path around the church to the back, where a gathering of five or six people were standing around a gravestone. One was a labourer with a pair of shears, who I surmised had come to work in the churchyard and had raised the alarm. A woman had her hand pressed to her mouth.

"Not again!" she said. "Oh, God, not again!"

"Does anyone know who it is?" someone said.

"I think it's Lucy!" the woman said. "Lucy Buxton!"

"What in Hell's name did that?" another voice said.

Looking back to the gate, I could see a police carriage drawing up.

I stepped forward to get a better look. A brunette in perhaps her mid-thirties was sprawled naked on a tomb, on her back. She was smeared in blood and had numerous gashes all over her body. Shredded clothing was scattered nearby. Nauseated, I looked away and stepped back for Mr Simmons who had hurried down the path.

He glanced at me and said in a commanding voice, "Unless you have any pertinent information, ladies and gentlemen, I'd be grateful if you could disperse."

I nodded at him and made my way to the gate, thanking the constable who waved me through.

My previous tranquillity was gone. Fear flooded my mind, not only to see a fellow human's life so viciously ended, but terror that my own failures might have allowed this to happen. Why had I covered up my suspicions about the origins of the book, as well as Mr Gardner's strange behaviour? Had Whickham recovered himself sufficiently to be capable of this awful thing? Why could I not have spent more time on Rosabel's murder, and less on Manners?

I had ridden for a couple of minutes, my body tense with dread and self-recrimination, when I saw movement in the corner of my eye. Assuming it to be a large dog, I looked more closely at the splash of colour in the side-street and was shocked to see a substantial orange, black and white creature. I realised that my eyes were not deceiving me, however much my rational mind wished to dismiss it: I was looking at a tiger, and he was looking at me.

I judged it best to continue at my steady pace in case any change of tack provoked him. I had not yet passed the police station, and when the animal was out of sight, I hurried Celeste on.

"A tiger, sir?" Constable Gawley said, frowning. "Did I hear you correctly? A big cat?"

"Yes, constable, a living, breathing tiger – I know how absurd that must sound," I said. "I expect it's from Tanner's attraction."

"Lord Almighty," he said. "Whatever next? That must be what killed that poor soul."

"Highly likely. It was at this end of Farrington Avenue, but God knows where it'll be now. Do you need help?"

"Thank you, but no, sir," Gawley said. "We'll get a search party together. Please be careful on your way home, sir."

"I will," I said. "Good luck!"

Phyllis! I could not leave her to wander innocently

through Hawksbridge with a blood-crazed wild animal on the loose. I stopped at the Drummond house, where the maid was alarmed at my intensity.

"I don't wish to come in," I said, "but I must warn you that a dangerous tiger is on the loose in Hawksbridge. Please stay in, and close your windows and doors."

"A tiger, sir? Are you sure?"

"Quite sure, and it has already killed a woman. So please take no chances."

With wide eyes, she nodded, and closed the door.

I considered stopping at as many houses as I could and warning the occupants to stay indoors, but I thought that the commotion and possible ensuing panic might aggravate the tiger, and necessitate the opening of doors that the animal could slip through. So I decided to leave that to the police, and hurried on. I startled a number of people I passed on the way with calls of, "Please take care! There's a tiger on the loose!" No doubt they thought I had lost my mind.

At last I was at the inn, and after tying Celeste up in the stable, I found Francesca in her parlour. She rose to greet me with a welcoming smile, which quickly disappeared when she saw my expression.

"Thomas? What's wrong?"

"Something terrible has happened," I said. "A woman – probably Lucy Buxton – has been killed, and a tiger is on the loose."

"Oh, gracious – Hercules?"

"I think so," I said, sitting down.

"Thomas, you look dreadful. A tiger loose in Hawksbridge! This is awful."

I suddenly leapt up. "We must secure all the doors and windows," I said. "I'll go and check them."

"Oh, yes, of course," she said. "Thank you. I'll make us coffee."

Having secured the house, I returned and gratefully

reached for my drink.

"You're in quite a state," Francesca said. "If I may ask, did you see the... the woman?"

"Unfortunately, yes," I said. "She was in the churchyard, all scratched, with her clothes torn off. It does look as though Hercules got at her."

"Oh, Thomas," she said. "The poor woman."

"And yet..." I hesitated and sipped my coffee.

"Yes?"

"Something about the scratches. They looked rather neat."

"Oh, must you?" Francesca said. "I feel faint."

"I'm sorry. It looked... well, not entirely as I would imagine."

"I'm sure neither of us has seen a mauled body before. Who knows what it would look like." She pulled a face.

"True," I said. "You're right." I no longer felt able to trust my own judgement.

"And I was feeling so bright and cheerful today," Francesca said. "We were going to have such an enjoyable morning, and then I was going to treat you to something nice at Myrtle's! But it's selfish to complain, of course, in the circumstances."

"I thought it was my fault," I said, running my hands through my hair. "Thank God it was a tiger. Thank God, even if that sounds heartless."

"Your fault?" Francesca said. "How could it possibly be?"

"Not paying enough attention to Rosabel's murder. I've been distracted..." I realised that I might seem to be blaming Francesca and her need for a solution to the Manners question, so I did not elaborate.

"You have had plenty on your plate, but in any case, it wasn't your responsibility to catch Rosabel's killer, Thomas," Francesca said. "And as you say, if it was an animal that killed this woman, no one could have stopped that from happening."

"Except perhaps whoever let Hercules out of his cage," I said.

"Accidents happen," Francesca said. "It could be criminal carelessness, of course. But let Mr Simmons look into that."

"After he's dealt with the tiger, that is," I said.

"Do you think they'll let Hercules live?"

"After he's got a taste for human flesh? I very much doubt it."

"Oh, what a terrible shame," Francesca said. "Tigers are such noble animals."

"Yes, and Hercules was looking a great deal more noble when I last saw him. Remarkably healthy, in fact."

"And he turned out to be a man-eater. Perhaps he was confused by being out of his enclosure, and lashed out."

"Perhaps," I said. "We'll have to stay here until we get word it's safe. I'm not having you ending up as another tasty morsel."

"Thank you. I think 'morsel' is a kind description in my case, though," said Francesca, pressing her hands to her midriff. "More of a feast. Oh, I shouldn't joke about something so grim."

I smiled. "At least we have a chance to catch up. How is John?"

Francesca got up and went to the window, and was silent for a moment.

"He has children. Lovely children. But he's younger than me, and... we are quite different. His children need a mother."

She turned to face me. "And I don't think that can be me. It's not fair on them, or John, who may want more children with a new wife. And I don't see myself as a mother to such young children, especially with my other commitments." She waved her hand in the general direction of her inn.

"I'm sorry," I said. "I truly am. John is a splendid fellow – I like him. But I see what you mean. Does he agree?"

"He's reluctant to say what he thinks. Perhaps he wants

to hedge his bets, and carry on with me until he finds a more suitable sweetheart. I can understand that, even if it's not an honourable position, strictly speaking. I'm half-inclined to go along with it, because he's... well, good company. But we have to be realistic. It may harm his prospects for marriage to be seen with me."

She turned back to the window and blew her nose. "But there is a bright side. I can spend more time with my other friends, and do more or less whatever I please."

"Let's go riding again soon," I said. "It's been far too long."

She came back to sit at the table, her eyes glistening. "Oh, what a good idea. Yes, I would like that."

I reached across the table and pressed her hand. "And you will always have my friendship, and my help if you need it," I said. "If that doesn't sound too melodramatic."

"Thank you, Thomas," she said. "It's not melodramatic. In any case, I love melodrama, as well you know! What a curious chance it was, sitting in the same carriage that day. You, in a dream and smashing your china, and me, being as impudent as ever. My life was never quite the same after that!"

"Nor mine," I said.

Francesca refilled our cups and we sat in silence for a while.

"Do you think you'll be summoned to London?" Francesca said.

"Unfortunately, I have been," I said.

"Oh, no!" she said. "But that's... It was so long ago, and you were obviously not to blame."

"Indeed," I said. "I'll just have to grin and bear it, and hope for the best."

"Please let me come with you!" she said. "You must have someone with you. I don't suppose Phyllis...?"

"No, she won't be there," I said. "I tried to talk to her, and only managed to make things worse."

"You poor nincompoop!" she said. "You will let me come, then?"

"Thank you. I would like that. But what a lot of trouble for you!"

"Nonsense. I haven't been to London for so long – there are people I can visit, if there's time. My tailor, for one – I need a new riding habit."

"Well, that will make it a hundred times more bearable," I said.

"Good," she said. "That's settled."

A shot rang out in the distance, followed quickly by another, and we looked at each other.

"Poor, poor Hercules," Francesca whispered.

"Perhaps he'll have a new vocation as a rug," I said.

Francisco frowned at me. "Oh, don't, Thomas! That's in atrocious taste."

"Sorry; but I was reminded of Whickham's tiger-skin rug. I noticed it was missing on my last visit. Walter Jenrick had borrowed it."

"Really?"

"Yes, it seems quite a coincidence, doesn't it?" I said. "Whickham said he'd borrowed it for a play. Do you know of anything else Jenrick is working on?"

She shook her head. "No, but he's restless – always coming up with ideas and schemes. So I wouldn't be surprised if he's putting on some play or other, given I've temporarily taken away his employment. You're not suggesting that was Walter you saw, disguised as a tiger?" She laughed. "I don't think he's *that* good an actor."

"No, it was definitely a real tiger. I was just thinking aloud, that's all."

There was a faint hissing sound.

Francesca looked at me. "Was that you?"

I shook my head, and we both listened. There was another, louder, hissing sound.

"A snake?" said Francesca. We looked around the room, and I went into the hall.

"I can't see anything," I said.

Francesca went to the window. "Thomas!" she whispered. "He's here!"

It was Hercules. He was trailing blood, and staggering around the courtyard, making the same strange hissing sound. He legs failed him and he collapsed on the ground, struggling to keep his head up. He soon gave in, and rested it on the cobblestones, his lungs heaving.

"Oh, Thomas!" Francesca said, horror on her face. "Whatever shall we do? We can't just leave him like that, to die alone."

"He might still be dangerous," I said, worried he might lash out in pain.

"Does he look dangerous?" she said. "I'm getting some water for him."

She fetched a bowl and filled it with water, and we both went cautiously out into the courtyard.

Hercules raised his head briefly, and gazed at us before once more resting his head on the ground. His breathing was ever more laboured, and he was wheezing.

"Hercules," Francesca said softly, "Hercules – we have some water for you."

She placed the bowl by his head, and tipped it a little. The tiger summoned enough energy to lap up some water before sinking back again.

Francesca gingerly put her hand out and stroked the tiger's head. "There, there, Hercules. You're with friends. Dear, handsome Hercules."

I was terrified the tiger would rally and grab her arm, venting his fury with the cruel humans who had first captured him, then paraded him, and finally hunted him down. But he had no energy. The wheezing was getting fainter, his breathing slower. It was not long until his breathing stopped entirely, his magnificent eyes now staring without seeing.

Francesca looked up at me, tears running down her face. "Why couldn't he be left alone in India to live out his life? Why must we ruin so much?"

I reached down and helped her off the ground, and she embraced me and wept. I wondered if this was for the death of her relationship with John as much as the tiger's, her suppressed misery having been forced to the surface.

"Do you think he understood?" she said, releasing me from her grasp and searching for her handkerchief. "Do you think he knew we wanted to help?"

"I think so," I said. "You did all you could. He's at peace now."

CHAPTER TWENTY-SIX

"Oh! It's Mr Rufford, isn't it? Come in, come in!"

It was pleasant to be greeted like an old friend by Miss Wooler.

"I was thinking about you just today," she said. "Let me make us some tea, and you can tell me why you've come! Make yourself comfortable."

"Thank you, Miss Wooler. It's a pleasure to see you again."

I settled myself in the parlour, and noted that the white crystals had been brushed off the wall, the pictures straightened, and the room had a generally more kempt air about it.

"Now, Mr Rufford," she said as she brought in the tea. "What brings you to Conundrum? Is your horse happy out there?" She peered out of the window. "What a beautiful animal."

"She'll be fine, thank you. Yes, I'm very fond of Celeste. She's served me admirably, and has the patience of a saint."

"What a pretty name," she said. "Let me see – what did I want to talk to you about? I'm sorry, it's gone clean out of my head. What a ninny I am! And after you've come all this way."

"No, I came to talk to you, Miss Wooler," I said. "I don't know if you remember what we spoke about last time – about the fact that there is a box of documents with your name on it – in a manner of speaking – that you can retrieve from a solicitor, Mr Andrew Barrowman. Documents pertaining to your ancestor, Richard Manners."

"Oh! Of course, of course, I remember now. And you wanted to see these documents. I'm afraid I wasn't terribly helpful, was I?"

"On the contrary, you said that if I could earn your trust, you might let me see them, on the understanding that I wouldn't share anything you didn't want me to share."

"Indeed, Mr Rufford," she said, pouring the tea. "I know that sounds a little harsh, but as I think I told you, I'm a cautious person. And the reputation of my family means everything to me."

"You didn't have a suggestion as to how I might earn that trust, as I recall," I said.

"No, and I'm afraid I don't have one now, even though I can tell you're a fine young man, and handsome too!" She laughed. "But I shouldn't let that sway me, should I? That's what a lawyer would say."

"You should not, indeed," I said.

"Oh dear," she said, picking up her cup. "I feel dreadful about it. What are we to do?"

"I do have an idea," I said. "What if I were to bring you the Manners Ruby?"

She coughed and spat our a mouthful of tea, shakily putting down her cup. Alarmed, I waited for her to coughing to subside.

"Bring me the – oh, Mr Rufford! What an odd sense of humour you have! Well, of course, if you were to do that, it would change my opinion of you. But not necessarily for the better!" She smiled. "Wouldn't that make a thief out of you?"

"Not if it belongs in the Manners family," I said. "Not if it's rightfully yours, because the wager that saw it go to the Whickhams was crooked."

"You think it was? I always thought so, but it might simply be wishful thinking."

"I believe it was effectively stolen from Richard," I said, taking a small bag out of my pocket and placing it on the table next to Miss Wooler's teacup. "That's why I've brought it to you."

Her eyes grew bigger, and she looked from me to the bag, and back. "I'm an old woman, Mr Rufford, with a heart that's no stronger than it should be. And I've never liked practical jokes."

"Please open it," I said.

With shaking hands, she pulled open the drawstring and carefully upended the bag. Out fell the ruby, complete with its clip.

"Heavens," she whispered. "Is it really...?"

I nodded. She picked it up gingerly, examining it and shaking her head. "How did you get this?"

"I plucked it from the eye of a basilisk," I said.

"I don't know what you mean by that," she said, "but I'm sure you'll explain." She got up, went to the window and held the jewel up to the light. "Such depth," she said. "Quite wonderful."

After a moment she came and sat down, and placed the ruby on the bag.

"You got it from Jacob Whickham?"

"Yes. Whickham hid it in the eye of a grotesque statue, and got a jeweller to make a replica for the other eye. The jeweller still had an eye that had a small flaw in it, forcing him to make another, and as we are acquainted, he kindly gave the flawed one to me."

"Ah! And you substituted it for the real one?"

"Yes. I had an opportunity, when I was alone with the statue after Whickham was taken ill."

She shot me a severe look. "You're a determined man, Mr Rufford. One might almost say ruthless!"

"Perhaps, but Whickham was in possession of looted property. He had a letter from Nathaniel to a cousin that boasted of gulling the ruby from Richard. Whickham proved his and Nathaniel's guilt by burning the letter. Perhaps your documents will shed more light."

"And you hope that presenting me with this will be the

act that ensures my trust in you?"

I nodded. "That was my plan, yes." I was losing confidence in it rapidly.

Miss Wooler sighed, and said, "I can truly say that no man has ever gone to such lengths for me. Not even Mr Fountain. But how does this guarantee your cooperation?"

"If I do something counter to our agreement, Miss Wooler, then you have a powerful weapon to use against me. You can destroy my reputation."

"Oh, my word, Mr Rufford! All this for a few papers, that may or may not be of any interest?"

"My friend Mrs Campbell needs to know the truth about Richard Manners," I said earnestly, "and the women buried on her property. Her peace of mind depends on it. And I feel I owe it to Manners himself, and to the women who died. Who else will bring justice and peace to them? The documents have come close to being destroyed, and we might never have known for sure who the women are and how they died."

"Well, I concede that they should be buried with their names and their dignity," Miss Wooler said. "Do you have any clue about them?"

"Yes, I believe they're Nathaniel's sisters, Caroline and Anne. But I can't be sure, and we don't know how they perished. They were supposed to have gone overseas, but this would appear to be misdirection on the part of their family."

"Dreadful!" she said, picking up the ruby and turning it in her hand. "Oh, Mr Rufford. How strange all this is. I do believe you deserve my trust. Who else would do such things for my family, and for these two tragic young women? Very well. We shall get the box, and read everything, and I shall tell you what the world deserves to know about Richard, be it everything, nothing or a little. Is that acceptable?"

"It is," I said. "Thank you!"

She smiled at me. "Mr Fountain wrote to me, you know."

"Really? I'm glad."

"He would like to see me. I don't know." She frowned, and stared into the corner of the room.

"Wouldn't you like to see him?"

"I think so," she said, slowly. "Perhaps. But it may be too painful after all these years."

"Things change," I said. "You're different people now. You can make a new friendship."

"Oh, I wish that were so, Mr Rufford," she said, smiling sadly. "I do wish it. But I've turned away from him for such a long time. How can he forgive me, or I him? Over fifty years of scorn can't be swept away!"

"Not scorn," I said. "Simply confusion, grief, perhaps some embarrassment? All understandable human reactions."

"Yes, I suppose embarrassment," she said. "Shall I tell you why we parted? I've never told anyone this."

"Please do, if you wish," I said. "After all, you have the power to make me keep your secrets."

"So I do," she said, looking pleased. "And so I shall. It was over a poetry book, can you imagine! A volume of rather racy poems by... let me see..."

"Allan Lawrence?" I said.

"Precisely! Allan Lawrence. How did you know? He gave me this book, and my parents found it, and told me how disgusting they thought it was. They didn't know I was seeing Leo, and they didn't think him good enough for me, especially some reprobate who corrupted a young woman with passionate, blasphemous verse. Leo's parents were also furious, for much the same reasons! I had to give the book back, and promise never to see him again."

"I'm sorry," I said. "That must have been devastating."

"It was," she said. "Oh, it was. We were so in love. But we were also afraid of our parents."

"Did you see each other after your parents died?"

"No," she said. "It seemed too late. And as you said, it was deeply embarrassing. Our families knew all about the poetry and it was quite, quite mortifying. It seemed too large an obstacle to surmount."

"But now all obstacles have fallen away," I said. "You may do as you please. You're not beholden to the past, nor any disapproving relatives. And it sounds as though Mr Fountain only thinks of you in warm terms. There is nothing he needs to forgive you for, nor you him. The path is surely clear."

"Oh, Mr Rufford! You make it sound perfectly simple."

"Perhaps it is. Perhaps you just need to write back, and arrange to meet. He strikes me as a lonely man, Miss Wooler. A man you have the ability to make happy. Is this not a wonderful opportunity for you both to have?"

She sniffed. "I'm trying to find a reason you're wrong. It cannot be this simple, after so many years telling myself it's impossible. If we can do it now, why not before? Why have I wasted so many long, tormented years of solitude? Excuse me!"

She hurried from the room, and I could hear sobs and nose-blowing. In a few minutes, she came back in.

"Dear, oh dear," she said. "Are you in the habit of making women cry? Bother you and your sound advice!"

She smiled and blew her nose once more. "I shall write back to Leo, and I'll accept his invitation to dinner. And I shall squarely blame you if I've made a dreadful mistake."

"Fair enough, Miss Wooler," I said. "You're doing the right thing. I wish you much happiness, whether for the duration of a dinner, or for longer."

"You're a sweet boy, Mr Rufford, and I forget whether you're married or not, but if you are, your wife is a lucky woman."

~

At the door, Miss Wooler said, "I shall write to the solicitor – what was his name?"

"Mr Andrew Barrowman."

"Yes, Barrowman, that's it. And I shall get his assurance that I may come in and retrieve my box – Richard's box. Then I shall write to you at..."

"Ramsburgh." I realised I was going to have to write her a letter with all the details.

"Ramsburgh! Indeed. I'll write and tell you when I have the box, and I shall make a cake, and we can go through it all together. How does that sound?"

"Splendid," I said. "And you can tell me how it went with Mr Fountain."

"Oh, I might, if you're good. And – Mr Rufford?"

"Yes?"

"Please return this." She thrust the bag containing the ruby into my hand. "I don't want you to be arrested, and all of a sudden, a jewel doesn't seem so important to me. What on earth would I do with it? Adorn myself?" She laughed. "Besides, I trust you now, jewel or no jewel. You seem to have won me over!"

~

How was I going to unsteal the ruby? On my previous visit to Whickham, I had come well prepared for serendipity, although I felt some remorse for taking advantage of Whickham's illness. A similar chance to be alone with the plaster Worm might not come again.

But there were more important matters to consider. Hawksbridge was in shock over Lucy's violent death, which Simmons appeared to be taking at face value, judging by his comments in the Herald. But in the wake of Rosabel's murder, and from what I saw of Lucy's body, I felt the police to be remiss. Something about the wounds did not seem right to me, although I conceded Francesca's point that I had no experience of this.

Dr Weldon, on the other hand, must surely have had sound grounds for his advice when the police had consulted him, and his office was my destination after seeing Miss Wooler.

As we shook hands in his room, its walls decorated with boxes of butterflies, I tried to forget what I knew about his personal life.

"Was it a medical problem you wished to see me about, Mr Rufford?" he said.

"In a manner of speaking," I said, "but not mine. I had some questions about Lucy, and her injuries."

"Ah," he said, frowning. "Well, as you must appreciate, my work with the police – as with my patients – is not something I'm able to discuss."

"I applaud your sense of professional responsibility," I said, "but when the lives of our citizens are at risk – particularly our young women – I believe some relaxation of this rule may be required."

He leant back in his chair and shrugged. "Well, you may ask your questions, Mr Rufford, and I'll see whether I'm able to answer them."

"Than you. My first question is, are Lucy's wounds entirely consistent with a tiger attack? Having briefly seen her body, there seemed something odd about it."

Dr Weldon looked uncomfortable. "How do you mean, odd?"

"I mean that the wounds seem strangely regular and neat, for a vicious attack."

He thought for a moment. "Perhaps. I have to confess the wounds were not as I expected."

"In what way?"

"In other circumstances, I might have concluded that they were caused post-mortem. There was surprisingly little coagulation around the outside of the wounds, despite a large quantity of blood being present. And..."

He paused again.

"Yes?"

"Well, as you point out, the cuts were quite consistent and precise, whereas the animal scratches I've seen tend to be more haphazard in their appearance. Although of course I've never seen the result of an attack by a tiger before."

"Interesting," I said. "So in fact, you have severe doubts that this attack was as it seems?"

He looked away. "I suppose there might be an explanation. The victim may have died of shock, before the animal attacked, and so the mauling was post mortem."

"But would that explain the amount of blood found?"

"Ah, no," he said. "Probably not, since the blood would not have flowed as freely after death."

"And the nature of the cuts might be explained by use of a knife?"

"That is a distinct possibility."

"And you explained all this to Inspector Simmons?"

"I did," he said, taking up a pen and twisting it in his fingers. "He was sceptical it could have been anything other than an animal attack. I was rather surprised, to be truthful. His mind seemed to be made up."

"I suppose it's natural to accept a convenient explanation, and one that doesn't require a lengthy investigation," I said. "But when a dangerous criminal is at large..."

"I have sympathy with your view," Dr Weldon said. "But I can only supply an opinion. It's for the police to follow the evidence as they see fit."

"Indeed," I said. "If I thought it would make any difference, I would try to persuade the Inspector to think again."

"I would not counsel against it," he said, gazing intently at me. "This is entirely between you and me," he continued, "but you might ask yourself: why would Simmons be so incurious? Is it to his advantage?"

"Good Lord!" I said. "That's quite an allegation. What makes you say that?"

"Oh, I make no allegation. I'm merely speculating. But there are rumours..."

"Yes?"

"You can ask Lucy's sister. She's a patient of mine. Naturally, this is already a breach of confidence. But I'll give you her address. Please destroy it as soon as you can, and don't mention my name."

He pulled out a pad of paper and started writing. "I have many female friends and patients, Mr Rufford. I want Hawksbridge to be a place of tranquillity for them once more, not one of fear."

~

The Buxton house stood apart from its neighbours in a quiet street on the east side of Hawksbridge. Dating from the last century, it was a far more impressive dwelling than I had expected for one of Lucy's occupation. As I approached, I could see all of the windows were barred, and the path to the front door was lined with railings to prevent the visitor from wandering off around the garden.

I pulled the bell, and immediately there was a loud barking. A hatch opened, and a hostile female face appeared.

"Yes?"

"Good afternoon, ma'am," I said. "My name is Thomas Rufford, and I would like to speak to Miss Ethel Buxton, if I may."

"On what business?"

"I wish to offer my heartfelt condolences."

"Thank you. Consider them accepted. Anything else?"

"Yes – I would like to see Lucy's killer caught. I mean, her actual killer. And I think you might be able to help."

There was a pause, in which the barking continued and I assumed I would be shooed away, and the hatch shut. But instead, I could hear bolts being slid, and the door opened. The woman, holding onto the collar of a huge mastiff, beckoned me inside. Her eyes were reddened, evidently from crying.

"Don't mind Brutus," she said. "He won't bite you unless I say so."

The mastiff turned its head to stare at me suspiciously as I followed her.

She shut the dog in the kitchen, and gestured for me to go into the drawing room.

I sat down in an armchair.

"I'm Ethel Buxton," she said. "I'm the staff now – I'm selling the place as soon as I can. Did you say Thomas Rufford? Didn't I read about you?"

"You probably did, ma'am," I said. "I've helped the police now and again."

"You don't want to go mentioning them, Mr Rufford," she said with a grimace. "Not the best friends, us and them. I mean, me and them, now."

"I was horrified about your sister, Miss Buxton. The whole town is in a state of shock and grief."

"Well, I don't know about that," she said. "Everyone knows what Lucy was. But she was my sister. I've done my share of bawling about it. Now I have to look to the future."

"You have a magnificent house to sell," I said. "That will be a wrench, I'm sure."

"Not a bit," she said. "I'll be glad to go. I've helped Lucy over the years, and she's helped me, but I was getting heartily sick of it all. Do you want a sherry? I've started already. Got into the habit of late."

"That would be most pleasant, yes please."

She poured our drinks and said, "Yes, it's all very well having a fine house, but there's a price to pay. Visitors of all kinds. Nastiness from drunken clients or just townsfolk who hate us – that's why we had bars put in. Brutus is our guardian angel, though the ugliest one you ever saw!" She laughed.

"Do you know," she continued, "I feel a bit light-headed? And it's not just the sherry. I loved my sister, despite everything, but I feel... it's awful to say it, but it's a relief. I don't want to live like this any more. I'm going to buy a little place in a village – away from wagging fingers and tongues – and there'll be enough left for a modest pension."

"I'm sure that will be delightful," I said. "I wish you the best of luck getting settled."

"I shouldn't be talking to you like this," she said. "I don't know what you're about and what you want with me. But as you can see, Mr Rufford, I'm slightly drunk."

She raised her glass. "If you're here for what Lucy gave, I'm afraid I can't oblige," she said. I smiled and shook my head. "She had her line of work, and I kept to mine, which was to mind the money and the house. And get her out of scrapes when need be."

"You have done admirably looking after the finances," I said, looking around the large drawing room with its handsome fireplace and lithographs of Northumberland castles. "I had no idea the business paid this handsomely."

"Oh, yes, well, for Lucy it did. An older gentleman settled a large amount on her, which helped us buy this place. And if you'd seen the gentleman in question, you'd understand why she charged so much!" She cackled at this.

"So you had no trouble with the police, operating out of here?" I said.

"Not really," she said. "Lucy got around. A policeman

isn't immune to feminine charms, and why would they want to poke a hornet's nest?"

"You mean the police might be embarrassed...?"

"Oh, indeed. Take that Mr Simmons. It was brief, but enough to make him well disposed to us."

"How fortunate for you," I said. "But I fear that it may work against Lucy now."

"How do you mean?" she said, refilling her glass.

"Well – is there anyone connected to Lucy that Simmons might fear? Enough to close down any investigation of her death?"

"But heavens above, Mr Rufford! It was a tiger! What more should he be investigating, other than that fool Tanner for letting the tiger out?"

"What if it wasn't a tiger, Miss Buxton? Was there someone else who might be able to reveal uncomfortable information about Lucy and Inspector Simmons?"

Miss Buxton became more serious. "I suppose Lucy was apt to talk sometimes. Perhaps someone else knew."

"Can you think of anyone in particular?"

"Not really."

It seemed that not all of Miss Buxton's inhibitions had been removed by the sherry, but I judged that she was thinking of someone. I tried another line of attack.

"I was at Jacob Whickham's house the other day. Is that a familiar name to you?"

"Oh, Lord yes!" she said, laughing. "Awful man. Lucy worked for him – well, him and his friends at the Wormers. They got up to all sorts. I said to Lucy, when she came home grumbling – I said, 'why do it? It's not worth it!' And she brought out a big roll of notes and said, 'oh yes it is!' Well, I couldn't argue with that. They pay well, I'll say that for them."

"Do you know what for, exactly?" I said.

"Well!" she said. "I'm not sure I could tell a gentleman."

"Not so much of a gentleman as to be completely

unaware that a man's interests can be... unusual," I replied.

"Their silly tales of monsters," she said. "That's what it was about, mainly. Do you know the story? Maidens get tied to a stake so a big worm can come and eat them. I would expect there to be a knight to rescue them, or some such, but oh no, they just get eaten. What a charming story!"

"I gather they re-enact it in some way?"

"Yes, but instead of a monster... well, there are several monsters, and they're all members of the Wormers! The maiden gets... you can guess, Mr Rufford. It ends differently from the story, let's put it that way."

"I see," I said. "Your poor sister."

She shrugged. "She didn't have to. She could have stopped, and we would have managed. But she liked the money, and some of the time, she even seemed to enjoy the work! Well, it takes all sorts to make a world."

"Did she mention a Peter McNulty?"

"That name rings a bell. I think that was the poor fellow with the Wormers. Oh dear, oh dear!" She giggled and knocked back the remains of her sherry.

"Poor fellow?"

"Apparently he couldn't rise to the occasion. Can you imagine – with everyone watching? He was so mortified, Lucy said, that he ran out of the house."

I shook my head. "Horrible. And he thought Lucy was his lover."

"What a simpleton," she said. "They'll have to find themselves a new maiden. But who'd take that job, apart from my mad sister?"

"Have there been others, to your knowledge?"

"Oh yes," Miss Buxton said. "Do you want to hear a sad tale?"

I nodded.

"Well, there was once a pretty young woman from a good family, from whom she became estranged. So she had nothing and no one, and fell in with the Wormers. She was offered a decent sum of money to come and play with them, and this she did. But of course, not knowing the tricks of the trade like Lucy, she became pregnant. And they encouraged a young Hawksbridge man to marry her, though he didn't realise she was with child."

"Did he find out?" I said.

"As far as I know, not even to this day. And that's why I can't say who it is. It might drive him mad if he knew."

"But perhaps the mother has information –"

"If she does," Miss Buxton said, "you'd need a seance to hear it. And as for her poor daughter..." She shook her head.

The dog started barking.

"I'd better deal with Brutus," she said. "He's getting restless. Bless him, he knows I've said too much already!"

CHAPTER TWENTY-SEVEN

I WOULD have to employ all the tact I could muster, I thought, as I sat waiting for Mr Simmons. My optimism that I could change his mind was draining away. It would be a brave man who could challenge the seemingly conclusive evidence of a mauled body and a tiger roaming the streets.

"I hope this is important, Mr Rufford," the Inspector said, taking a chair in the room with whose bare walls I was now far too familiar. "I have a full day ahead of me." He softened his tone a little and added, "Although we are, of course, grateful for the warning you gave about the escaped animal."

I nodded. "I'm aware you're a busy man, Inspector, but I believe this is crucially important," I said. "It's about Lucy Buxton."

"A great tragedy, of course," he said, "but I can't see what else there might be to say about it, unless you have information about the negligent keeper. It was an appalling accident, though certainly an unusual one in my experience."

"I don't think it was the tiger that killed Miss Buxton," I said. "As you know, I saw her body, and the marks were... suspicious."

Simmons smiled. "Surely you're not an expert on animal attacks, now, Mr Rufford? How many big cat maulings have you seen?"

"None, of course," I said, "but –"

He held his hand up. "I see what's happening here. You're rightly concerned about Rosabel Gardner's murder – and yes, that was clearly a murder, even if we don't yet have the culprit. And this puts you in a certain frame of mind to judge other violent deaths in the same light. Perfectly understandable. But a policeman can't let his judgement run along such rigid lines. Not all evil in this world is caused by humans, Mr Rufford. Sometimes accidents happen, and there isn't a person directly to blame. Although we will of course come down severely on the keeper, who appears to have a reputation as a drunkard. But he's not a murderer."

I found this admonishment patronising and frustrating.

"Is it possible, Inspector, that in trying not to be seen to jump to one conclusion, you may have jumped too far the other way? The evidence of the wounds is surely enough to rouse suspicions. Did you not think it curious how neat the cuts were?"

"As I said, Mr Rufford, you're not an expert in these matters. You're simply trying to fit the facts to your prejudices."

"Then at least listen to Dr Weldon," I said. "He has severe doubts about it. He has opinions about the presentation of the wounds and the blood that I believe you have dismissed."

"I beg your pardon?" he said, evidently astonished. "You have spoken to Dr Weldon about this? That is simply outrageous!" He stared at me, his face reddening. "It seems to me I've given you far too much leeway in your interference with police work here. I'm a patient man, Mr Rufford – I must be, in my profession. But this is too much. How dare you suggest that I can't be trusted to judge the evidence in this case? This is impertinent, Mr Rufford! Grossly impertinent!"

Hearing the Inspector's raised voice, Constable Taylor put his head around the door. "Is everything in order, sir?" he said.

"Perfectly," Mr Simmons said. "You may show Mr Rufford out. Our meeting is concluded."

"I'm afraid it isn't," I said, not moving. "I have more to say."

Constable Taylor stood frozen in the doorway, an expression of horror and fascination on his face at my insolence.

"I would like to speak with you alone," I said.

"No," Simmons said. "My constable will stay."

"Very well," I said. "It concerns your interest in Lucy Buxton. Other than a professional interest, that is."

Simmons went a deeper shade of red, hesitated, and then made a gesture with his head to Taylor, who nodded, withdrew, and closed the door.

"What the devil are you playing at, sir?" he growled.

"I have no interest in judging you," I said. "I just ask you to consider that a brief friendship with the deceased may have inadvertently influenced your thinking. It would be convenient to close the case quickly, in a way that few would contradict. It would reduce the risk of embarrassment – and perhaps the end of your career."

I did not dislike Mr Simmons, even if I did not always agree with him. And so it gave me no satisfaction to see the fear and distress in his eyes.

"You might not even be conscious of thinking like this," I added. "I simply propose the notion for your consideration, in the hope of a balanced decision."

The Inspector drew a deep breath. "And what makes you so sure of this slur on my character, Mr Rufford? It's an extraordinary accusation, especially for one with the sword of Damocles hanging over his head due to his own adventuring."

"I've spoken to Lucy's sister," I said. "She strikes me as a reasonably reliable witness."

He sighed with exasperation – partly, I suspected, at his own weakness.

"You really are an infuriating busybody, sir. Damn you! Yes, I knew Lucy Buxton briefly. It was foolish, but there it is. But if you think that has affected my judgement on this or any other case, you're deluded, sir. Perfectly deluded!"

"Were you not slightly afraid that if Lucy's killer were to be human and not feline, and you went after them, they or their associates might try to interfere with all of your important work in Hawksbridge? Or that it might simply emerge during the course of a trial?"

He sighed again. "Lucy had connections that were... unsavoury. But it was not a deliberate train of thought on my part."

"And then there's the fact," I said, "that the victim was Lucy – someone who might be easy prey to a man, given her line of work – and not anyone else in Hawksbridge. It's too convenient."

The Inspector rubbed his face. "God damn it," he said. "I thought Dr Weldon's conclusions more than a little fanciful. I've always said that the simplest explanation is usually the correct one, and to imagine a conspiracy involving a tiger... it's absurd. But perhaps an alternative explanation might be considered."

I nodded. "You could have another word with Dr Weldon," I suggested.

"I might," he said. "Well, sir, I shall review all the possibilities, regardless of the consequences, even though I still favour an animal attack."

"Thank you," I said. "Obviously I'll betray no confidences from Lucy's sister."

He nodded. "This changes nothing in regard to the London matter, Mr Rufford. Is that understood?"

"Perfectly," I said.

~

Mr Harris' visit two days later was a welcome one, as gloomy thoughts were squatting in my brain. We settled down in the suitably masculine environment of my study.

"We've missed you," he said. "You and Phyllis. Olivia tells me to tell you not to be a damned fool and throw away your wonderful marriage."

"So you're on a mission?" I said. "And she said 'damned fool'?"

"No, no, those are my words," he said. "She was much harsher than that! Ha! No, of course not, she was as tactful as ever. And it's not really her mission. I wanted a chin-wag anyway. And some of your delightful Cognac," he added, raising his glass to the afternoon light. "Olivia says this is too strong for me and makes me crotchety."

"I'll watch out for it," I said, "and switch your glass for a coffee cup if necessary. You probably know I made a complete hash of my last conversation with Phyllis."

"Yes, that did come back to us – bad luck, old boy. Sometimes the ladies misunderstand us. I expect it was something like that, no?"

"Partly," I said, "and partly an unwise remark or two. I can be a complete idiot. Maybe even a damned fool."

"We all can, we all can," said Mr Harris. "A hazard of being human. But I'm sure you can reverse it. Phyllis dotes on you."

"The question, is that enough? But thank you. I'll try again, as many times as it takes."

"That's the spirit," he said. "Now, I may have some news for you, on the subject of poor Miss Gardner's death. And perhaps even Miss Buxton's." He paused for dramatic effect.

"Yes?"

"Strangely, Mr Tanner has been arrested! At least that's what I've heard. Apparently an article of Miss Gardner's clothing was found at his Wonderland."

"Good Lord," I said. "So his arrest can't merely have been for negligence. I didn't think I'd really get through to Simmons."

"How's that?"

"Ah – I went to see him, to ask if he might review the evidence surrounding Miss Buxton's death. I felt uneasy about it."

"Well, I'll be jiggered!" Mr Harris said. "Getting grumpy old Simmons to change his mind? What *can* you have on him?" He laughed.

"But I've been encouraging Louise to work with Tanner," I said. "Another blunder of mine."

"No harm done," he said. "Where is the estimable Miss McNulty? I was hoping to have a word about millipedes."

"She's in Newcastle for a few days, being treated to a tour of the Natural History Museum. She's lodging with the director of the Society and his wife, no less!"

"All on account of some ancient marks on a rock! Wonderful," said Mr Harris. "She and the children would get on so well," he added, his expression turning glum. "When will we see them again? The house is so quiet and tidy. It needs a family, and all their noise, which I used to find annoying and now I crave! But they had to spread their wings, of course."

I nodded, thinking of Flora, and how much she would have changed when she returned. If she returned. Hawksbridge would seem parochial, and not all her memories of it were good.

"Anyway – may I?" he said, helping himself to more of the Cognac and refilling my glass. "I've been passing the time by writing some verse. Trying to, at least. I thought I'd write one about fossils. Does the millipede have a scientific name, I wonder?"

"I'm not sure they've come up with one yet," I said. "But I suppose you could use the word 'invertebrate'."

"Ah, yes, invertebrate. What rhymes with that... Celebrate? Congregate? Vacillate? Inebriate? No, no, that's no good."

"Scintillate?" I suggested.

"Aha!" he said. "Let me see... 'A tiger bold may terrify, and snakes may scintillate, but nothing chills our human blood like huge invertebrate.' How about that?"

"With work, you may have something," I said.

He gave me a look of mock offence, and then said, "I know, it's not exactly Keats. We shall change the subject. I hear Francesca has gone away for a couple of weeks."

"Oh? Do you know where to?"

"To stay with a friend in Edinburgh, apparently. But can you blame her? That poor animal dying in her yard, on top of everything else. A complete change will do her the world of good. And then she'll return, and we can all enjoy her energy and schemes again."

"I look forward to that, assuming I'm not in jail," I said.

"Oh, my dear fellow, that won't happen, surely?"

"It's all too possible," I said. "All this" – I waved my hand – "could vanish like a mirage. Phyllis will find someone else. I'll linger behind bars – or worse – until I'm utterly forgotten."

"Oh, pull yourself together, man!" Mr Harris said. "A good lawyer will sort you out. I'm sure there's no real evidence."

"Please excuse my self-indulgence," I said. "I think Olivia may be right about the Cognac."

~

Louise returned from Newcastle the following Tuesday evening, but was too tired to say much except that she had had a fascinating trip, and would tell me all about it in the morning. Before retiring, she had taken from the hall table a letter addressed to her in an unfamiliar hand.

I had been imprudent enough to down three-quarters of a

bottle of wine that night, and by the time I had arisen in the morning, there was a note waiting for me on the breakfast table.

Dear Thomas,

Apologies for rushing off again so soon. I slept like a petrified log and feel much refreshed. I will tell you all about my trip later today, but Francesca has written to say that she is back early from Edinburgh - it seems due to a quarrel with her friend! - and she wants my opinion about the theatre today. I do not at all know what I can offer, but I will be happy to see her and exchange our news.

Affectionately,

Louise

It seemed a shame for Francesca to have cut short her much-needed break. But apparently it had been just sufficient to put her back in the saddle. I wondered with a certain pique why she had not invited me as well; but after all, I had enjoyed male company with Mr Harris, and women were likewise allowed to seek out their own kind.

Then it struck me that the letter I had seen on the hall table was addressed to Louise in a hand that was not Francesca's. That could be explained by her housekeeper or butler addressing the letter: perhaps she had dictated it.

But the urgency of Francesca's letter was curious. Could it not have waited until Louise was better rested from her trip? Would she not normally have delighted in the excuse to call at Ramsburgh? And surely she did not know Louise so well as to solicit her opinion in this fashion.

As I ate my toast, I grew more anxious, and when Mrs Felton came in with more coffee, I asked how long Louise had been gone.

"Oh, only about an hour," she said. "She was in a cheery mood! I've never seen her cheeks so rosy."

"She took the trap?"

"She did – she said she wanted to drive it herself and not keep anyone waiting if she and Francesca were there all day, as she thought they might be."

"Did she say anything else?"

"No, my dear. Is there something wrong?"

"I don't suppose so," I said, "but I want to check anyway. Can you ask Howard to get Celeste ready, please?"

~

The fact that Tanner had been bailed on Monday – according to the staff grapevine – did not help my nerves. But having been freed, would he immediately make plans to commit a crime? I doubted it, and someone else was on my mind. A person who had had dealings with Rosabel; who was known to participate in disgraceful acts of sensual indulgence; and who had met Louise, albeit briefly.

Celeste was happy to gallop for short bursts, but I did not want to over-exert her, and so I failed to catch up with Louise on the road.

As I came into the courtyard of The Angel Arms, the cart was there, and the pony had been tied up in the stable. I tied Celeste up, and looked over at the theatre. Its door was shut, and I could hear no unguarded female chattering and laughing as I had hoped, either from the theatre or the house.

I had had the foresight to grab my keys for the inn and all

its buildings before leaving. I approached the theatre door, and put my ear to it: to my horror, I heard a familiar male voice delivering a kind of incantation. All my suspicions were confirmed. It was Walter Jenrick.

CHAPTER TWENTY-EIGHT

"HAVE you prayed tonight, Desdemona?" I heard Jenrick declaim from behind the door. "If you bethink yourself of any crime, unreconciled as yet to heaven and grace, solicit for it straight."

There was a pause. "Say your line!" he hissed. "Alas, my lord!"

I heard Louise whisper. "Louder!" Jenrick said.

"Alas, my lord, what do you mean by that?" Louise said, in a quavering voice.

"Well, do it, and be brief," Jenrick said. "I will walk by: I would not kill thy unprepared spirit; no; heaven forfend! I would not kill thy soul."

I unlocked and opened the door as quietly as I could, and slipped into the theatre. On the stage, which was raised a foot or so above the floor, Louise was kneeling on a tiger-skin rug before Jenrick, who was dressed as a soldier. Louise had her hands behind her back, presumably bound, and Jenrick held some sheets of paper up to her.

"Say it!" Jenrick commanded.

"Talk you..." Louise faltered. "Talk you of killing me?" Tears ran down her cheeks.

I walked towards them with trepidation, and they both stared at me, Louise with a mixture of torment and relief.

Jenrick shot me a look of disgust. "Oh, Mr Rufford. This is most inopportune. Can't you see I'm busy?"

I could now see that Louise had a rope halter around her neck, which Jenrick tugged.

"No closer, please," Jenrick said. "If I pull this any tighter, your friend will die, rather unpleasantly. I'm afraid she's not a natural on the stage. And alas, she has so little time to improve."

"Let her go, Jenrick. We will talk about how to end this to our mutual satisfaction."

"Since you have just robbed me of my satisfaction – albeit momentarily – I'm not in much of a mood to parley. Now place your hands on your head, and walk slowly towards me."

I obeyed.

"Stop there," he said when I was a few feet away from him. "This is not a stage sword." He drew the sword halfway out of its scabbard, flashing it in the light, and replaced it. "I have a choice of how I might dispatch my Desdemona. If you try to run, she will instantly die."

I looked towards the door, wondering if I might make a dash for help.

"Ah – you left the door open," he said. "Please go and lock the door, and come back to this spot."

I did so, though it was terrifying to seal myself in with a homicidal madman. But I knew Louise would certainly be killed if I left the theatre. I returned, and handed over my keys.

"Thank you," he said. "I do hope Mrs Campbell is well, Mr Rufford. Unfortunately I have to tender my immediate resignation from the company, for obvious reasons. You have interrupted the pleasure I was hoping to take from this novice before her untimely demise – such a scandalous rewriting of the Bard's instructions, although I think in the spirit of the play! However, I shall restrain you, and you may watch, as your final entertainment." He stepped back, his eyes still fixed on me, and reached down for the remaining coil of rope.

"What is the purpose of all this, Mr Jenrick?" I said.

"Purpose?" he spat. "That's a word that has no meaning to me. There's no purpose to anything, so I must take satisfaction where I may. I suffer from a terrible sickness, Mr Rufford – I'm plagued by profound ennui. And I've always been attracted to Shakespeare's darker creations. The role of the villain fascinates me, and to play it for real is a true joy."

"But what did Rosabel Gardner do to you? Or Lucy, for that matter? They were innocent young women with their lives ahead of them."

"Lucy, innocent?" he said, smiling. "You're quite the humorist. There was nothing innocent about Lucy. She was anyone's – Tanner's, mine, even carrying on with that idiot friend of yours. She was happy enough to blame Tanner for the spanking I gave her. She got no more than she deserved, so spare me the tears over that conniving trollop. Now Rosabel – you may be more on the mark, although no woman is truly innocent. Anyway, a virgin is a far more interesting quarry. I made her a woman, albeit for a tragically brief time, before giving her the supernatural frame of the Devil's Teeth. A whimsical touch, I know, but what a beautiful painting that would have made. Her father gave me the opportunity by bringing her to me, and who am I to reject good fortune?"

"Why would Mr Gardner do that?"

"Ah, because Mr Gardner has delusions that I don't have time to go into. You'll have to ask him. Oh – you won't be able to, will you? How thoughtless of me."

"Just tell me this," I said, racking my brain for ways to delay Jenrick's next move. "Why was Jacob Whickham so interested in Rosabel?"

"Now that I *will* make time for," Jenrick said. "It's an amusing tale. Poor Jacob got it into his head that he was her father. Her mother was no better than Lucy, at least for a spell when she was penniless, and she played our maiden when we were younger. Any of us could have been the father, but no, he insisted it was he. And so began a tedious obsession, first with the mother, then with the daughter. It was pitiful. And he had that garish statue built in the image of Mrs Gardner!"

"So it was Whickham who sent Rosabel the Lawrence volume?"

"Oh, no, that was me. I took it from his library. As

numerous people can attest, he was unnaturally taken with Rosabel. The authorities, had they looked, would have found a painting of Rosabel. It should have been enough to have had him arrested."

"So why implicate Tanner?" I said.

"I was in two minds about Jacob. I felt this plan was weak. So I thought of Tanner, and how I could satisfy a long-standing itch. I befriended the animal keeper and got him drunk, so it was easy to steal the keys and duplicate them. I enjoyed thinking about how I would dispose of Lucy, who held far too many secrets about me. The poor whore trusted me to the end, when I suffocated her in the churchyard by pushing a stocking into her mouth, and faked the mauling."

"Is that what you used the tiger-skin for?" I desperately tried to think of ways I might overpower Jenrick without imperilling Louise.

"Unfortunately the claws were not as sharp as I had imagined, but it gave me a guide for where to slice. And I had to go back for some pig's blood because hers hadn't flowed nearly as dramatically as I wanted. Still, it's been highly instructive, for future adventures."

Jenrick selected a length of rope, and still holding Louise's leash, withdrew his sword, and cut it.

"And how did you implicate Tanner?" I said. I wondered if I could grab the halter from him in time, before he could bring the sword down on me. Time was quickly running out and I would soon lose the freedom of my hands.

"For that, I decided to sacrifice two delightful keepsakes – Rosabel's shift and drawers. To hedge my bets, I planted the drawers in Whickham's house – inside a piano that was never played – and when I released the tiger, I planted the shift at Tanner's in case of need. I had hoped Hercules would get the blame for Lucy's death, but when I heard Simmons had changed his mind and was going to investigate the death as murder, I knew I could hardly pin both deaths on sickly Jacob.

But Tanner was perfect for it. So I let it be known about the shift. Having Lucy be seen with Tanner before her death, and now in possession of Rosabel's shift, this should be more than enough to earn him the noose. But enough explanations. Put your hands behind your back and turn around."

I stood my ground. "By murdering us, you'll lead the police straight to your door. They will find the evidence here."

He laughs. "The police! They are buffoons, sir, and unable to tie their own bootlaces, much less know a criminal when they see one. For you are a criminal, Mr Rufford, whether you killed that butler or simply covered up your escapade. As for evidence, I shall place Louise's shift at Tanner's, and perhaps a token from you, since I still have the keys and his tawdry folly has been shut down. Tanner will once more get the blame. You will both pay a visit to the ice house, which, as I recall, has room enough for two, and I doubt you'll be found any time soon."

"Multiplying your crimes is a show of arrogance that will get you hanged," I said. "If you leave us alone now, and never return, you have a chance of escape – and perhaps your existing crimes will not be traced to you."

"Oh, I have no fear of that, Mr Rufford. You see, despite my precautions, I've decided to go travelling before I risk the inconvenience of a police interview. I'm a wealthy man now, and may go where I please. I have the Manners Ruby. I had to nudge Jacob along to meet his maker, but it didn't take much, given his lamentable state of health. I only had to admit to my night of pleasure with Rosabel, and his stupid, failing heart broke. And in the confusion I was able to take the jewel – which is now my destiny, opening any door I wish. What do you find so amusing?"

"That you can't tell a priceless jewel from a worthless piece of paste," I said, summoning as much bravado as I could. "You're holding a fake, Mr Jenrick. Perhaps as a dramatist and actor, you can appreciate the irony!"

"You're desperate, Rufford," Jenrick said irritably, "and I can understand why. How could you possibly know such a thing?"

"Because I have the original," I said, "which I swapped with a rejected copy I obtained from the jeweller. I'm able to tell you precisely from which monster's eye I took it. I will even give you the real ruby, if you let us go."

"Ha! It's an imaginative bluff, considering you're no writer, Mr Rufford, but I'm afraid it will make no difference. Turn around."

"Then take a look," I said. I detected uncertainty in his voice, and hoped to force a chisel into this chink. "It's an ingenious copy, but if you look closely, you will see the truth. You can find the small crack Mr Belford made when fixing the mount."

He stared at me for a moment, and then sheathed his sword. He reached awkwardly beneath his breastplate into a pocket and withdrew a small bag. Fumbling with the drawstring, he dropped the bag and the jewel fell out.

"Blast!" he cried, and dived for the jewel, but it disappeared into a large gap between the old paving slabs.

I leapt forward onto the stage and pushed him over so he cracked his head on the flags, then grabbed the rope connected to Louise, and she rushed off the stage.

The only route open to us was the gallery, so we ran up and went as far forward as we could. While Jenrick rubbed his head and searched in vain for the jewel on his hands and knees, I untied Louise's hands and removed the halter. Shaking, we looked around for how to protect ourselves.

"God damn it," Jenrick said, unable to find the ruby, and stood up. "Never mind, I'll look for it after I've dealt with you."

He unsheathed his sword and mounted the steps to the gallery. We attempted to hide behind the chairs, but they offered precious little protection, and Jenrick spotted us at once. He advanced, removing his sword, which he lifted above his head as he approached me.

"Let us remove the irritant, and be left with the pearl!" he cried, at which Louise, now closest to him, pushed the chair in front of her with all her might. It slammed into him; the sword flew out of his hand, whereupon it gouged a groove through the flesh of my left cheek and clattered to the ground.

For a moment, Jenrick tried to regain his balance as his body swayed over the low parapet. His arms flailed balletically, but it was no use. Gravity pulled him over the wall and he fell with a scream to the ground, his breastplate clanging against the stone flags.

There was a silence, and then a groaning sound. I looked over the parapet; blood was flowing from Jenrick's head, and bone was protruding from one shoulder. And yet he was moving, crawling painfully towards the door like a half-crushed spider. Louise and I watched, horrified, at his slow progress. He managed to find his key with his good arm, and hauled himself up with an almighty groan to unlock the door. Opening it, he sank back to the ground and crawled out of sight, a trail of blood marking his path.

Louise and I held each other for a short while, despite the blood flowing down my cheek and onto the nightdress Jenrick had provided for her, and then made our way down from the gallery.

"Stay there," I said, and Louise gratefully sank into a chair, nursing her bruised throat.

The trail of blood led to the ice house, which was a short distance away. I could see Jenrick's twisted legs disappear into the neck of the building, and then he was still. I cautiously approached. Jenrick was face down, motionless. I waited for any signs of life but there were none, so overcoming my dread, I rolled him over. His dead eyes were staring and his mouth, covered in loose soil, was open in a silent scream. What had those eyes seen, or his aberrant imagination created, in his final moments? I turned him back over, and quickly withdrew from the ice house to be violently ill.

CHAPTER TWENTY-NINE

We were too shocked to say much to each other. I retrieved my keys from Jenrick's body – an unpleasant task – and took Louise into Francesca's parlour while I went to get her clothes from the theatre.

I waited outside the room while she dressed, and decided that I could send someone to fetch Celeste later. I held a cloth to my face to staunch the bleeding and drove the trap to the police station, trying to absorb the events of the last hour. I was deeply worried about Louise's state of mind. She was wrapped in a blanket and shivering; I wanted to distract her with innocuous conversation, but I struggled to find a suitable topic.

Simmons and two constables listened to my explanations with growing dismay.

"That is most distressing, sir, ma'am," he said. "We'll go to the theatre directly. I suggest you get your face seen to by Dr Weldon and then go home, and I shall visit tomorrow for a fuller description, if I may, sir."

"Please do, Inspector," I said. "If you think you'll be up to it?" I added, to Louise. She nodded.

"I was having my doubts about Mr Tanner, sir," Simmons said. "I shall of course drop the charges. There's a lot to straighten out." He shook his head. "But thank God our killer is accounted for. I'm glad you came to no serious harm, Miss McNulty."

~

Mrs Felton was carrying a tray of dirty crockery when she looked in on me in my study.

"She's sleeping," she said. "What a dreadful shock she's had. And you, of course, my dear, and your poor face! But, mercy – imagine if you'd decided to have another piece of toast this morning..."

"Or slept a little longer," I said. "I know."

"It doesn't bear thinking about," she said. "Her ending up like poor Rosabel, or Lucy Buxton!"

"Quite," I said. "But it's frustrating that Jenrick has evaded proper justice."

"That devil got what he deserved," she said, the crockery rattling with her vehemence. "And to think Louise delivered the fatal blow, with that chair! Good for her."

"I'm not sure that will help her recover," I said. "It's awful to be responsible for taking a life, no matter the blackness of the soul concerned. I'm not sure one ever really gets over it."

"Yes, of course," said Mrs Felton. "The poor, dear girl. Is there anything else you need?"

"A small glass of sherry to steady my nerves would be splendid. But I assure you, one glass only. My head needs to be straight for the Inspector tomorrow."

~

"Good morning!"

I raised my head from the notes I had been scribbling. "Oh, good morning, Louise! I didn't expect you to be up so soon. How are you feeling?"

"Better," she said, touching her neck. "Still rather sore, though. And you? Your cut looks painful."

"Thank you – it's not as bad as it looks," I said. "Dr

Weldon did a decent job with the stitches."

"Good. Anyway, I couldn't bear to be on my own. I want to get over this business with the police, and then try to think of other things. I still haven't told you all about Newcastle."

"Indeed!" I said. "I'm looking forward to it."

Mrs Felton came and fussed over her, and insisted she had bacon and eggs to keep her strength up.

"I killed a man," Louise said, toying with her bacon. "I can't believe it."

"If you hadn't, I wouldn't be here now. Neither of us would. It was entirely necessary, and incredibly brave."

"I suppose there was no other way," she said.

"None at all."

"How strange to think we could be lying where those sisters lay, perhaps undiscovered for just as long," she said. "Who would think to search in a grave so recently vacated?"

"I hope Simmons would, or Francesca," I said. "Anyway, that's too grim. We are both alive. I believe there are cultures in which a man whose life is saved must follow his deliverer wherever they go, to protect and serve them. Is that my future now?"

Louise smiled. "I don't think Phyllis would approve. And you *will* win her back. Besides, it sounds rather eerie and inconvenient. I release you from that duty. And if you hadn't come after me... well, we are all square."

~

"So if I've understood you correctly," Inspector Simmons said, having written copious notes, "Jenrick first intended to frame Jacob Whickham for Miss Gardner's murder, hence the book of poetry, and then changed his mind, and framed Philip Tanner instead."

"Correct," I said. "You may still find evidence inside a piano at Whickham's, which he planted as a precaution."

"But Whickham had in fact been interested in Miss Gardner?"

"As far as I know, only because he believed himself to be her father, Inspector. I've no idea if this is in fact true. I hope it won't be necessary to mention this to Mr Gardner."

"I don't see any good coming from that," Simmons said. "Might I ask you to give me your opinion on a motive for Jenrick's crimes, sir?"

"Certainly," I said. "I think Jenrick had an unnatural interest in the idea of restraining women." Simmons glanced uncomfortably at Louise. "Perhaps it stems from the myth of the Hawksbridge Worm. I believe that story has caught his already perverted imagination, together with the thrill he got from acting out villainous behaviour on the stage. He confessed to boredom with life, and this is how he dealt with it. Naturally, he must already have had debased morals to countenance what he did."

"Yes, that all rings true," Simmons said. "But why pick his particular victims?"

I thought for a moment. "Jenrick was contemptuous of Whickham's obsession with Rosabel's mother and insistence that Rosabel was his daughter. So when Rosabel became available to him, as it were, via Mrs Campbell's theatre production, and perhaps the pretext of extra acting tuition, he had the perfect opportunity. He could indulge his own perversions as well as hurt Whickham just for the malicious pleasure of it. At least that's my interpretation of it." I deliberately omitted the detail of Mr Gardner's as-yet unexplained role shortly before her death.

"I see," said the Inspector. "What a disgusting man he was. And Miss Buxton?"

"I think three motives were at play," I said. "They had an association going back some years, involving many secrets. He didn't want to have to rely on her discretion in the coming years, and killing her also enabled him to indulge his lusts. He and Tanner were sworn enemies, so implicating Tanner in the murders would give him the ultimate revenge. He was nothing if not economical, Mr Simmons – he liked to solve several of his problems at once."

Simmons nodded and scribbled.

"Finally, if this is not indelicate – have you any idea of the reason he went after you, Miss McNulty?"

Louise shrugged. "When he brought my brother back in a drunken state, he leered at me in rather a horrible way. So he may have formed some kind of notion at that point, to feed his awful impulses and – as Thomas says – to implicate Mr Tanner. I think it was largely a matter of convenience – I trusted Francesca, and her inn and theatre were both unoccupied, so he was able to trap me. Far too easily, I must confess."

"Not your fault, ma'am, not your fault," said Simmons. "Now then, sir, you said he intended to make off with this jewel – the Manners Ruby. That he would make a new life for himself."

"Yes, Inspector," I said. "I was heartily sorry when Jenrick said Whickham had died."

"Another tragic victim, to be sure," he said. "But we heard nothing about a stolen jewel when we went to Whickham's house to investigate. Perhaps the servants were unaware? Or complicit?"

"Ah!" I said. "I think I may know what happened. The jewel may appear to be still in its place, due to the presence of copies Whickham had commissioned. The jewel should have been in the right eye of the Worm and the Maiden statue. Presumably he had an extra made in case the original ruby needed to be removed for cleaning, or some other purpose. The staff must not have noticed the switch."

"Oh, that hideous thing," Simmons said. "Gave me the

fright of my life. And he told you exactly where he kept this valuable jewel, sir? Seems a bit unwise."

"Yes," I said. "He was quite drunk, and extremely proud of both the statue and the ruby. I'm afraid he was in need of a friend. I was not really suited to that role."

I drew the bag from my pocket and placed it on the table, glad that I finally had the opportunity to return the ruby. I merely had to tell a small, harmless lie.

"I retrieved this from the theatre, Inspector, and kept it for safekeeping."

Simmons looked at me with raised eyebrows. "Indeed, sir?" He emptied the bag onto the table.

"And you say this is the genuine Manners Ruby? Interesting."

Giving me another quizzical look, he brought out another small bag from his own pocket.

"Then what do you suppose this is?" He tipped the bag out, and the ruby's doppelgänger rolled onto the table.

"One of my sharp-eyed constables spotted it shining in a crack on the floor earlier this morning," he said.

"Goodness," I said, innocently. "How extraordinary." I mentally kicked myself for not making a search, but we were in no condition to do this after our close call, and in any case it had slipped my mind.

"Yes, sir," Simmons said. "Do you have an explanation?"

"Well," I said, with only momentary hesitation, "I can only suppose that Whickham had a number of copies, and Jenrick was hoping to pass off the fake jewel as real, and double his fortune. Or he didn't know which the real one was, so he took both just in case, for later identification."

"And he dropped both of them in the theatre?" said Simmons.

"It seems so," I said.

Simmons thought for a moment, looking from me to the jewels and back again, and then sighed. "Very well." He wrote a couple of phrases on a page in his notebook, ripped the page out, tore it in two, and placed one half in each bag along with the corresponding jewel. "We wouldn't want them becoming confused, would we, sir?"

"No, Inspector, certainly not."

He smiled and looked at me intensely. "Of course, we don't know which is really the genuine ruby, do we?"

Had he deliberately trapped me? "Ah – no, I suppose we don't," I said. "I only assumed..."

"Yes, sir," he said, after a brief pause. "You weren't to know." Did I detect sarcasm? It was sometimes hard to tell with Simmons.

He put both bags in his pocket.

"The important thing is, sir, ma'am – you're both safe, and so is the ruby, whichever one it is. I won't take up any more of your time. You've both been most helpful."

"Our pleasure, Inspector," I said. "I'll see you out."

At the front door, I hoped that if he had any doubts about me, he would confront me with them now. Instead, he simply said, "Thank you, sir. I do hope Miss McNulty's nerves are quickly restored to full health. I may see you in London soon."

Standing by his carriage, he turned and said, "Good luck, Mr Rufford."

~

The following day, I received one letter, and Louise two. Phyllis had written to each of us expressing horror and sympathy about recent events, and I was discouraged to find that the tone of my letter was not substantially different from that of Louise's.

However, I did not have time to dwell on this, since

Louise's other letter was from Peter's new employer, a Mr Riddle, expressing grave concern at Peter's health. He had a bad fever, and it was, he said, of the utmost importance that we come to his bedside before it was too late. It was a blow to the prospects of Louise's recuperation from her ordeal, and once more she was distraught.

The address was a farm at Pygden, some fifteen miles south of Hawksbridge, and, hiring a carriage and pair, we determined we could manage the round trip in a day if we set out first thing the next morning. When we arrived just before midday, at one of a string of farm labourers' cottages, it was a shock to see Peter's condition. Even through his thick beard he was visibly gaunt, perhaps due to the exertions of his job as well as his illness. The fever had stolen away his usually ruddy complexion and his bedclothes were damp with sweat.

Mr Riddle's daughter, Maud, had taken the part of nursemaid, mopping Peter's brow and bringing him soothing broth when the fever abated.

Waiting by Peter's bedside for him to wake, I cast my gaze over his new lodgings. The little terraced cottage was only a decade or so old and therefore not as decrepit as I had expected, although still drab inside. It seemed extraordinary that Peter had willingly swapped a life of hedonism for physical labour in modest surroundings. And yet his indulgence had only made him miserable; here, he had purpose, honour and distraction.

Finally, he murmured, turned over restlessly and opened his eyes.

"Oh!" he grunted. "Louise! and Tom! You came."

"My poor brother," Louise said, holding his hand. "I've been so worried. We both have. You're so hot! How long have you been like this?"

"Can't remember," he said, wiping his forehead. "A day? A week? I pay time no heed. I have sloughed off all. I work, I sleep, I work again – such bliss! Give me the shovel! Let me slice the earth." He laughed. "I embrace the earth now, Tom. We are great friends, and one day, she'll embrace me. Such glorious sleep..."

He drifted off again, and I exchanged an alarmed glance with Louise.

When he came to again, he seemed calmer, and slightly cooler.

"Peter," I said gently, "Jenrick is dead."

"What?" he said, raising his head. "That devil gone to Hell? What hero did God's work? Let me shake his hand!"

I placed Louise's hand in his. "This is her hand. Your brave sister was forced to fend him off."

Tears rolled down Peter's cheeks. "Thank you, sister. Thank you. It was my fault. If I had only said something... Maud told me about Lucy. Was that really the tiger, or...?"

"Jenrick," I said.

He groaned. "She should not have died, if I'd simply been honest. Instead, I ran away, and walked, and walked until I lay in the muddy road, and Mr Riddle found me. My salvation! I've been able to repay a speck of their kindness, and have saved a little more, to repay you, Lou, and you, Tom."

"There's really no need," I said.

"I will!" he said, with spirit. "I must. Don't take that from me."

"If you wish it," I said. "Why did you run, Peter?"

"Prop me up, please," he said, and I rearranged the pillows so he could sit up, which he did with some difficulty. This position helped to clear his head.

"So many reasons, I've lost count. My debts were piling up. Jenrick threatened to tell the police about Oliphant if I was ever indiscreet. Damn my loose tongue. Then he bragged about his days in London, acting and directing. About how when playing Othello he found himself squeezing the life out of some poor actress in a rehearsal. He had an urge to carry on squeezing, and had to be pulled off her before he killed her."

He coughed and signalled for some water, which Maud helped him drink.

After having his fill, he continued: "His company refused to act with him, and that's why he came back to Hawksbridge. I should have followed my instincts and had nothing to do with him after that."

He paused for breath. "But I was weak. He persuaded me to join the Wormers, and then he humiliated me. What would Lucy not do for money, when I had stupidly thought... I was beside myself. I had to get out of that hell. Something broke inside me. So I went back to Ramsburgh, and to my eternal shame, made your beautiful wife give me money and take me into Hawksbridge. In my bitterness, I even tried to poison her against you about Oliphant. Dear God, I hope I didn't succeed."

I remained tactfully silent while he wiped a tear from his face.

"I had intended to get a coach somewhere, anywhere – perhaps Newcastle, or London where I could utterly lose myself. But in town, I had the misfortune to meet one of my creditors, who became unpleasant – in short, I was left with no money and in a state of despair. What little was left of my pride did not allow me to return to Ramsburgh. So I walked until I could walk no more. I had intended simply to die. But Mr Riddle found me."

He smiled and squeezed Louise's hand. "It was the best thing that could have happened. I'm only sorry I may not be able to repay you, if this fever..."

"Oh, don't say that!" Louise said. "You seem stronger than when we arrived."

"Perhaps," he said. "Do you have somewhere to stay?"

"We've only hired a carriage for the day," I said. "But we could –"

"No, no," he said. "There's no point. I don't like to be seen like this anyway. You must be getting back, before the light goes."

Louise held Peter's hand to her cheek. "Oh, Peter..."

"I'm well cared for," he said. "Maud is a remarkable nurse, and an even better friend."

Maud, who had been standing discreetly in a corner, smiled and looked down. I had formed the distinct impression of tenderness between the two.

"If I get better, I'll be happy," Peter said. "If I don't, I'll have had more than most miserable souls in this world. You don't need to worry about me. Thank you for coming to see me. I need to sleep..."

Maud helped him into a comfortable position, and he quickly fell asleep, wheezing rhythmically.

"I know he's done wrong in the past," Maud said to us, "but he has such a good heart, bless him! I'll look after him, as long as it takes."

"I've no doubt you will," I said. "You have been so kind."

CHAPTER THIRTY

FRANCESCA'S staff had sent word to Edinburgh to say that her property had become a crime scene.

"I really couldn't enjoy Edinburgh," she said, when we had started our journey to London, "knowing what you and Louise had been through!"

She held onto my arm as the coach sank into a large rut in the road. "To think Jenrick – our own trusted employee – was responsible for that mayhem! And that I was talking to a callous murderer, and even sympathising with him over the loss of Rosabel. I must have been blind."

"He fooled a lot of people," I said. "I had my doubts about him, but John Hutton had the keenest instincts."

"The more John complained about him, the more I assumed he was simply jealous! I should have listened. And I confess when Jenrick's reference never arrived, I thought little of it. Dear Lord! We might have saved Miss Buxton, at least, and avoided your anguish in the theatre."

"A more dramatic scene will never be played out there, I think," I said.

"I hope to God not," Francesca said. "How is Louise?"

"Recovering well," I said, "and sanguine about her brother. She's heard nothing yet, since we visited."

"I must say I couldn't stand Peter," Francesca said, "but if he's really changed, as you say..."

"It seems so," I said. "Whether he has much time left in his new incarnation, I don't know."

"I hope the fever passes soon," she said.

"Will you try again with the theatre?"

Francesca looked at me reproachfully. "Of course,

Thomas! You should know by now that I don't give up so easily."

"You would be justified, given –"

"Nonsense," she said. "The best way to purge Jenrick's odious ghost from the theatre is to use it, with as much noise, colour and laughter as possible. I shall find another director. But one play will never be performed there: Othello."

~

Our overnight stay in Newcastle, and then in London, had the strange quality of a pleasure trip, since I stinted neither on accommodation nor food.

It was the day before my hearing, and our London hotel seemed to mock me by embodying the opposite of all the qualities I might have to get used to if incarcerated. There was an excess of light from the enormous windows, the furnishings were sumptuous, and the many staff were impeccably polite.

"The last meal of the condemned man," I remarked at dinner.

"I won't allow you to get gloomy, Thomas," Francesca said, elegantly cutting a sliver of roast beef. "You will go in with your head held high, and they will see you for what you are."

"Yes, a trespasser and a thief!" I said.

"A thief? Whatever can you mean?"

I lowered my voice. "I stole the Manners Ruby."

"You did *what?*"

Some of the other diners stared at us. "Don't worry," I said. "I gave it back to the police."

"Thomas, whatever possessed you...?"

"I had to earn Miss Wooler's trust, or we would never see the Manners papers. It was the only thing I could think of.

And I'm pretty sure that ruby is rightfully hers anyway."

Francesca put her cutlery down and pressed her fingers to her temples. "You're giving me one of my headaches. You silly, silly boy, Thomas. Do you *want* to be sent down tomorrow?"

"I agree it was reckless," I said, picking up my wine glass. "But I felt I had little to lose, what with the prospect of incarceration, and Phyllis having left. I was in a bleak, almost nihilistic state of mind. I wanted to feel more in control of things, and that gave me the opportunity, and something of a thrill. Anyway, I don't think Inspector Simmons was any the wiser, although he was a trifle confused by the presence of two rubies."

"Two?"

"Including the copy Jenrick stole, thinking it to be the genuine article."

She shook her head. "I should be grateful, as you have done this for my benefit, but I'm really very cross with you."

"I'm sorry," I said, draining my glass. "How can I make amends?"

"Well, I dare say you could make yourself useful," she said. "After we've eaten." And she tapped her aching temples.

~

Blackheath Magistrates' Court was designed to inspire respect for the establishment and the rule of law, from the long flight of stone steps culminating in a columned portico, to the lavish panelling in the corridors and courtroom. The Royal Arms insignia hanging over the magistrates' bench provided a welcome and almost incongruous splash of colour, and under it, the three magistrates sat reviewing their notes.

I was instructed to stand in the dock, which made me feel

the fate of Richard Manners and the Whickham sisters, and second, an unresolved strand of Jenrick's rampage through Hawksbridge.

For a third time I knocked on Mr Gardner's door. He put up no resistance and ushered me in. In the parlour, a sturdy bag was in the process of being packed, and the room was even barer than before.

"I'm going away, Mr Rufford," he said as he gestured to the single tatty chair remaining in the room. "It's for the best. I'll not be missed."

I sat down. "I came to see if you had any questions about Jenrick. There is perhaps some satisfaction, if not entirely a sense of justice, to be had from his death."

He shrugged. "I thought he were my friend. That's how I met my Clara. I was obliged to him. I'd heard stories, of course – he could be a wild one. But so can a lot of lads. He thought I should be the one to have Clara, and she consented, which I didn't dare hope for. How could I not see him as my friend when he made the both of us happy?"

I nodded. It seemed Mr Gardner might still be unaware of Jenrick's motivation for marrying Clara off.

"You'll be wanting to know the truth now," he said, looking at his feet. "Since you helped kill him, it's fair. But God, is it hard to tell!" He put his hands to his face.

"My Clara died of the stone," he said. "It went from here" – he placed his hand on his breast – "to her mind." He shook his head. "All I wanted – except Rosabel – was took from me, and cruelly so. I couldn't stand it. I thought the pain would go, but it didn't. Years and years of it. I tried things..."

He paused. "What kind of things?" I said.

"Mushrooms," he said. "Walter knew where to get them. They sent me strange places, sometimes to the place where Clara was. A few months ago, I gave some to Rosabel too. I wanted us to both see Clara. I dreamed of all sorts, of being in Clara's arms and knowing bliss, and then when I woke I were in..."

He clutched his face again, and wiped away tears. I waited for him to continue, fearful of what he would reveal.

"I were in Rosabel's bed, with my arms around her, and no nightshirt. I didn't know what I'd done. I began to think I had... but she couldn't remember anything. It tormented me, something dreadful."

"It would," I said. "A terrible thing for any decent father to imagine."

"I thought I had spoilt her whole future life. What man would want her? And Rosabel is – was – all I had in the world. I drank with Walter. Like a fool, I told him of my fears, and he said he knew an old woman who could... make it whole again, for a price. I heard nothing for a long time."

"And then," I said, "Rosabel's interest in the theatre gave him an opportunity."

"Damn him to Hell, and me with him," he said, his voice cracking. "He said to bring her along that afternoon, and to tell her she would be having a lesson with him. He would persuade her to see the old woman at his lodgings, and be healed. And I trusted him. Rosabel was suspicious of going to see him at that hour, and didn't want to go, but I persuaded her, God help me. I trusted that snake, as if I were a newborn babe with no whit of sense!"

He struck his fist repeatedly against his skull.

"I didn't want to believe it were him who killed her. Not the man who gave me my wife. So I told myself something else must have happened to her. She must have wandered off, and been snatched by... who knows what. Navvies, fairies, anyone but him."

"So you didn't suspect Jenrick at all?" I asked.

"Perhaps at the back of my mind. And I feared for what Walter might say if I mentioned his name. The sickening shame of it! I could never show my face here again. That's if he didn't simply kill me."

"I see," I said. "I can perfectly understand your fear."

"But if I'd spoken up, Lucy Buxton might still be alive. I can't live with all this any more. That's why I've taken the Queen's shilling."

"You've joined the army?" I said.

"Aye," he said. "I'll do my penance, and if my maker should take me, then I have no quarrel with Him. That way I'll be in peace. But I'll do some good before then, God willing, and kill a few of our enemies."

"Are you sure that's necessary?" I said. "There must be other ways you can come to forgive yourself."

"It's for the best," he repeated. "I don't know any better diversion than fighting to the death, and I must have ease from my terrible thoughts."

Which would be all the more terrible, I realised with dismay, if he knew the irony of Jenrick's brag in the theatre: that Rosabel had retained her innocence up until Jenrick's attack.

CHAPTER THIRTY-ONE

"DID you hand it back?" Miss Wooler asked as she led me to the parlour. "Please tell me you did."

"The ruby? Yes, I found a way to return it, I'm glad to say."

"Oh, splendid. And you weren't caught?"

"Fortunately not," I said.

"Thank goodness!" she said. "Leonardo told me about that awful man Mr Jenrick. Good riddance, I say. I was taught never to speak ill of the dead, but there are exceptions!"

"Aha, Miss Wooler!" I said. "So you've seen Mr Fountain! May I ask –"

"Oh, stop it, young man," she said, playfully slapping my arm. "All in good time. But first, the box, the box!"

I sat while she pulled a shabby wooden object towards her, with trembling fingers.

"All this trouble about a battered old box!" she said. "I do hope you won't be disappointed."

"Me also," I said. "Perhaps Richard is playing a joke on us."

She smiled. "Wouldn't that serve us right for getting so preoccupied with it? For my own sake, I wouldn't mind a bit being teased by my great-grandfather. Oh! I promised you tea and cake! Let me get it."

She made her way into the kitchen, and, tantalised, I hoped that Miss Wooler would not now have to make the cake from scratch.

The box was satisfyingly blackened and cracked with age: it had evidently been antique even in Richard Manners' time. No doubt many precious items had once been stored there –

perhaps lay there still – and the box had become a treasured possession in its own right. A key was in the lock, and I saw that the fading ribbons and red seals had not been removed. Miss Wooler had been remarkably patient.

"There was no key when I went to see Mr Barrowman," said Miss Wooler, as she carefully placed the tea tray on the table. "But he had a hunt around and managed to find one that fitted."

"May I pick it up?" I asked.

"Of course," she said.

It was quite heavy, and shaking it gently, I felt objects move inside.

"There's certainly something in there," I said. "Not just documents."

"How exciting!" she said. "Well, go on, then! You may open it."

A strange reluctance had come over me. Manners had planned for this moment over a century earlier, and I felt his ghostly scrutiny. What right had I to judge his keepsakes, much less express disappointment if they did not give up all of his secrets?

I broke off the seals, removed the disintegrating ribbons, and turned the key. I looked at Miss Wooler, and lifted the lid.

Inside, several objects were wrapped neatly in linen cloths, on top of a pile of documents. I lifted the first out and removed its swaddling: it was a well-executed miniature portrait in a plain wooden frame. I recognised the sitter at once from the two lockets. On the back, faded, curvaceous lettering identified the subject as 'R. Manners'.

"Behold, your great-grandfather," I said as I passed it to Miss Wooler.

"Oh! Richard!" she said, staring intently at the portrait and unable to speak for a few moments. "I've never seen a picture of him. How handsome he is!"

"Yes – I recognise him," I said. "Each of the Whickham

sisters – if they are indeed the bodies found in the ice house – had a locket with a portrait very much like this man. Of course, I could be mistaken."

"Both women?" said Miss Wooler. "Surely not. I think you're letting your imagination run away with you!"

"Quite possibly," I said.

The next linen mummy contained two little bags, and from each bag I drew a glass vial, stopped with a cork. I held them up to the light.

Each vial contained a lock of light brown hair, of different shades. Around the neck of each bottle was a label with faded lettering; on one was written 'Anne', and on the other 'Caroline'.

Were they love tokens, or gruesome trophies?

"You may be giving too much credit to my imagination," I said to Miss Wooler as I passed her the vials. "This hair belonged to Anne and Caroline."

"My word," she said as she peered into the vials. "Richard, what have you been up to?"

I looked into the box, and after retrieving a bundle of documents, I removed the top one and started to read aloud. I had difficulty with some words, as they had been blurred with liquid splashes, the source of which I could guess when I reached the end.

Dearest Richard,

I clasp your letters to my wretched bosom, and consume your loving words over and over. I dare not think of the cottage! - and our embraces within.

Three things are clearer to me than ever. First, that my love for you burns as fiercely as the sun. Second, that it can never truly be consummated. Third, that you must take Caroline as your wife. I have watched you together with tears of love, and hopelessness, and happiness to know that you and she will know the joy of marriage. She is the older, cleverer and more worthy of this inestimable prize.

Do not think of me as a friend lost, but rather as a champion found - a champion for the blessed union that you and my beloved sister will know. There is a beauty in my sadness, just as a song in a minor key bestows joy on the weeping listener.

Go to her, my already-bygone love! Go to her with the knowledge that you are double-loved. I renounce you, my darling, though I burn forever on the pyre of my ardour for you.

Yours ever and never,

Anne

We stared at each other. "Well!" said Miss Wooler. "I really... this is... My word. The poor creature."

"Shall I read another?" I said, and she nodded. I unfolded the next letter, written in a similar but not identical feminine hand.

My dear friend,

I must start with the stuffiness of a beneficiary to

her patron with a thousand thanks for your generosity. How much further can we now extend our help for those many unfortunate females in marital distress! You have been so attentive to our humble endeavours, and we can never repay our obligation to you.

There is another obligation I must speak of: the duty of love which we must now both cast off. I believe you understand my passion for you, and I have seen in your eyes the love you likewise bear for me. I should thus regard with jealousy my sister's love-lorn look, a tenderness you return unconcealed. And yet, I do not.

My little sister, who has blossomed so gloriously, is now the bride you deserve and must take: you are the master she has dreamed of, and to whom she longs to submit. Of the two, I may be the more calculating, my mind more inclined to making order. Anne has always followed her heart. And so it is easier - although still the hardest task of my life - for me to take off the cloak of my passion, and lay it down so that the proper marriage may be made.

If this sounds cold, I assure you I am quaking as I write this; because I thrust a knife into my own

Whickham sisters' death. Perhaps Mr Fountain had been right to fear a considerable scandal on behalf of the Church.

"Thank you," I said. "May I enlist Mrs Campbell's help? She can be trusted."

"Of course, of course," she said. "I only ask for her discretion. Who knows what you may yet find! And then you can come and tell me all the details, to save my aching eyes."

~

"If you have sympathy for Richard," I said as I removed the box from my leather bag at Halfpenny House and placed it on the parlour table, "you may need to steel yourself."

To my surprise, Francesca leapt from her chair, and putting her hand on my arm, said, "Then let's delay the moment of truth. I'm in too good a mood for it. You promised to ride with me, and there could there be no better day for it!"

There was joy in her eyes as she raced me across the fields, down to the ruined mill and back. For those minutes, the gloom of the last few weeks was forgotten, leaving only exhilaration. The reassuring pound of hooves, the swirling air, the smell of earth and grass: and above all, the sun's precise, intense exhibition of every object, as if every stone, branch and blade was exquisitely significant. This vigorous existence from one second to the next seemed, momentarily at least, to provide all the meaning required from life.

All too soon, the horses were stabled, and Francesca, her face healthily rosy, led me to a garden bench with a view of the house.

"I hope you have quite made up with Phyllis," she asked as she sat down.

"I have," I said. "And yes, I've told her all about the

ruby."

"Good boy," she said, as though I were an obedient dog. "But how did she take the revelation that her husband is a thief?"

"Obviously she was not entirely happy about it, but she accepted the notion that the sisters – and Manners – might be able to rest in peace once the truth was known. And that taking the jewel was necessary to achieve it. And my insistence that the ruby doesn't rightfully belong to the Whickham family – I hope I'm right about it."

"Not to mention the fact you were crazed with melancholy," Francesca said.

"Well, perhaps I have no real excuses," I said. "But it has at least unlocked the box of secrets."

Francesca sighed. "I think I'm ready for them now. What did you find?"

I told her about the sisters' letters, and the little I had read of Manners' letter to his dead correspondent.

"Oh!" she said. "What a tragic, romantic pair. Could Richard really have taken their lives? And that of his poet friend? Surely not. Did the impossible choice between the two women drive him mad?"

"Well," I said, "Richard had mentioned his fear of losing the ruby – that it might kill him. So if you give credence to such things, losing it to Nathaniel could have cursed his life, and those he loved. Or he could have believed the curse, and that was enough."

"Perhaps. We shall have coffee," Francesca said, "and then we'll tackle the box."

~

Francesca was entranced by Richard's portrait, the sketches, and the locks of hair. I picked up Manners' letter, and found the superior light in Francesca's parlour speeded my comprehension of it.

To my dear, dead friend, Philip,

How fare you in Heaven? You have surely earned your place, unlike me. I miss you and our letters, so I will continue to write in the hope that you will look down with a Heavenly telescope (no doubt far superior to our mortal playthings) and read my words. Besides, I have no one left in whom I can confide my darkest thoughts.

When composing my prior letters, I have often wished for more to say, to decorate the tedious recital of my life's events. Now I long for the opposite.

First I must explain about the Anaukpetlun Ruby and how I came to lose it. As you know, I have entertained a belief in a kind of curse on with the jewel, whereby its loss, not directly its possession, would be my undoing.

I was reckless, half-believing my life depended on it, yet feeling a need to break such an unholy and irrational dependency. So when Nathaniel suggested a wager, I was compelled to let fate take its course. It was in a rare moment of revived friendship with

Nathaniel - for it had been dwindling for some time - that we drank and looked into the fire, and spoke of the old times.

Presently, he sprang up and took hold of the coal bucket. "Let us mark our friendship with a wager!" he cried. "Let us say a number, and whoever has the number closest to the true number of coals shall win. If I win, you shall give me your ruby. If you win, I promise to withdraw to my farm and you shall have this inn. And I will no longer stand in your way in the matter of marriage - if you can only make up your mind!"

I had a glimpse of my own future happiness, a freedom to visit those wonderful creatures if they agreed to stay on at the inn. Indeed, they would be helped in their charitable undertakings, with rooms aplenty for distressed folk. And if I lost the wager, I would be freed once and for all, and come what may, from the shadow of that wretched jewel, as would my daughter Julia to whom I did not wish to pass an accursed inheritance.

Added to which, I had drunk immoderately. So I accepted, we spoke our numbers and counted the coals, and I roundly lost. Nathaniel made a show of regret, but held me to our bargain. I handed him the jewel, and I was not struck by lightning or afflicted with a pox, or any of the other things I had dreaded.

A week later, my sense of relief abruptly ceased when I received a letter from Caroline, in distress at Nathaniel's treatment of her and Anne. A maid had told Caroline that she had seen Nathaniel counting the coals on the evening of the wager, before I arrived. So Caroline and Anne had remonstrated bitterly with Nathaniel, receiving in return a whirlwind of fury.

To my distress, Caroline spoke of a fever that had taken hold of the three of them. Alas, I have been confined to my desk with a thousand tasks, but I shall go and visit them as soon as I can. What shall I say to Nathaniel? We have only the word of a maid. The Church would not sanction my appearance in court over a drunken wager. There may be little I can do, and perhaps it is for the best.

As if this were not enough; with a heavy heart, I have killed my friend Allan Lawrence! But he was a false, wicked friend. What think you, Philip? There will be no more venom towards the Church, no more wild, carnal imaginings or tales of rapacious *monsters. It is long past time to put him to rest, and I think he had but little wit left in him.*

Yours perpetually, though you are an angel in Heaven and I a miserable sinner,

Richard

"You are vindicated!" Francesca said when I had finished the letter from Manners. "The ruby should no more belong to the Whickhams than to the Campbells. But why have we never heard anything about Lawrence being murdered?"

"He veers from reason to insanity," I said. "It reads strangely."

She took up the packet of letters. "May I?" she said. "You can rest your eyes."

I nodded, and she began to read the next letter.

Philip, my patient confessor,

All is lost. My loves are both dead. It is the ruby, I know it is! What a fool I was to let it go. Why did I not take heed of the curse? All over a bucket of coal!

"Good God," I exclaimed, and Francesca took a deep breath before continuing.

I worked long nights and burned many candles to finish my tasks, so that I might hurry to the inn. The Devil take me - had I not been so conscientious, I might have saved them!

I found Nathaniel feverish in his bed, tossing and

turning and muttering. I could not find Anne and Caroline - they were not in their beds - so I shook Nathaniel and gave him water until his tongue was loosened. He admitted that he had fallen out with his sisters, and he had bid them fetch ice for their fevers, and then locked them in the ice house to teach them the rightful respect and submission that he said should be accorded to him. He then stared up at me with horror on his face, saying "Oh! What day is it? How long have I lain here?"

He stumbled to his feet and he led me to the ice house, which he unlocked. There we were met with a ghastly sight. Anne and Caroline were clasping each other, but they were white, and cold to the touch. Nathaniel had slept for nearly two days, and his sisters, already having the fever, had succumbed. Nathaniel fell to his feet in grief, and by God's grace I did not kill him, although I was sorely tempted.

"I will be hanged," he said, again and again. After his agitation subsided, he implored me to help conceal the manner of their deaths. When I refused, he threatened to implicate me - he would say that rejection by both sisters had made me angry, and that I had locked them in the ice house. He further reminded me of other confidences I had disclosed to him over many years, and suggested reasons we could give for the women's absence.

I knew that I would lose my position in the Church by association with this calamity, and all prospect of employment. Indeed, I could hang in Nathaniel's place, or on the same gibbet, leaving my darling Julia fatherless. And so - Philip, forgive me - I at length agreed to his plan, and we buried both women in the ice house.

We have burned their clothes and possessions, and will say they have gone to seek a new life in the Colonies.

I know I will go to Hell, on many accounts - I dare not hasten the end of my forfeit life. So my torment will be unendurable, and forever. And I will not meet you again in that sublime existence that, despite my many doubts, I had always hoped to attain.

Your miserable, wicked, and cowardly friend,

Richard

CHAPTER THIRTY-TWO

Not long after dawn, the screech of a peacock disturbed us. But it was more than pleasant to lie together, listening to Nature waking up, and clawing back lost time.

"My muse didn't follow me back to my father's house," Phyllis said. "She seemed to like it better here."

"You're inspired again?" I said, clasping her hand.

"Yes! Gloriously," she said, turning her head towards me. "I'm so lucky. And then I think of poor Rosabel, and how few chances she got. I feel terribly guilty, and even guilty for not feeling guilty enough!"

"She would hardly want that," I said. "But yes, it's utterly unfair. I hope Jenrick is burning in Hell."

"Oh, let's not think of that monster. I have a plan to distract us. Perhaps in the spring..." She hesitated.

"Yes?"

"We might go to Venice? It's such a shame we didn't manage it in the summer."

"Venice..." I said. "Yes, we should. You need the stimulation for your writing, and I need a change. And of course it's the most romantic place on Earth, if you avoid the more malodorous canals."

"Oh, wonderful!" Phyllis said. "But you must take on no obligations before we go."

"I'll be on my guard to avoid any situation that promises to be remotely interesting."

"Thank you," she said. "We can take a wonderful old palazzo."

"Yes – where you may lean on the bedroom window sill and gaze at the sunset over the canal, while being amorously attended to by your dashing husband."

"You're so crude," Phyllis said. "But I dare say that might not be completely objectionable."

Titian jumped up next to me and circled before resting his chin on my arm, which I indulgently offered.

"He's getting more affectionate in his old age," Phyllis said. "Is that sweet, or slightly sad?"

"A little of each," I said. "I trust you'll be like Titian and your love will only increase. When you're fifty, you should be draping yourself over me at every opportunity."

She raised herself on one arm. "But then at sixty, I might suffocate you."

"The loving squeeze of death," I said. "A mixed blessing; but there must be worse fates. Better that than to have no release for one's affections at that age." I paused, and then added, "I must go and visit Mrs Tambard and tell her what I've discovered about Manners."

"I'm not sure I like the association of those thoughts," Phyllis said, with an exaggerated pout. "She needs no excuse to show her admiration!"

"Actually, she's much more your admirer than mine. And I promise I won't let her steal any more kisses."

"I'm sure the one she extorted from you is sufficient for many pleasant imaginings," Phyllis said. "I won't begrudge her that, when I can get all the kisses I want."

"How many is that?"

"Oh," Phyllis said, "so many, that I must make a start immediately."

I rolled onto my back, to Titian's disgust, and Phyllis slowly, delicately touched my lips with hers.

~

The previous day, I had not enjoyed watching Francesca's cheerful disposition evaporate as she had read Manners' shocking letter. But to balance the awful circumstances of the Whickham sisters' last hours, we now knew that Manners was not responsible for their deaths. A double murder of passion would have been far worse a revelation.

We were cheered, as much as was possible, by the bitter-sweet letters of love from Anne and Caroline: their intensity was moving, and we could not condemn Manners for his inability to choose between them. Richard's strange claim to have murdered Allan Lawrence still baffled us, and Caroline's mention of Bram needled me, since this name appeared in one of Lawrence's poems. I did not say it aloud; but had Manners simply borrowed the name, or had he taken Lawrence's cat after dispatching his friend?

Francesca brightened up, and she was able to send me off with a smile and a plea to visit her again soon with Phyllis. I had returned with the rest of the papers unread, but a glance had revealed them to be mostly poetry, which I assumed to be unpublished.

The morning's pleasures still fresh in our minds, Phyllis and I took a turn in the garden with Fox, before I let my wife rejoin her muse. I returned to my office with a jug of coffee to decipher the remaining papers. Manners wrote of his affection for his daughter, and there were speculations on the nature of love. But there was one poem of particular interest, which I read with relief as well as astonishment, and which prompted me to write to Francesca immediately.

The Scapegoat

When a child, the days shone brightly
Pleasures many, woes worn lightly
Evil was a story tell'd me
Whilst my loving mother held me.

Expell'd from childhood's chrysalis,
Gorg'd I on the heady bliss
Of wisdom borrow'd, men to follow
Notions brave to mould tomorrow.

Seeping in with fact and theorem
Came a dark and oily serum
Doubt, despair, it sought my weakness;
Pox of mind, a boil of bleakness.

Passion's guilt I took for sinning
So my scapegoat had beginning:
Acts and thoughts condemning me
Flowed from sinner, poet, he.

Vanity, though once remov'd

Meant this creature must be prov'd
And thus achiev'd a cheating fame:
The one I made to take my blame.

EPILOGUE

"I TRUST you intend to continue with your play, Francesca?" Mr Harris said, nodding at the butler who topped up his wine. "I gather your script is excellent – it would be a pity to waste it."

"Oh, David," said his wife, "after all that's happened? You can't expect her to –"

"I shall indeed," Francesca said firmly. "I'll strip out every vestige of that man's work from it, and I shall put it on in honour of Rosabel. I promise everyone in this room, so I cannot possibly go back on it!"

"What about finding another director?" Phyllis said. "Perhaps you can inveigle one from Newcastle?"

I looked at my wife in gratitude to be forgiven and once more with her, amongst our friends.

"I've found one," Francesca said, standing up. "Behold!" she said, and gave a bow.

"Oh, bravo!" said Mr Harris, raising his glass to her.

"I'm a novice, of course," she said, sitting down, "and I'll make many, many, mistakes, but my actors will guide me. I believe I have a little instinct for it. And it's not so unusual for a woman to direct."

"You'll be wonderful at it," I said.

"Hear, hear," said Phyllis. "I gather the theatre is nearly ready."

"It is," said Francesca, "and I'm opening The Angel Arms next week. Please, everyone – come and fill it with friendly noise! We must frighten away every last bad memory."

"It will be a privilege," said Mr Harris, to general agreement.

"I shall also say a few words at the ice house," Francesca said, "for Caroline and Anne. They will soon finally be at peace in their new home in the graveyard, along with their lockets. I insisted they lie near Richard, and happily, Mr Benton has found a way."

"Miss Wooler has agreed for all to be revealed?" Mrs Harris said.

"She has," Francesca said. "She's concluded that it's time for the true history of her great-grandfather to be known, however painful it is. And despite his weaknesses, Richard has shown an admirable capacity for love, and a dreadfully stricken conscience."

"Yes," I said, "the poor man was so tormented by melancholy and the fires of his own passion that he invented a means of separating his better, devout side from his darker self. Now we know why there's so little written about the life of Allan Lawrence: he was a figment of Richard's imagination."

"How strange," said Mr Harris. "I'll see Lawrence in an entirely new light when I next read him. Especially 'Twice Damned'!"

"Oh, goodness, yes," Mrs Harris said. "I'm sorry, but that one is most ungallant."

"I think we should take it with a pinch of salt," I said. "I can't believe it truly represents Richard's relationship with Caroline and Anne. After all, Manners himself spoke of 'wild, carnal imaginings' in one of his letters. Lawrence was a way to express everything a man of the Church could not, and to air doubts about his faith. And eventually, Richard was disgusted with what he'd written, which is why he decided to kill Lawrence off."

"But it can't be easy for Miss Wooler to accept that her ancestor was responsible for Lawrence's books," said Louise. "It's brave of her to face it, and have it publicly known."

"Yes," I said, "but she discussed it with her friend Mr

Fountain and they have a particular perspective... that the truth, and human passion, cannot be denied indefinitely."

"May we infer...?" said Mrs Harris.

"Alas," I said, "I'm not at liberty to say."

"Oh, you utter tease," said Mrs Harris. "Then tell me this: what of the Veiled Sisters? Where do Caroline and Anne fit into the myth? Or perhaps they don't?"

"There is nothing in the box to tell us," I said. "I don't think we'll ever know for sure. But my strong suspicion is this: that in Nathaniel's confused mind, the notion of the Veiled Sisters was a homage to his sisters – hidden in plain sight, as it were – but also a convenient way of increasing his income. It must have been torture for Richard, of course, who would no doubt have regarded it as a cynical exploitation of the tragedy, and a harrowing reminder."

"Of course, of course," said Mrs Harris. "How awful."

"And if I may ask – do you know what prompted Richard's... final actions?" said Mr Harris.

"I can only speculate," I said, "but when his daughter married and moved away, I think poor Richard must have been unable to bear the torment and guilt. And he had put aside his Allan Lawrence character that allowed him to vent his frustrations. The inn had been sold, Nathaniel having died or moved back to his farm. Richard arranged his affairs, including the box with some of his most treasured mementoes, and letters to enable a future understanding of his predicament. Then he went to the place where his two, true loves still lay and took a room. He cried out in misery, scrawling on the wall, before taking his life in a manner that thankfully we have no means of knowing."

There was a hush as everyone grappled with this dreadful scenario.

"And the Church authorities covered it up," I added after a moment, "giving him a Christian burial and ordering the writing to be removed. But at the inn, a sympathetic soul – or a devout one – panelled over it instead, not wanting to silence a man of God and erase the truth."

"Without which, the sisters might still be lying in the ice house," Mr Harris said. "What will become of the message?"

"It's still there, but I had it covered – carefully – with new panelling," Francesca said. "I don't feel disconcerted to know it's there – we have answered his cry now."

"And what of the ruby?" said Mrs Harris. "Thomas, Francesca told me you held it in your hand!"

"I did," I said, smiling. "It's impressive. I expect the lawyers will find a relative of Whickham's to give it to – Miss Wooler is not making any claim on it and I don't blame her. Her house is not conducive to the necessary security, and – cursed or not – I doubt it could bring her any more happiness than she has recently found."

"Well, it brought Richard no happiness at all," said Mrs Harris. "I dare say without it, Anne and Caroline would not have quarrelled with Nathaniel, and then perhaps one of them would have married Richard."

"Indeed," said Francesca, "if he'd been able to make his mind up. What a bitter man Nathaniel must have been to swindle his friend. Perhaps he still blamed Richard for the failure of their theatre."

"If one were superstitious," said Mr Harris, "one might say that Richard's fear of losing the jewel was amply justified."

~

The ladies moved to the drawing room, while Mr Harris and I lingered in the dining room to finish our wine.

"I don't wish to be ghoulish about it, Thomas," said Mr Harris, "but do you have any idea what made Jenrick do the disgusting things he did?"

"Jenrick said himself that he suffered from boredom," I said. "He had already indulged his baser instincts by perverting the original intentions of the Folklore Society. And Peter McNulty told me that Jenrick had confessed about a significant moment. Playing Othello in London, he enjoyed strangling his Desdemona, almost fatally, and he evidently wanted to repeat it and go further. What started as mere play-acting and debauchery, ended in utter wickedness. The thrill was never enough for him."

He shook his head. "I hope we're not all susceptible to such a progression, if suitably provoked."

"Absolutely not," I said. "From my experience, there is a congenital evil in certain people, who are in constant need of sensual excitement and are indifferent to the pain of others. And we have another line of defence: our beliefs and taboos keep the majority of us from degeneracy."

I thought of Mr Fountain's warning that this defence was under attack from a general scepticism in our society, but that seemed too weighty a topic for this occasion.

"True," he said. "You spoke of Peter – I gather he had a severe fever. I wasn't at all impressed by him, but I don't wish him ill. What is his condition?"

"We didn't expect him to live," I said, "but a week or so ago, we had a letter from him. He had the temerity not only to recover, but to become engaged to the daughter of the farmer who had employed him! And it seems I'm to be the best man at his wedding, which will be an intriguingly rural affair."

Mr Harris pulled a face. "Really?"

"He has become less obnoxious than he was," I said. "At least, I hope this is a permanent change. We shall see. But as he wishes to continue his work at the farm, I won't be expected to provide accommodation. That makes me generously disposed towards him."

"Well, that's all rather remarkable," Mr Harris said. "And Louise seems much better, despite her unspeakable ordeal.

Thank God you arrived in time."

"Quite," I said, "although we could still so easily have ended up in the soil that Caroline and Anne had recently left."

"I wonder if Jenrick would have succeeded in framing Mr Tanner," said Mr Harris, "if you hadn't dispatched him. Without you to correct Simmons' errors..."

"I dread to think," I said. "Tanner must be pleased to be back in business and building his new sculpture garden."

"But that poor animal – Hercules," Mr Harris said. "He was quite beautiful. And slaughtered for a crime he didn't commit."

"Yes – I saw him with Mr Tanner. They had a touching bond. He will be distraught." I thought of Titian; though disparate in size, the two cats were strikingly similar in their nature and capacity for affection.

Mr Harris rose from his chair. "Come, Thomas. We are in danger of becoming maudlin. Let us think of such things no more and join our beautiful and clever ladies."

~

After we had arrived in the drawing room, Phyllis rose from her seat and said, "Ladies and gentleman – Louise has an announcement to make," and sat down.

Blushing, Louise said, "It's nothing much, really, but – I've found employment!"

A cheer rose up, and Mrs Harris said, "How intriguing! With Mr Tanner, my dear?"

"No," Louise said, "although I'm glad to have been helpful to him. My position is in Newcastle, at the Natural History Museum! I'm to be a junior curator in their Palaeontology Department."

"Oh, well done, well done indeed!" said Mr Harris. "And

good for the Society and their museum for recognising the precedence of your discovery over mere qualifications."

"David, they're employing Louise, not a fossil," Mrs Harris said firmly. "And I'm not sure that –"

"Quite, quite," Mr Harris said, "but the story of the find and its finder does the Museum no harm in attracting attention. And a female to boot – they will be rather in the vanguard of influential opinion!"

"My dear," said Mrs Harris under her breath and through a forced smile, "a boot is exactly what will be coming your way if you keep this nonsense up."

Francesca went over and shook her hand warmly. "This doesn't surprise me at all, Louise. I'm so happy for you!"

I smiled at Louise, having already learned of her change of circumstances.

"Wonderful news indeed," said Mrs Harris. "But where will you stay?"

"The Director and his wife have a free attic room," said Louise, "and are kindly putting me up until I find something permanent. Since they have already shown me great consideration and hospitality, I'm not at all afraid of moving to the city. Although I hope not to be a disappointment at the Museum, of course."

"You'll be sorely missed," I said, with feeling. "You must promise to come and stay as frequently as you can bear."

"Thank you!" she said. "And you must come and see me in my new surroundings, amongst the bones of the long dead! Oh – how alluring that sounds!"

There was laughter, and Mr Harris stood up.

"This may be an appropriate time to indulge your host's clumsy attempts at verse," he said, "and make amends for his even clumsier remarks earlier. If I may, Olivia?"

"Oh, very well. I could no more stop you than a herd of buffalo," Mrs Harris said. "Pray continue, house bard."

He cleared his throat and unfolded a piece of paper. "It's called 'A Frightening Vision'."

A Frightening Vision

We often act, we men, as though
There's little left for us to know
We strut and preen, and put on airs
Master of our world's affairs.
Now comes maid, upon a mission
To unearth a frightening vision
Of an age before all creeds:
When crawled monstrous millipedes.

What ghastly maw does satiate
Pangs of this invertebrate?
What of faith, what use to pray
When writhing serpent comes this way?
Tremble at these marks on stone
Cower at the length of bone
Men bow down and ladies curtsy:
Fear these beasts, devoid of mercy!

Many legged worm of terror
Could you be Creation's error?
Clerics sweat to see their sermon
Nullified by ancient vermin.
Learned journals host debate:
What means this grim invertebrate?
Still, all parties are agreed –
We're glad you're dead, vast millipede!

Mr Harris bowed and sat down to smiles and applause. Immediately from behind the half-open door a disembodied but familiar voice said, "Put on airs, Pa? Speak for yourself!"

"Victor?" said Mr Harris, in astonishment. Mr and Mrs Harris looked at each other, and then rushed to the door as Victor, leaning on a cane, revealed himself. The prodigal son was so fussed over that it was a moment before they noticed Flora hanging back in the doorway.

"And Flora!" Mrs Harris said. "Oh, my dears! How can this be? How truly wonderful! But Victor – you're injured! What happened?"

"I fell from a tree, mother," he said. "My curiosity got the better of me. But don't worry, it's healing, and doesn't prevent my most important duties." He nodded towards Flora.

"Oh, Victor, you're as dreadful as ever!" scolded Mrs Harris.

I went to Flora and we embraced heartily. "I've missed you dreadfully, sister! Have you changed?" I said, clutching her hands with both of mine. "You seem more self-assured. And you have a healthier colour."

"I think our travels have been beneficial for my health, on balance," she said. "Not quite so much for Victor's. But how well you look! What a pleasure to be back with you all," she said, as Phyllis came to enfold her old friend in her arms. "I have thought of you so much."

"We have a charming addition to our circle," said Mrs Harris. "Louise McNulty – a palaeontologist, no less!"

Introductions were made and hands were shaken. "I must speak with you professionally, Miss McNulty," said Victor. "I'm engaged in an attempt to understand the mechanisms behind – oh, my apologies! This is not the time."

"You two will come to Ramsburgh," I said, "and we'll make time for talk of bones. But you must have so much to tell about your journeys!"

"Give me a brandy," Victor said, "and I'll make a start."

Mrs Flora Harris: niece of Ramsburgh's previous owners, the Kingtons, and wife of Victor Harris

Mr Peter McNulty: a former friend of Thomas

Miss Louise McNulty: Peter McNulty's sister and aspiring palaeontologist

Inspector Ralph Simmons: a detective

Constable Taylor: a policeman

Constable Gawley: a policeman

Mrs Bess Shannon: the proprietor of Myrtle's coffee shop

Mr Frederick McPhee: a director at the Pottery

Dr Philip Weldon: a doctor

Mr John Belford: a jeweller

Mrs Florence Tambard: a wealthy widow

Mr John Hutton: a builder

Mr Leonardo Fountain: an antiquarian

Mr Nathaniel Whickham: a landlord and friend of Richard Manners

Mr Jacob Whickham: a descendant of Nathaniel Whickham

Miss Lucy Buxton: a woman of easy virtue

Miss Ethel Buxton: Lucy Buxton's sister

Miss Rosabel Gardner: an aspiring actress and worker at the Pottery

Mr Mark Gardner: Rosabel Gardner's father

Mrs Clara Gardner: Rosabel Gardner's mother

Miss Mabel Bailey: a friend of Rosabel Gardner

Mr Philip Tanner: a local entrepreneur

Mr Richard Manners: a late 17th/early 18th century rector

Julia Manners: Richard Manners' daughter

Mr Allan Lawrence: a late 17th/early 18th century poet

Miss Ruth Wooler: a descendant of Richard Manners

Mr Luke Paxton: Scottish neighbour of the Gardners

Mrs Moira Paxton: wife of Luke Paxton

ABOUT THE AUTHOR

Julian Smart was born in Nottingham, England, and studied Computer Science at the University of St Andrews. He has a doctorate from the University of Dundee. Julian has worked for the University of Edinburgh, the Artificial Intelligence Applications Institute, the Scottish Crop Research Institute, and Red Hat UK.

Julian started the wxWidgets open-source GUI toolkit project which is used by many organisations and individuals worldwide, and by Julian for his own projects, including the e-book editing software Jutoh. Jutoh was used for creating all books by Julian and Harriet Smart.

Julian collaborated with Harriet Smart to write *Emma Vernon's Northminster Ghost Stories*, a spin-off from Harriet's Northminster Mysteries which he has edited since 2010.

Julian is currently working on *The Thomas Rufford Mysteries*, a series set in nineteenth-century Hawksbridge, a fictional town in the north east of England.

Printed in Great Britain
by Amazon

GW01608019

REFLECTIONS OF ME

KIRSTY "KIRZART" LATOYA

First published in the United Kingdom by:
OWN IT! Entertainment Ltd
Company Registration Number: 09154978

Cover Illustration: Kirsty Latoya

Design: Caroline Lee

ISBN: 9780995458970

WWW.OWNIT.LONDON

Dedication

To my mother and guardian angel Rose.
Thank you for making me the woman I am today.

INTRODUCTION

Eagerly, I burst into my classroom with a signed copy of 'Lola Rose' by Jacqueline Wilson. I showed everyone in my class and even had a photograph with my favourite author. I adored my ever growing collection of her books, especially because of Nick Sharratt's colourful and kid friendly illustrations- I was obsessed. I asked my teacher about his occupation and she replied "He's an illustrator" the 8 year old me beamed up in excitement to her 'That's what I want to be when I grow up".

This childhood dream somehow got lost and although I always drew my passion died down. I wasn't encouraged academically to pursue art so I began to think I wasn't good at it. My mum would always tell me I was amazing though and would buy me paint by number sets and colouring books that I'd spend my evenings completing. My dad on the other hand would encourage me to be more academic and would do maths and science activities and questions with me. He had dreams of me becoming a doctor, which I had to let him down gently about.

As I grew, my mother continued to be my biggest supporter but she faced her own challenges which sometimes made that difficult.

Before I was born she was diagnosed with Marfans Syndrome, a genetic disorder of the connective tissues which can affect the heart, eyes, skin, skeletal system and more. Most of my childhood was watching her in and out of hospital; undergoing major operations, receiving treatment and regular appointments.

I recall this one time when my mum was in intensive care and couldn't even breathe for herself, she was connected to what seemed like a million machines. I watched my older brother sit at her bedside, clasping her lifeless hand in tears. At that moment I thought we were going to lose her but my mum would always fight and overcome everything life threw at her.

My own diagnosis of Marfans syndrome came when I was a child, then puberty started I began to notice the physical differences the disorder had on my body. I was very tall and thin with extra long limbs, my chest bone protruded and I started developing scoliosis. I had a difficult time coming to terms with the fact that I was different, I hated it. I felt tall and ugly and thought that nobody would ever love me. In secondary school it got worse as my scoliosis became more prominent. I would hide away in baggy clothes and overcompensate for my sadness with my loud and bubbly personality. At the time I didn't realise it but I was falling into a deep depression.

In college I had corrective surgery for my scoliosis which left me in hospital for my 18th birthday and learning how to walk again. My depression began to spiral as I had other personal issues and my ever growing poor self esteem. In uni I finally decided to seek counselling which helped me in a way I never thought. I walked into my first appointment and was greeted by a middle aged, middle class white man with a firm hand shake. Instantly I judged him thinking what would he know about my life as a young black women with a serious health condition but he surprised me and was so easy to talk to. He understood me and helped me to help myself, I was able to fall in love with me again.

Uni as a whole was a very positive experience, I had left with new skills and amazing memories. My unforgettable study year abroad in New York allowed me to study art on an academic level, learning the technicalities of painting and drawing. This refuelled my creative fire and after graduating from my English Language, New Media Publishing and Creative Writing degree I decided to venture into the art world again. I quit my full time customer service job and launched into the freelance life with the full support of my mum. At the time it was just me and her living at home but she encouraged me to go for it if it was what I really wanted.

January 2016 was going to be an important month for me, the start of my full time freelance career. I was filled with excitement, nerves and anxiety but I was ready. It started out great, I had a few clients and was working on a couple of projects. On January 21st my mum brought me along with her to a doctors appointment at the hospital, she had been feeling unwell and they had diagnosed her with an aneurysm on her heart which needed immediate medical intervention.

At the appointment we were expecting to get a date for surgery but as the doctor fumbled through his notes he realised key information hadn't been passed onto the relevant doctors, resulting in no date being booked. Quite frustrated I asked him "Well how serious is this?" I had felt let down by them "She could drop down dead tomorrow" he snapped back. My mum didn't flinch, she sat quietly with her hands calmly in her lap. We left the doctors office and didn't discuss what had been said. As we waited for our taxi she called over one of the receptionists in the waiting area. I had been drawing on my iPad and my mum started to show off my work to the young woman with a proud look on her face as she explained my drawing process, pointing out my technique as I created.

The next day came around and my mum was in high spirits despite her pain but by evening she became quite ill. I called my brother around and we decided to call an ambulance, after waiting an agonising 40 plus minutes it finally arrived and we went with my mum to the hospital. "Lord, not today" I quietly prayed as I thought about the terrible possibility. We sat in the family waiting room for a while and a teary eyed doctor came in and sat down next to me. He started to explain that they had been on their way to take her to some scans and her heart had suddenly stopped, he explained they had done everything they could but she had died. Confused I argued with the doctor, telling him it wasn't true and to go try again. The disbelief continued as I was led to the room where she was laying, her skin still warm. She had fought for the last time. The coincidental prediction of the doctor from the day before now resonating in my head as I stroked her skin. She was gone.

The next few weeks and months were tough, my depression and anxiety started to increase to the point where I began having suicidal thoughts. Nothing made me happy and I felt I had no purpose, the only thing that stopped me was seeing the pain everybody was in and not wanting them to go through it again. I was at my wits end and a friend suggested I try to draw my feelings. At this point I was adamant that I would never draw again because I felt guilty doing something I loved when I should be grieving. The pain of this loss was so great that it was almost indescribable, I didn't eat without my friends reminding me to, I didn't go outside unless it was to do with the funeral. I wanted nothing more than to be alone with my thoughts but decided to listen to my friend and draw.

I created a self portrait of a crying Kirsty, holding a mask that was smiling. When I released this private moment to the public on social media, it unexpectedly went viral and I began to see the impact it was having, somebody even got it tattooed on them! I created more pieces focusing on mental health which became a form of art therapy for me, I had found a way to get out my negative feelings in a positive way and I was helping others. This new turn in my art caused my followers and attention to spike online, I even started to do press interviews about it. The first time the majority of my family and friends heard about my mental health struggles was on BBC Breakfast news when I revealed all. My new found openness allowed me to speak about what I was going through and how I used my art to help me. I was asked to do a multitude of interviews and spoke to ITV, BuzzFeed, Huffington Post, Evening Standard and much more. I was invited into corporate spaces and prisons to deliver motivational talks and presentations with my art and was tasked with educating others about mental health and the stigma it holds in African and Caribbean communities. I held 2 of my own art exhibitions and was part of some amazing ones which allowed me to target larger audiences with my work. I had turned my pain into my passion and all from expressing my creativity. I created my digital paintings on my iPad so I could draw wherever I was and I used my finger as a stylus because it felt natural. I had taught myself how to paint digitally by studying digital paintings and doing trial and error to figure out the intricacies of them. I started on a free drawing app called Sketchbook Pro but soon upgraded to the industry leader Procreate which proved itself worth the small one off payment. Within this one app I was able to create magic that will hopefully stand the test of time, which brings me to this book. I wanted to tell my story through the use of art and poetry, exploring important themes like mental health, love, identity and womanhood. Each art and poetry piece is a reflection of me in some way and I hope they resonate with you. Like the illustrator Nick Sharratt inspired me, I hope to inspire upcoming artists and creatives to believe they can be whatever they want to be. You are the master of your own destiny so don't let anyone or anything stop you from achieving your goals and dreams.

Fight on valiant fighter and proceed to succeed!

ALONE

DROWNING IN EMOTIONS

DISTRESS

INTRUSIVE THOUGHTS

CHALLENGING

FEAR

PANIC

OVERWHELMING

SUSPENSE

I HAVE ANXIETY

UNEASE

NEGATIVITY

NAUSEA

SUFFOCATING

TENSION

UNCOMFORTABLE

NERVOUSNESS

DEPRESSION

How are you?
I'm fine

A LETTER
TO MY FRIENDS

When you ask me how I am and I say that I'm fine
I have a confession and it's that I have been lying
It's easier to lie than to explain my mood
Easier to turn to other vices like comfort food

I don't know how to explain the way I've been feeling
Everyday I wake up wishing I was still dreaming
Because the dream world is easier, no complications
Nothing can stop me I have no limitations
Back in the real world, depression is real
It makes me withdrawn and incapable of saying how I feel
It eats me up and life becomes a chore
And sometimes I just don't wanna talk about it anymore

I don't want to worry you with all of my issues
So I tend to just confide in my box of tissues
Your love is not disputed, I know that you care
You're one call away and will always be there
But sometimes it's difficult to be so transparent
Especially when my behaviour becomes so abhorrent

So I'm sorry for lying but at least now you know
That I'm not being difficult it's just hard to show
My feelings inside and how they're affecting me
I'm learning to deal with my problems effectively
Next time you ask how I am, I won't say I'm fine
Unless it's the truth, I'm so done with lying
I'll tell you the truth if my tears are falling
And if a bad mood comes on without warning
I'll give a text if I need an ear
Or give you a call if I need you here.

DEPRESSED

YOU'RE TOO SKINNY

"You're too skinny, you're too slim"
"Thick girls always win"
"Wow I can see your bones"
"Doesn't your mother feed you at home?"
"You look like the wind would blow you away"
"You're a size 8? No wayyy!!"
"A real woman has curves"
Ugh the nerve!

Who gives you the right to comment on my features
You suck the good out of everything you bunch of leeches
I'm happy with my size
Stop being a bully in disguise
I'm not skinny because I starve myself!
I eat everything in the fridge and on my cupboard shelves!
I've just been blessed with the slim gene
Sometimes I eat crap and sometimes I eat clean
Jealousy doesn't suit you I'm afraid
So how about you stop throwing shade

You can be shamed for being fat, skinny, short or tall
For being too dark or not having any melanin at all
Someone will always have something to say
But it's up to you if you give them the time of day.

TOO SKINNY
MATCHSTICK
BOY FIGURE
FLAT
SKINNY BITCH
EAT MORE
UGLY
TOOTHPICK
MARGA
SKELETON
boney
NO CURVES
TOO TALL
Anorexic
SKIN &
BONE

IDENTITY

TRANQUILITY

PAIN
IN YOUR EYES

I can see the pain in your eyes
Your contour and highlight does not disguise
Your battles and bruises
The heart sees what it chooses

It ignores the wrongs
Your love is so strong
But it's blind to abuse
He's tying your noose

Please open your eyes
And identify the lies
From the devil in disguise
You need to be wise

You're stronger than this so walk away
And live to see another day.

PAIN IN YOUR EYES
PAIN

MR. WRONG

The pain in my chest is incurable
Excruciating, piercing, not durable
No doctor can save me
This load is too weighty
My heart is tearing
My patience is wearing
This question reoccurring
The answer I'm yearning…

When will you love me back?

My soul aches as it searches for a reason
Why I'm not good enough every passing season
My heart stands alone, an empty flask
Craving your liquid love, in it I will bask
I need you to feel what I am feeling
Every day and night, I find myself kneeling.
Praying to God with all my might
Begging for love, for Mr. Right

But you never come so I settle for less
In turn become used to being second best
Mr. Right now tells me he likes me and that's good enough
So I give him my body, my love and my trust
He abuses it and the pain starts again
Wondering if he'll love me and if so when?

My chest tightens as the pain increases
Neglection, rejection they're tearing me to pieces
An unwanted toy, I sit on the shelf
Wishing I knew the worth of myself
Wanting the love I rightly deserve
Requited and pure, my heart now reserved

So I'll sit here and wait for my happiness to appear
And hope it comes soon 'cos I've been waiting for years.

LOST LOVE

Patience
Is a
Virtue
RESERVED

RESERVED

Sorry sir this space is reserved for a king
Not somebody looking for just a quick fling
Somebody who's serious and won't waste my time
A man full of love, who'll keep me on cloud nine

This space is reserved for a man who is loyal
One who'll sing Tarrus Riley 'She's royal'
A man who's compassionate, romantic and fun
The type of guy you can take home to your mum

I don't want my impatience to lead me to settle
'Cos I'm looking for a love, stronger than any mental
I'll be a God fearing woman to match my God fearing man
A couple that prays together stays together so that's the plan

I want to build a life with somebody like-minded
Because I don't want to end up being blindsided
I have hopes of marriage and kids in the future
So I need to choose carefully when picking a suitor

I wanna look at my king and think 'Issa snack'
And I want him to look at me and think the same back
I don't want Mr Right Now, I want my Mr Forever
Someone who's ambitious, caring and clever

Patience is a virtue although it can be hard
But one day your king will appear and catch you off guard
So don't give away your heart prematurely.
Have faith and be patient and he'll come along, surely!

ROSES FOR ROSE

I write this with teary eyes
…sometimes the lows are more frequent than the highs
Sometimes the pain dances around my chest
Sometimes I wonder how much fight I have left

I remember when I lost you I couldn't cope
But I had to be strong and hold onto hope
I planned your funeral and read the eulogy
Fought back the tears and read with fluency

At your graveside I didn't break down
I threw a rose on your coffin when I should've thrown a crown
I was strong for everyone because I had to be
But the weakness inside has been escaping rapidly
I haven't grieved for you properly because I can't let you go
I love you and miss you and I hope that you know
I think about you every single day
And keep your memories alive in my own special way
But it breaks me you won't be there at my wedding
And I won't be able to complain to you when my kids do my head in

I can't accept that you've left me
Your only daughter is now empty
A passive being, just existing
The voice of life constantly insisting I give it another try
So I keep living, although it's hard
My heart forever broken, forever scarred

The doctor's voice still in my head repeating
"I'm so sorry, her heart stopped beating"
He told me with teary eyes
…sometimes the lows are more frequent than the highs

I touched your skin, it was still warm
You looked fast asleep, my heart was torn
My precious mother, my precious Rose
You were an amazing person which everyone knows
I write this with teary eyes
…sometimes you have to turn the lows into highs
I've channelled my pain through my creativity
And strive to be the best like you told me to be.

MUM IT HURTS

THE WORLD IN HER EYES

PTSD
BODY DYSMORPHIA
PHOBIAS
DEPRESSION
ADDICTION
BPD
SCHIZOPHRENI
TRAUMA
STRESS
ANXIETY
BIPOLAR
ADH
EATING
DISORDER
LOW SELF ESTEE
PARANO
SUICIDAL
THOUGHTS
ALCOHOL/SUBSTANC
ABUSE
OCD

CHE LINGO
WAKANDA

POSITIVE LOVE

Yo I'm feeling kind
of depressed

Bro, you need to man up

A LETTER TO MEN

They tell you "Man up"
And boys don't cry
Show no weakness
Wipe the tears from your eyes

They say that you're feminine when you show any emotion
You must display dominance or there will be a commotion
You can't be depressed you must keep it together
Put a brave face on whatever the weather

The social expectations forced upon men
Continues to emerge over and over again
We cannot place gender into a box
'Cos anyone who doesn't fit is ridiculed and mocked
Not every man will be the alpha male
We cannot continue to let toxicity prevail
Don't tell your friend he needs to "Man up"
He's definitely man enough!
Get educated, get smart
Don't be ignorant and laugh

Men can cry, they can be depressed
They can break down, they can get stressed
Be there for your friends, with a listening ear
Don't judge, be open and be kind to your peers.

DARK THOUGHTS

YOU
ARE
STRONG

STRENGTH

She escaped from the darkness
She knows her strength now
The light beckons her

You
Are
Enough

ENOUGH

You've spent your life wanting to be someone else
Wondering why you have no sense of self
Looking at Instagram beauties
Wanting their booties but not appreciating your own

You envy the straight European nose
Think to yourself "I need me one of those"
But not realising the story behind your own

You don't believe your kinky hair is desirable
Look at straight hair and deem it admirable
And you want to cover up your own

You hate your curves, think there's too much lumps and bumps
You want Dr Miami to smoothen out the humps
Not realising the power and beauty you own

Your rich melanin is a problem which you want to fix
You buy bleaching creams, from dark to light you want to switch
Your natural skin tone you want to disown

Why do you always want more? You think you're incomplete
An unfinished project you try to compete
With unrealistic beauty ideals
When your true beauty needs to be revealed

The woman in the mirror is enough
Stop wanting what others have, jealousy will cause you to combust
You're beautiful and smart
A perfect work of art
You are enough!

LONDON MIST

MEDITATION

ISLAND GIRLS

TIGER STRIPES

I trace my tiger stripes with my fingers
True beauty's exploration
The unruly lines, a story book
Line by line it reveals itself
True poetry on my skin
A gift from growth
I embrace
I am not ashamed
I have earned my stripes

TIGER STRIPES

Go Home
£474
BRITISH JAMAICAN

HOME

Born into a country I call my own
But I've lost count the amount of times
I've been told to "go home"
A British Jamaican my identity is clear
My parents fled home for a better life here

Over time my mum's accent didn't fade at all
But an English one would appear
When she made certain phone calls
Sometimes she'd ask me to pass the 'cling flim'
So I learnt to understand her creative synonyms
Overgeneralisations happened from time to time
Cotton buds become 'Q-tips' a favourite of mine

Growing up I loved fish and chips, shepherds pie- the lot
But I also loved Jamaican food, cooked up in a Dutch pot
I loved the fried dumplings made especially for me
The cornmeal porridge, saltfish and no forgetting ackeee
Stew peas, ox tail, festival and jerk chicken
Delicious is an understatement, the food was finger lickin'
Fish on a Friday and Soup on a Sunday
If there was leftovers I'd even have some on Monday
I'd vibe to the greats like Beres Hammand
Sing classics from Bob Marley like 'Jammin'

The first time I went to Jamaica I was under the age of one
And that's when my love story really began
I loved the magical sun and the cool island breeze
The beautiful scenery, the exotic palm trees
Fried fish and bammy on Hellshire's shore
A true paradise you can't help but adore

So when the English tell me to go home, I go
But in Jamaica I'm seen as a foreigner. I have no home.
Too Jamaican to be British, Too British to be Jamaican
But I know that I'm both I'm not confused nor mistaken
Despite the rejections that seem to appear
I'm a British Jamaican and my identity is clear.

Original
9780 80

Ghetto
17
0

QUEEN

FADED

KAINE BUFFONGE

WINNIE HARLOW

MISUNDERSTOOD

YOU CAN

When they tell you "you can't"
Remember everything you've ever achieved
They don't even know the magic you have up your sleeve

When they tell you "you'll fail"
Remember every time you got back up
You have perseverance and determination not luck

When they tell you "you won't"
Remember that everything is in your hands
You are the master of your own destiny, they just don't understand

And when they tell you "you'll never"
Remember that you were born to be great
Nothing is impossible, your magnificence is not up for debate

The rose That grew From concrete

CONCRETE ROSE

Beautiful
Fighter
SCARRED

ME TIME

It's okay not to be
perfect

ACKNOWLEDGMENTS

I would first like to thank God for blessing me with this gift and allowing me to share it with so many people.

With God all things are possible – Matthew 19:26

I must thank my family for their support, especially my brother and sister-in-law who've been so patient with my constant disappearing to work on this project.

Thank you to my better half for all your love and encouragement through this process. When I felt like I couldn't do anymore you pushed me to continue, I'm incredibly appreciative.

I can't individually name all my friends ('cos there's like a million) who've supported me through this process but you know who you are, from the bottom of my heart I'm grateful. A special thank you to my best friends for your patience and putting up with me complaining when things got tough. Jade, my 'manager' thank you for reading every contract, poem and extract as well as reviewing every art piece. You reminded me of my purpose constantly and kept me going.

Word on the Curb, my fellow creatives, thank you for dedicating your limbs to many hours as my personal mannequins. You provided me with constant motivation and a great working environment.

A big thank you to all of my inspirations and muses; the various photographers, artists, models and designers who have inspired the art in this book.

To my supporters, every person who's ever liked, shared, commented or bought my art, you've brought me a step closer to my dreams, I appreciate you.

This project would not have been possible without my amazing publishers Crystal and Jason, I can't believe you actually allowed me to publish a book! You believed in me and gave me a chance and it means the world to me. Thank you eternally.